A FOREST

Recent Titles by James Follett from Severn House

THE TEMPLE OF THE WINDS TRILOGY

THE TEMPLE OF THE WINDS
WICCA
THE SILENT VULCAN

DOMINATOR
THE DOOMSDAY ULTIMATUM
EARTHSEARCH
MINDWARP
SECOND ATLANTIS

A FOREST OF EAGLES

James Follett

This first world edition published in Great Britain 2004 by
SEVERN HOUSE PUBLISHERS LTD of
9–15 High Street, Sutton, Surrey SM1 1DF.
This first world edition published in the USA 2004 by
SEVERN HOUSE PUBLISHERS INC of
595 Madison Avenue, New York, N.Y. 10022.

British Library Cataloguing in Publication Data

Follett, James, 1939-
   A forest of eagles
   1.   World War, 1939-1945 - Prisoners and prisons, British - Fiction
   2.   Prisoner-of-war escapes - Great Britain - Fiction
   3.   Germany - Armed forces - Officers - Fiction
   4.   War stories
   I.   Title
   823.9'14 [F]

   ISBN 0-7278-6062-3

Typeset by Palimpsest Book Production Ltd.,
Polmont, Stirlingshire, Scotland.
Printed and bound in Great Britain by
MPG Books Ltd., Bodmin, Cornwall.

Part One

'A U-boat Will be Waiting.'

1

Considering that he was blessed with an inventive turn of mind, jumping out of a moving train was not one of Karl Moehe's better ideas.

It would be best, his inner voice advised him, to come up with a method that does not involve the possibility of a broken leg. *Ungluckish* Moehe! Unlucky Moehe! You might break more than a leg – you'd break your neck!

But those thoughts that counselled prudence were drowned by a more powerful voice that had gnawed at Karl ever since his capture.

You must escape!

You must escape!

You must escape!

The staccato rhythm of the train had beaten its insidious message on Karl's consciousness since he and his two guards had left London that morning. He had considered making a break at Euston Station but Corporal Elwin had handcuffed him until they were on the train. Karl had protested that handcuffing prisoners of war was contrary to the Geneva Convention, to which the soldier had replied that Geneva was a long way away and that his sergeant wasn't. Furthermore, if U-boat officer Leutnant Karl bloody Moehe hadn't shown such a predilection for escape bids since his capture, the handcuffs at Euston would not be necessary.

1

You must escape!
You must escape!

Private Morgan rose, clutching his rifle in one hand and the luggage rack with the other. The train was moving fast, swaying and clattering. They had come a long way north: the gangs working on the bombed lines around Birmingham had been left far behind. The soldier announced that he was going for a pee, left the compartment and pushed his way along the crowded corridor. A passenger who didn't see the compartment's reserved notice backed hurriedly out when Corporal Elwin snarled at him. Karl slid across to the vacated window seat. Corporal Elwin tightened his grip on his rifle and glared at the fresh-faced young man sitting opposite. 'You watch it, Sonny Jim,' he warned.

'Fields,' said Karl, gesturing at the window. His English was poor but the corporal's hostile tone needed no translation. 'Fields. I like. My parents, my father is *der Abbauer . . .*' He groped for the right English noun and made a digging gesture.

'Fucking swede-bashers,' said Corporal Elwin sourly.

'Pardon? My English – not good.'

'I said, fucking swede-bashers.'

Karl committed the phrase to memory. He was convinced that his atrocious English was improving quickly. A good command of colloquial English was essential for his escape to succeed.

He stared out of the window at fields bathed in the sunlight of a bright afternoon in late March. It was 1942. On leaving London, the young U-boat officer's spirits had been lifted by the sight of the widespread bomb damage that had been inflicted on the capital by the Luftwaffe. But now, eight hours after leaving Euston, they were far from the war, passing through rolling fells dotted with countless sheep contained in fields defined by drystone walls that laced the landscape like grey varicose veins. The grass in the shadows of the dry walls bore the white haze of permanent frost. Now and again there were U-shaped glacial valleys in which gangs of women were preparing fields for cultivation. Karl was intrigued; the British made much greater use of women than he was accustomed to

2

seeing at home. It had been the same in London – everywhere there were women driving ambulances, staff cars, even trucks, setting up barricades around bomb craters. It was low-grade information. No doubt the intelligence services back home knew all about the use the British made of their womenfolk. But the OKM – the German navy's high command – and its technical experts would not have the priceless information that he had that was fuelling his desperate need to escape to get the knowledge home.

The train plunged into a tunnel. Corporal Elwin hauled on the broad leather strap that lifted the drop-down window closed before sulphurous fumes and hot cinders from the locomotive filled the compartment. Much to Karl's relief, he lowered the window again to permit a small gap when the train emerged from the tunnel. He preferred coal fumes to the stink of the cheap cigarettes that his captors had smoked incessantly since leaving London.

Private Morgan returned to the compartment, slung his rifle on the overhead luggage rack, and flopped down beside Karl without insisting on reoccupying the window seat. He fished a crumpled packet of Woodbines out of his battledress breast pocket and offered it to the corporal. Both soldiers lit up.

The train thundered northwards.

The distance they had travelled worried Karl. He was being taken further north than he had imagined possible. When his interrogators in London had finished with him, having frustrated them by divulging nothing of value, or so he thought, they had said that he was to be sent to Grizedale Hall – a prisoner of war camp for officers. He had asked where it was but their reply had been that it was somewhere in England.

Of the many subjects that were not his strong point, geography was a prime candidate. He had always thought of England as a very small country and yet they had been travelling north most of the day and there was no sign of the Scottish mountains he had once seen on a postcard.

He turned to Private Morgan. 'Excuse me, sir.' He had learned to call everyone 'sir' even though he sensed it was

3

incorrect in the case of officers addressing soldiers. 'But England . . . Much big?'

The soldier looked puzzled and glanced at his comrade, who shrugged.

'England,' said Karl, using his hands to indicate height. 'Much tall? Long? Many kilometres?'

'I read somewhere that Land's End to John O' Groats is one thousand miles,' said Corporal Elwin.

The last three words hit Karl between the eyes because the English was similar to German. *One thousand miles!* One thousand six hundred kilometres! His head swam. He had no idea that England was so large.

You must escape!

'We go up? All way?' Karl used his hands to convey his meaning.

'You'll find out soon enough, Jerry.'

Karl didn't understand Corporal Elwin's meaning and assumed the worst. Doubtless this Grizedale Hall would have barbed-wire fences, and lookout towers full of trigger-happy Britishers manning machine-guns and searchlights. There would be little chance of escape. He had no choice but to make a break from the train. He twisted into the corner of his seat, dropped his chin on to his chest, and pretended to doze, his thoughts a whirl. Through half-closed eyes he watched Private Morgan pitting his wits against the *Daily Sketch*'s crossword-puzzle writer. He could see only Corporal Elwin's knees but he guessed that the NCO was staring boredly out of the window. The train reduced speed and screeched loudly and harshly over temporary repairs. Workmen with pickaxes and sledgehammers stood clear and watched the train clattering by. The window caught his attention by rattling in its frame.

Karl's body remained relaxed but what he saw electrified every nerve in his body. The hole in the leather strap that held the window up was badly frayed and the vibration had dislodged it slightly so that it was barely hooked on its retaining pin. One jolt and the window would slam down. His mind raced, weighing up possibilities. Diving through the window head first was asking for trouble. It would have to be feet first. Not in itself a problem: he was wiry, fit, and athletic. If he grasped the window frame low down with his left hand and higher up with his right hand, he would be able to twist his body sideways and so clear the frame. The trouble was that his seat was on the right side of the train and the English, as with their roads, drove their trains on the left. He would land on the southbound track. The chances of him landing in the path of an oncoming train were slim – thinking back, there hadn't been that many trains going in the opposite direction.

The violent shaking of the train as it passed the engineering work made it easier for him to turn his head left or right to take in his surroundings. Through half-closed eyes he studied the blur of the southbound lines and sleepers. With the train moving at even his estimated forty kilometres per hour, his chances of escaping a crippling injury when he hit the tracks were nil.

Then the train slowed to a crawl but the jolting got worse. The leather strap jumped. The train swayed, the coaches jerked and jostled against their couplings, and the down line on his side disappeared to be replaced by a steep, grassy embankment that fell away to deciduous woodland.

Karl could scarcely credit his good fortune: the train had been diverted on to the down line. Certain that his captors would hear his hammering heart, he noted that Private Morgan held his pencil in his right hand as he frowned over his crossword puzzle, and Corporal Elwin used his right hand when taking drags from his cigarette. Karl reasoned that his jumping from the right-hand side of the train would put both men at a disadvantage after his leap: they were right-handed and would have to aim their rifles from their left shoulders.

'Landslide,' was the word passed along the crowded corridor.

The train began to pick up speed and the track became smoother. The window strap gave no sign of budging. Karl remained slumped, feigning sleep – praying for the window to drop while running a mental frame by frame movie rehearsal of exactly what he had to do when, and if, it did drop. That was beginning to look less likely with each passing second. It was only a matter of moments now before the train returned

5

to the correct side of the tracks and his opportunity would be lost. His brain worked feverishly, using his skills and training as a torpedo officer to calculate his mass, the train's velocity, the likely trajectory his body would follow, and the angle and impact of his body on the embankment. At least the grass looked long and there was a fringe of dead bracken where the embankment rose out of the bare-branched woodland. His two-sizes-too-large navy-blue greatcoat that the Red Cross had supplied worried him but there was nothing around the window that it would be likely to snag on and maybe the thick material would afford some protection. He stirred in his sleep, gathering the voluminous garment more tightly around him.

The locomotive reached the temporary track switch that diverted it back on to the up line, sending shock waves the length of the train.

The window fell.

Karl's nerves were so keyed up that his hands were reaching for the window frame even before the window had completed its drop.

His mental rehearsals paid off. In one smooth, flowing movement, he grabbed the frame at an angle, bunched his knees up to his chin, and straightened his body like a coiled spring bursting out of its housing. The greatcoat caught on something but it didn't impede his departure from the train.

He found himself flying. Flying for longer than he had expected and the steep embankment was racing up to greet him much faster than he had calculated. Other calculations let him down, too, because the human body isn't a torpedo and doesn't behave like a torpedo in flight. He had estimated that he would bounce twice after hitting the ground – in fact he bounced four times. The first impact drove the breath from his body like a steamroller dropped on a barrage balloon. It seemed brutally unfair that ground covered in long grass should be so hard but he had not taken the effect of late, hard frosts of northern England into account. The final bounce that brought his body nearly to a stop was more an untidy cartwheel, his arms and legs flailing like a rag doll fired from a cannon. All motion ceased when he generously permitted the frozen ground to deliver a haymaker to his jaw.

Pain filled every corner of his consciousness and invaded every muscle and bone in his body. It was the sort of all-pervading pain that by its intensity announced its intention of providing him with life-long companionship. The blue sky looked inviting, from whence friendly chariots of fire would be sure to swoop down to end his torment and bear him away.

No friendly chariots arrived, but unfriendly bullets did, and quite quickly, too: the loud crack of .303 rounds zinging above his head and smacking into the nearby trees. There were harsh, metallic screams as the locomotive's wheels locked and skated on the track. Men were shouting. Another crack of rifle fire. The sudden eruption of grass and soil not four metres from where Karl lay spiked his bloodstream with adrenaline, doubling the power of his punished muscles. He staggered to his feet and half ran, half fell down the rest of the bank towards the doubtful safety of the winter-stripped trees. He stumbled and fell but the pain, particularly in his right ankle, was nothing compared with the demon of terror snapping dementedly at his heels. His greatcoat caught on brambles that slashed at his face but he pushed blindly on, heedless of the wracking agony. Once in the trees he stopped briefly to take stock, doubled over to get his wind back, his lungs clawing down frozen air, making clouds of telltale vapour. He straightened and tested his arms and legs. That he was able to stand was a good omen. His jaw throbbed where it had helped break his fall, his hands were grazed, his right ankle an agony but it could take his weight, and he could move his arms – all meagre indications that he hadn't broken or dislocated anything.

The train had stopped and he could hear Corporal Elwin bellowing orders, his voice drawing closer. Karl stumbled blindly on deeper into the woodland, tripping over tree roots. The woodland gave way quite suddenly to open fields with no cover. There was a ploughman driving a pair of heavy horses but he was far enough away for Karl to risk leaving the trees and run along the edge of the woodland. He surprised himself by managing to keep up a shambling but steady pace for some minutes despite the numbing pain in his right ankle, and

7

reckoned he had covered half a kilometre before exhaustion forced him back into the trees to rest, flopped out on the ground, oblivious of the pain where his body made contact with the frozen soil, conscious only of his throbbing ankle.

He brought his gasping breathing under control and listened. There were distant shouts. The train had been crowded with servicemen. It was likely that Corporal Elwin had pressed a number of them into forming a search party. If they strung out, it would be only a matter of time before they found him.

Karl resumed his hobbling run along the edge of woodland. He reckoned that he needed another two kilometres to be well clear of the centre of the search. Despite the bitter cold, after thirty minutes jogging, sweat was pricking his eyes. He kept wiping his face on the sleeve of his greatcoat without pausing in his stride and didn't see the steep bank that dropped down to a stream until it was too late. He tumbled down, his fall cushioned by an avalanche of half-rotted and dead leaves, and frost-dried bracken from the previous autumn. He climbed wearily to his feet and was about to resume his flight when his keen nose picked up an evocative scent from happy childhood days playing with his brothers in the woodlands on their parents' farm.

Badger scat.

He followed the stream into the woods. His experienced eye quickly located the entrance to their sett. It was in a clearing, well above the stream, set into the bank and partially concealed behind a tangled mass of exposed alder roots. Karl dragged some of the roots and debris aside and examined the opening. It was larger than was usual for badgers and had probably once been used by foxes. He decided that it would serve his purpose admirably and he set about gathering armfuls of leaves and bracken, which he piled up near the entrance. The cold seared him when he took off the greatcoat, rolled it up, and crammed it deep into the opening. He winced in pain as he wriggled backwards into the hole and pulled the leaves and bracken after him, packing them as best he could to conceal the entrance.

The relief at no longer having to run was offset by the insidious cold that pressed all around him. No doubt the owners of the sett would be annoyed at finding their front door blocked but badgers usually provided their homes with several emergency exits, and the occupants were unlikely to emerge on foraging sorties until after dark.

Karl waited, cramped and miserable, listening as the birdsong returned to normal. The warning *chirp-chirp* call of a blackbird alerted him. He heard voices drawing near and then they faded away. There was the sound of the train moving off. A motor vehicle passed by on the edge of the woods. And then silence apart from the harsh cries of rooks and crows.

The cold was a slowly tightening vice of misery. His arms and legs were numb. The temptation to crawl out of his hiding place while his limbs were still capable of movement was almost irresistible but he stayed put. The English were devious – quite capable of using a deliberate straggler. On his first and last patrol, he had been officer of the watch when he and his U-boat's lookouts had spotted a convoy straggler. An ideal candidate for one of Karl's new torpedoes. He had gone after it. The straggler turned out to be an armed merchantman, bristling with depth charges, and with a well-trained gun crew. *U-684* had spent several hours in the 'cellar' before giving the trawler the slip.

'*Ungluckish* Moehe,' commented his skipper teasingly. 'Now we know why you're called that, eh, leutnant?'

Karl moved his arms and legs as best he could in the confined space to maintain his circulation. He stopped occasionally to listen intently. An hour passed and he heard new sounds: men calling to each other, the blast of whistles. This, he guessed, was a more organized search party, probably strung out in a line as they moved through the woods. A horse neighed. And then a sound that stilled his heart: the excited yapping of dogs.

The search party drew nearer his hiding place. Curses as men tripped over roots concealed under the leaves. They were scrambling down the bank. The choked panting of dogs straining against their leashes.

'For Christ's sake keep spread out and keep moving!' yelled a voice. 'We've only got another hour of daylight.'

The dogs whined excitedly and began snuffling through the leaves near the sett. Karl braced himself, mentally rehearsing: 'No shoot, please! No shoot, please!'

There was a sudden commotion and the dogs were dragging their handler away from the badger sett.

'Your bloody dogs!' the voice complained. 'I said they'd be useless. All they're interested in is bleedin' rabbits.'

The search party pushed on through the undergrowth, seemingly more intent on arguing about the respective merits of different breeds of dog rather than hunting for an escaped German officer. They were followed by the man on horseback who seemed to be in charge, judging by the way he yelled orders at his reluctant volunteers.

It was twilight and the daytime temperature, such as it was, had plummeted when Karl extricated himself from the burrow on his elbows. He recovered his greatcoat and wrapped himself in its folds while hobbling up and down, slapping himself to restore his circulation, and contemplating his next move.

The hopelessness of his situation – that he was an enemy in strange land, without money, and with only a rudimentary grasp of English and no knowledge of the geography of this country – never occurred to him. As a lad, he and his brothers had been tasked by their father to rebuild a large, dilapidated barn. It had seemed a huge, impossible task and the boys had protested.

'But you only have to do the roof,' their father had said. 'Just concentrate on that. Think of it as the only job and it'll be finished in no time. Then you do the front and that's the only job and you don't worry about anything else. And so on. You break a big job down into little jobs and before you know it, the whole job is done.'

That sound advice coloured Karl's thinking now. There was no point in worrying about how he was going to get home with his priceless information. His immediate concern was to survive one day. If he could survive one day, he could survive two days. But survival meant getting warm and that meant making a fire. He had no matches but that didn't deter him. He set off up the bank in the failing light and came upon a large, recently fallen oak that he had noticed on his flight. The main branches had been sawn off but the root ball, where it had torn out of the ground, had not been touched. He broke off a digging stick and attacked the soil around the roots. The outer pan was frozen hard but it was soft underneath. He unearthed a squirrel's cache of chestnuts and cobnuts – not what he was looking for but he filled the greatcoat's pockets and continued digging. The two large pieces of fine chalcedony – flint – were exactly what he wanted. One would have been enough but two made the job easier. The smaller piece had a flaw of inclusion. He struck it and the flint fell into two large, wedge-shaped flakes with razor-sharp edges. He used the broadest wedge to prise up and break off two saucer-size sections of bark from the underside of the oak's trunk, where it was reasonably dry. Hacking at an ash using the flint as a hand axe provided him with a long, flexible wand. The other flake served as a plane which he used to shave silver birch bark into a large, wool-like ball, which he thrust into a pocket.

He had enough materials to make a start and set off down the bank to his burrow. The little valley, cut by the stream, and the surrounding trees would screen his fire at night. He spotted an empty cigarette packet. It was dry, most likely dropped by the search party. The silver birch would make good kindling but the cardboard would be better. He gathered an armful of dry leaves, some dead sticks, and broke up a branch into short lengths as logs. Large stones from the stream provided a bed for the eventual fire and would retain heat.

With his trophies set out in easy reach, Karl made himself as comfortable as he could and sat cross-legged to begin work. The flint's sharp point made easy work of gouging a recess in the centre of both pieces of bark. He cut a short length off the thick end of the ash wand to serve as the fire stick. Next he removed his shoelaces and knotted them together into a long lace. Each end was secured to the ash wand to make a loose-stringed bow, which he looped around the fire stick with a single turn. He made the largest piece of bark secure on the ground and located the fire stick in its recess. He held the other piece of bark in his hand and used its recess to hold the upper end of the fire stick. He began sawing the makeshift bow so that the fire stick twirled back and forth. He was careful not to apply too much pressure. His aim was not to make a fire just yet because it wasn't dark enough, but to dry out the sap in the bark and the fire stick. Water vapour curling from the end of the fire stick rewarded his efforts. He kept this up for a further five minutes and stopped to carefully tear the cigarette packet into fine strips. With everything laid out so that he knew where it was, he waited for darkness.

He started work in earnest as the last of the daylight drained from the sky. It took two minutes vigorous sawing with the bow to produce the acrid scent of wood smoke. He settled down to a steady rhythm, taking care not to get too carried away and break the shoelace. The glowing ember that eventually appeared showed up clearly in the gathering gloom but Karl didn't stop work until smoke was stinging his eyes. He gathered the strips of cardboard around the glowing recess in the bark and blew gently, and then a little harder when the first tongue of yellow flame appeared. The warmth on his cheeks was the touch of God. The silver birch shavings followed by dry leaves got the fire going safely, and a carefully built wigwam of larger sticks to aid their drying soon had it well established.

With larger logs spoked around the fire and a handful of chestnuts roasting in the ashes, he wriggled out of the greatcoat and allowed his numbed body to absorb the fire's blissful warmth. He threaded the shoelaces carefully back into his shoes – they were a valued possession. The firelight enabled him to forage nearby for small branches to make a lean-to shelter against the bank, which he covered with leaves and bracken weighted down with handfuls of sphagnum moss. While gathering armfuls of bracken for his bed he heard an indignant snort accompanied by a scuffling in the undergrowth and guessed it was one of the occupants of the sett leaving by an alternative exit while expressing grave displeasure at this invasion of home and habitat.

He washed in the stream and ruefully examined his bruises. His right ankle was now swelling so he made a cold compress of moss and leaf loam and bound it firmly with ivy pulled from nearby trees. A couple of days of severe aches and pains lay ahead of him but he counted himself incredibly lucky not to have broken anything.

A meal of roast chestnuts and edible mushrooms followed by a drink of water further lifted his spirits. He made up the fire so that it would keep in for a few hours and decided to at least try to rest even if his bruises and swellings militated against sleep. It was three hours after sunset when he crawled into his bivouac, scratched a hole in the leaf mould for his hip and rested his head on a pillow made by stuffing his vest full of bracken. Karl liked his creature comforts, had strong views on the subject of pillows, and considered sacrificing the vest well worthwhile.

He listened to the stirrings of nocturnal creatures, deliberately not allowing his thoughts to dwell on the problems of staying free and escaping from England. That left only his aches and pains demanding to be catalogued. His sprained ankle hurt like hell; the nagging pain was certain to overcome his exhaustion and make sleep impossible.

And so he slept.

2

Having submitted his department's weekly naval intelligence summary to his chief, Admiral Godfrey, that morning, Lieutenant-Commander Ian Lancaster Fleming, Royal Navy Volunteer Reserve, had been expecting trouble all day. Big Ben was chiming five o'clock and the blackout curtains were in place when his phone rang. He winked at Sally, his secretary, and picked up the receiver.

'When you've a moment please, Fleming.'

'Right away, sir.' Fleming replaced the phone, yawned, and caught Sally's eye. 'Delay my coffee, angel. G wants to see me.'

'It'll be that report, sir,' said Sally. 'You went a bit far. It reads more like a Dashiell Hammett thriller.'

'That's quite a compliment to pay a former journalist,

13

Sally,' said Fleming. He rose, buttoned his jacket and smoothed his hair. 'Although I've heard that Dashiell Hammett has drink and woman problems. I don't have a drink problem except when I can't get hold of Dom Perignon for my dinner parties.'

The girl smiled and admired Fleming's aristocratic, broken nose profile as he removed his cap from the bentwood coat stand and tucked it under his arm. She reflected that she wouldn't mind being one of his problems. A view that was shared by most of the girls in the Admiralty building. 'When this lot is over, you ought to think about writing thrillers,' she said.

Fleming gave her a disarming grin as he left Room 39. 'Great minds think alike, angel.'

He made his way to Admiral Godfrey's office. 'What sort of mood is he in?' he asked the naval intelligence chief's secretary – a frosty-faced, middle-aged woman, her hair pulled into a tight bun. It annoyed her that she was attracted to Fleming and therefore she strongly disapproved of him.

'It was quite good until he read your report. Go right in.'

Admiral John Godfrey, head of the Directorate of Naval Intelligence, looked up from his desk as Fleming entered. He nodded to a chair, picked up a pink flimsy and handed it to his visitor. 'Signal from the War Office. Those clowns have lost one of your clients. A Leutnant Karl Moehe. He was being escorted to Grizedale Hall when he hopped out of the train a few miles south of Lancaster like a damned flea. Moehe. Mean anything to you?'

'Vaguely, sir. I didn't handle his interrogation. Moehe . . . I think he tried to make a run for it when he was landed at Gib.'

'That's him. I've just been talking to Jenkins. Seems the bounder has made another two escape bids since leaving our care. Third time lucky because they haven't caught him yet. They're resuming the search at first light tomorrow.'

'The train was moving, sir?'

'About thirty miles per hour. Damned fool.'

'I thought the army had rules about escorted POWs being sat on the right-hand side of trains?'

Admiral Godfrey grunted. 'There was a landslide. The train was diverted on to the down line so our friend took a header out of the window, down an embankment. Even so, he took a hell of a risk.' The senior officer leaned forward. 'Take a look at his file, Fleming. See if there's anything in there that might account for him being so damned desperate to escape or if he's just a brainless hothead. Don't waste too much time on it.'

Fleming promised to look into it right away. As he was leaving, Admiral Godfrey's parting shot was: 'A brief, succinct report by tomorrow evening if you please, Fleming, and try not to make it read like *The Thirty-Nine Steps*.'

Fleming returned to Room 39. He flipped his cap on to the bentwood coat stand so that it spun on the peg like a hoopla ring – he rarely missed.

'Phone call while you were out, sir,' said Sally, smiling sweetly. 'A Cathy Standish. She says she's done something quite shocking to bribe a butcher and don't be later than eight o'clock for dinner otherwise she won't be responsible for her actions.'

'Thank you, Sally,' said Fleming, refusing to be drawn. 'Would you get the file on POW Leutnant Karl Moehe for me, please.' He wrote the name on a slip of paper.

'Oh, yes,' said Sally as she was about to leave. 'Miss Standish said that you owe her two shillings for a garlic crusher.'

'Sally.'

'Sir?'

'She's a Mrs.'

Sally was too well-bred and disciplined to go as far as slamming a door when she left a room, but she knew how to close it with just sufficient force to express disapproval. She returned ten minutes later, placed a bulky manila file in front of Fleming and made him his evening cup of coffee.

'Anything else before I leave, sir?'

'No. That's fine, Sally. Thank you.'

The girl put on her hat and coat and bid her boss goodnight, adding, 'Have a nice dinner . . . And dessert.'

'Goodnight, Sally. Oh – one thing. She's a widow.'

For a moment the girl was tempted to ask if she was a merry widow, but that would be pushing even Fleming's good nature too far.

'One of the biggest landowners in the Lake District,' Fleming added.

It seemed to Sally that Fleming was trying paint this Mrs Standish as a homely, matronly country guest. If so, it didn't work: there was nothing homely or matronly about the husky voice on the phone that radiated sexuality like a burning firework factory.

She confined her answer to a polite 'Yes, sir' and left.

Fleming settled down with his coffee to read Moehe's file. The interrogation of the missing U-boat officer at the London 'Cage' in Kensington had been handled by Matthew Hodges and Geoffrey Cape, otherwise known as Mutt and Jeff. They were a good team. Hodges played the hard man and Cape was the softy whose Munich accent was so perfect that it fooled Bavarians. And he had a deadly interrogation technique to go with it. Fleming turned to the transcript of Cape's first session with Moehe. He read the German transcript in preference to the English translation because the hard-pressed DNI translators often skipped Cape's idle chit-chat, mistakenly thinking that it was unimportant.

3

Geoffrey Cape jumped hurriedly to his feet when Karl was marched between two soldiers into the interrogation room. He spilled papers on to the floor, which the soldiers helped him recover. He stammered out embarrassed 'thank yous' in poor English. The soldiers withdrew, leaving Karl sat at the table, gazing in some curiosity at a bespectacled, prematurely bald man who was intent on sorting his papers. Karl guessed he was aged about forty. Small, pink hands that had never known manual work.

Cape looked up and smiled sheepishly. He radiated nervousness. 'Good morning, Leutnant Moehe. I'm Max Stiller.

You can call me Max if you wish. I take it you don't mind if I call you Karl?'

Karl shook the offered hand. The interrogator's grip was limp, non-existent, but what astonished him was the man's Bavarian accent. He snatched his hand away.

Cape looked nonplussed. 'Is something the matter?'

'I don't talk to traitors,' said Karl coldly.

Cape seemed lost for a moment. 'I do hope you're not going to make things even more difficult for me than they are, Karl.'

Karl folded his arms. 'What happened to the other one?'

Cape fumbled in his pocket, produced a packet of cigarettes, which he dropped on the floor. He recovered them and offered the open packet to Karl.

'I don't smoke.'

'Do you mind if I—?'

'I don't care what you do,' Karl interrupted, determined to be uncooperative. 'But I don't like the smell of cigarettes.'

Cape looked uncertain and returned the cigarette he was about to light to the packet. 'In that case, I won't.'

The concession gave Karl the impression that he had a level of control over this traitor. It built his confidence. He repeated his question about the other interrogator.

'Herr Hodges needs to rest his voice now and then,' Cape answered. He smiled self-effacingly. 'I'm a little different.'

'You're very different. Hodges may yell and bang the table, but he is not a traitor. I don't talk to traitors.'

'But you didn't talk much to Hodges.'

Karl shrugged. 'So why are you working for the British?'

A sad look came into Cape's eyes. He seemed reluctant to speak for a moment. 'I am always asked that, therefore the British have allowed me to answer it. I have no choice. My wife and I and even our two children were arrested the day after Chamberlain declared war on us. We were here on a camping holiday in the Scottish highlands.' Cape glanced at the door, felt in his pocket, and slid a photograph across the table. 'Magda, my wife, and Helga and Anna.'

Karl looked down at the photograph but didn't touch it. It showed a pretty blonde sitting on a car's running board with her arms around two curly-haired girls aged about eight. He didn't believe Max's story. On the other hand the English were known for their deviousness. Perfidious Albion, Napoleon called them. The English preferred to learn French as their second language rather than German, which would be more sensible, so it was possible that they would make ruthless use of any German-speakers they could lay their hands on. They seemed to have got hold of a bit of a bumbling idiot in this Max Stiller.

'People think Helga and Anna are twins,' Cape continued. 'But they're not. Hard to believe. Their dates of birth are on the back.'

The slight pleading note in the interrogator's voice prompted Karl to turn the photograph over. The message on the back read:

> I don't know where my wife and children are. The British have promised that no harm will come to them if I work for them. Please do not give me any important information. There is a microphone and a recording machine.

'You see?' said Cape, 'born just over a year apart. But you can understand why people think they're twins, can't you? You understand?'

Karl pushed the photograph back. 'Yes. I understand. They are lovely children. I can't say the same about their father.'

Cape looked sadly at the picture before returning it to his pocket. He fumbled nervously through his papers. 'The British don't tell me much. We'd better start at the beginning. You're Karl Moehe—'

'I have been giving my name, rank and service number, and no more,' said Karl firmly. 'I am Karl Paul Moehe. Leutnant. My service number is—'

'Let's not talk about the Kriegsmarine, Karl. What else can we talk about . . . What was your first paid job?'

The question threw Karl. He thought for a moment and decided that there was no harm in answering this traitorous fool's questions so long as they dealt with innocuous matters. 'Working on my parents' farm.'

'Did you enjoy the work?'

'Yes.'

Cape nodded. The report by the corvette that had picked up Moehe said that he was a strong swimmer and had helped several of his fellow crewmen to the scrambling net. U-boatmen who could not swim were not uncommon. Unlike the British, Germans were not a nation of weekend sailors and tended to spend their childhood summers hiking and camping. 'I can understand,' Cape replied. 'I sometimes used to help out during the holidays on an uncle's smallholding. Such hot work, too, but I never fancied cooling off in his pond. His pigs used to wallow in it.'

'*We* had a lake.'

'Lucky you.' Cape smiled happily as though the reminiscing was providing a brief but valued respite from his troubles. 'All uncle's pond was good for was sailing model boats he used to make for us. Did you ever sail model boats on your lake?'

'Yes,' said Karl, wondering if all this idle chat would get his interrogator into trouble. He hoped so and would do his best to lead him on.

'Did you make them yourself?'

'Yes. But that was when I was about ten. Making sailing boats is kids' stuff. I was interested in making powered boats.'

'I was never much good with my hands,' said Cape ruefully. 'Anything I made that was meant to float, didn't.'

Despite his feelings of hostility towards this man, Karl couldn't help but smile at his woebegone expression.

'So what sort of models did you make, Karl?'

'Everything. Electric boats. Clockwork boats.'

Cape looked at the prisoner admiringly. 'They all worked?'

'Of course.'

'What was the most difficult?'

'A Mississippi stern wheeler,' Karl replied. Cape's disbelieving expression put him on the defensive. 'I had to build everything – even the steam engine. The plans were in an American model-making magazine. Father has a big lathe – for repairing farm machinery. It wasn't very good for model work – too big and clumsy – but I managed.' He settled in his chair. If this idiot was prepared to let him talk about nothing,

19

that was fine by him. 'The magazine came out monthly. You made a few bits each month. And the last parts were how to assemble it and test it. The steam boiler was the most difficult. All the joints had to be brazed.'

'Brazing? Is that like soldering?'

Moehe looked faintly contemptuous. 'It's nothing like soldering. Brazing requires much higher temperatures and special solder and flux.'

'Flux?'

'A sort of paste that excludes oxygen so that metals can bond together when heated.'

'I'm surprised that you didn't go to technical college.'

'Oh, but I did,' Karl replied. He added proudly, 'I passed the entrance examinations and was accepted for the Kriegsmarine Technical Academy in Kiel.'

While automatically answering his interrogator's next question about his father's farm produce, Karl wondered if he had said too much. He had never mentioned his technical background to anyone, not even the table-thumping Hodges, but this stupid Max didn't seem interested. He was now asking about the farm! What would a Bavarian know of seafaring matters? The British were stupid to use him and, no doubt, would be mad at him for not following up his admission. Feeding him a few more tantalizing snippets here and there would probably get him into serious trouble if he didn't recognize their value and follow them up. Serve the traitorous bastard right.

Karl continued answering Max's casual questioning about his boyhood and even mentioned the toy torpedoes he used to make for his youngest brother using his father's aluminium cigar tubes.

'How did they stay underwater?' Cape queried. 'Surely cigar tubes float like corks?'

'They needed some ballast but not much. They were powered by elastic bands with a little propeller at the end – just like real torpedoes except that real torpedoes have two contra-rotating propellers. It was their speed that kept them dynamically submerged – by water pressure acting on the hydroplanes. When the elastic bands ran down, they came to the surface. It was great fun launching them in one spot in the lake and seeing them pop up to the surface in another.'

'Good job they weren't fitted with warheads,' said Cape wryly, 'otherwise you would've been blowing up ducks.'

Karl smiled at the thought. 'Warheads on toy torpedoes would've been difficult for me then. But I could probably manage it now.'

Cape blew his nose. 'How old is your youngest brother?' he asked, neatly folding his handkerchief before returning it to his pocket.

'He'll be seventeen now.'

'I wish I'd had brothers,' said Cape wistfully. 'You seem to have had an idyllic childhood with them.'

'It was a lot of hard work. Real work – not sitting in an office,' Karl replied pointedly.

The door opened. One of guards barked three words in English that Karl had no difficulty understanding:

'Phone, Stiller. Now!'

A fleeting look of anxiety crossed Cape's face. He made his apologies to Karl and left the room, leaving the guard to glower fixedly at the captive. Karl could hear Cape's voice raised in anger in the next room, even shouting during one exchange, but the one-sided conversation was in English so he had no idea what the argument was about.

Cape returned to the interrogation room looking a little chastened. 'The British are cross with me for all the chit-chat.' He gathered up his papers. 'Mr Hodges is to take over. I might be back this evening but I'm not sure. Thank you for your understanding, Karl. I've enjoyed our chat.'

As he left the room, Cape glanced questioningly at the guard, who had moved behind Karl's chair. The guard gave an imperceptible shake of his head. It was what Cape had expected.

Karl remained seated, uncomfortably aware of the guard standing behind him. After five minutes Hodges barged into the room. A short, thickset man with a permanent scowl that increased in intensity as he sat.

'I've been listening in,' Hodges grated in his atrocious accent. 'Waffle. Waffle. Waffle. You may fool that idiot

21

Stiller with all your childhood rubbish, Moehe, but you don't fool me. I want facts from you. What was the purpose of your patrol?'

'To sink your ships,' Karl answered coolly. 'I would've thought that that was self-evident.'

Hodges's face reddened. He banged his fist on the table. 'Don't play the goat with me, you Nazi scum! We're in the process of questioning all the survivors in your crew – victims of bungling, incompetent officers like yourself. It's no wonder your Admiral Doenitz had no confidence in *U-684* and didn't send it to American waters as he is doing with all his operational U-boats. What's the matter, Moehe? Your skipper's navigational skills not up to finding your way across the Atlantic so you had to feel your way along the kerb to North Africa?'

'You've got it in a nutshell,' Moehe replied, adopting a crestfallen expression. 'They were so convinced that we couldn't read charts that we were given school exercise books with a map of the world on the back. We found Africa quite easily really – it's that big place south of Europe. We figured that if we kept the sound of tribal drums on our left all the time, that we should be able to find our way down to Cape Town.'

Hodges's apoplectic expression pleased Karl. He was so easy to wind up. Really, the British were incredibly stupid in their choice of interrogators. He sat back, arms folded and returned the interrogator's hard stare. He decided that he liked Hodges; he knew where he stood with the belligerent little Englishman.

4

It was after 7 p.m. Fleming was about to call it a day when he became aware of the shadowy figure in the doorway of his office. In accordance with Admiralty power-saving rules, the desk lamp was the only light in the room. He pushed it to one side and rose.

'Good evening, sir.'

'Burning some midnight, Fleming?' Admiral Godfrey enquired, entering the office. He was wearing his coat and scarf.

Fleming gestured ruefully at the piles of manila folders and documents strewn across his desk. 'I decided to clear up this Moehe business right away and got a bit involved.'

The senior officer reflected that it had to be interesting for Fleming to allow it to eat into his womanizing hours. 'Anything I need to know about?'

'We need more analysis staff, sir.'

Admiral Godfrey glowered.

Fleming handed him a grainy photograph that showed a fresh-faced young man saluting as he received a scroll from Admiral Karl Doenitz, the commander-in-chief of Germany's U-boat arm. 'A blow-up from some newsreel footage,' said Fleming. 'Graduation day at the Kiel Technical Academy. Summer 1936. That's Moehe receiving a double diploma. Note the two tabs on the scroll. He must be a bright lad. They send the best ones to the torpedo research station at Wilhemshaven. Geoff Cape wormed out of Moehe that he was interested in torpedoes and that he knew the best beer gardens in Wilhemshaven.'

'So you've learned that the U-boat arm has officers who know something about torpedoes,' Admiral Godfrey observed dryly. 'I'm impressed.'

Fleming positioned another photograph under his desk lamp – a group photograph of ten smiling young men in Kriegsmarine coveralls. In the centre was an older man. They were standing in the gardens of a palatial mansion. The Germans' love of taking group photographs was matched by the British intelligence services' love of collecting copies of German group photographs. If you could identify one person in a group picture or knew what he was doing, the chances were that the others in the picture were doing the same thing or helping him do it.

'This arrived from Stockholm yesterday,' said Fleming. 'Our naval attaché says that the gentleman in the middle is Professor Wolfgang Braun – the head of T5 research at

Siemens. And that building is definitely Siemens's research labs. And the gentleman to Braun's left is definitely our runaway Karl Moehe, wouldn't you say, sir?'

Admiral Godfrey bent over the picture. 'Not much doubt about it,' he grunted.

'And Moehe is wearing coveralls, so he's not just visiting. He's part of Professor Braun's T5 team.'

There was a silence in the office for a few moments as the older man considered the implications of Fleming's ferreting. The Directorate of Naval Intelligence had strong evidence that T5 was the code name for an acoustic torpedo that the Kriegsmarine were known to be developing. A deadly weapon that could home in on the engine noises of ships.

'The rest is conjecture on my part,' Fleming admitted. 'I've checked with Sefton Delmer at Milton Bryan and he's confirmed that Moehe's *U-684* hasn't been mentioned in dispatches on Goebbels's news-service Hell-Schrieber teleprinters. There's a big gap between when it was commissioned at Kiel and it being sunk off Portugal. Doenitz wouldn't keep a nice new operational Type VIIC U-boat out of the fun off the US coast without good reason. My guess is that it had been carrying out tests of prototype T5s in the Baltic and that its trip into the Atlantic was to test the torpedoes under operational conditions. According to the corvette that picked up survivors after the U-boat was bombed, the scuttling charges were no ordinary charges. They made a hell of a bang and the U-boat sank within seconds before the boarding party in a dinghy got near it.'

Admiral Godfrey considered that Fleming was pushing supposition to its extremes but he had learned to respect his subordinate's intuitive flair and shrewd assessments.

'The chances are,' Fleming continued, 'that Moehe was the technical officer in charge of the trials and he has vital information on the behaviour of the T5 torpedoes that he has to get home. Hence his frequent escape attempts. He's certainly no hothead making breaks out of sheer bravura like von Werra.'

'Any luck with the interrogations of other crew survivors?'

Fleming leafed through some papers. 'The few that have

been processed so far have refused to say anything. Name, rank and number. Nothing else.'

'All of them?'

'All of them so far, sir,' Fleming affirmed. 'Right down to the diesel mechanics. Looks like they'd all received some intensive briefing by Moehe before they were picked up. He was the only officer to survive.'

Admiral Godfrey pressed his lips together in a hard line. Fleming's reasoning made a lot of sense. 'So you're angling for me to sanction petrol for you to go to Grizedale Hall tomorrow and have a long chat with the fellow?'

'That's assuming he'll be caught tomorrow,' said Fleming carefully.

'Of course he'll be caught. He doesn't speak English, does he?'

'No, sir. We're certain of that. Cape had a fake telephone conversation in English in Moehe's hearing saying that it would be wrong to stand Moehe against a wall and have him shot. Moehe didn't react, and he was never caught out.'

'Well, then – he'll be picked up,' said Admiral Godfrey irritably, moving to the door.

'Perhaps not, sir. During Cape's second session he learned that before Moehe joined the navy he had spent a couple of years in the Hitler Youth and had liked going on their toughening-up extended survival training trips without taking as much as a knife. He always seemed to draw the short straw and get the toughest assignments and the worst instructors. He picked up the nickname Unlucky Moehe.'

5

The pain in his ankle and cramp in his calf woke Karl. It was still dark but what concerned him was that forest creatures of the night must have encased his body in concrete while he slept because he was unable to move. It required careful planning before he was able to ease himself on to his stomach and use his elbows to drag himself out of his bivouac. Each muscle set in motion was the result of intense concentration. Eventually he was able to sit up and take stock, trying to ignore the demons that were gleefully thrusting red hot lances into his ankle. The fire consisted of a single ember no larger than a burning cigarette end but everything was brittle dry from the heat so it was easy to coax it back into cheering light and warmth by gentle blowing and feeding it with a few leaves. From the remains of the spoke pattern of half burnt-out logs he guessed that he had slept for about five hours. There were still several hours before daybreak. Losing his watch when *U-684* went down was a nuisance. He preferred not to think about his fellow officers, all of whom had perished.

He peeled away the compress he had tied around his ankle and was alarmed to see how badly swollen it was. Walking was out of the question – he couldn't even get his shoe on. There was nothing else to do but prop himself against a tree root and consider his options. There was only one: he would have to remain here another twenty-four hours to rest his ankle. The sound of a train reminded him how close he was to the railway. Maybe that was a good thing: the British were sure to think that he had got much further away when they resumed their search.

But first he had to get reasonably mobile. With the aid of his flint hand axe he hacked away at a forked hazel and shaped it into a crude but serviceable crutch. He used the bark shavings to make a torch and hobbled to the stream. The handful of heavy clay he dug out of the bank felt promising – just the right moisture content for the crude bowl he hand-moulded to hold its shape. He made a larger version and placed both efforts near the fire, turning them now and then so that they would dry out evenly without cracking. Next he took a close look at the navy-blue greatcoat the Red Cross had given him. He turned it inside-out and slit through the outer layer across the back. As he expected, the inter-lining that gave the garment its shape and bulk consisted of tough sackcloth-like woven hessian. He napped a new flint hand knife. It was good flint and provided razor sharp flakes. Slicing the inter-lining into bandage-width strips was easier than he had anticipated. He joined them carefully together with a series of small knots across the material's warp and ended up with a two metre long bandage.

Making the hot poultice was more difficult. The larger bowl wasn't really dry enough to stand being filled with water and stood on the fire. Instead, he filled it half full and used two pieces of bark to grip one of the big stones that formed the base of the fire. The water spat and seethed as he lowered the hot stone into the bowl. Another hot stone brought the water to the boil. He added handfuls of sphagnum moss, which he stirred into a thick porridge and proceeded to slap it on to his swollen ankle as hot as he could bear while winding the makeshift bandage tightly around the injury to keep the poultice in place. The pain eased almost immediately. He rested to contemplate his handiwork and reflected that his old Hitler Youth instructor would've been proud of him. An hour later he redid the hot poultice and was pleased to see that the swelling was going down.

Careful not to overdo things, he foraged for fuel, breaking longer saplings into suitable lengths by levering them between forked branches, and placing them around the fire to dry and so reduce the amount of smoke they gave off when they burned. Breakfast as the first light of dawn stained the eastern sky consisted of roast chestnuts and hazel nuts, and he even made some tea by steeping ground elder in boiling water. He risked one more hot poultice, doused the fire and hid evidence of his occupation of the area under leaves and bracken. He passed an hour improving the camouflage of his lean-to and making it waterproof because a sullen black sky held the threat of rain. He had just finished moving his carefully dried fuel under the bank's overhang and covering it as best he could when the sky carried out its threat.

The deluge lasted all day and kept Karl confined to camp. No bad thing, he decided: he needed to rest his foot as much as possible. He was cleaning his teeth, using the chewed end of a twig as a toothbrush, when he caught a glimpse of a low-flying single-engine light aircraft that seemed to be square searching the area. Probably an RAF trainer with the pupil pilot being given some practical experience of ground reconnaissance. It stayed around for about an hour, droning back and forth before losing interest and returning north. It was the only high point in a crushingly boring day spent dozing and daydreaming.

The rain stopped and nightfall brought clear skies and the warmth of a fire and a hot meal of edible roots, horseradish and ground elder soup with the last of his nuts thrown in for good measure. His ankle was much better and needed only an occasional cold compress. He could now wriggle his foot into his shoe.

Tomorrow, he decided, he would be fit enough to walk. His plan was to head east, walking only at night and sleeping where he could during the day. He had to avoid coming into contact with locals at all costs. He reckoned that he'd have no trouble maintaining an easterly heading if he kept Jupiter on his right and Polaris on his left. England being an island meant that he was certain to reach the east coast which he would then follow south until he came to a port. Finding and stowing away on a ship sailing for neutral Sweden would be a problem. Maybe there would be an opportunity to steal a boat. Mindful of his father's advice about breaking large projects down into smaller tasks, that worry could wait. He was confident that a means of escaping England's shores would present itself so that he would be able to return home with his vital information. Never again would he be called *Ungluckish*. In the meantime, he would play each day as it came.

6

Karl slept soundly that night and was awake shortly before dawn. After a thorough wash in the icy stream he felt refreshed and ready for anything. While cleaning and polishing his nails, using a sandstone pebble as a nail file, he decided to risk foraging along the railway track in the half light – a lucky decision because he came across a workmen's hut protected by a flimsy padlock. He levered the hasp and its wood screws popped out of the door. Inside the hut was a real find: the repair gang's working clothes. A tough-looking pair of battered, scuffed boots were too large but they would be better than his shoes. An oilskin cape was thrust into his greatcoat's cavernous pockets plus a woolly hat together with lengths of string and even an old ivory-handled table knife and matching fork. He went through all the workmen's pockets and found a shilling, a few pennies, and best of all: a box of Swan Vestas matches. A packet of stale cheese sandwiches provided a welcome breakfast. A screw-top lemonade bottle and an enamel drinking mug would certainly be useful. He rummaged in an old oil drum that served as a litter bin that hadn't been emptied for months. It yielded paper that he could use for kindling, a comb, a small handbag mirror, lengths of wire that he could use to set rabbit snares, and a couple of crisp packets with their twists of blue paper containing salt intact – a particularly lucky find. Also there were fragments of soap, a smelly face flannel, a rusty but sharp safety razor and various other small items that might be useful. All disappeared in his pockets.

He secured the padlock hasp in position, wedged the screws in place with spent matches, and returned to his camp where he set out his trophies to admire them, pleased with the results of his expedition. His ankle had hardly troubled him. A few minutes spent honing the razor on a flat stone restored a usable edge. With the mirror held in position on a root by a knob of clay, and with the aid of a piece of the soap, he managed to give himself a reasonably clean shave. He was particularly glad to be rid of his three days' stubble.

Three days! He had evaded capture for three days, nor was there any sign that the British were looking for him now: he was living down that damned unfair Hitler Youth nickname.

The day was unseasonably warm, so he peeled off the greatcoat and moved to the edge of the woods adjoining the farmland, where he would be able to remain hidden and sit in the sun. He spotted the worn track of a rabbit run and used some of the wire he'd found to set a couple of snares. About a hundred metres from his hiding place was a row of humps like giant mole hills with a tuft of straw sticking out of the top of each mound. He recognized them immediately. They were earthen clamps – overwintering stores to keep root vegetables fresh. He noted their position for an after-dark visit. A meal of baked potatoes would be a good start to his hike.

The sun was fast losing its strength when he saw a lone figure striding across the fields, vaulting confidently over drystone walls with the aid of a stout staff, whistling tunelessly. The figure drew nearer. Karl crouched and watched him. His first thought that the man was a shepherd was quickly dispelled. He didn't think English shepherds wore shorts and carried rucksacks on their backs with a mug hanging from a cord. He passed within twenty metres of Karl's hiding place, his muscular legs shortening their stride as he went up the rise and disappeared from view.

A hiker!

Now *there* was an idea. He had noticed hikers during the train journey and chided himself for not thinking of it earlier. What appeared to be a lone hiker making his way across country in the daytime, or at any time, would be unlikely to attract attention.

He hurried back to his camp and set to work. He restored the black sheen to the workman's boots by rubbing them with pine resin that oozed from nearby trees. The process also helped make them waterproof. They looked quite smart by the time he'd finished. Some experimental folding of his greatcoat and securing it with string provided him with a realistic-looking rucksack, especially with the poultice bandages serving as shoulder straps. The dangling enamel mug would be a nice touch. He decided against cutting his trouser legs to shorts – not all hikers wore shorts. A stout length of straight hazel trimmed with his hand axe made a good staff. Shaving off the bark and working pine resin into it gave it a professional sheen. He cut three notches into it with his flint knife. One for each day of freedom; each notch representing a victory.

At dusk he set off to investigate the clamps and returned, staggering under the weight of the greatcoat slung from his shoulder bulging with parsnips, potatoes and carrots. The earthen mounds with the straw chimneys were a veritable larder. To add to his run of good fortune, one of his snares had caught a large rabbit.

He lit a fire when night fell and used another flake struck from his flint to skin and gut the rabbit. He spitted it over the fire while the vegetables baked in the hot ashes. Next he washed his underclothes and decked them around the fire to dry. He kept his foot near the fire's warmth while preparing his meal because his busy day had set off the throbbing again – a reminder that he still wasn't a hundred per cent fit for walking; nevertheless his plan was to set off when he had eaten. The rabbit sizzled cheerfully and dripped fat on to the fire. It smelt good. And it tasted even better, too, as he discovered thirty minutes later when he tucked into the first meal of fresh meat and vegetables that he'd had since spending his Christmas leave with his parents. He used a large piece of oak bark as a plate, and a real knife and fork, the rabbit and vegetables flavoured with a sprinkle of his precious salt. There wasn't a scrap of meat left on the small pile of bones by the time he had finished gorging himself.

He climbed to his feet and gingerly tested his weight on his ankle. It hurt. But he was in good spirits, feeling decidedly but satisfyingly bloated. It would be better, he decided, to rest and be on his way at first light. Besides, he would need daylight to be certain of clearing the campsite and hiding all traces of his occupation.

7

K arl opened his eyes to a bright blue sky and sunlight filtering through the trees. His prayers before falling asleep for the good weather to hold had been answered. The bivouac was dry and he felt snug and warm. There was no tell-tale smouldering from the fire, so he allowed himself the luxury of a lie-in – two or three hours dozing and then to work. The first job was to add another notch to his staff.

Bathing in the icy stream was an unpleasant but necessary

business. He hated feeling dirty. He shaved, being careful to conserve his soap, scrubbed his teeth as best he could with a twig, and cleaned his nails. Once dressed, he buried all the waste he had accumulated and tossed his fire stones back in the stream. The lean-to's materials were scattered around the clearing. He stowed all his belongings in his greatcoat rucksack. He had already tested the boots and found them reasonably comfortable but they needed packing with leaves until some suppleness returned with use. He took about ten kilos of vegetables, which was as much as he felt he could carry. The rest he lobbed into the trees.

No one seeing the clean-shaven young man emerging from the trees into the bright sunlight would have suspected that he had been living rough for nearly a week. He looked smart and well scrubbed, his step confident, his boots gleaming, his grasp on his staff firm, the rucksack, with its dangling mug, sitting comfortably on his shoulders. A woolly hat completed his outfit.

Karl walked eastward for four hours across the rolling fells, taking as straight a line as possible although he soon learned to take care in valleys where the sun didn't reach because the ground could be soft and even dangerously boggy.

The land changed subtly as he pushed eastward. The few arable fields gave way to sheep-rearing country, and what trees there were in folds and hollows seemed more stunted. The ache in his legs suggested that he'd been climbing the whole afternoon. Thankfully his ankle had held out. Seeing several parties of hikers was a relief and on one occasion he saw a solitary fell walker carrying a sketch pad.

An hour before dusk he made camp in a dank, gloomy patch of woodland on the north side of a fell. Rather than make a bivouac, he arranged some short stakes to set up his greatcoat as a makeshift tent, helped by two sheets of rusting corrugated steel that he dragged out of a stagnant pond. He decided not to risk drinking the water and was glad that he had taken the precaution of filling his lemonade bottle whenever he came across a clear tarn or stream. His evening meal consisted of two potatoes and two carrots from his stock. He hadn't seen any clamps that day – just fells and sheep. The extra weight of vegetables in his pack had turned out to be a wise investment.

Before falling asleep, he went over the day's march and estimated that he had travelled twenty kilometres. He knew that England got narrower to the north, and the train had taken him a long way up. Based on a considered guess, he hoped to reach the coast in five days but the important thing was to take one day at a time in the certain knowledge that he would reach the North Sea eventually. He was a seaman and saw the sea not as a hindrance, but as a path that led to freedom and home.

He spent a restless, uncomfortable, night and was glad to be up and busy at first light such as it was because a heavy, leaden cloud base lay low across the fells like a damp funeral shroud. Another notch – another victory. The meagre daylight was so diffused when he set off that it was impossible to determine the position of the sun. He maintained his heading by point-to-point navigation – fixing on a distant landmark and walking towards it although even this became difficult as the mist closed in. The conditions improved as the day wore on but having to skirt a small town took longer than he expected. At one point he walked along a well-used farm track enclosed by drystone walls. It offered some respite from the wind although he tried to avoid tracks for fear of meeting someone. A concern that was borne out when he breasted a rise and saw two farm workers repairing a cart that had a broken axle. They were only about fifty metres away and had seen him. There was nothing for it but to keep walking while rehearsing an English-accented 'good morning' under his breath. Good. Good. Good. Not *guten*. Morning! Morning! Morning!

They stopped work and watched his approach with interest.

'Hey opp,' one of them called out as Karl drew level with them.

Karl smiled and doffed his woollen hat. 'Good morning, fucking swede-bashers,' he responded in a friendly tone and kept walking. He reached a bend and glanced back at the men. They hadn't resumed work but were glowering at him in undisguised hostility.

8

The weather was appalling the next day. Icy cold, wind-driven unceasing rain that swept in vicious bone-numbing squalls across the high fells. Karl's greatcoat, which he was now wearing, became a heavy, sodden mass that slowed his pace. Eventually he was forced to abandon his trek and seek refuge in a shepherd's stone hut that was built into a moss-encrusted wall. He sat huddled, cold, wet and miserable while doing his best to dry out the greatcoat but there was no fuel for a fire, and his food for the entire day consisted of three raw carrots. He wished that he had thought to bring more carrots than potatoes because they could be eaten uncooked. Some rusty cans that he wedged upright on the wall caught some rain for drinking and shaving. Keeping reasonably smart-looking was an essential part of his disguise.

Freezing fog compounded his misery the following day. Contemplating another day of inactivity, spent shivering in the shelter, was out of the question but he had no choice. The notch he cut into his staff was a hollow victory.

There was no improvement in the weather the next day. He decided that it would be better to keep moving and rely on his sense of direction to hold his eastward course. After two hours' trudging, he sensed that his general path was downwards. His soaring hope that perhaps he was nearing the coast was soon dashed when he started climbing again.

He crossed several roads and even followed one for a while in the hope of coming across a signpost. He found one, the British hadn't been that efficient in removing them all this far north, but the name on the finger board, 'Satterthwaite', meant nothing to him. He guessed that the village was near because there were more scattered buildings and farmhouses around, and he even heard a clock in a house chiming two o'clock as he passed it – his first indication of the time other than the sun's position since his escape. He came upon a well-worn road that probably led down to a village. If there was a church its orientation would give him a bearing, but he dismissed the idea as being too risky.

He drove himself on into the unseen wilderness and kept going until every pace became forced, aching labour. A stand of tall and forbidding pine trees loomed out of the heavy mist. He veered towards them. Those tree trunks on the edge of the woodland exposed to the sun would have moss growing only on the north-facing side of their trunks. It would give him a rough bearing. To his dismay, he discovered that the moss was not growing where he expected. He had been heading north.

With his spirits lower than at any time since his capture, he decided that further progress in this fog was impossible so he pushed a little further into the pines and made camp. Lighting a fire was also impossible. The cloying fog had soaked through everything and had even penetrated the cellophane wrapping around his box of matches. Two heads crumbled to paste when he tried to strike them and he dared not waste any more. He still had his two pieces of bark and the fire stick but gave up after fifteen minutes' ineffective sawing back and forth with the bow. The technique depended on dry kindling; everything was wet in this godforsaken place.

Rather than lie down, he propped himself against a tree and chewed slowly on his last carrot to make it last. How many days had he been free? Nine? Ten? The cold was playing tricks with his memory. He counted the notches on his staff and realized that he couldn't remember if he had added one that morning. Perhaps the appalling weather would ease tomorrow. This dreary, soul-eroding, freezing fog could not last. And with that little spark of optimism to sustain him, exhaustion brought the merciful relief of sleep.

9

Karl woke and immediately realized that his nickname had reasserted itself. The fog was now so thick that it had permeated the pines. Visibility was less than fifty metres and the straight column-like brooding conifers gave the impression that he was standing in the middle of a giants' chess game. Packing with frozen fingers took a long time. He tried to carve a notch but the knife kept slipping from his numbed grasp. A deep scratch would have to suffice.

Breakfast was a swig of water from his lemonade bottle. With hunger and cold as his sole companions, he set off out of the woods and stopped dead when it dawned on him that he could not remember his route into the woods. The trees were no help: each pine looked exactly like its neighbour. He retraced his footsteps to where he had camped and tried to visualize his movements of yesterday evening. The springy pine needles did not retain footprints. It was ridiculous: he had been too tired to have penetrated much more than fifty metres, if that, and now he couldn't find his way out. All he had to do was spiral out from his camping site and he would be sure to find the edge of the pines. But dense clumps of undergrowth, huge spreads of rhododendrons, and the need to make frequent detours soon got him hopelessly lost. What he had first supposed was a small stand of pines turned out to be a large forest.

And the fog got worse.

Karl spent the rest of that day stumbling through that hellish place, getting progressively weaker and even reduced to licking moisture off rhododendron leaves now that his water was gone. There were no trees other than the conifers and their ground-sterilizing needles. No hazels with their crops of nuts that could usually be scratched out of the soft loam that carpeted forests. No pig nuts – nothing.

But for the scratches on his staff, he would have lost count of the several days of aimless wandering in that terrible forest, sleeping fitfully when he could, not caring if it was day or night while his strength ebbed away. Yet deep down in his soul, his iron will kept his fierce resolve to escape burning like a bright flame in the darkness of his misery. His blinding hunger and thirst induced crazy hallucinations. At one point, when half asleep, he imagined that he heard the sound of distant axes, men singing a German folk song, laughter. But despite his wretchedness, his spirit never fully deserted him; the priceless knowledge that he had to get home drove him on through the misery of unending fog-shrouded days and nights.

It was late afternoon or early morning, he didn't know which, when he suddenly realized that the hated conifers were no more. He stopped and stared. There were no trees within the radius of his fog-limited vision. Underfoot was grass and he could hear a nearby stream. He wheeled around. The edge of the forest was fifty metres away, its perimeter marked by a broad firebreak track that he hadn't noticed crossing, so confused were his senses. The compulsive sound of the stream was easy to follow. He fell on his stomach on the bank and sated his raging thirst. As he raised his head to take in his surroundings he felt the touch of a breeze on his face. The fog was swirling, forming into ghostly tendrils, and for a few moments a watery, low sun appeared for the first time in over a week.

About two kilometres ahead, across a valley and a narrow road, a grey stately mansion appeared. The fog closed in again but those few moments were enough for Karl to take in most of the mansion's details. It was big, and stood in its own grounds protected by a high wall. Best of all, there were no major obstructions between him and the vision – just a long, downward slope across fields criss-crossed by a few low walls, and littered with the inevitable grazing sheep.

He remained motionless when the fog thickened again, not daring to move because his body was aimed straight at the point where the mansion had appeared. Such a large building would be certain to offer many hiding places while he searched inside for the kitchen. The ground's frozen touch penetrated his clothes but he hardly noticed. Only when darkness had fallen did he rise to his feet and move forward while concentrating desperately on keeping to a straight line. He came to the first drystone wall where he expected to find it and climbed over, hope enabling his exhausted muscles to draw on unsuspected reserves. Some sheep sheltering on the far side scattered in alarm. He ignored them, not taking his eyes off the point in the featureless curtain of fog where the mansion lay. Another field crossed, another low wall encountered, again, where it was expected. His heartbeat quickened when his nostrils picked up the faint scent of cooked food.

So intent was he on keeping his eyes fixed straight ahead that he almost fell into the ditch that bordered the road.

Beyond the ditch was the high wall that seemed to surround the mansion. It was much higher than it had looked during his brief glimpse – at least three metres and built of close-fitting granite blocks. He decided to skirt it in the hope that he'd find a place where it would be low enough to climb. The direction he took didn't matter – he couldn't lose the mansion now, and the heady smell of cooking was stronger. An hour's searching along the high wall brought luck. There was severe frost damage on a corner where the wall turned abruptly and climbed a steep rise. There was a gap that had been spanned with several strands of barbed wire, but the surrounding mortar was weak, crumbling to dust in places. Despite his hunger-weakened state, Karl scrambled up the pile of fallen masonry and feverishly yanked several more blocks away, making a gap below the barbed wire that he could wriggle through.

The large, imposing mansion was on the far side of some large shrubs and an expanse of lawn that had been mostly turned over to growing vegetables. Yellow light shone around gaps in the curtains in upstairs windows. There were even a few ineffectual, low-wattage floodlights on one side of the building that illuminated the shrubbery. He had noticed on his long trek that the locals weren't as blackout conscious in this part of the world as they were in London although he had never seen floodlights in use. As if reading his thoughts, a distant air-raid siren sounded its mournful, wailing lament. Karl waited, crouching behind a rhododendron bush to see what would happen and to familiarize himself with the layout of the mansion and its grounds. As far as he could make out, the mansion had a balustraded terrace that spanned the full width of the house. He reasoned that if the place was anything like similar to great houses at home, the kitchen would be separate from the main building, probably adjoining a stable yard or outbuildings. He heard the distant drone of bombers. Although pleased that the Luftwaffe were taking the war against the English this far north, he felt that his comrades' timing left much to be desired because at that moment all the guiding chinks of light and the floodlights were extinguished as though a master switch had been thrown. The darkness was now total. It would be dangerous in his present state to do anything other than wait for first light.

Two hours later the siren sounded the all clear and the lights came back on.

Karl decided to act. He darted diagonally across the lawn towards the side of the mansion and froze when he heard voices and the crunch of boots on gravel – glowing cigarette ends marking the progress of the two men as they talked in low tones. He waited until they had passed and raced to the side of the mansion, heedless of a painful trip on steps because the smell of food was now overpowering – clamouring at his reason.

He was drawn to a dimly lit ground-floor window. He peered in at a large scullery with stone sinks and draining boards like aircraft-carrier decks lining two walls, stacked with enough plain white dinner plates to feed a hundred people. That the occupants of such a fine house were reduced to eating off such cheap crockery was indicative of the state that the English were in. All they had left were their fine houses and estates, and even these would soon be redistributed to his victorious countrymen. The soft light came from an adjoining room which *had* to be the kitchen. He cautiously tested the door beside the window and found that it was unlocked.

Ungluckish Moehe indeed!

The first thing he noticed was the warmth. He had almost forgotten what warmth was and risked a minute spent savouring the bliss emanating from an ancient cast-iron radiator. The radiators in the big house in London where he had been interrogated had always been cold.

He pulled off his boots, crossed the scullery in stockinged feet to the door, and peered around the jamb when he was satisfied that the adjoining room was unoccupied. His surmise that it was the main kitchen proved correct. It was a large room with a flagstone floor. Down one wall stood a row of gas cookers, and the other walls were lined with plain dressers and cupboards. In the centre was a large, plain deal food preparation table. A sleeping black cat, curled in the middle of the table, raised its head and stared fixedly at him with unblinking amber eyes. The place, lit by a solitary low-wattage light bulb hanging from the ceiling, had the clean-scrubbed, tidy look of a busy kitchen that had been put to bed for the night.

Karl seized the cat's bowl and crammed the remains of its meal into his mouth. English shepherd's pie. He had been fed on it during his captivity in London. The cat regarded him speculatively. During a long and largely criminal career the cat had often stolen from its 'staff' but this was the first time that one of them had stolen from it.

The meagre leftovers aggravated Karl's ravening hunger. Not only did he need food now, but supplies that would sustain him on his eastward trek. He opened and closed cupboards. They were bare. He found a larder, its shelves stacked with catering tins of peas, dried milk and dried eggs – all too large to be of any use.

Back in the main kitchen he spotted a large food-mixing bowl draped with mutton cloth. It had been placed on the top-most shelf of a high dresser, doubtless to be outside the cat's sphere of thievery.

There was no sign of a stepladder, so Karl climbed on to the dresser's lower ledge and reached up. The cat watched with interest. Karl considered that the wretched creature

40

must be a hardened villain for anyone to go to such trouble to put food out of its reach: he could only just grip the bowl by standing on tiptoe. It tilted slightly. Tepid stew ran down his arms and dripped on to the ledge he was standing on. The heavenly aroma of cooked meat and vegetables was overpowering. He shifted his footing and felt the onset of a problem in the making as his stockinged foot encountered the spilt stew and started sliding away from under him. The dresser's upper section moved away from the wall. The problem turned into a disaster with terrifying rapidity. The bowl slipped out of Karl's hands, drenching him in about three litres of lukewarm Irish stew. He felt himself falling and lashed out, grabbing the first thing his flailing hands encountered, which happened to be the light flex.

Karl managed to fall without crying out as he hit the flagstone floor amid a shower of sparks. He rolled clear of the falling dresser, which made up for his stoic silence by coming down with a tremendous crash while unleashing a cascade of crockery that seemed to shake the building. The bowl containing the Irish stew never reached the floor because it finished its fall upended on Karl's head.

The cat, sensing that it would be involved in blame apportionment during the inevitable accounting that was sure to follow, did the sensible thing and fled.

There were shouts. Boots thundered into the kitchen. The unmistakable sound of rifles being cocked. Blinded by Irish stew, and by the bowl over his head, Karl shot his hands up and cried out: 'No shoot, please! No shoot!'

'On your feet, Jerry! And keep those hands up!'

The bowl fell off Karl's head and shattered on the flagstones as he climbed to his feet. He wiped stew from his eyes and blinked in the flashlight beam that was trained on his face. Five Lee Enfield rifles held by five unsmiling, khaki-clad British soldiers were aimed at him. One of the soldiers wore sergeant's chevrons and a hard expression. His name was Sergeant Finch and he didn't like Germans. He gave an order and a soldier turned on the kitchen's main lights. Karl stood amid the wreckage of the fallen dresser

41

and smashed crockery. He sensed that even if he had a good command of English, talking himself out of this one would not be easy.

There was a footfall outside and Major James Reynolds, Canadian Army Corps, DSO, entered the kitchen. He was wearing a dressing gown and a black patch over his left eye. His lone eye surveyed the mess and glittered angrily at Karl. He had been sitting in his office-cum-workshop making flies and spinners when he had been interrupted by the commotion in the kitchen.

'Caught this one stealing food, saar!' yelled the sergeant, as though the officer were several parade grounds distant.

Reynolds winced and wondered, not for the first time, if it might be possible to arrange Sergeant Finch's transfer to the coastguard service to make up for any likely wartime shortages of foghorns.

'He doesn't look like one of ours,' Reynolds observed. He studied Karl. 'Name?'

'Karl Moehe, sir.' Karl saluted. His stockinged feet rendered his heel click inaudible.

Reynolds frowned.

'Bleedin' liar!' Sergeant Finch's voice dislodged flakes of ceiling plaster. 'Major Reynolds wants your real name!'

'Leutnant Karl Moehe, Kriegsmarine?' Reynolds enquired.

The question depressed Karl. It suggested that the English were on to him; he would not have given his rank unless asked. 'Yes, sir.'

'We don't have anyone of that name, saar!'

'I think we do now, Sergeant.' Reynolds folded his arms and regarded the young German officer. He said in slow, careful German, 'How did you get in here?'

Normally Karl would not volunteer any information that easily, but his spirit was crushed by this latest capture. He answered, 'I was hungry. I saw lights and found a hole in the wall, and made it bigger.' His voice trailed away.

Reynolds's thoughtful expression gave way to the beginnings of a smile that played at the corners of his mouth.

'Well, Leutnant Karl Moehe. Welcome to Grizedale Hall. Prisoner-of-War Number One Camp, Hawkshead, for officers. You were due here two weeks ago.'

10

'Two weeks!' Fleming echoed incredulously, and started laughing.

'I fail to see any humour in the situation,' said Admiral Godfrey frostily. 'E.F.T.S. 15 logged three hundred flying hours looking for the blighter.'

'Which they would've probably spent on flying experience for their pupil pilots anyway, sir,' Fleming pointed out.

'And over one thousand hours by war reserve constables. Damn fellow dressed as a hiker and strolled across England in broad daylight bold as brass. According to him, no one challenged him. Not one.'

'So he's been questioned?'

'Just the usual camp debriefing.' Admiral Godfrey rooted around on his desk and produced some papers. 'Pack of lies if you ask me. Look at this. He says he lit a fire the first night by rubbing two bits of wood together. Everyone knows that that's not possible.'

'Mutt and Jeff's reports from the "Cage" point out that although Moehe did his best not to provide much information, what information he did provide was truthful.'

'And you think that you can get more information out of him?'

'We've now got all the interrogation transcripts from his other crewmen,' said Fleming.

'And not one of them has mentioned as much as a whisper about the T5,' Admiral Godfrey observed.

'Precisely, sir. Sherlock Holmes's point was that the dog didn't bark. All the POWs we've captured so far mention harmless snippets about their service life, but not the crew of *U-684* – they've been kept isolated from one another

43

and yet they've not even said as much as what their *smut* was like.'

'*Smut*?'

'Their cook, sir. We know from what the naval attaché in Stockholm has gleaned that the T5 acoustic torpedo is at the trial stage. We know that *U-684* set out from Kiel and not the U-boat bases at Lorient and Brest, therefore it wasn't part of an Atlantic group. We know from decoded signals traffic that it maintained radio silence – the dog didn't bark. We know that Moehe was the U-boat's first watch officer and that he's a torpedo specialist.' Fleming paused and smiled ruefully. 'The one thing Moehe hasn't kept from us is that he's desperate to escape.'

'As are they all, Fleming. And you want me to send you to Grizedale Hall to talk to him?'

'It's our best shot, sir. We know next to nothing about the T5.'

Admiral Godfrey didn't like the Americanism but let it pass. 'What makes you think that Moehe will talk to you, Fleming, when he's hardly talked to anyone else?'

'My irrepressible self-confidence, sir.'

The older man smiled thinly. Well, it was an honest answer but it didn't convince him. 'You may be right, Fleming, but I think you're building too much on too little – reading too much into this Moehe's escapes. Sorry to disappoint you, but I know from experience that once I send you to the Lake District, its charms are such that we won't see you again for days.'

It was an unfair comment but Fleming knew better than to argue the point beyond observing that the fishing season hadn't started.

'The answer's still no. You're needed here in London.'

'Very good, sir.'

'Besides,' said Admiral Godfrey when Fleming reached the door. 'From what I've heard, you've brought some of the Lake District's charms to London.'

Fleming inwardly cursed the Admiralty rumour mill. It seemed at times that it was more effective at the dissemination of intelligence about the private lives of its staff than gathering information about the enemy. He was about to explain that Mrs Cathy Standish had come to London on a shopping visit and to visit relatives, and that he had agreed to put her up in his flat, when Admiral Godfrey's phone rang. The senior officer picked it up, listened, and muttered a slightly surprised 'really?' before thanking the caller and replacing the handset. He looked fixedly at Fleming.

'I've changed my mind, Fleming. Maybe I had better sanction the use of petrol for that absurd car of yours to visit Grizedale Hall after all. Our friend Moehe has escaped again.'

11

Leutnant Willi Hartmann stopped on the second-floor landing and mopped his chubby face with a stolen handkerchief while he got his breath back for the final flight of stairs – the steepest and narrowest because the third floor had once been Grizedale Hall's servants' quarters.

Willi was one of the camp's most remarkable prisoners because he was the only one who had, according to Nurse Brenda Hobson's camp records, managed to put on weight during the fourteen months he had been a prisoner of war. In civilian life Willi had been a small-time crook. Then he joined the army, was sent to occupied France, and became a big-time crook, using his position as a supplies officer to sell motor transport spares to a lucrative and grateful black market.

Willi's service life had been a catalogue of misfortunes of which the most unfortunate entry had been his application of a moderate amount of blackmail to secure a flight in a Heinkel on a daylight raid on the Isle of Wight because he wanted to see England. The Heinkel had been shot down and now Willi was seeing more of England than he had anticipated. The only comfort was that at least he was beyond the reach of the military police in France, who were anxious to discuss a number of issues with him: namely their belief that supplying garages around Chartres with army-issue tyres, petrol and other spares was taking the concept of maintaining good relationships with the civilian populace a little too far. His relations with the camp guards was also good, with the possible exception of Sergeant Finch, who had once declared: 'That fat little Bavarian bastard has got his thieving, pudgy fingers into every pie and one day I'm going to break them off one by one.'

Many of Sergeant Finch's assertions about Willi were monstrous calumnies. Willi would never dream of selling his grandmother. A scandalous notion – he was much too good a businessman to entertain any deal that might undermine the market value of his mother.

Willi's most recent misfortune was that the senior German officer at Grizedale Hall, Commander Otto Kruger, had made Willi his adjutant – an official-sounding term for general dogsbody. Willi didn't mind that so much: the job gave him a little power which was always useful. What he resented was that the U-boat 'ace' had made two adjoining rooms on the top floor of Grizedale Hall his office and quarters. That Willi had to toil up and down the stairs at least ten times a day made his weight gain as a prisoner of war even more remarkable. But this time he had information: a Leutnant Karl Moehe, who had been recaptured only the night before, had escaped. Information was power and imparting it would help with a favour he needed from his commanding officer.

Willi rapped three times on the door of what had once been Grizedale Hall's butler's quarters and entered. The fug created by the fumes from the poisonous black cheroots that Kruger smoked stung his eyes. The single dormer window set into the slate roof was shut. It was an austere office for an austere man. A cheap wooden desk in the centre of the room and a wooden filing cabinet against the wall were the principal items of furniture. Not even family photographs adorned the bare, distempered walls although it was unlikely that they would have survived the fumes. The only touch of luxury was a square of Axminster carpet under the desk. Willi was hot from his climb and grateful that Kruger never turned his radiator on. The clouds of cheroot fumes were emanating from behind a two-day-old copy of the London *Times*. The hands holding the newspaper were slender and capable looking.

Willi cleared his throat. The *Times* was lowered slowly and Otto Kruger's inscrutable dark eyes regarded him dispassionately. He was a lean, spare man in his early thirties. Black hair slicked straight back. Clean shaven and always immaculately turned out because the British had kitted him out with a new Kriegsmarine uniform so that he would look good for propaganda purposes when paraded before newsreel cameras. A Knight's Cross gleamed at his throat. But it was the eyes that captured attention. To Willi it seemed that that penetrating, all-knowing stare was probing all his guilty secrets, analysing them, classifying them – forgery, blackmail, extortion, fraud, theft, black-marketeering – before moving on to more serious crimes.

'Good morning, Willi,' said Kruger in English.

Willi was preoccupied and answered in German.

'A good start to the day, Willi,' said Kruger icily, continuing in English, folding the newspaper carefully. 'There are two days of my English-speaking week left.'

Willi started to apologize in English but Kruger interrupted him. 'The whole point about this time of year when little work is needed on the vegetable plots is to concentrate our minds on other matters, Willi, such as perfecting our English.'

'Yes, Commander.'

'Now what is it you wish to tell me about Leutnant Moehe's escape that I don't already know?'

Willi was suitably crushed; the toil up three flights of stairs had been in vain. 'So you know, Commander?'

Kruger relit his cheroot. 'Only that he escaped from the solitary confinement block this morning. He seems to be a remarkable man. Two weeks on the run. He breaks into the POW camp he was being sent to, and then escapes again. I was looking forward to meeting him. Has he been recaptured?'

'Not according to my information, Commander.'

Kruger exhaled a cloud of poisonous fumes in Willi's

direction. 'Well, you'd better go back to spying through keyholes, and your tumblers pressed against walls, and your bribes and blackmail and extortions, and set about bringing your information up to date.'

Willi was incensed by the accusation: he never spied through keyholes – listening through them was much more effective.

Kruger opened a desk drawer and passed a handwritten form to his adjutant. 'I'm running short of POW questionnaire forms. I'd like another dozen by lunchtime, please.' Kruger picked up the *Times*.

'There is another matter, Commander,' said Willi, moving to the door.

'Which is?'

'It is complicated. My English—'

'In German.'

'I've been tipped – er – advised that there might be a surprise inspection of my room at 1400, Commander.'

Kruger raised an eyebrow. 'I thought your bribes of chocolate to the guards always ensured that your room was left alone?'

'I've been given to understand that Sergeant Finch is insisting on supervising the search himself this time.'

Kruger permitted himself a rare smile at Willi's woebegone expression. Trying to bribe Sergeant Finch would be like asking Churchill to change sides. 'And you'd like to move your stock of Hershey bars in here?'

'There's not so many of those coming through now that America is in the war, Commander. But we're getting a reasonable supply of Toblerone bars from the Swiss Red Cross, from Swiss sympathizers, and South America. I'll move everything back once the inspection is over.'

'Very well. Don't forget my questionnaire forms.'

Alone again, Kruger returned his attention to the *Times* and a story tucked away on an inside page that had caught his attention. It consisted of a few lines about an unnamed escaped German naval officer who had been on the run for two weeks. The story could only be about the remarkable Leutnant Moehe. Although Kruger had every confidence in Willi's ability to unearth more information about this extraordinary officer, he looked forward to hearing all the details from Leutnant Karl Moehe himself.

It could only be a matter of time.

12

Major James Reynolds quickly inserted cotton-wool plugs in his ears when the door of his office swung open and Sergeant Finch marched in two privates.

'Left! Right! Left! Right! Halt!' Three pairs of boots shook the office; three right boots crashed down on the bare boards. The shock startled a cuckoo from behind its doors in a cuckoo clock made by the POWs. It uttered a sad squawk and dangled forlornly on its spring. 'Private White and Private Jones reporting, SAAR!'

Reynolds tipped back his chair and treated the two sheepish guards standing in front of his desk to a one-eyed glare of deep displeasure.

'At ease,' he ordered.

The two men stood easy and kept their eyes on the wall map of Canada behind their commanding officer but Sergeant Finch remained rigidly to attention, chest thrust out, eyes straight ahead, forage cap on his head at the regulation angle. No one had ever seen Sergeant Finch standing at ease in the presence of an officer. Some POWs maintained that he had been born standing to attention.

'Every war reserve constable from two counties is out scouring the fells for Moehe thanks to you two,' said Major Reynolds abruptly. 'What really annoys me about this is not so much that I'm not allowed to dock your pay to help cover the cost of your bungling, but that you allowed a prisoner to escape before I'd a chance to give him my standard "Welcome to Grizedale Hall and escape is impossible" chat.' The earplugs made his voice boom hollowly in his head. He decided that he didn't like them.

'Yes, sir,' said Private Jones miserably. 'We're very sor—'

'You will remain silent until given permission to speak!' Sergeant Finch bawled.

Major Reynolds decided that maybe the earplugs weren't so bad. 'All right. Tell me what happened. You first, Jones.'

Private Jones swallowed nervously. 'Well, sir. Me and Chalk – I mean Private White – took him his breakfast at 0800. Private White unlocked the door to the SC block and locked it behind us. Then he unlocked the door to Leutnant Moehe's solitary confinement cell and stood back when I took the tray in. Only Leutnant Moehe wasn't there.'

'A cell measuring six feet by eight feet was empty?'

'Yes, sir. I couldn't believe it.'

'But the cell wasn't empty, was it?'

Private Jones nodded miserably. 'No, sir.'

Major Reynolds's unfriendly eye turned on Private White. 'And your role in this shambles?'

'I followed Private Jones into the cell to help him search it, sir. Suddenly there was a crash behind but before I could turn around, I was shoved into Private Jones and me keys were snatched. By the time we'd sorted ourselves out, we was locked in. He must've wedged himself across his cell above the door.'

'In other words,' said Major Reynolds dryly, 'you fell for the oldest trick in the book?'

'Yes, sir.'

'And Leutnant Moehe fell on you?'

'Yes, sir.'

'Well, now it's my turn.'

13

Fleming steered his Bentley tourer on to the verge in response to Cathy Standish's plea and stopped the engine. The huge car, with its hull of a bonnet, wasn't so much parked as moored.

Cathy jumped out of the passenger seat and leaned against a drystone wall. They were at the brow of a hill that overlooked

Grizedale Hall's wooded valley with its man-made swathes of Forestry Commission conifers, with a fire-watching tower here and there, made from the pine trunks of the trees they were guarding. She pointed to a glint of blue, sparkling in the noon sunlight.

'Look, Ian. You can just make out Windermere. I haven't seen it from here for years. It must be all that clearing by the POW working parties.'

'Possibly,' said Fleming, more interested in watching Cathy. They had broken their long drive from London by spending the night at a hotel. Cathy had forsaken her smart city clothes and now wore a headscarf, a tight sweater, and equally tight jodhpurs. She knew how to lean over a low wall.

'Grizedale's such a lovely building, Ian. It's a shame it's no longer a family house. Harold Brocklebank used to give some fabulous summer parties. There'd be a marquee, a band, and the dancing used to go on all night. Then the Holiday Fellowship took it over. They ruined it. All the lovely oak panelling and decorated ceilings plastered over. Cheap holidays for mill workers and best not to intimidate them with ornate surroundings. I made a small fortune out of those mill workers. Half a crown a day each for a fishing licence. Another half a crown to rent tackle.'

Fleming smiled. 'I heard that the War Office were a bit sensitive about you locals calling it a holiday camp when they requisitioned it as a POW camp.'

Cathy turned to face him. She managed to look provocative despite her heavy riding jacket. 'When my uncle was captured in 1917, he was sent to a proper POW camp with rows of huts, barbed-wire fences, and watchtowers everywhere. Why don't we build proper camps, Ian?'

'To save money. Why go to the expense of building camps when the War Office can requisition empty properties? We're not short of disused stately homes.'

'We never do anything right,' said Cathy, turning back to study Grizedale Hall. 'Always half-baked measures. We'll never win the war at this rate. Look at that wall. Any agile prisoner could climb it, and it's crumbling to dust in places.'

'Churchill's view is that the coast is the real fence,' Fleming commented.

'And meanwhile we locals have these panics every now and then when a prisoner escapes. How many times were we stopped and checked on the way here? Three times.'

'Not that many escapes since Otto Kruger became senior German officer,' Fleming pointed out. 'From what I've heard, an escape has to be planned right down to the smallest detail before he'll approve it.'

'Trouble looms,' said Cathy warningly.

The chauffeur-driven Rolls-Royce had come up on them unawares. It purred to a stop beside Fleming's Bentley. An elderly lady wound down the rear passenger window.

'Good afternoon, Mrs Heelis,' said Cathy politely.

Beatrix Potter, or Mrs Heelis as she preferred to be called, was a formidable 76-year-old Lake District landowner. As usual, she was dressed in grimy, ill-fitting tweeds, a moth-eaten bonnet that looked as though it had once served as a horse's nosebag, and several layers of old cardigans – the few remaining buttons of which were fastened to the wrong buttonholes. She looked exactly like her own illustrations of Mrs Tiggy-Winkle, the character she had created many years before. Unlike Mrs Tiggy-Winkle, Beatrix Potter was a phenomenally rich woman, thanks to the royalties that her children's books continued to earn, even though she had given up serious writing many years before. The great interests that now dominated her cloistered life were her Lake District estates, her herds of prize-winning Herdwick sheep, and the National Trust, of which she was a founding member and one of its principal benefactors.

'So you're back,' said Beatrix Potter sternly.

'Very nearly, Mrs Heelis. In about ten minutes.'

'About time, too. This is a busy time of year.'

'I left Jeff Morgan to look after everything. I needed a break.'

Beatrix Potter snorted. 'I used to employ him as an odd-job man at Hill Top Farm. He was useless.'

'Well he's very capable now.'

'You found a respectable hotel in London, I hope?'

'I had an extremely comfortable room, Mrs Heelis. Every convenience a girl could wish for. Excellent room service.' There was a slight teasing note in Cathy's voice. She liked Beatrix Potter and didn't resent the cross-examination.

The elderly lady's gaze fixed disapprovingly on Fleming.

He put on his most engaging smile. 'Good afternoon, Mrs Heelis.'

'I know you.' She made it sound as if knowing Fleming was one of life's more grievous misfortunes.

'This is Lieutenant-Commander Ian Fleming, Mrs Heelis.'

'We met at one of Cathy's parties last year,' said Fleming.

'You professed a desire to be a writer after the war, as I recall.'

Fleming gave a little bow. 'Indeed I did, Mrs Heelis. You made me promise to write a children's book.'

'Well, see that you keep it. Children are a most discerning and rewarding readership, Commander.' She looked him critically up and down. 'You look a fit young man. Why aren't you helping chase after this wretched escaped prisoner of war? We've been stopped twice by the police already.'

'It's a police and army matter, Mrs Heelis.'

'I've a good mind to visit Major Reynolds and tell him what I think of his security. Luckily I've had those Germans working on my farm. I know that they haven't got two heads, but a lot of people can't sleep at night thinking that there are Nazis rampaging on the loose.'

'None of them are Nazis, Mrs Heelis,' Fleming observed. 'I'll give you my word on that.'

'I know that, you silly man. But a lot of the locals don't.'

'I'll call in over the weekend and give you a full account of my London trip,' Cathy promised.

Beatrix Potter nodded and ordered the chauffeur to drive on.

'Not too full, I hope,' said Fleming, watching the receding Rolls-Royce. 'She doesn't look well. You might finish her off.'

Cathy laughed and slid her arm around his waist. 'You're right about her not looking well, though.'

Fleming didn't answer. Cathy sensed him stiffen. He was

staring intently at a clump of trees further down the slope, not ten yards from where they were standing.

'What's the matter, Ian?'

Fleming lowered his voice. 'There's someone hiding on the far side of those trees.'

'The escaped prisoner?'

'His clothes fit the description,' said Fleming, still keeping his voice down. He glanced left and right along the wall. 'Listen carefully, Cathy. I'm going to move away as if I've got into the car. I want you to stay here, in this spot, and pretend to have a blazing row with me.'

Cathy looked both bemused and worried. 'What are you planning?'

'I'm going to circle around and nab him.'

'But he might be dangerous.'

'More likely he's bloody hungry. He's watching us and listening to us. Now do as I say and don't watch where I go. Pretend I'm in the car.'

'What shall I say?'

'Anything you like. If it is Moehe, he doesn't speak English. A nice blistering row to keep his attention, make him think we're still together.'

'Blistering?'

'Really blistering,' Fleming affirmed, backing away from the wall.

Cathy wasted no time. She spun around and let fly at the empty car. 'You're disgusting,' she railed. 'I'm a sweet, innocent country girl, yet you had no compunction about luring me to London to satisfy your villainous lusts and filthy perversions! Do you really think that you can get around a girl like me, or any girl for that matter, by taking them to expensive restaurants night after night? Treating them to shows, cooking breakfasts for them every morning . . . ?'

Fleming was a little taken back by Cathy's acting skills. It was all very convincing, and he hoped the fugitive hiding in the trees thought so, too. He ducked down and ran half-crouched for some fifty yards alongside the wall.

'. . . I should've listened to my mother! She knew all about evil men like you – dazzling simple country girls . . .'

Girl? thought Fleming as he vaulted over the low wall and ran down the slope towards the clump of trees, swinging an arc so that he could come up behind the mystery figure. You're forty-two if you're a day, my angel!

'. . . I know what you were after! My eggs! Three dozen you made me take to London just to satisfy your disgusting, perverted cravings for scrambled eggs every morning and me every night!'

Fleming considered that that was a little harsh. He edged around the clump of trees and there was Karl Moehe not ten yards away, his back to Fleming. A greatcoat was draped across his knees and he appeared to be scraping it to get rid of mud stains as he peered through the foliage, watching Cathy holding forth. She was certainly worth watching: hands on hips, her riding jacket unbuttoned, breasts heaving with indignation, blonde hair streaming out in the breeze from under her headscarf as she laid into her imaginary lover with extraordinary gusto and wholly unexpected vehemence. Her riveting performance enabled Fleming to creep to within four yards of Karl. He could see the side of the fugitive's face and was surprised that he was clean-shaven. For a moment Fleming thought that he had made a mistake – prisoners in solitary confinement weren't allowed to keep shaving tackle. He edged a little closer. No mistake – it was definitely Karl Moehe.

The splendid sight of Cathy Standish in her stride was a temporary distraction from Karl's immediate dilemma. He now realized that his escape from Grizedale Hall had been premature – a case of an irresistible seized opportunity. Two weeks on the run had eventually convinced him that sheer determination wasn't going to work. It would've been better had he joined his captured comrades. They would be certain to have an escape organization that could provide him with adequate clothing, money and documents so that he stood a better chance of getting home with his information. He had just decided to give himself up when a voice spoke to him in German.

'Good afternoon, Leutnant Moehe. I don't blame you. I could watch her all day. A remarkable woman.'

Karl's head snapped around as though it were on a greased swivel. His eyes went wide with shock and his stunned, disbelieving stare of horror switched rapidly back and forth between Fleming and Cathy.

'No point in your trying to run, Karl,' said Fleming affably, patting his jacket pocket. 'I doubt if you could outrun a bullet.' He held out his hand to the German officer. 'Lieutenant-Commander Ian Fleming, Royal Navy Volunteer Reserve, and you're Leutnant Karl Moehe, *U-684* of the First U-boat Flotilla.'

Karl was too numb to think of anything to say, or anything more sensible to do other than to shake the offered hand.

'I expect you could use a spot of lunch, Karl. I know I could. There's an excellent inn not far from here where they serve up the most delicious shepherd's pie. Have you tried shepherd's pie since you've been in England?'

'I don't have any money,' said Karl.

'You'd be my guest.' Fleming called out to Cathy, who was getting round to a general description of her lover's parentage and how he had been conceived standing up in a vomit-splattered alley beside a docklands pub on St Patrick's night. She stopped in mid-flow and regarded the two men. They talked for a few moments, the stranger pulled on a shabby greatcoat and they trudged up the rise towards her, the stranger in the lead. She helped them climb over the wall.

Fleming made the introductions in a mixture of German and English. Cathy regarded the young, crestfallen German officer appreciatively.

'You're sure he doesn't speak English?' Cathy asked Fleming as he steered Karl into the back of the Bentley.

'Hardly a word. And you can't have him.'

'I could do with an extra pair of hands on the farm . . . Just for a couple of days. Getting hold of strong, capable help is getting impossible.'

Fleming started the Bentley's engine and piloted the car back on to the road. 'I'm taking him back to Grizedale Hall, but I'd like a chat with him first. I'm sorry, Cathy, but would you mind if I just dropped you off at the farm? I really do need to get back to London otherwise my chief will want my guts on a plate.'

'Sometimes I feel that I'd like a lot more than just your miserable guts served up on a plate. Okay – home, James.'

Cathy turned around and smiled engagingly at Karl as the car moved off. He was scratching with his fingernails at dried mud caked into his greatcoat. He looked up and responded with a rueful, half smile before returning to his cleaning.

'How do you know he won't try to escape again?'

'Because he gave me his word.'

'Ian – he looks much too clean and smart to have been on the run.'

Fleming felt in his pocket and passed Cathy a sliver of flint. 'He napped his own razor. Careful – it's sharp. And he made a hairbrush out of pine needles stuck in a piece of clay.'

'Clever,' Cathy commented.

'Clever and resourceful,' Fleming replied.

A few minutes later he pulled up outside the entrance to Cathy's farm just as an elderly, rheumatic police constable wheeling a bicycle emerged. He was almost bent double and didn't see the Bentley until his front wheel encountered the car's bumper. He straightened and nodded to Fleming and his two passengers.

'Good morning, Mr Pritchard,' Cathy greeted him. 'You old fraud. I contributed to your retirement clock at least two years ago and now I catch you back in uniform. Shame on you.'

'Part time, Mrs Standish. The constabulary is short-handed. I've left a leaflet in your letterbox to be on the lookout for an escaped German prisoner of war from their holiday camp. He's not thought to be dangerous.'

'He's been recaptured,' said Fleming.

His accent and uniform carried weight with the ancient policeman. 'Thought he wouldn't last long, sir. Thanks for letting me know.'

Karl didn't understand a word of the exchanges but it seemed that this Ian Fleming had some influence because the constable tried to mount his bicycle and got stuck with his leg halfway over the saddle. Cathy jumped out to help him complete the manoeuvre and gave him a push to get him on his wobbly way.

She smiled at Karl as she retrieved her baggage. Karl looked politely away while she gave Fleming a long, passionate and somewhat unladylike kiss. It seemed to Karl that the English weren't as reserved as he had been led to believe.

'There is one thing, Cathy,' said Fleming anxiously. 'That little performance you put on just now was a bit unfair. You asked if there was anything you could bring down to London and I said a few eggs would be appreciated if you could manage them. Three dozen was your idea.'

Cathy's eyes sparkled mischievously. 'But, Ian, my darling. It was only play-acting. I created a fictitious lover – an uncouth, arrogant, possessive, philandering heel. Not a bit like you.'

Fleming smiled, reassured.

'You're far worse,' Cathy finished.

14

M ajor James Reynolds was having a bad war. Losing an eye at Dunkirk had not been a good start, but he was getting over that, whereas it was unlikely that he'd ever get over the sheer perversity and pigheadedness of Major-General Somerfeld of North-Western Command, the officer in charge of prisoner of war camps, who behaved as though he were personally responsible for bearing the cost of running them. All Reynolds's previous month's requisitions for materials had been bounced. Not by a supplies clerk at the Central Ordnance Depot, but by General Somerfeld himself. A hundred-yard reel of barbed wire – refused; six garden spades – refused; axes – refused; six exterior floodlights – refused. Reynolds swore softly to himself. That was the second request for replacement floodlights that had been turned down. There was a comedian among the POWs who was a crack shot with a catapult. The guards had never found the weapon despite frequent searches.

'Send in a req for two,' General Somerfeld had scrawled on the form, 'and it will be considered.'

Why couldn't the miserable, sarcastic old bastard have altered the forms himself? It was a waste of paper having all this bumf flying back and forth. As if that wasn't enough, another handwritten note from the General observed that six more POWs would be sent to Grizedale Hall the following week and it would be appreciated if Major Reynolds could make a special effort and try to keep them within the confines of the hall at least for a week or so, but preferably for the duration of the war if it wasn't too much trouble.

The last document in the morning signal envelope was a two-page memo stressing the need to save paper by using both sides of the paper. Reynolds turned it over. The verbose memo had been stencilled on one side of the paper.

His intercom buzzed once. Two buzzes were for Sergeant Finch in the adjoining office. He picked up the receiver. It was the guard house at the main gate. Lieutenant-Commander Ian Fleming had arrived with a guest who had been signed in as a visitor.

Probably Cathy Standish, thought Reynolds morosely, replacing the receiver. Lucky devil. And why couldn't he have warned him that he was coming? There'd be a helluva row if General Somerfeld discovered that the Director of Naval Intelligence occasionally sent Fleming to Grizedale Hall to scratch around for snippets of information from the inmates. Nevertheless, he liked the naval intelligence officer and always enjoyed his visits. There was the familiar sound of Fleming's Bentley burbling across the courtyard and stopping outside his office. Reynolds sighed and dumped the papers in his out tray for Sergeant Finch and Private Knox to deal with.

The door opened and Fleming breezed in, debonair and beaming. 'Hallo, James. Good to see you.' He started unbuttoning his jacket. 'Every time I pop in here I think how I'd like to transfer my office up here. Always so damned warm. We're freezing in the Admiralty.'

The two men shook hands. 'Great to see you, Ian. How's London?'

'Slowly being flattened from the odd raid.' Fleming placed a slim volume before Reynolds. 'There we are, James. *The Compleat Angler.* Only a third edition, I'm afraid.

The first edition went under the hammer for a king's ransom.'

Reynolds didn't notice the second man who had followed Fleming into the office. He seized the antique book and leafed reverently through it. 'Gee, Ian – this is great – just great. A dream come true.'

'A dream that's made you five pounds poorer,' Fleming observed, placing a box of cheroots on the desk. 'And these are for you know who. How is he, by the way?'

'Huh? Who? Oh – Kruger? Okay, I guess. Just look at these illustrations, Ian – they're incredible.'

'James – I have someone I think you'd like to meet.'

Something in Fleming's tone caused Reynolds to take his attention off his prized book and look up. Fleming had stepped to one side so that nothing impeded Reynolds's view of the clean-shaven figure standing before him. Karl's attempts to keep himself looking smart were largely negated by the shabby, stained state of his greatcoat. It is of moments like these that fiction writers are fond of describing how their character's jaw dropped. Reynolds's jaw didn't merely drop but nearly bounced off his desk.

'I found him wandering on the fells,' said Fleming cheerfully, savouring the Canadian officer's open-mouthed expression. 'I thought that you might like him back. He's been fed and watered.' He placed a small, blue form on Reynolds's desk. 'And this is his visitor's pass. It says that he has to be off the premises by four o'clock, but I don't think that that would be a good idea. And it might be a good idea to have his entry in the visitors' book deleted. He put 'Kriegsmarine' in the organization column. I'm sure General Somerfeld wouldn't approve if he noticed it on one of his inspections.'

Karl stepped forward. He gave Reynolds a crisp salute and offered a speech in English that he had been mentally rehearsing. 'Good afternoon, Mr Reynolds, sir. Leutnant Karl Moehe reporting for duty.' He gestured to his dirty greatcoat. 'This I am much sorry. I think I am looking like a fucking swede-basher.'

15

'Eight shillings for lunch, Fleming?' Admiral Godfrey enquired, interrupting his junior officer's verbal report. 'What did he eat? A horse?'

'More like two horses, sir. Three portions of the land-lady's shepherd's pie. He hadn't eaten properly for over two weeks.'

'And what sort of information did we get for our eight shillings?'

Fleming had been avoiding that subject. 'Nothing, sir,' he admitted. He added quickly, 'But the fact that I could get nothing out of him certainly points to the fact that he has something to hide. He refuses point-blank to discuss anything to do with his U-boat. Not even idle tittle-tattle.'

'As always, Fleming, your logic passeth all understanding. Well – we're certainly not going to learn anything now, are we? He'll do twenty-eight days in solitary, by which time any information he might have on the acoustic torpedo is likely to be out-of-date. Somehow I can't see General Somerfeld allowing us to talk to a POW in solitary confinement. He's none too happy about the navy capturing one of his escapees.'

'I don't think Karl Moehe will do twenty-eight days solitary, sir.'

'Why not?'

'I suggested to Major Reynolds that in view of Moehe's desperation to escape, that he'd almost certainly make another madcap attempt.'

'You deserve a medal for putting your finger on the bloody obvious, Fleming.'

'I stressed Moehe's resourcefulness . . . His ability to live off the land, to stay at large.'

'Add a bar to that medal.'

'Not giving him solitary but putting him in with the other POWs right away would place him immediately under Otto

Kruger's discipline. As we know full well, sir, Kruger doesn't sanction escape bids unless they're carefully planned. Moehe won't accept our discipline but he will accept Kruger's discipline. I reasoned that that would be the best way of stopping Moehe's crazy breaks.'

'How the army run their camps isn't a navy matter, Fleming. You had no right to interfere.'

'It was only a suggestion I made to Major Reynolds, sir. Nothing else.'

'And if he ignores your suggestion?'

'I don't think he will, sir.'

'But what's the damned point anyway?'

'If Moehe is in possession of vital information about the acoustic torpedo, he'll tell Kruger and doubtless beg Kruger to allow him to escape. If it's that important, Kruger will be equally keen to get Moehe and his information home.'

'Meaning that if Moehe does escape, it'll confirm that he is in possession of information?'

'Yes, sir.'

'Something we suspect already, but that doesn't provide us with the information, doesn't it?'

Fleming recognized danger signals indicating when his chief was getting mad. 'As you've often pointed out, sir. It's not gathering intelligence that's difficult, it's effective dissimulation of what information we do gather. If Moehe escapes, we'll have a focus. We'll be able to tip off agents in Doenitz's Atlantic U-boat ports. Get them to be on the look-out for new torpedoes – changes in serial-number prefixes. Once they know what to look for—'

'Fleming!'

'Sir?'

'Get out.'

Fleming returned to his office, feeling depressed, not understood. He sat brooding, organizing his thoughts, while Sally concentrated on her work.

There was one thing he was certain of, as were many of his colleagues, and that was that a shrewd, far-sighted man like Doenitz – a brilliant planner – would be certain to have devised some sort of method for captured U-boat officers to communicate with home – to warn Doenitz of new techniques and weapons devised by the allies for the hunting and destruction of U-boats. The previous year the POWs at Grizedale Hall had even managed to build a short-lived radio transmitter. The damnably maddening thing was that in setting up POW camps for captured officers, the British had ensured that many highly intelligent Germans with advanced skills were concentrated in relatively few places.

Radio communications were impossible now that new monitoring procedures were in place. That left the prisoners' letters to and from home as the only means of making contact. He asked Sally to fetch Otto Kruger's file from the registry. It was a bulky manila wallet. He unhooked the red tape and leafed through the file's contents until he came to Kruger's letters. All the correspondence of VIP prisoners of war was photographed after routine assessment by War Office censors, and prints were sent to the Director of Naval Intelligence.

Kruger's letters home, written in his precise, spiky handwriting, made for dull reading – particularly his infrequent but lengthy letters to Alice at a genuine address in Wilhemshaven, although who Alice was and her relationship to Kruger was unknown. There were few endearments in the U-boat 'ace's' letters to this Alice, but, then, they were rare in all his letters, even those to his parents.

In general, his topics were accounts of his day-to-day routine as a POW senior officer; how his comrades' vegetable plots were progressing; minor lapses of discipline among subordinate POWs – nothing that the War Office censors ever considered necessary to scissor.

Fleming checked the official 'sent' and 'received' date stamps – sometimes difficult to read because the letters were printed on to cheap photographic paper. Alice always responded quickly to Kruger's missives. An average of eleven days lapsed between Kruger sending a letter and receiving a reply from her. The Red Cross postal service was efficient. He needed a magnifying glass to read her tiny handwriting.

The file also contained a report from the crypto-analysis branch, who had studied the letters. They had turned Kruger's and Alice's correspondence inside-out, looking for word

63

patterns, substitution codes, numeric conversions, and had concluded, in the limited time that they had been allowed to devote to the letters, that if they did contain a code, it was probably based on a one-time pad system using a book available to both parties as the key. Fleming knew that this was unlikely. It would be almost impossible for Kruger or any POW to retain possession of a book throughout capture and interrogation. What he did notice was that Alice's letters were always in response to a letter from Kruger – she had never written a letter to him of her own volition.

Fleming drummed his fingers on his desk. Kruger was certain to be in possession of Karl Moehe's full account by now. It would be interesting to see if he fired off a letter to Alice within the next few days.

His depressed spirits were even lower as he walked home. An empty flat would be awaiting him. After two weeks of Cathy Standish's vivacious company, he realized that he was missing her. More often than not they had been content to stay in during the evenings, listening to a concert on the radio or playing chess – she had a formidable endgame, and also played a mean hand at poker. Her eclectic Girton education had ensured that she was equally at home in dungarees mucking out pigs, or acting as a sparkling hostess at dinner parties for his friends.

Fleming wondered if he ought to confound everyone, especially his mother, who was forever introducing him to debutantes, by getting married. The thought of her horrified reaction to Cathy Standish cheered him up.

16

'Right,' said Reynolds in poor but adequate German after he and Karl had exchanged salutes. 'First things first. Consider yourself extremely fortunate that you've served only one day of the twenty-eight days of solitary confinement you should serve for your senseless escape attempt. Builders are due to carry out some work on the solitary block, therefore it won't be available for a while.'

He fixed Karl with a hard, one-eyed stare that most new-arrival prisoners of war found intimidating. This wretched Moehe stared right back. Insolent devil. Reynolds marked him as a troublemaker.

'Doubtless you have noticed how remote we are here. The pikes and fells may look beautiful on a day like today, but in winter they can be deadly.'

'Yes,' said Karl politely. 'I have had some experience of them.'

Reynolds suspected that the German officer was being facetious. He pressed on. 'I'm from Montreal and thought I knew something about hard winters, but here they can be really something. A German escapee has already died of exposure on Heron Pike. He'd spent two days wandering in a blizzard. And if the pikes and tarns don't get you, then the bogs certainly will. Another thing – the Home Guard and war reserve constables and forestry wardens here are all locals who know the fells like the backs of their hands. It never takes them long to round up runaways.'

Karl decided that it would be politic not to mention that none of them had found him.

'One last point on escapes. Grizedale Hall is built on rock. Granite. So you can forget about tunnelling. Understood?'

'Yes, Major. Escape from Grizedale Hall is impossible. Does that apply to breaking in as well?'

Reynolds considered that personally skinning this Moehe and roasting his hide would be almost as enjoyable as angling.

'This is a camp for non-Nazi officers,' the Canadian officer continued coldly. 'London have decided that you're politically colourless, which is why you're here. The border-line cases and the hardliners go to special camps run by the Free Polish in a manner that the War Office turn a blind eye to. Any suggestion of Nazi bullying and you'll be packed off to one of the other camps and no right of appeal to the Red Cross commissioners or any of that nonsense.

'Secondly, as you have seen, Grizedale Hall is a magnificent country mansion. One of the finest in the country and I aim to keep it that way. After the war, the War Office will have to hand it back to its owners in its original condition. If the hall comes to any harm, we'll be happy to rehouse you in huts. Your commanding officer and I have an agreement on this.

'The prisoners have freedom of movement in the hall and grounds during the day but do not step over the boundary marker wire or you are liable to be shot. You are locked in the hall between sunrise and sunset.'

'But I found an unlocked door at night, Major.'

Reynolds refused to be drawn, ignoring the remark. 'How prisoners organize their accommodation is up to your senior officer. He's responsible for internal discipline – we look after security. It's a simple system and it works.

'There's a Queen Alexandra's Royal Army Nursing Corps sister, Brenda Hobson, who has a sickbay next to the showers. She works here three days a week and looks after the medical records of all hundred and twenty prisoners. As a result of an agreement with Commander Kruger, all prisoners are required to help out in the kitchen. In fact they *run* the kitchen. Commander Kruger is responsible for the duty rosters. There are voluntary working parties who work in Grizedale Forest under the supervision of armed guards – repairing fire-watching towers and suchlike. We're allowed to use wind-damaged and fallen trees for our central-heating boiler. We also have exercise walks for prisoners who behave themselves, and working parties that are taken out to local farms. There's a morning roll-call at 0800 every morning. Snap roll-calls can be called at any time. Any questions?'

Karl thanked Reynolds and saluted.

'Commander Kruger's aide is Leutnant Willi Hartmann. He's the one to see regarding your quarters.'

Sergeant Finch appeared and marched Karl into the courtyard, where Willi was waiting to accost the elusive new arrival.

17

'First name?' said Willi.

'Karl.'

Willi filled in the answer in the hand-ruled box. 'Middle names?'

'This is ridiculous,' Karl exclaimed. 'I have important information for Commander Kruger. It is imperative that I see him immediately.'

'When we've finished this questionnaire,' Willi replied. 'Then he'll spend an hour going through it, then he might want to see you. Middle names?'

Karl answered in bad grace.

'Any known nicknames?'

'This is absurd!'

At that moment Kruger entered his office. Willi half rose from the desk but the senior officer motioned him to remain sitting. Karl jumped to attention and was about to salute but Kruger interrupted him.

'Remain seated, please, Leutnant Moehe. Carry on, Willi.' Kruger stood with his back to the tiny, unlit fireplace, regarding Moehe thoughtfully.

'Commander – I have some vital matters to discuss with you.'

Kruger's brooding eyes bored into Karl. 'Later.'

'But—'

'I said *later!*' Kruger sounded mild but there was underlying ice in his tone. 'One point, Leutnant Moehe. Why aren't you in solitary confinement?'

This is crazy, thought Karl. What did it matter? 'I was told that I was lucky, Commander. That builders are due to carry out alterations to the cell block.'

Kruger nodded. 'Carry on, Willi.'

'Any known nicknames?' Willi repeated.

'No.'

'*Ungluckish,*' said Kruger succinctly, lighting a cheroot.

'We have an officer who remembers you from Wilhemshaven. He recalls that you were known as Unlucky Moehe.'

'I don't think it stuck, Commander.'

'Sometimes they do, sometimes they don't. Sometimes they're so apt that they follow you about all your life.'

With that, Kruger left the room, leaving Karl to resentfully answer Willi's searching questions for thirty minutes. The questions about friends and relatives in neutral countries were Willi's own additions. He was always on the lookout for new sources of supplies for his bribery and blackmailing operations.

'That's a lot of sensitive information I've given you,' Karl complained when they had finished. 'Are you sure that it won't fall into British hands?'

'Quite sure,' Willi replied. 'Take yourself off for an hour or so and the Commander will send for you when he's had a chance to study this.'

18

Karl mooched moodily around the camp, stared up at a small fire-watching tower that served as lookout for the guards. He watched a violent, no-rules football match between the Luftwaffe and Kriegsmarine and turned his attention to the neat rows of vegetable plots that some prisoners were preparing for spring sowing. One gardener went out of his way to make himself agreeable by introducing himself as Oberleutnant Heinrich 'Harry' Busch.

'Leutnant Karl Moehe, Kriegsmarine,' said Karl as they shook hands.

'Oh – so you're *Ungluckish* Moehe?' said Harry. 'The only prisoner of war to break into Grizedale Hall.'

'It was an accident.'

'Well, I didn't think you did it deliberately. And you escaped. Why aren't you doing solitary?'

'Some building work is to be done on the cells.'

'How about giving me a hand with this hoeing?'

Karl politely declined, saying that small, individual plots did not make efficient use of the available land.

'They'll seem big enough when you're allocated one,' said Harry cheerfully. 'Commander Kruger likes to keep us all busy.'

Karl was tempted to point out that he would be escaping, but wisely kept silent. Judging by the indifference that Kruger had displayed so far, he decided that escape acting on his own initiative was the only option. It was ridiculous – the man was more interested in his damned nickname than information that could speed up the fatherland winning the war. Maybe it would be possible to bypass Kruger altogether?

'Is there an escape committee, Harry?'

The prisoner laughed. 'Of course.'

'When does it meet?'

'God knows. You'll have to ask Commander Kruger.'

'Oh . . . Is he a member?'

Harry laughed again. 'Commander Kruger *is* the escape committee. It has one member and that's him. Chairman, vice-chairman, secretary and treasurer. Not that I think it has any money. He's never sanctioned an escape since I've been here although there were some last year.'

The news further depressed Karl. He realized that he needed information and fast, therefore cultivating Harry Busch's friendship, and his allotment, seemed a sensible idea. He picked up a spare hoe and set to work.

'That's the idea,' said Harry approvingly. 'The devil and idle hands et cetera.'

An hour passed quickly as Karl worked while telling Harry about his two weeks on the run.

'Leutnant Moehe!' It was Willi, perspiring after his search for Karl. The vegetable plots were the last place he'd thought of looking. 'Commander Kruger wishes to see you in his office now, please.'

Karl followed the stocky Bavarian as he laboured up the stairs.

'Do you enjoy your work, Willi?' Karl enquired.

Willi was unable to answer immediately because he was

69

convalescing after the long climb by clinging to the newel on the top floor, almost bent double.

'Working for the Commander is a great honour,' Willi wheezed when he had nearly recovered and had passed the mime phase.

'Why does he have his quarters right up here? It can't be the view. It's a tiny window and you can't see anything out of it for cigar smoke.'

'Used to be the servants' quarters up here. Three flights of stairs, and this last flight is steep and narrow. Surprise searches are never surprising.'

Willi tapped on Kruger's door when he had regained his full health.

The room was filled with cheroot fumes. Kruger's attitude seemed slightly less hostile. He dismissed Willi and waved Karl to a chair. 'Please excuse me, Leutnant, but I haven't quite finished reading this.'

Karl sat in silence while surreptitiously watching Kruger. It seemed incredible that he was actually in the presence of the famed U-boat 'ace'. Kruger, Joachim Schepke of *U-100* and a handful of other commanders had revolutionized U-boat warfare by utilizing the superior speed of their diesel engines to carry out surface attacks against convoys at night, actually penetrating the destroyer screens to get into the convoy lanes. It was a deadly tactic that negated much of the allied efforts to develop equipment such as ASDIC to detect submerged U-boats. Kruger's maxim of 'one torpedo – one ship' had resulted in him becoming Germany's top-scoring 'ace' in terms of tonnage of enemy shipping sunk. A career that had ended when his *U-112* had been rammed at night by a British destroyer.

Kruger finished reading the questionnaire and fixed his brooding gaze on Karl. 'A remarkable catalogue of extreme foolhardiness and bad luck, Leutnant. Your nickname is well earned. You managed to remain at large for two weeks only to break into this camp, escape again, and then be recaptured. Will you be staying for dinner this evening?'

'I was anxious to get home, Commander,' Karl replied,

adding boldly, 'And I still am, as I've made plain in those answers.'

'Tell me about your boat's last patrol.'

At last! 'Have you heard of the T5 acoustic torpedo, Commander?'

'A rumour at Lorient. Nothing definite. I was captured over a year ago. Some recent arrivals here think that it had been successfully tested in the Baltic.'

'That was my boat, Commander. *U-684*. We were assigned to trials of the torpedo. We sank an allied armed trawler in the North Sea. It had an extremely noisy engine and stern gear. Probably an unbalanced screw. We sank it with one torpedo from a bow tube with a fifty-degree lay-off angle.'

Kruger was astonished but remained silent. Such an angle meant that *U-684* would have been travelling on virtually the same heading as the trawler – the U-boat did not have to get into a favourable position for an attack.

'For our last patrol,' Moehe continued, 'we had struck down fifteen pre-production T5 acoustic torpedoes at Kiel. Our orders were to test the T5 under operational conditions in the Atlantic but we were not to take part in wolf-pack attacks against convoys.'

'Why not?'

'Our batch of T5s weren't electric – they had compressed-air motors. The bubble tracks would have given us away to convoy escorts. Compressed-air motors were used so that we could see how the T5 torpedo behaved when it was running. All allied shipping in the North Atlantic shipping is convoyed and we did not have the range to carry out tests in American waters. So our skipper took us south – off North Africa – where we were more likely to come across lone sailings for surfaced attacks in daylight . . . Also we needed calm conditions so that the Siemens scientist we had on board could film the tracks with a cine-camera.' Karl smiled. 'He used to climb up on to the periscope standard.'

Surfaced attacks in daylight under calm conditions, thought Kruger. About the most dangerous type of attack imaginable for a U-boat to attempt. It renewed his respect for those U-boatmen who were prepared to take huge risks to ensure that Germany's U-boat arm had the finest weapons possible. 'Did you find any targets?' he asked.

'Ten ships. We sank four,' Karl replied.

Kruger's eyebrows went up.

'But we only managed to sink two at first – as with the trawler, they had noisy stern gear and were old and slow. We could've just as easily sunk them with our main gun. The T5's hydrophone steering system had no trouble locking on to them. After that our luck changed. Six lone-sailing allied ships got away. They were all fast, modern cargo ships. Turbines, according to our hydrophone operator. One of them came close to ramming us. It gave us a difficult time.'

'So what went wrong with these quieter ships?'

'The T5s would veer towards them, over-correct two or three times, and then veer right off target and be lost. I used to spend most of my time off watch going over the problem with the Siemens man. We used to annoy the old man by having bits of stripped-down T5 acoustic gear on the wardroom table.'

As Kruger had hoped, much of the junior officer's initial self-consciousness was slipping away as he warmed to his subject.

'I was looking at the array of microphones when the possible cause of the problem occurred to me,' Karl continued. Without asking for Kruger's permission, he picked up a pencil and started sketching rapidly on the back of a piece of paper. 'There are five microphones arranged in a semicircle in the pistol chamber in front of the torpedo's warhead. They're very directional and give the torpedo a flat, fan-shaped "area of interest" ahead of it. The microphone picking up the strongest sound sends signals to the servos that control the torpedo's rudder so that it swings towards the target. As you know, Commander, when a torpedo turns, it banks like an aircraft. I reasoned that the banking twisted the microphones' fan from the horizontal and caused them to lose positive contact. I suggested to the Siemens man that if we altered the torpedo's depth-keeping hydroplane controls to keep it upright as it turned, that would keep the microphone array horizontal, and maybe the torpedo wouldn't lose contact.

72

'The Siemens man thought that maybe I had the answer, so we drew up some new servo links that the chief engineer made up for us and we fitted them to a torpedo so that its hydroplanes could move independently of each other. Going up or down as the torpedo turned to keep it upright – no turn banking.' Karl paused in his sketching and looked askance at the piece of paper and pencil he had purloined. 'I'm very sorry, Commander. I didn't think—'

'It doesn't matter,' Kruger interrupted. 'Did your modification work?'

'It was a week before a target presented itself. A three-thousand-tonne merchantman – *Walvis Bay Queen* – registered Cape Town, making twelve knots. Fast. By that time we had modified four torpedoes, so we chanced a ninety-degree lay-off shot at a range of eight thousand metres. She saw us and the bubbles, cranked up her engines and zig-zagged like crazy. It didn't do her any good – that torpedo kept right after her. It hit and we finished her off with the gun.'

Kruger's expression rarely displayed his feelings but this time he could not disguise his surprise. 'Ninety degrees?'

Karl nodded. 'We were on the same course, on her quarter but we had stopped our engines. Had we missed, we had three more torpedoes in the bow tubes and ready, and would've closed in for a closer shot if we had to . . . We didn't have to. The torpedo ran straight ahead of us for about five hundred metres, and then picked up the scent and headed straight for the target. We sank a smaller cargo ship the next day using the same technique.'

'Range?'

'Ten thousand metres. We wanted to test at maximum range.'

Six miles! And an attacking boat did not have to get into a favourable position. There was a brief silence as Kruger weighed up the consequences. 'You seem to have been responsible for turning a prototype into a deadly weapon,' he observed at length.

Karl nodded, pleased at the recognition. 'Now you understand why I have to escape, Commander. I have to get the information home somehow. It's possible that another boat

73

on similar operational trials patrol may encounter the ideal weather conditions that we had for us to work out what was going wrong, but I doubt it.'

'Did you radio a report?'

'No, Commander. We had orders to observe radio silence throughout the entire patrol. From what our old man had heard at Kiel, there were rumours that the British have developed a system for long-range radio-direction finding.' Moehe indicated the sheet of paper that he was gradually covering in intricate sketch plans and columns of figures as he talked. 'Once we knew what was wrong, the Siemens man and I spent hours on the calculations for resetting the T5's hydroplanes so that it would remain horizontal but the depth-keeping would not be affected. It would be impossible to convey such detailed information in a radio transmission.'

The same thought had occurred to Kruger. He asked a few questions about the sinking of *U-684* and lapsed into silence. He lit a cheroot and inhaled on it while seemingly lost in thought. Karl began to get restless.

'About my escape—'

'I don't sanction any escape attempt unless it has been properly thought out. Tunnelling is out of the question because Grizedale Hall is mostly built on rock, as Major Reynolds would've pointed out to you in his standard welcoming speech. Nevertheless, escaping from Grizedale Hall is not difficult – several have succeeded. But none have succeeded in remaining free for long – as you have already learned the hard way. Escaping is one thing, Leutnant Moehe. Getting home is quite another.'

At this point Karl was so wound up that he overstepped the mark. 'But it is vital—'

'Nothing is vital unless I decide it is vital!' Kruger snapped. 'The only vital thing for you to remember is that I am your commanding officer and that you are still subject to Kriegsmarine discipline. Is that understood?'

'Yes, Commander,' said Karl, suitably crushed. 'Please accept my apologies.'

'Accepted,' Kruger replied in bad grace. He inhaled deeply

on his cheroot and picked up the piece of paper with Karl's sketches. His tone became more conciliatory as though he regretted his outburst. 'You have demonstrated a great deal of courage and initiative since your first capture, Leutnant Moehe, and considerable skill and ingenuity before you were captured. In the light of what you've told me, your desire to escape and reach home is highly commendable and understandable. What I want you to do now is apply those characteristics to exercising patience. A lot of patience. I want you to write down all the details of the modifications needed to the T5 and make all the necessary sketch plans. Could you get everything on one sheet of paper, using both sides?'

'Yes – I'm sure I could if I had mapping or drawing pens. I can draw and write very small.'

'Just like all engineers,' said Kruger, standing, signalling that the interview was over. 'See Hauptmann Dietrich Berg. He's our technical officer. His workshop's on the ground floor near the kitchen where you were caught. He'll supply you with writing materials. I won't insult your intelligence by asking if you divulged anything to the British about the T5 trials during your interrogation, but have you discussed this with anyone here?'

'No, Commander,' Karl replied, also rising.

'See that you don't.'

'Thank you, Commander,' said Karl exchanging salutes.

'One small point, Moehe,' said Kruger when Karl reached the door. 'When I said that I don't sanction escapes unless they're properly worked out, that's not to say that you can't plan one. Just don't make it obvious, and don't tell anyone.'

Karl's spirits were riding high when he went in search of Dietrich Berg.

19

Hauptmann Peter Paulus Ulbrick studied Karl Moehe's meticulous sketches and notes concerning modifications to the T5 torpedo. The tables and neat drawings had been crammed on to a single sheet of paper. It was the work of a skilled draughtsman. He listened intently to Kruger's account of his interview with the torpedo officer. The senior officer finished talking and lit another cheroot. 'So what do you think, Paul?'

'I can't think straight in this fug, Otto. That's what I think.' With that Ulbrick crossed to Kruger's window and wrestled the sash up. He leaned out and breathed deeply of the crisp air, carried on the southern breeze across Furness Fells. 'God only knows how you manage with this stink.'

Kruger smiled faintly. 'You've never had to endure the stink in a U-boat. The smell of urine, sweat and heaven only knows what else from forty-four men can be formidable.'

'No – thank God I haven't,' said Ulbrick with feeling. 'U-boatmen. You're all slightly mad. You have to be to do what you do.' He inhaled. 'God – I think I can smell the sea.'

'You can when the wind's in the south,' Kruger replied. 'That's why I like the window shut.'

Ulbrick tried to close the window and gave up. He turned to face Kruger. The army officer had been the camp's senior officer until Kruger's arrival. Ulbrick's style had been very different from the way Kruger did things. Ulbrick had sanctioned every hare-brained escape scheme going. His view was that it was the duty of every officer to cause the maximum disruption and inconvenience to the enemy. As a result of ill-planned, impromptu escapes, two well-liked officers had died.

The authoritarian Otto Kruger had changed all that. His first concern had been the low morale of the prisoners, largely due to boredom, which degenerated into resentment when he introduced training courses on every conceivable subject. Where his questionnaires detected an expert on a subject, that person became a course lecturer. Every prisoner was required to attend at least two courses. A group of craftsmen under Dietrich Berg made cuckoo clocks and profitable toys that Willi sold, and six of them were even learning unprofitable Sanskrit. A drama group made costumes, and staged plays and revues in Grizedale Hall's spacious great hall, now the common room that had once been Harold Brocklebank's ballroom and main dining room.

Kruger had persuaded Major Reynolds to agree that every man could have a vegetable plot. Some prisoners had objected and others had been glad of the chance to occupy their minds. Gradually Kruger had won them all over to his way of thinking, including Paul Ulbrick, now Kruger's second-in-command, who had been his most outspoken critic. Kruger was not really liked – he was too aloof, too distant, to encourage friendship, but he was well respected and the prisoners in his charge knew that he placed their interests above all else.

'Well, Moehe certainly is a remarkable officer,' said Ulbrick. 'Clever, resourceful, tough, and slightly mad, of course, like all U-boatmen.'

'And obsessed with getting this information home,' said Kruger, tapping the document.

'This acoustic torpedo is important?'

'Very. We've had nothing but disasters with the magnetic firing pistols.'

Ulbrick grinned disarmingly. 'I suppose any gadget that enables drunken U-boat crews to fire torpedoes without having to go through the tedious business of aiming them must have something going for it.' Then he was suddenly serious. 'Could you bury that information in one of your letters?'

'Could you?'

'The trouble with the Luftwaffe high command is they'd look upon your letter code system as defeatist. They don't expect their fliers to get shot down. Our top brass are not as bright as your Admiral Doenitz.' Ulbrick picked up Moehe's sheet of drawings. 'Anyway, I'd say that burying this lot in a letter would be next to impossible.'

'Exactly.'

Ulbrick looked speculatively at Kruger. 'As I say, we don't have a system to ask Hermann to land a Heinkel on the lawn here, so it's down to you. A U-boat in Morecambe Bay is the obvious choice.'

'Precisely.'

'Can Moehe swim?'

'He's an exceptionally strong swimmer. He fired the scuttling charges in his U-boat when the control room was half underwater, and he helped get most of the crew into the life rafts and up the scrambling nets when the British picked them up.'

Ulbrick met Kruger's gaze. 'So there's your answer, Otto. You'll have to write a letter to Alice.' He turned to the open window and gazed south over the rolling fells. His nostrils detected the faint scent of ozone and seaweed borne on the breeze. 'Lucky bastard,' he said softly.

'Don't forget his nickname,' said Kruger. He moved Ulbrick aside and slammed the window shut.

20

The photograph of Kruger's letter to Alice arrived on Fleming's desk two days after the original had been cleared by the War Office censors and had disappeared into the Red Cross's postal system. The handwriting was slightly blurred owing to the cheap paper but legible, and made for the usual dull reading. Kruger was complaining that books in German on vegetable growing were scarce. He described the soil conditions and locations of the vegetable plots and wondered if Alice could look up what manner of soil treatment was needed for the coming growing season and what would be the best vegetables to grow and what density, and could she please send some seeds? There was a long description of what vegetables had flourished the previous year, and crops that had fared less well.

Fleming was elated that his prediction that Kruger would

soon write to Alice had proved correct. It was obviously a coded letter but a concerted effort at breaking the code without Admiral Godfrey's consent would be impossible. It would be best to await Alice's reply.

He didn't have long to wait. Alice answered Kruger's letter within five days – a record – and Fleming was reading her letter the day before Kruger was due to receive it. It was long, covered two sheets, and was filled with gardening information such as how many grams of lime per square metre should be applied to acid soils; the amount of wood ash and humus needed to help condition soil, tips on composting, crop rotation to avoid diseases, planting distances, and so on.

'Christ,' said Johnny Benyon, a crypto-analysis expert, during a meeting in Admiral Godfrey's office. 'It positively screams code. She might as well have printed "This is a coded letter" in inch-high block capitals on the envelope. But, as we've said before, sir, we've done everything possible to these letters in the time we've been allowed. Even if you authorized a team to work on them for a week, I'm sure we wouldn't get anywhere. They're using the equivalent of a one-time pad.'

Although Admiral Godfrey sensed that Fleming was on to something important, he had to make the best uses of his slender resources, and that meant making tough, unpopular decisions.

'I'm sorry, Fleming,' he said when they were alone. 'But you will have to drop this one. The "Cage" have got six interrogators on sick leave with this blasted flu outbreak. I've promised them that you'd help out for a few days.'

The two men looked at the photographed letters. 'So we let Kruger receive his letter, sir?'

'I don't see why not.' Admiral Godfrey chuckled. 'You know, Fleming, it's possible that we're running with the wrong end of a large stick in our mouths. All those words might mean just what they say. Lots of complicated gardening hints.'

Where Admiral Godfrey, his code experts, and Fleming were mistaken was to attribute importance to the words in the Kruger–Alice correspondence. The hidden messages were not so much contained in the actual words or the letters that made up the words, but in the spaces between the words and letters.

21

Dealing with Kruger's correspondence was Willi's twice-weekly job after mail distribution in the common room. He bustled into Kruger's room with an armful of post and announced that the letters included one from Alice.

'I'll deal with it, Willi.'

'But you've shown me how the encoding works, Commander,' Willi replied, handing the letter over.

Kruger broke the War Office censors' seal and opened the letter. He glanced at the date at the top of the first page. 'This isn't in the "Ireland" code, Willi. I'll need your magnifying glass.'

The little Barvarian knew better than to express his disappointment at not being party to any secrets. He gave Kruger his magnifying glass, sat at his card table that served as a desk on mail days and set to work, glancing surreptitiously at Kruger now and then in the forlorn hope of gleaning information from the senior officer's inscrutable expression. He hadn't known until then that there was more than one type of letter code.

Kruger frowned over the letter. Alice had written the name of the month in full and not used the usual abbreviation. This meant that letters rather than whole words would be used. Decoding the missive was going to be a lengthy job.

He pulled his desk closer to the window and set to work, moving the magnifying glass along the line of neat handwriting until he found the first tiny break in the flow of cursive script. It was dated the twenty-fifth day of the month, therefore he ignored the first five similar breaks. The sixth break came before an 'A' so he wrote an 'A' on a blank piece of paper. The next break preceded an 'L'. The first word he assembled spelt 'Alice' which meant that he had established the correct start point for the decoding key.

Kruger worked steadily for thirty minutes. Such was his concentration that he even forgot to light a cheroot. The listings of amounts of seeds and fertilizers that Alice had provided concealed dates, times, and a position. He turned to the windowsill, felt underneath the protruding board for the two knots that covered release clips and pushed them in. The windowsill could then be wriggled forward exposing a cavity in the masonry that was home for a large number of potentially useful items ranging from passes, identity cards, and Ministry of Food ration books, to the more mundane such as bus and train tickets. Most had been found by working parties of prisoners on litter-clearing teams sent to picnic areas and Lake District beauty spots at Beatrix Potter's behest. Quite a few were the result of Willi's bribing activities. Among the material was the sheet of drawings that Moehe had produced. One of the most prized items was a large-scale map of the Lake District, which Kruger spread out on his desk. He measured the distance from Grizedale Hall, following a line almost due south through Satterthwaite village to the triangular tongue of Morecambe Bay where it reached into Furness Fells to form the estuary of the mouths of the River Crake and the River Leven at the triangle's apex. He plotted the exact position where a U-boat would be waiting some two miles offshore during the next lunar cycle when high tides would be occurring in Morecambe Bay between midnight and an hour before dawn.

He made a few notes, put everything away and glanced at the cuckoo clock that Berg and his craftsmen had made for him. 'Willi!'

Willi jumped. 'Commander?'

'I want Moehe in here in exactly thirty minutes and Hauptmann Ulbrick in exactly forty minutes. Also I want window-cleaning lookouts at each end of the corridor. You can be one of them.'

'Right away, Commander,' said Willi glumly, heaving himself to his feet.

22

Fleming spun his cap in the direction of his office's bentwood coat stand and missed.

'Bugger.'

'Not like you to miss, sir,' said Sally, looking up from her typewriter as Fleming dropped into his chair, loosened his tie, and eyed the pile of papers in his in tray with distaste.

'God – how I hate interrogation work. I've been playing the hard man all week.'

'I'm sure you can be a very effective hard man, sir,' said Sally, stone-faced.

Fleming grinned. 'They've let me off early today. Look at all this bumf. Do you think we'd lose the war if I were to dump this lot?'

'It couldn't make things any worse, sir. The top papers are the latest shipping loss figures.'

Fleming made a start on his paperwork, got depressed and bored in that order, and took the two Alice letters from his desk drawer. He never tired of studying them.

A thought occurred. If Kruger had managed to pass important information to the fatherland in his letter, why was Alice's reply so long-winded? Maybe it was requests for clarification? He turned the letter over and read through the lists that itemized quantities of fertilizers and seeds. They were nearly all numbers.

And it came to him. Alice wasn't asking for clarification – she was supplying a time and a position for a rendezvous! He thumped his desk in excitement.

'Sally. I want you to visit the hydrographers' office and get me charts of Morecambe Bay. Er . . . What else?'

The girl seized her notepad and pencil while her boss was thinking.

'Yes – I'll need one-inch-to-the-mile maps of the area around Morecambe Bay, and tide tables for Morecambe Bay for . . .' Damn! How long ahead? A wild guess. '. . . for the next two months. Take some money for a taxi. Come back if you can't find one and I'll fix up a car. It's urgent.'

While she was gone Fleming tried to see Admiral Godfrey and learned from his secretary that he would be away for the rest of that day. Sally returned three hours later laden with all the documents that Fleming required.

He set to work immediately, spreading the charts out on his desk and immersing himself in the tide tables, hardly noticing when Sally bid him goodnight. He quickly realized that he was tackling the problem from the wrong end. Start at Grizedale Hall. The best time for a prisoner to escape would be as soon as it was dark. Around 2000. Grizedale Hall's nearest point to the sea was Morecambe Bay. The route from the hall to Morecambe Bay was easy country. About fifteen miles from the hall to the east side of the bay, where there was at least eight metres of water relatively near the coast at high tide. A U-boat couldn't risk anything less shallow than that if it wanted to remain mostly submerged. A fit man could cover that distance from Grizedale Hall to the sea in four to five hours. Then he'd have a two-mile swim at the very least. Moehe was fit, he had proved that, and he was a strong swimmer, he had proved that, too.

Fleming's pulse quickened. He had the who; he had the where. Now for the when. The tide timetables answered that question. In three days high tides occurred in Morecambe Bay on three consecutive nights between midnight and 0400. The next favourable time would not be for another month, and that would take the escape bid nearly into June, when there wouldn't be as many hours of darkness, and the high tides in the bay would be a metre less anyway. No – if there was to be an attempt, it would have to be within three days – starting next Sunday night. If that rendezvous failed, there would be one or two or three more opportunities at the most, provided Moehe could lie low during the hours of daylight. The resourceful German officer had already shown that he was good at that.

After an hour's work and reasoning, Fleming reckoned that he had everything: the who, the where, and the when. Everything, that is, except confidence in his guesswork. The doubts crept in. Maybe he was building too much on too little? Maybe the Alice letters were, as Admiral Godfrey had suggested, merely complicated gardening hints.

Too complicated!

Fleming had only to look at Alice's tables to know that he was right.

It would happen on Sunday night.

He searched through his contact book and telephoned Commander Michael Havers at Western Approaches Headquarters. They pressed their respective scramble buttons when they had established contact.

'Listen, Mike. Are you interested in catching a U-boat?' Fleming listened to the reply and chuckled. 'In that case, have you got a corvette or a sloop you could spare next Sunday night and Monday morning for a spot of lurking in Morecambe Bay? And maybe Monday night and Tuesday morning as well?'

The reply from Liverpool was a resounding and emphatic negative.

'Well, anything, Mike? Christ – even an MTB would do . . .' This time the negative was accompanied by expletives. 'Okay – how about a tug? Surely you've got something, old man? I'm handing you a U-boat on a plate, for God's sake!'

After a few minutes of earnest pleas, Havers promised faithfully to call right back. Fleming sat at his desk, fiddling nervously; he smoked two cigarettes and almost snapped his pencil in half when the phone rang. He snatched up the receiver and listened. His tense expression gradually relaxed. His initial chuckle degenerated into laughter. 'She's available, Mike? I had no idea . . . Training? Well – yes. That had never occurred to me. It's a bloody marvellous idea. She'd do very nicely. Very nicely indeed.'

An hour later Fleming was hammering his Bentley north, driving as fast as he dared in the meagre illumination from his cowled headlights. Every now and then he couldn't help laughing out loud.

23

'You're escaping on Sunday night,' said Kruger curtly, without preamble.

Karl gaped.

'Have you worked out an escape plan?'

'Well . . .' Karl was too flustered to organize his thoughts. 'I've been looking at possible—'

'It doesn't matter. You're being provided with a ready-made plan. In fact you're being given everything on a plate, Leutnant. Clothes, papers, an identity card, compass, a waterproofed torch and a watch, some money – not that you should need it. You'll be a Dutch seaman on shore leave. Seamen usually pick up some English, so between now and Sunday night you'll be coached in some elementary phrases. Hopefully the need to use them won't arise.'

Kruger crossed the room to his map of the Lake District that was pinned to the wall. He pointed to Grizedale Hall. 'That's where we are.' His finger moved south to the east side of Morecambe Bay. 'And that's where you'll be swimming out at high tide where a U-boat will be waiting.'

Karl forgot himself. 'A U-boat, Commander!'

'I trust you've heard of them, Leutnant. It will pick you up south of this headland. You'll be breaking out of the hall at 1930 – earlier if the weather is bad, heavily overcast. You'll have a fourteen-mile trek ahead of you. You will have to get to the coast by 0115 at the very latest. High tide is an hour later. You will have thirty minutes of slack water either side of high tide when swimming will be safer and there'll be enough depth for the U-boat. At other times the currents in Morecambe Bay are dangerous, even for a strong swimmer. And in any event, the U-boat will not risk waiting once the tide turns. You'll have one more opportunity the following night. If you miss that, my strict orders are that you must destroy your information and give yourself up.' The senior German officer gazed fixedly at Karl, his eyes searching yet expressionless. 'Is that clearly understood, Leutnant?'

Karl realized that he was trembling. 'Yes, Commander.' He looked at the map. 'Will I be able to make a tracing of the map, Commander?'

'No. And this map remains in this office. You will study it in here. There's not a great deal to remember and I'll be questioning you until you're familiar with every detail. The only other thing you will have to remember are high-tide times.'

'I'm sure I'll have no trouble remembering everything, Commander.'

Kruger's tone softened. 'There's something else I want you to remember, Karl. As a U-boatman, I doubt if I have to remind you that many people will be taking considerable personal risks to get you and your information home. If it comes to a question of your having to decide on your safety, or their safety and the safety of the boat, you will be expected to treat your safety as a matter of secondary importance. Next there is the question about the information that you've written out. You've said that you would be able to remember everything. But that's not enough. U-boat crewmen can get killed in action. You could get killed and your information would be lost. Therefore you must hand over your information to the U-boat's captain.'

'I understand, Commander,' Karl replied, momentarily astonished at Kruger's use of his first name. Thinking that he was being dismissed, he saluted and turned to leave.

'And where do you think you're going?'

'I'm sorry, Commander. I thought—'

'There's much to be done in very little time. You're going to make a start on memorizing this map. Hauptmann Ulbrick will be along in a minute. He'll teach you to read those contours so that you'll be able to draw pictures of the terrain from them by the time he's through.'

After two days of intensive preparations, Karl's escape from Grizedale Hall on Sunday evening was an anticlimax. The worst bit was climbing down the makeshift rope made from plaited clothes lines from the first floor while a fierce wind and driving rain slashed at him like demented bread knives. It had been raining all day and water must have leaked into two of the feeble but crucially positioned floodlights because they did not come on at dusk and the British seemed disinclined to do anything about it in the appalling weather.

They also seemed to have abandoned their routine foot patrols. Karl waited, crouching in the shrubbery, icy rain-water streaming uncomfortably down his neck despite the sou'wester that had been found for him before he had shaken hands with Kruger and Ulbrick. After two minutes he decided that the guards weren't going to appear, so he made his dash for the damaged section of wall where he had first broken into the camp.

Fear lent him strength. He had little difficulty prising back the temporary planks that had been nailed across the gap so that he could wriggle through because someone had thoughtfully left a garden spade where it would be of use. He repositioned the planks so that they looked undisturbed and set off south, maintaining a steady jog into the driving rain. The chances of anyone being out and about in this appalling weather were remote, so he risked staying on the road, determined to have plenty of time in hand for when he had to take to the country, meanwhile a long, uphill climb lay ahead before the descent to the sea – best tackle it with a short-paced but steady jog.

His boots pounded rhythmically on the road that led to Satterthwaite village and freedom.

The U-boat was carried slowly through the driving rain into Morecambe Bay on the flooding tide, its twin Blohm and Voss diesel engines silent. It was running on its electric motors – an electrician rating in the motor room aft of the engine room operating the big rotary controls in response to the bell telegraph signals from the helmsman. The last order had been for dead slow ahead on both.

The boat was hull down, its ballast tanks partly flooded so that the deck casing was nearly awash. A rating was hanging on to the jumping wire at the bow, calling out depth readings using an old-fashioned but reliable sounding line.

The U-boat's captain was hunched on the conning tower, listening to the soundings while the lookouts quartered an invisible horizon with binoculars, rainwater and spindrift streaming off their foul-weather clothing. They paused occasionally to clean their lenses with chamois leathers. Immediately below them in the attack kiosk came the occasional whirr of the electric motor that spun the rotary saddle chair as the U-boat's first officer used the attack periscope's superior height to scour the surrounding black sea.

The U-boat's skipper was edgy about taking his craft this close to land in a bay noted for its tide-scoured, shifting sands. But so far the charts showing that he was in a reasonably deep channel on the eastern side of the bay seemed to be reliable.

He looked at his watch. The moon would rise in fifteen minutes. They would need it to find landmarks to be certain of their position. He hoped the cloud would clear but there was still plenty of time.

High tide would not be for another three hours.

26

K arl skirted Satterthwaite village without difficulty. The only vehicle he encountered was a truck filled with singing soldiers but he had heard its approach in good time and crouched behind a wall until it had passed. The low, drystone walls of the fells provided excellent cover for a fugitive.

The rain began to ease and finally stopped when the steep, uphill climb mercifully flattened out. The cloud was clearing and a half moon broke through, briefly causing the tops of the surrounding pines to glow in the ethereal light. It was a good moment to check everything. The sheet of paper bearing his information on the acoustic torpedo was still in place. It had been folded and wrapped in a lead toothpaste tube that had been split open, flattened and thoroughly cleaned. The resulting package, sealed in candle wax to waterproof it, had been lightly sewn into the pocket of his trousers so that he wouldn't lose it when swimming, but he could rip it out quickly and dispose of it if necessary. His torch was a bicycle rear light, its body shrouded in a rubber glove and sealed with electrician's tape to make it waterproof. His vest was uncomfortable. It was a buoyancy aid that had been made from two vests that had been stitched together with split corks trapped between the two layers.

He checked the time by his watch and pictured Kruger's map of the area in his mind. He was three miles from the sea and only five miles from the point where he would have to enter the water and swim. His elation helped him forget the numbing cold, and sucking on a boiled sweet provided a much-needed energy boost.

Rather than pass the fronts of a row of cottages, he climbed a wall on the far side of the road and continued running, crouching low. Water draining off the hill had collected at the foot of the wall, making the ground boggy and hard-going. The pain that lanced through his right ankle when he fell badly was such that he was unable to prevent himself crying out. He rolled on to his back in the mud, grasping his right knee to his chest, his face contorted in pain at the night sky. It was the ankle he had sprained badly when he had jumped from the train.

He rested for a few minutes. The pain diminished slightly and returned with renewed vigour when he pulled himself to his feet and resumed his journey. Jogging was now out of the question, all he could manage was a shambling gait, but he drove himself on, trying to ignore the agony in every step while being thankful that he had made such good progress until then.

But the pain proved impossible to ignore. Minutes were suddenly precious and he spent five of them wrestling a short, stout post from a picket fence to serve as a crutch.

He pressed blindly on, trying to shut out the pain. Just take it one step at a time. Each step taken was a torture and a victory, and the victories eventually triumphed. Somehow he reached the sea but he still had three miles to go to get south of the headland where he was supposed to enter the sea. The sheer effort of every step exhausted him. He sank to the ground at the edge of a stretch of dunes, sucked on a boiled sweet and decided that he had no alternative but to get his right boot off before the swelling made it impossible to remove. The effort cost him another five minutes. By the time the boot came free he could hear the incoming tide, probing its way rapidly across the expanse of marshes, oiling its way among the dunes, an advancing menace that shone silvery-black in the weak moonlight. One tiny comfort was that the wind had dropped.

He pressed on for half a mile, putting all his weight on the makeshift crutch, each step a drunken lurch, each lurch a shaft of blinding pain that dulled his reason and his sense of time. He was now on sand. The crutch kept sinking. The advancing water seemed to be ending its massive invasion of the bay – it had become silent. It came as a shock when he stopped to check his watch to discover that it was already high tide. Twenty minutes of slack water had passed, there was only forty minutes left, and he had a mile to go. There

90

was nothing for it but to start swimming now and try to keep to a south-westerly heading. He struggled out of his left boot and crawled into the sea. The icy water closing around him made him gag for breath. The pain in his ankle became a background feature of the general agony that wracked his entire body as he fully immersed himself. He waded out, launched himself forward in an energy-conserving breast stroke and was relieved to discover that kicking with his right foot was far less painful than walking on it. The buoyancy in the vest proved a blessing and his confidence returned.

27

The U-boat's quartermaster appeared on the bridge with a chart. He and the skipper crouched below the coaming and checked it with the aid of a penlight torch. They talked quietly, the quartermaster pointing out landmarks. Two miles ahead on the U-boat's starboard bow quarter lay the dark spit that marked the low headland. The crewman with the sounding line called out decreasing water under the U-boat's keel. Also the sea here was calm, protected by shores on each side that hemmed in too close for comfort. All these factors confirmed the captain's feeling that he dare not go any further. He gave the order to stop electrics and directed the lookouts to concentrate on a quadrant from ahead to ninety degrees starboard.

The U-boat lay motionless. The eerie silence now that wind had gone was marred only by the sound of slack water lapping at its deck casing and gurgling from the drainage holes.

28

A combination of the terrible cold and the exhaustion as a result of the energy he had expended hobbling for such a distance on his crippled right ankle eventually defeated Karl. His strokes weakened and eventually he stopped swimming and drifted, his buoyancy vest keeping him afloat and barely alive. To do nothing was heavenly luxury, to just relax and let the freezing water support him while it eroded his reason and awareness was pure bliss.

A tiny corner of his brain told him he was dying. Very well, then, he would die; let the pale sergeant come for him. It would be another uniform; another voice barking commands. He saw Kruger's expressionless eyes before him, boring into him. Then the icy gaze became filled with contempt. It restored a flicker of reason. There was one last hope. The torch. He had forgotten it. His numbed fingers groped for it. He waved it weakly back and forth, then remembered that it had to be switched on. There was no sensation in his fingers but somehow he managed to operate the switch. The feeble light it gave off was a flickering uncertainty like his will to live, but waving it enabled the battery terminals to make better contact and it glowed more steadily and a little brighter.

29

It was the U-boat's first officer in the attack kiosk who first spotted the tiny point of light. He worked the foot controls to turn the rotating chair and centred the periscope's graticule on where he thought he had seen it. There it was again! Bearing ten degrees starboard – almost dead ahead. He called out the bearing to the captain on the bridge.

On the conning tower all binoculars swung towards the U-boat's bow. Two of the lookouts saw the light. The captain passed the bearing to the helmsman. In the motor room the electrician answered the telegraph by setting the rotary switches to dead slow ahead both – one hundred revolutions per minute on each screw.

The U-boat's shark-like bow cleaved gently through the oil-black water. The forward hatch near the main gun clanged open. Several crewmen emerged and spread themselves out along the deck casing.

K arl slipped into semi-consciousness. The torch fell from his fingers. A wave rolled him on to his back. As his head went under he heard a faint, high-pitch whine. The sound brought him to. Perhaps he had imagined it. He dipped his head under water. The whining note was louder. A black shadow was moving towards him. His cry was a strangled croak. A powerful searchlight stabbed out of the darkness, sweeping back and forth before finding him and blinding him. The shadow loomed large and close. Then hands were grabbing at his collar and arms. He felt himself being lifted out of the water. His instinct was to yell at the fool responsible for the searchlight but he was paralysed by cold and could make no sound or even move. The roar from the bridge exhaust vents as the diesels suddenly started drowned the voices of the men who were lowering him into a warm, red-lit interior. He was passed through a hatch. To his joy he recognized the overhead pipework of a Type VIIC U-boat. A glimpse of the radio man's cubby hole and he was being laid on the long settee berth in the petty officers' mess. Someone started cutting away his clothes. He was about to say that a lot of work had gone into making them but the sudden divine sensation of hot towels being wrapped around him stilled his protests. His jacket was pulled clear and more hot towels went around his shoulders and over his head and neck. Unseen hands sat him upright and pulled his sodden trousers off.

'Good evening, Leutnant Moehe,' said a voice in German. 'Or should I say, good evening, Unlucky Moehe?'

It was a voice that Karl knew. He snatched the towel from his face and stared aghast at the owner of the voice. It was Ian Fleming, resplendent in his lieutenant-commander's uniform, wavy gold bands on the sleeves of his carefully pressed jacket. He was propped nonchalantly against the bulkhead. He smiled as Karl's frantic gaze darted around his surroundings.

'Don't worry, Karl. You're on board a genuine Kriegsmarine U-boat. Welcome aboard His Majesty's Submarine *Graph* – formerly *U-570* before it surrendered off Iceland in 1940. The British newspapers made a tremendous fuss at the time, so I'm sure you must've heard about it. Its former skipper, Hans Ramhlow, was at Grizedale Hall – he's probably in Canada now. I don't suppose it's giving away any secrets when I say that this boat is proving useful in training boarding parties.'

Karl was too dumbfounded and his mind was galloping off in too many directions for him to think of anything to say.

'I can't tell you how pleased I am to see you, Karl,' Fleming continued cheerfully. 'If you hadn't shown up I'd be in worse trouble than you're in. In case you're concerned, there was a U-boat in the area a few hours ago. Unfortunately it saw us first and made off. The navy are hunting for it now.'

Karl saw a rating searching through his trousers and pulling out the lead-wrapped package. He handed it to Fleming and what was left of Karl's shattered spirits plummeted to the bottom of a bottomless pit.

'I think I can guess what's in this,' said Fleming, glancing at the packet and slipping it in his pocket. He looked sadly at the hapless U-boat officer. 'First you escape by jumping from a moving train. Then you break into the POW camp that you were being sent to anyway, then you escape a second time and get caught while eavesdropping. For a glorious finale, you escape a third time and try to hitch a lift home in a British submarine. You really have earned that nickname, *Ungluckish.*'

Part Two

The Shackled Men

1

'Good morning, Commander,' said Reynolds, rising as Sergeant Finch showed Kruger into his office. 'Please take a seat. Not such a fine morning this morning and it looks like it's going to get worse.'

'Good morning, Major,' Kruger replied, returning Reynolds's salute and sitting. 'You wished to see me?'

Damn the man, thought Reynolds. A man of few words. Always wanting to get down to business. No pleasantries to give him time to think. He indicated the teapot and cups on his desk. 'Can I offer you a cup of tea?'

'You can when I've heard and considered whatever it is you have to say. But please go ahead. Don't let me stop you.'

As always, the German officer's condescending, slightly sardonic manner annoyed and unsettled Reynolds. Kruger had a knack of making him feel small by always seeming to assume control, and that gaze could chill a blast furnace. That Kruger looked so damned superior in that immaculate, tailor-made uniform didn't help. It had been Fleming's stupid idea to have it made. Reynolds didn't see why he should wait, so he poured himself a cup of tea and stirred it, conscious of Kruger's unblinking stare on him.

'I've had a signal from the War Office,' Reynolds began. 'I confess that what I have to say doesn't make me happy.'

Kruger remained silent.

Reynolds toyed with his teaspoon. 'Last week two British officers were landed on the Channel Islands under the cover of darkness. They were wearing raincoats over their uniforms. Unfortunately something went wrong and they were arrested by the occupying military police. Photographs appeared in the German press showing them handcuffed.' Concentrating on what he was reading meant that he didn't have to meet that cold stare. 'As I'm sure you know, Commander, the handcuffing of captured soldiers is a gross violation of the Geneva Convention concerning the treatment of prisoners of war. His Majesty's Government is extremely angry that the convention has been so disgracefully flouted by the German authorities and it has ordered that ten German officers held in a British POW camp should receive similar treatment. This is the Number One camp for German officers, therefore this camp has been selected. I am required to handcuff ten officers for five days.'

Reynolds was about to continue but broke off in surprise when Kruger rose without a word, pulling on his gloves. He saluted Reynolds, and strode towards the door.

'I haven't finished, Commander!'

Kruger pulled the door open. The two guards who were posted outside heard their commanding officer and crossed their rifles in front of Kruger when he appeared.

'Major Reynolds says he hasn't finished, sir,' said Private Allen, a fresh-faced nineteen-year-old.

Kruger's icy stare unnerved both guards. He raised extended, kidskin-gloved forefingers, pushed the rifles apart, and continued towards the main building. The soldiers' rifles had been touched by the enemy, therefore they were in their rights to cock them and point them at Kruger.

'Halt!'

Kruger kept walking. Prisoners playing squash against the wall by the main entrance stopped their game and watched the astonishing spectacle as their commanding officer walked towards them.

Sergeant Finch heard the sudden commotion and appeared in Reynolds's office.

'Commander Kruger has left without permission, Sergeant. I want him stopped and brought back here immediately!'

Sergeant Finch raced into the courtyard, blowing his whistle and yelling orders. Ten soldiers poured out of the guards' mess. They formed a line across the courtyard between Kruger and the main entrance.

'Commander Kruger!' Sergeant Finch called out. 'You are to return to Major Reynolds's office!'

Kruger kept walking.

On a word from their NCO all ten soldiers closed their rank and cocked their rifles but Kruger kept walking. Bad news travelled faster at Grizedale Hall than dragon's breath through a field of paper flowers. Prisoners were appearing in the courtyard from all directions.

'Halt or we fire!'

Christ! No! No! No! Reynolds's thoughts almost shouted as he frantically signalled his NCO.

Kruger's iron will and hard stare were enough for one of the soldiers in the centre of the line to give way and let him through.

Sergeant Finch's yelled order to fetch Kruger back, by force if necessary, was not that easy for his squad to carry out. As Kruger entered the hall, prisoners spilled across the guards' path, blocking the entrance. The scene deteriorated with extraordinary rapidity. There were shouts and curses. Prisoners eager to bring the whole thing to the boil started fighting among themselves, appearing to exchange hard blows, covering their receipt of pulled punches with convincing roars of rage and pain. It was the sort of thing they excelled at. Some punches were not pulled and connected with soldiers, the more hot-headed of whom responded with kicks. One soldier even started swinging his rifle like a club. The shambles was prevented from degenerating into a riot by Major Reynolds unholstering his revolver and firing two shots into the air.

The silence was immediate as fighting stopped and alarmed faces turned to the camp commandant.

'Sergeant Finch! Diversion roll-call, please.'

'Saar!' The NCO gave three long blasts on his whistle – the signal for a snap roll-call. Everyone seemed glad of the sudden ending of the affray. The prisoners who were present shuffled into lines, other prisoners came running in response to the soldiers pounding through the hall, yelling 'Roll-call! Roll-call! *Rouse! Rouse!*' and blowing their whistles. One keen gardener arrived carrying his rake and had to be disarmed.

Hermann, the camp's black cat, appeared, trailing behind his idol, Leutnant Walter Hilgard, a giant of a man who had been the leading chef on the *Bismarck* and was now in charge of the camp kitchen. He and his six sous chefs were wearing white coveralls. Hermann relied on Hilgard to keep him supplied with titbits. Also, he disliked being left out of anything and watched with yellow-eyed interest as the prisoners tidied their lines with outstretched arms. The clock built into his stomach told him that this roll-call was being held at the wrong time. Muttered questions about a possible escape at the front of the parade became substantiated rumours by the time they reached the rear.

Sergeant Finch had found his clipboard and took the file count from Corporal White. He counted the ranks himself, totted up the figures, and marched to the regulation distance in front of Reynolds, crashing his boots to smart attention and saluting.

'One hundred and thirty-one prisoners present, saar!'

'And one cat,' said a voice in clear English from the middle of the phalanx.

Sergeant Finch glowered at the sea of bland faces before him. One day he was going to find out who it was that made that comment at every roll-call and personally strangle him. 'One prisoner missing, saar!'

A roll-call by name was not necessary. Kruger was not in his customary position at the head of the parade.

Reynolds approached Ulbrick in the first row. 'Hauptmann Ulbrick. Will you take over in your commanding officer's absence, please.'

Ulbrick did not move. There had to be a good reason for Kruger's uncharacteristic behaviour, so he stood his ground. 'With respect, Major. I have no reason to believe that Commander Kruger has escaped or is indisposed. I cannot assume command unless he authorizes me to do so.'

Reynolds set his lips in a hard line but did not press the matter. He moved to the second row and fixed his lone eye balefully on Willi, perspiring freely from having just raced down three flights of stairs.

'Leutnant Hartmann. Will you please find your commanding officer. Give him my compliments and say that his presence is required at roll-call immediately. On the double, if you please.'

There wasn't much double in Willi but he did his best as he scuttled off.

'We will keep all the prisoners here until we have a full count,' said Reynolds grimly to Sergeant Finch.

'Saar!' The NCO conveyed the camp commandant's wishes to the gathering in his best scathing, foghorn style.

The men remained standing to attention. Willi appeared in the main entrance five minutes after he had disappeared. His face was bright red. He leaned an outstretched arm against a pillar to get his breath back, stumbled up to Reynolds and gave him a clumsy salute.

'Commander Kruger is in his room, Major. He thanks you for your compliments, which he returns, and suggests that if you wish to discuss anything with him, that you send him an agenda for a meeting, which he will consider attending.'

Reynolds looked at his watch. 'Thank you, Leutnant. Will you please inform Commander Kruger that if he's not down here in five minutes, that he will be brought down by force.'

Willi's moonlike face went even rounder in alarm. 'Now, sir?'

'Yes, please.'

'But it'll take me five minutes to get up there, sir,' Willi protested.

'Just be as quick as you can!' Reynolds snapped.

Willi puffed into the hall. This time ten minutes elapsed before he reappeared and he leaned against the pillar for even longer than before. He staggered across the courtyard, his face puce, and forgot to salute Reynolds. In fact he hardly had the strength to stand, never mind lift his arm.

'Commander Kruger sends his compliments and has asked

99

me to repeat his last message,' Willi managed to gasp. He looked pleadingly at Reynolds but the Canadian was staring past him.

Willi had become an atheist on his third climb to the top of the building. He followed Reynolds's gaze, saw Kruger emerging from the hall, and decided that maybe there was a god after all. He returned to his place in the parade, offering prayers of thanks.

There was a murmur among the prisoners as Kruger strode unhurriedly to the head of the parade. He spoke briefly to Ulbrick, whose jaw tightened, and took his place without saluting Reynolds or acknowledging his presence.

On a word from Reynolds, Sergeant Finch and the corporal again went through the ritual of counting heads.

'One hundred and thirty-two prisoners . . .'

'And a cat.'

'. . . present, saar!'

Reynolds thanked the sergeant and turned to Kruger. 'Would you dismiss your men, please, Commander.'

Kruger faced the parade and gave an order in German. The men began to disperse, some reluctantly. The upset had made a welcome break in their routine and they were keen to find out what had caused it, and what would happen next. They drifted away when Kruger spoke sharply to them. Only Willi remained hovering within earshot.

'Perhaps we can now resume our discussion in my office, Commander,' said Reynolds coldly.

'There's nothing to discuss. You want to handcuff ten of my officers, contrary to the Geneva Convention, and I refuse to allow it or participate in any way.'

The Canadian contained his mounting anger. 'You realize that someone could've been shot just now as a result of that debacle?'

'None of my officers are armed,' Kruger replied coldly. 'None were trying to escape, and none were disobeying orders. Had an officer been shot, the responsibility would have rested entirely with you.'

Reynolds's manner became informal. He lowered his voice. 'For Chrissake, Otto. Be reasonable. I've argued for a concession that the men need only be handcuffed between roll-call and teatime. The point is that I don't like the situation any more than you do, and I think there's a way out so that I don't have to carry out this stupid order. Can we discuss it my office, please?'

'The only way out for you is to refuse to obey what is an illegal order, Major. No discussion between us can change that.'

'I don't have to refuse to obey it,' Reynolds snapped, his patience wearing thin with this obstinate man. 'I can't obey it because we don't have ten pairs of handcuffs!'

2

A week passed before Reynolds had to deal with the problem again. It was in the form of a telephone call from an aggrieved civilian with flat feet destined to fight the war as a clerk in an army central ordnance depot.

'You've put in a requisition for eight pairs of handcuffs, Major.'

'That's right. We're allowed to refer reqs for urgent supplies directly to you now.'

'That's not the point. According to our supplies schedule, you're not entitled to any handcuffs.'

'That's crazy. We've already got two pairs.'

'That's what your Sergeant Finch has just told me. Your allocation of handcuffs is most irregular. How did you manage to obtain them?'

'I've no idea. They were probably here when I was posted here.'

'Our OiC is most annoyed.'

'Tough,' Reynolds sympathized. 'So what do we have to do?'

'The situation will have to be regularized before we can action a replacement req.'

'Another one!'

'You will have to return the handcuffs you're holding.'

'Will you put that in writing?'

'We've already done so. This requisition is being cancelled. You should have the signal tomorrow. We'll need a supporting returns docket saying that—'

'I'll put you back on to Sergeant Finch,' Reynolds interrupted. He pressed the button to drop the call back in Sergeant Finch's lap, replaced the receiver, and relaxed, hands clasped at the back of his neck.

Excellent. So now he was going to end up with no handcuffs. So far, so good.

Two days later it got better.

Captain Moyle was General Somerfeld's aide. His telephone manner was abrupt because he didn't have flat feet and he was resentful because it looked as if the war was going to pass him by. 'The General wants to know why you haven't acknowledged his order regarding the handcuffing of ten officer POWs.'

'I haven't been able to carry out the General's order.'

'Why not?'

'I haven't got ten pairs of handcuffs.'

Captain Moyle said he would call back immediately and did so two days later. 'You should have two pairs of handcuffs, Major Reynolds. General Somerfeld said that you don't have to have ten POWs handcuffed simultaneously.'

'I haven't got two pairs of handcuffs.'

'But it says here that you have.'

'I did have. But not now.'

'Have you lost them?'

'No.'

'Stolen?'

'No.'

'Then where are they?'

'They had to be returned to the COD.'

'On whose orders?'

'On the orders of the OiC at the COD,' said Reynolds. 'I've got it in writing.'

'So put in a req to the COD for a new issue!'

'I did.'

'And?'

'But it had to be cancelled and a new one issued.'

'For God's sake! How did that happen?'

'It's a long story,' said Reynolds, putting his feet on his desk. 'It all started when I put in a req for eight pairs of handcuffs to supplement the two pairs that I already had. It was then that I was told that I had to return my original two pairs to regularize the situation. I did so. Are you with me so far?'

'I think I'm ahead of you.' There was a resigned note in Captain Moyle's voice.

'Returning my two pairs of handcuffs,' Reynolds continued, 'meant that I had no handcuffs at all and that my req for eight had to be cancelled and resubmitted as a req for ten pairs because I'd returned my original two pairs. And that's the situation as it stands – I've no handcuffs at all.'

There was a long silence. Reynolds thought he could hear deep breathing at the other end of the line.

'This is a ludicrous situation,' Captain Moyle fumed. 'An absolute shambles.'

'I agree, Captain. Naturally I'm most concerned that I'm unable to carry out General Somerfeld's orders.'

'The orders came from the highest level.'

'In which case it's extremely embarrassing all round,' said Reynolds sympathetically.

'I'm going to look into this mess right away,' Captain Moyle growled. The line went dead. Reynolds resumed making flies. Hermann had caught a woodpecker, therefore he had a good selection of brightly coloured feathers to choose from.

An idyllic week slipped by. It ended with a phone call from Captain Moyle. 'General Somerfeld has been rolling heads at the COD. They're dispatching ten pairs of handcuffs to you today.'

'That's excellent news,' said Reynolds suavely. 'Please assure the General that I'll carry out his orders as soon as they're delivered.'

The clack of a typewriter from the adjoining office reminded Reynolds to check that the procedure he suggested to Sergeant Finch to 'guard our asses' was in place. He pressed a button on his intercom. 'Did you get all that, Sergeant?'

'Yes, sir. Private Knox has a full shorthand transcript.'

Reynolds thanked him. Having a former press reporter on his admin staff was so goddamned useful.

An hour later the flat-footed supplies clerk at the Central Ordnance Depot phoned, sounding aggrieved. 'There's a discrepancy on your req, Major.'

'Surely not? Sergeant Finch and I checked it most carefully before it was sent.'

'Do you want ten handcuffs or ten pairs of handcuffs? In the description column you've put "Handcuffs, pairs" and in the quantity column you've put "10 off".'

'Ten pairs, of course,' Reynolds replied, not altogether sure what the fellow was talking about. He added hopefully, 'Would you like us to cancel that req and raise a new one?'

'That's the correct procedure,' snapped the clerk. 'But there's been a lot of trouble here over your handcuffs. We're having to short-circuit all the correct procedures. I can't tell you how much extra work we're having to do.'

'We'll be more than happy to follow the correct procedures,' said Reynolds blandly. 'We don't want you to get into trouble on our account.'

'I'll alter the req but it's most irregular. Please ensure that your pink flimsy is also amended.'

'I'll see that it's done,' Reynolds promised, wondering if he had come to the end of the delaying tactic road, not knowing that the journey had barely begun.

3

'I think you'd better take a look at this delivery, sir,' said Sergeant Finch ominously, putting his head around the door.

Reynolds sighed and entered the NCO's domain. Private Knox continued typing at his desk, pretending not to be listening. Sergeant Finch had cleared his desk to make room for a wooden crate about the size of an ammunition box. He had already prised out the nails and removed the cover. The handcuffs were sandwiched between strips of heavy, greaseproof paper, held together with thick, black grease. He used a piece of blotting paper to protect his fingers and lifted out one of the heavy strips.

'Two handcuffs to each strip, sir. Mucky things to count but we've got ten strips here.'

Reynolds sat in Sergeant Finch's chair. 'Meaning we've got *twenty* handcuffs!'

'That's right, sir. Ten pairs. Looks like the depot's idea of a pair of handcuffs isn't the same as ours.'

The Canadian officer stared at the wooden box while Sergeant Finch laid out one of the sandwiched pairs of handcuffs across old newspapers and peeled away the brown paper. Two unusually large handcuffs lay accusingly in their bed of gleaming, treacle-like gunk.

'Twenty fucking handcuffs,' Reynolds muttered morosely. 'Aren't they a bit on the large size?'

'That's what I thought, sir. They're a lot larger than the two pairs we had to return, which I'm sure were the standard type that the redcaps are issued with.'

Sergeant Finch separated one of the handcuffs from the greaseproof paper while he was talking and dangled it from a pencil. The broad iron cuffs were joined by a nine-inch length of stout chain.

'That chain's far too long,' said Reynolds.

'There's some chalk marking on the bottom of the crate, sir,' said Sergeant Finch, prodding through the thick grease with his pencil. 'Looks like they were returned to depot from Durban in 1910.'

'You mean Durham?'

'Durban, sir. South Africa.'

'Good heavens.' Reynolds watched in silence as Sergeant Finch took all the handcuff strips out of the box one by one and felt carefully along the outside of their wrappings, pinching them with his fingers. 'A damned nuisance these turning up, Sergeant.'

'Yes, sir.'

'It's a crazy order. It's certain to cause trouble when we implement it.'

'I think that can be guaranteed, sir.'

'Meaning you disapprove? You can speak freely.'

The NCO finished checking the outsides of the handcuffs' wrappings. He glanced at Private Knox, who was engrossed in his typing. 'It's not for me to say, sir,' he said stiffly, keeping his voice down – not easy for Sergeant Finch.

'Meaning you don't approve. I said you could speak freely.'

'I've no liking for the Jerries, sir. But I have some regard for their senior officer.'

Reynolds sighed and stood. 'Well . . . Get ten of these things cleaned up, Sergeant. The sooner we carry out this crazy order and get it over and done with, the better.'

'I don't think we can carry out the order, sir,' Sergeant Finch replied, wiping his hands on a newspaper.

'Why the hell not?'

'There aren't any keys, sir.'

4

'No keys!' Captain Moyle yelled in Reynolds's ear. 'What do you mean, no keys?'

'I can't think of any other way of putting it,' Reynolds replied. 'We have twenty handcuffs and no keys.'

'Twenty! You're supposed to have only ten!'

'It's a long story.'

'I don't want to hear it. Have you checked the packaging?'

'Meticulously, Captain. There definitely aren't any keys.'

There was a string of audible expletives followed by a silence. 'Okay,' said Captain Moyle at resigned length. 'You'll have to indent COD for more handcuffs. I'll call them now and make damn sure they check them before dispatch.'

'Unfortunately we can't do that,' said Reynolds.

'Can't do what?'

'Put a req for more handcuffs.'

'Why not?'

'Our requisitioning pad is empty. It's had a bit of a caning over the last month.'

'I'm beginning to think you're doing this deliberately, Major.'

Reynolds put on his best outraged tone. 'That's a monstrous allegation, Captain Moyle. If you look at the records you'll see that we've been thwarted at every turn.'

'Okay. Okay. I apologize. So why haven't you got a new requisition pad? No. No. Don't tell me – let me guess. Because stationery supplies such as new requisition pads have to be requisitioned using a requisition pad?'

'Got it in one,' said Reynolds admiringly. 'I've called the COD and explained the situation. I promised to send them a retrospective stationery requisition if they send me a pad in lieu. And before you come out with any more unfounded allegations, Captain, we put in a req for three pads through you last month under the old system and the number was cut to one pad which is now empty.'

'Now listen,' Captain Moyle grated. 'I'm going to clear everything up from this end once and for all. No stone will be left unturned. No hide will go unroasted. Don't do anything. No phone calls, no paperwork – nothing. Just sit tight and the handcuffs will be on their way to you.'

'With keys?'

'With keys!' Captain Moyle was close to shouting.

'Have you got a magic wand, Captain Moyle?'

'I haven't! But General Somerfeld has a particularly large magic wand.' And then the Captain was shouting. 'And if his orders aren't carried out, and soon, he'll visit you in person and insert it somewhere painful!'

The line went dead. The phone rang again just as Reynolds was replacing the receiver.

'Sideways!' yelled Captain Moyle.

5

C aptain Moyle demonstrated his remarkable hide-roasting and stone-turning skills because the handcuffs arrived at Grizedale Hall two days later. This time they had been cleaned in advance. Each one came with two keys and a COD inspection certificate – two copies – the pink flimsy had to be signed and returned.

Sergeant Finch and Major Reynolds regarded them in silence. They were lined up on the NCO's desk: ten large handcuffs, gleaming and black, fine examples of the black-smith's craft, and strikingly similar to the first consignment with large cuffs and a long length of linking chain with a central swivel. The underside of their box said that they had been returned to the COD from South Africa in 1910.

Reynolds was the first to break the silence. 'Are you thinking what I'm thinking, Sergeant?'

'I hope not, sir.'

'Who's the smallest man we've got?'

'That would be Private Jones, sir.'

'Who else?'

'Private White, sir.'

'Those two. Very well. Have them brought to me, please. I'll be in my office.'

Five minutes later Reynolds was behind his desk, inserting cotton wool in his ears when the door was flung open and Privates White and Jones, wide-eyed with fear, were marched into the office by Sergeant Finch.

'Left, right! Left, right!*ATTEN-SHUN!'*

Three pairs of boots crashing to the floor shook the building.

'Private Jones and Private White reporting! *SAAR!'*

Reynolds rose and fixed his eye on Private White. The colour of the soldier's expression matched his nickname, 'Chalky'.

'Put your hands out, Private,' Reynolds ordered.

Private White gave his comrade a frightened glance and did as he was told. Reynolds picked up a pair of handcuffs and clicked the cuffs in place around the soldier's wrists. 'Keep your hands like that. Now you, Private Jones.' Reynolds secured the soldier's wrists with a second pair of handcuffs.

'Sir—' White began to protest but was cut off by Sergeant Finch bellowing that he wasn't to speak unless spoken too.

'It's all right, Sergeant,' said Reynolds, regarding the two soldiers who were standing before him, looking forlorn, their manacled wrists held out like beggars exhibiting deformities. 'What's the problem, White?'

'Me and Jones didn't think there was no harm in it, sir. I mean – it was all ripped up.'

'No harm in what?'

Private White swallowed. 'The parachute, sir.'

Reynolds caught Sergeant Finch's eye and said, 'Well . . . If you're prepared to confess, I might be prepared to reconsider the charge.'

'The prisoners found it on a litter-clearing detail, sir,' Jones volunteered. 'Chalky and me let them keep it in exchange for some bars of chocolate. My girlfriend will do anything for chocolate. It was only afterwards that we found out that they was made of silk.'

'Girlfriends?'

'Parachutes, sir.'

'And did she? Do anything, that is?'

'Yes, sir,' the soldier answered sheepishly.

Reynolds nodded, struggling not to smile. Even Sergeant Finch seemed to be having difficulty keeping a straight face. 'Well, I daresay that that's something that Sergeant Finch may want to look into. Right now, Private Jones, I want you to try escaping from those handcuffs.'

The soldier blinked. 'I'm sorry, sir?'

'Major Reynolds wants you to see if you can escape from those handcuffs!' Sergeant Finch bellowed in Jones's face. 'Tell me which words in his order that you don't understand and I'll explain them while exercising my customary patience and good humour!'

Still looking surprised and bemused, Private Jones hooked

his thumbs into his palms to fold his knuckles and shook the handcuffs off without difficulty. They fell on to the desk with a clatter.

'Now you, White.'

Private White did the same with the same result – his handcuffs clattered on to the desk.

'Thank you, men. Dismissed.'

The two soldiers left the office, looking as worried as when they had entered.

'Looks like we've got a problem,' said Reynolds ruefully, picking up one of the handcuffs and examining it. 'These goddamn things aren't adjustable. What sort of prisoners were you British dealing with in South Africa? Gorillas?'

'Maybe there's something missing from them, sir? An inner sleeve perhaps?'

'I'd like to be certain before I go chucking blame about,' said Reynolds grimly. 'There's going to one helluva row over this.'

'I think I know someone who might be able to help us, sir,' Sergeant Finch volunteered.

The following day, Police Constable Ian Pritchard (retired), formerly of the Royal Military Police, was ushered into Reynolds's office, and plied with whisky-laced tea by Sergeant Finch to help unlock his back and to compensate for his bicycle ride to Grizedale Hall. 'Cycling does me rheumatics good,' he had declared deprecatingly on arrival. Sitting sideways on a chair with his tortured back pressed against a hot radiator was heavenly bliss.

Reynolds produced one of the handcuffs and passed it to the policeman. 'What do you make of these, Mr Pritchard?'

'Bless my soul,' said Pritchard, turning the handcuffs over in his hands. 'These take me back a bit. Must be twenty year since I last saw a pair. Suez. We needed them there, I can tell you. There was a riot in '25 that—'

'What can you tell me about them, please, Mr Pritchard?'

'Well . . . Let me see now. Looks like a Froggart job.' He peered closely at one of the cuffs. 'Yes. Thought so. See those letters? F.D.L.'

Reynolds and Sergeant Finch looked and could just make out the letters stamped into the forged steel.

'Froggart Darby,' said the policeman. 'Wonder what happened to them? They made some fine restraint equipment—'

'What we'd like to know, officer,' said Reynolds patiently, 'is why did they make handcuffs that are so large? Is there anything missing from them? Some sort of inner sleeve, padding or lining that the depot didn't send us?'

'Handcuffs?' Pritchard echoed in surprise. 'Wherever did you get that idea? These aren't handcuffs, sir – they're leg irons.'

6

'*They're what!*' Captain Moyle yelled.

'Leg irons,' Reynolds repeated. 'Shackles.'

'For God's sake,' Captain Moyle muttered, sounding like an officer on the point of resigning his commission. 'I gave specific instructions. I told the COD that they were to check and double check before dispatch.'

'That's no good with CODs – you have to stand over them.'

'Very well. Use the shackles. Clap 'em in irons.'

'Not only does that sound regrettably naval,' said Reynolds blandly. 'But it would be in breach of my orders. It states quite clearly that ten POW officers are to be handcuffed.'

'For heaven's sake use your initiative! What's the difference between leg irons and handcuffs?'

'Leg irons are bigger and they're spelt differently. Also you're inciting me to disobey orders which is an offence under—'

'I am doing no such thing!' Captain Moyle howled. 'All I'm suggesting is that a little common sense would solve the problem once and for all. It's perfectly simple—'

Reynolds pretended to get angry. 'If everything is so perfectly simple, Captain Moyle, then why don't you get General Somerfeld to change his orders so that I can use shackles?'

The line went dead. The next person to join the battle was General Somerfeld himself. Reynolds took the phone call in some trepidation. Despite his reputation, the General was not an unreasonable man and listened to Reynolds's account without interruption.

'What particularly annoyed me was the clumsy attempt by your Captain Moyle to persuade me to disobey your orders, sir,' Reynolds concluded, figuring that there was no harm in spreading dissent in North-Western Command's HQ.

'He did what?'

Reynolds outlined his last telephone conversation with Captain Moyle.

'Thank you for being frank with me, Major. I shall be having a word with Captain Moyle. Meanwhile, we still have a problem. Very well – use the leg irons.'

Reynolds swallowed. Damn! 'With respect, sir, and please don't think I'm being difficult but—'

'I've read your report, Major. Full transcripts of telephone conversations. Quite remarkable. Your conduct throughout this wretched business has been exemplary. You've had obstacle after obstacle placed in your path in your valiant attempts to obey orders. I've decided to cut this Gordian knot that others have tied you up in by sending you a revised order to use the shackles. I'll send out a dispatch rider so that you'll receive it this afternoon.'

Reynolds sat brooding at his desk for some minutes after the phone call had ended. He had hoped that, after a month of delaying tactics, the order from the War Office would be rescinded. There was nothing for it but to confront Kruger with the news. He pressed the intercom button to call Sergeant Finch.

'I take it you heard all that just now, Sergeant?'

'Yes, sir. Private Knox has got it all down.'

'It looks like the end of the road. Take some guards and tell Commander Kruger that I wish to see him now. Don't hesitate to bring him here by force if he proves difficult.'

Force wasn't required but Kruger's face was set harder and colder than normal when he confronted Reynolds, standing between two guards, with two more behind him. He refused an invitation to sit. The month of strained relations between the two men had inexorably reached breaking point.

'Starting tomorrow morning at roll-call, ten German officers will be shackled for the day and released at teatime,' said Reynolds flatly. 'The procedure will continue for five days. They must be the same officers each day. Those are my orders. I intend to see that they're carried out.'

'Shackles now?'

'Yes, Commander. Shackles. And before you raise any objections, shackles are much easier for all concerned rather than handcuffs. They'll be able to move about, go to the bathroom, eat – do everything that they can't do when wearing handcuffs except play football.'

Kruger regarded Reynolds in icy contempt. 'Your explanation reminds me of the girl who tried to justify her illegitimate baby on the grounds that it was a very small baby. Shackles are a barbaric, medieval anachronism.'

'Give me ten names at roll-call tomorrow morning. Whether you select by lot or by volunteers is up to you but I want ten officers.'

'You will have to select them yourself, Major. I've already made my position clear. I will not be party to this illegal act.'

Reynolds was unmoved. 'Very well. I will select them. There's something I want you to consider. The original orders were that the men were to be shackled. Period. I stuck my neck out by getting the order changed so that they could be released each evening until roll-call the next morning.'

Kruger shrugged. 'As I said, a small baby but still a baby. There will be no co-operation.' He glanced at the guards flanking him. 'There is nothing further to discuss. I wish to leave.'

The atmosphere at roll-call the next morning was so electric that harnessing it would have met the power needs of a small town. Alternatively, an imaginative taxidermist could have stuffed it and mounted it.

One hundred and thirty-two prisoners, and one cat, were counted. They watched uneasily as a guard carried out a small wooden crate and placed it on the ground at the head of the parade. Kruger had briefed them the previous evening at a meeting in the common room. That some thirty guards were on duty – the camp's entire contingent – instead of the usual ten brought home the seriousness of the situation even though the guards had their rifles slung across their backs.

Reynolds stood on the crate and addressed the POWs in his slow, halting, and – at times – excruciating German. He outlined the orders he had been given and said, glaring around at the prisoners of war with his solitary eye, that he intended carrying them out.

'Ten officers have had their names selected by lot. I'm going to call them out and I want them to come forward and form a new rank at the head of the parade.'

He then produced a list of names and started reading them out, stumbling over some pronunciations. There were POWs on the list who had surnames that used every letter in the alphabet. None came forward. The faces of the prisoners stared blankly at him.

'May I help, Major?' Kruger enquired, holding out a gloved hand.

Reynolds did his best not to show surprise. It was unlikely that the senior German officer would ever capitulate, but there was no harm in hoping. He nodded his thanks, and gave the list to Kruger, who faced his men and launched into a stream of rapid German that left Reynolds floundering. The grins and nods of men in the front rank confirmed the Canadian officer's suspicion that Kruger was up to something. And then

Kruger started calling out the names, slowly and succinctly. As one the prisoners started regrouping, forming new lines, men ran back and forth to take up fresh positions. They spaced their ranks and files into neat lines using outstretched arms and the entire parade came to smart attention. The entire manoeuvre took less than thirty seconds and at the end of it not one of the men on the list was in the front row.

Reynolds took the list from Kruger. 'I want all the men whose names were called out to raise their right hand!'

Kruger confirmed the order in German.

The tight group of arms that went up confirmed Reynolds's suspicions: Kruger had ordered the ten men into the centre of the phalanx.

'Those men will all come forward!' Reynolds ordered.

No one moved except for Hermann, who got bored with the charade and sloped off. For a few seconds there was silence in the courtyard until Reynolds nodded to Sergeant Finch, who, in turn, barked an order to the guards. They closed in on the parade and that was a signal for the prisoners to do something wholly unexpected. Without a word of command from Kruger, and moving as though they had been under the guidance of a skilled choreographer, they gathered into a tight circle around the ten chosen men. Then they linked arms to form two even tighter outward-looking concentric circles. Their faces were grim, jaws set in determination. Kruger remained outside the circle, his gaze fixed on Reynolds.

Sergeant Finch wasn't thrown. He summoned his men into a group to give them brief instructions. Some looked nervous, uncertain. On a blast of his whistle they charged the human laager. The circle heaved and distorted like an electrocuted amoeba but the line of linked arms held, even when some prisoners went down under the onslaught. They were quickly hauled to their feet by neighbouring comrades.

The soldiers frantically grabbed at arms, twisting, pulling, cursing as they tried to break the human chain. The shouting and yelling reached an intimidating crescendo but none of the prisoners offered any violent resistance, not even retaliating when they were kicked. At one point three burly guards managed to break the outer circle's link. Had the other guards spotted it and concentrated their efforts there they may have broken through completely but the entire scrum of heaving humanity suddenly moved backwards causing the attackers to flounder forwards and lose their advantage, and prisoners to re-establish their determined laager of muscle and bone.

There were two more abortive charges with the same result except several prisoners and guards suffered cuts and bruises, not as a result of direct violence but from the rifles that were slung across the soldiers' backs. During the lull, injured front-line German officers, one blinded by blood, were moved to the centre of the tightly packed group and replaced by uninjured comrades.

The circle of set faces confronting Reynolds looked even more determined than before. He was uncomfortably aware of Kruger's gaze on him. Sergeant Finch was also watching him, awaiting further orders. A guard was sitting on the ground, clutching his temple, while a mate tried to staunch the flow of blood with a wadded handkerchief.

'Only a scratch, sir,' said the injured guard when Reynolds stooped to speak to him. 'I'll be okay.'

Reynolds squeezed the man's shoulder. He straightened and turned to Sergeant Finch. 'Return your men to normal duties, Sergeant.' He crossed to where Kruger was standing to attention. 'Dismiss your men, Commander.'

With that, Reynolds turned on his heel and strode to his office. Only when he was inside did he let his emotions show. He swore angrily to himself, flung himself into his chair, yanked a desk drawer open and poured himself a generous slug of Canadian bourbon. His hands were shaking. He hadn't felt like this since Dunkirk with Stukas diving down on his position, sirens screaming. This was worse. At least he'd been able to do something at Dunkirk, even if it was feverishly scratching a foxhole in the dunes with his bare hands. Here he was impotent.

Sergeant Finch entered the office carrying the box of leg irons.

'How are the men?' Reynolds enquired.

'All okay, sir. The one you spoke to – Dawkins – will need a couple of stitches when Nurse Hobson comes on duty. It wasn't the Jerries, sir. It was falls and that. Getting hit with each other's rifles—'

'I was there, Sergeant!' Reynolds snapped. 'I may have only one eye but I'm not fucking blind!' He immediately regretted his outburst and apologized.

'If I may venture a suggestion, sir.'

'Let's hear it.'

'It should be easy enough to nab prisoners one at a time during the day.'

'Kruger will make damn sure that those ten men will make themselves scarce.'

'With respect, sir, it doesn't have to be them. Any Jerry will do so long as there's ten of them.'

'That would amount to letting Kruger dictate terms to us. I won't tolerate him calling the shots. We do this my way – the proper way. I'm damned if I'm giving in to that goddamned Jerry.'

'In which case, sir, we're going to need reinforcements. My troops are outnumbered four to one.'

'I realize that,' said Reynolds, picking up his phone.

8

The prisoners had just assembled for roll-call the following morning, the box of leg irons was ready and waiting, when two Bedford covered trucks and a police Black Maria rolled into the courtyard. On a word from a red-faced brigadier who jumped out of the lead vehicle, the tailgates of the trucks dropped down to disgorge a hastily mustered collection of military police and basic-training conscripts, all carrying batons. A mixture of twenty regular police and war reserve constables piled out of the big police van. They lined up and produced their truncheons. The reinforcements numbered some fifty men. They stared at the recalcitrant prisoners, some wide-eyed and nervous – for some these were the first Germans they had ever seen – but the majority looked eager, ready for battle.

'Sorry we're late, Major,' said the brigadier brusquely after introductions. 'Had a spot of MT trouble. Right – let's get down to it and give these damned Jerries a thrashing they'll never forget.'

'Roll-call first, sir,' said Reynolds firmly.

Brigadier Hubert Dayton was an impatient but clever man who preferred action to words. 'You'd better get on with it,' he growled.

The roll-call passed off smoothly: 132 men present. No cat this time because Hermann had decided that there was nothing to benefit him in these new charades. Reynolds called out the ten names and not a prisoner in the parade stirred.

'No truncheons or batons, sir,' he said firmly to the brigadier.

The senior officer glowered. 'What the hell do you mean? We're here to teach these bounders a lesson, and, by God, that's what we're going to do.'

Reynolds repeated his request and cut short the brigadier's protests. 'With respect, sir. I'm the officer in charge of this camp and I say, no truncheons or batons.'

Brigadier Dayton looked set to argue the point, but changed his mind, and gave orders to his platoon sergeants and the officer in charge of the police contingent. The batons were returned to the army vehicles and the police slid their truncheons into their trouser pockets. All eighty men stood awaiting their orders. On a word from Reynolds they began to encircle the parade but the prisoners changed their tactics. Instead of forming a circle, they moved quickly as a single body to the broad rear of the hall that flanked the courtyard and formed themselves into a compact semicircle against the wall, arms linked as they had the previous day but, with almost half the perimeter to defend, their lines of men with linked arms were now five deep.

There followed four charges. Three minutes of mayhem; three minutes of yelling and cursing; three minutes of determined passive resistance by the prisoners in which the attackers, too crowded together and tending to get in other's way, failed to dislodge a single prisoner from the group. A long blast on Sergeant Finch's whistle caused the attackers to stand back from the embattled group, chests heaving, helmets scattered across the courtyard. Both sides had suffered minor physical injuries, but British pride had been the worst casualty.

'So now do we use the batons and truncheons?' said Brigadier Dayton in a quiet aside to Reynolds.

'Under no circumstances,' Reynolds said categorically.

The senior officer shrugged and ordered his reinforcements back to their vehicles. 'You're a fool, Reynolds,' was his parting comment. 'This situation cannot be allowed to continue, and I very much doubt if it will be allowed to do so after I've made my report.'

9

In the crowded common room Nurse Brenda Hobson finished treating prisoners' wounds with iodine, lint and sticking plaster, and sought out Kruger. He and Ulbrick were sitting in battered armchairs in earnest conversation. Both men rose, bowed and clicked their heels.

Brenda Hobson had been widowed the previous November when a U-boat had torpedoed the battleship *Barham* in the Mediterranean. Her seven-year-old son was now fatherless, yet it was a measure of her character that she found it impossible to harbour hatred towards Kruger and his fellow U-boatmen, or any of the prisoners.

'What's going on, Commander?' she demanded. 'And please don't come out with the nonsense about rough games that your men have been giving me. I wasn't born yesterday. This is the second day I've come on duty and found customers waiting for me.'

'There have been rowdy altercations between my men and the guards,' Kruger admitted.

She frowned. Kruger's command of English was always a little disturbing. 'You mean fighting?'

'Altercations, Nurse Hobson. My men were not involved in any fighting. I give you my word on that.'

'Well I hope that there won't be a repeat tomorrow morning.'

'So do I,' Kruger replied impassively.

She was about to leave when a thought occurred. 'Of all those wonderful toys your men made for my boy last Christmas, the big engine is his favourite. But a wheel broke yesterday. Could I bring it in to be repaired, please?'

Kruger bowed. 'Please give it to Hauptmann Berg. I will ensure that it is repaired immediately.'

The nurse thanked him, gathered up her first-aid box and left the room, aware of the admiring glances that followed her. It was strange that she felt safer with these men than she did when working in the casualty department at the Barrow military hospital.

'And how do you propose avoiding a repeat tomorrow morning?' Ulbrick enquired as the two men settled back into their armchairs.

Kruger lit a cheroot and exhaled. 'I can only hope that Reynolds sees reason.'

Ulbrick snorted. 'He's not the one who has to see reason. You've made your point, Otto. As Reynolds said, leg irons are a lot more convenient than handcuffs. Let's get this entire messy business behind us as soon as possible. We're never going to win. And if this camp gets a reputation for being troublesome, the British will pack us all off to Canada as they did with the Shap Fell camp. It's now only a matter of time before Britain falls and we're liberated. But Canada and America will fight on for years – we'll never beat them and we'll all be old men by the time we're sent home.'

The army officer had a valid point. Nothing sparked off escape fever quite as much as rumours of an impending transfer to Canada, but Kruger was unmoved.

'No German officer will be put in leg irons as long as it is within my power to resist it,' he declared emphatically. 'The matter is closed.'

Kruger might well have had a change of mind had he been party to the telephone conversation that Reynolds had with General Somerfeld later that day. When it was over,

Reynolds stared ashen-faced down at his blotter. Marshalling his thoughts was best achieved with a shot of bourbon.

10

The absence of Major Reynolds at roll-call the next morning and the appearance of a Humber staff car made all the prisoners uneasy. Brigadier Dayton stepped on to a large ammunition box that had been found to serve as his podium. The box containing the leg irons was on a card table with a chair beside it and two corporals standing guard. The brigadier initialled Sergeant Finch's clipboard when the count was complete. There was a buzz of conversation among the prisoners that was silenced on an order from Kruger. The non-appearance of vehicles loaded with reinforcements was also disturbing. Kruger caught Ulbrick's eye and raised an enquiring eyebrow but his second in command looked equally baffled.

'Commander Kruger,' said the brigadier, staring down at the German officer with undisguised hostility. 'I trust that your misplaced scruples will not prevent you translating what I have to say?'

Kruger agreed to act as interpreter. He didn't consider it appropriate to observe that most of the prisoners understood English. Brigadier Dayton had a forbidding presence that discouraged unnecessary comment.

The brigadier glanced at his watch and cleared his throat.

'That's the tenth time he's looked at his watch,' Ulbrick muttered.

Kruger made no reply. He, too, had noticed Brigadier Dayton's obsession with the time.

'Prisoners-of-war!' the brigadier began. 'Doubtless you have noticed that Major Reynolds is absent this morning.' He paused to allow Kruger to speak and continued, 'This is because for the next two hours I am the acting commanding officer of this camp. I am here to ensure that the orders of His Majesty's government that requires ten German officers to be shackled for the next five days are carried out.' He looked at his watch again. There was the distant rumble of an approaching vehicle. 'I will also be assuming temporary command during morning roll-calls until Friday to ensure that the orders from the War Office are carried out.'

His statement provoked a buzz of comment that Kruger made no attempt to silence.

A Bedford army truck roared into the courtyard. It swung towards the administrative block and reversed rapidly to the head of the parade to within a few yards of where Kruger and Ulbrick were standing. There was the metallic rasp of a handbrake, the engine stopped, but no soldiers jumped out of the vehicle. Instead the tailboard was dropped down with a loud crash and the canvas covers across the rear of the vehicle were thrown back to reveal two young soldiers, each one crouching behind a Bren gun. The weapons were on close-quarter battle tripods mounted on large wooden crates, their muzzles trained on the parade. One weapon was fitted with the standard curved magazine, the other had the much larger anti-aircraft drum magazine. Two more vehicles appeared and parked at the far end of the courtyard. Large red crosses were superimposed on their camouflage paint. They were military ambulances. They stopped their engines but no one got out.

There was a total hush in the courtyard as 132 prisoners-of-war stared in white-faced silence at the threatening machine-guns.

'Paul – what are those guns?' Kruger demanded through clenched teeth, noticing that the soldier manning the gun with the drum magazine was wracked with nerves, his knuckles bone white. His companion was relaxed, chewing gum.

'Three-oh-three Brens.'

'How many rounds in their magazines?'

'Twenty-eight in the standard magazine. God knows what that drum holds. Over a hundred at a guess.'

Brigadier Dayton surveyed the stunned parade in satisfaction. The timing of the vehicles' arrival had been perfect. 'When you have finished your chat, Commander.' He produced a paper from his battledress pocket and unfolded it slowly and deliberately. He regarded the ranks of silent men before him. 'I'm going to call out ten names,' he announced. 'I want—'

Kruger broke in prematurely to translate, adding clearly in German. 'Do not break ranks! Remain where you are!' He tried to make his voice sound calm but he could not hide his urgent note. The nervous soldier manning the Bren gun looked as though he were about to faint. His fingers around the trigger guard were trembling noticeably.

'I want each man to raise his hand when his name is called and to come forward,' said the brigadier. 'No one else is to move. Any form of resistance or wilful disobedience of my orders will be treated as insurrection and I will not hesitate to give the order to open fire. Your days of fun and games are over.' His tone was matter-of-fact, almost casual, but none of the prisoners doubted his word.

'Handel, Joachim, Sub-lieutenant,' Brigadier Dayton called out. 'Come forward!'

No one moved.

Kruger saw that the young soldier's finger on the Bren's trigger had renewed its trembling, turning white as it hooked tighter. The trigger actually moved.

'Leutnant sur Zee Handel!' Kruger suddenly snapped, loud and clear. 'Step forward immediately!'

Brigadier Dayton permitted himself a fleeting smile of satisfaction as a young, fresh-faced prisoner raised his hand and made his way to the head of the parade. The puzzled prisoner gave Kruger a questioning glance before obeying Sergeant Finch's gesture and sitting in the chair. One of the corporals in charge of the leg irons snapped the shackles in place around Handel's ankles and the other made sure they were secure. Sergeant Finch jerked his thumb at the parade. The young Kriegsmarine officer shuffled back to his place, the chain of his leg irons grating on the cobbles.

'Muller, Peter, Senior Lieutenant! Come forward!'

Kruger ordered the officer to go forward. The performance with the leg irons was repeated. The tension was draining visibly from the nervous young soldier by the time the fourth man was shackled. With the last prisoner manacled and shuffling back to rejoin his comrades, the soldier had taken his hands off his Bren gun and was talking in a low voice to his companion.

'I'm delighted that common sense has prevailed,' said Brigadier Dayton, looking pleased with himself. 'We shall return for tomorrow's roll-call and each day until Friday.' He turned to Kruger. 'Please dismiss your men, Commander, and thank you for your co-operation.'

The courtyard was empty of prisoners when Brigadier Dayton emerged from Reynolds's office. The ambulances had left. The two soldiers who had manned the Bren guns were busy in the back of the truck, dismantling their weapons and stowing them in the canvas holdalls. They did not notice the senior officer's approach.

'Private Walker.'

The soldier whose white-faced fear had alarmed Kruger stopped what he was doing and gave the brigadier a salute. There was no trace of his original nervousness. If anything his grin and salute had an impish, almost cocky quality.

'A very creditable performance, Walker,' Brigadier Dayton complimented the young soldier. 'It certainly had me fooled and it most certainly fooled Commander Kruger.'

'Weren't nothing to it, sir. Pleased to have been of help. I've always liked a bit of play-acting.'

'Ah. You have ambitions to be a thespian?'

The question seemed to surprise the young soldier. 'Not really, sir. I'd sooner leave that sort of thing to women.'

11

If Hauptmann Dietrich Berg had existed in fiction he would have served an aspiring writer well as a mad scientist although he was neither mad nor a scientist. He was an extremely clever, eager to please, young technician who happened to be accident-prone on a scale best described as monumental. He first blew himself up at the age of six with the aid of a children's chemistry set that its manufacturer had guaranteed was harmless. At school he decimated a chemical laboratory in addition to losing two fingers during his first attempt at building a perpetual-motion machine. His three years at university were punctuated by an assortment of minor explosions and a number of major ones.

When asked by the army for a reference, his university authorities had recommended that Berg should be posted to a department dealing with some form of research – possibly explosives. The German army, with its remarkable ability to put square pegs in round holes – a talent it shared with the British army – sent Berg to an infantry regiment as a wireless operator because they discovered that he had been an amateur radio enthusiast until Hitler had revoked all 'ham' radio licences in 1936 on the day after Berg had been issued with his.

After that, Berg had to content himself with blowing up the odd radio valve here and there although he did succeed in shooting off his big toe during rifle drill. The injury left him with a slight limp that contributed to his capture at Dunkirk and later being run over by a Post Office van at Euston railway station while in the company of two guards who were quicker on their feet than he was.

Despite the loss of two fingers, he was an accomplished engineer and was Grizedale Hall's technical officer in charge of a small workshop and a team of ten craftsmen that officially produced cuckoo clocks and toys, which Willi sold unofficially, and unofficially produced virtually anything else to order.

Two hours after roll-call, Kruger and Ulbrick, and some of the shackled prisoners crowded into Berg's workshop. Lookouts had been posted. Joachim Handel sat on a bench and hiked his feet on to the back of a chair so that Berg could take a close look at his leg irons.

'I think it would be easier if I took them off,' said Berg apologetically, conscious of his audience, and Kruger's presence in particular. He selected a length of stout wire from the clutter on the bench, twisted it deftly into the left iron. It sprang open. He repeated the operation with the right iron. Handel rubbed his freed ankles appreciatively.

'Ah yes, Commander,' said Berg, holding the leg irons for Kruger to see, too engrossed to notice that everyone present was gaping in surprise. 'They have to use a special barrel lock. I suppose the security of leg irons is more important than handcuffs because a prisoner is likely to have his hands free.' He looked up apologetically. 'I'm very sorry, Commander, but it would be difficult to reproduce these. We don't have a forge. We could make one, but it would be difficult to hide.' He stroked a file across one of the links in the chain. 'It's been hardened, too. We'd definitely need a forge.'

'Berg,' said Kruger carefully, taking the leg irons and inspecting them. 'Why would I want you to make more of these damnable things?'

Berg blinked, his expression crestfallen. 'I don't know, Commander. I did wonder.'

'I wanted to see if you could unlock them.'

Berg brightened. 'Oh, I'm sure that won't be a problem, Commander.'

Kruger handed the leg irons back. 'Excellent, Berg. You've done well. My apologies, Handel, but you'll have to put these back on. Can you lock them, Berg?'

'That won't be a problem either, Commander.'

Kruger thanked him and asked Ulbrick and Willi to accompany him on a stroll around the grounds.

'Willi,' said Kruger as they went down the terrace steps. 'There's a guard who used to be a journalist.'

'Private Alan Knox, Commander. He works in admin.'

'I want you to employ your undoubted skills in devious ferreting to find out if he's maintained his contacts in the newspaper world. I'd be surprised if he hasn't.'

'Now, Commander?'

'Now, please, Willi. It's urgent.'

The order alarmed Willi but he scuttled off.

'What are you planning, Otto?' Ulbrick asked as he and Kruger crossed the lawn.

'I've not given up on this business, Paul.'

'Why not? You've made your point. You've inconvenienced the British and have earned their respect rather than their enmity. The order came from London and it's quite obvious that it's not liked at local level.'

The two men reached the wall and strolled along the trip wire, passing the point where there were temporary repairs to the frost-damaged section of the wall.

Kruger spared it the briefest of glances. 'It's an illegal order and I intend to fight it,' he replied.

'And we get packed off to Canada?'

'All battles are a risk, Paul.'

'Calculated risks. You can fight as hard as you like, Otto, but you can't win.'

'That's a defeatist attitude.'

'Because we, personally, *are* defeated! The British hold all the aces. Aces in the form of guns as you learned at roll-call.'

'That we forced the British to behave in an uncharacteristic manner is a small victory.'

Ulbrick snorted angrily. 'Uncharacteristic, my foot. Read what they did in India. They mowed down hundreds of unarmed men that stood up to them. Look, Otto – there's a lot we could do to register our protest.'

'Such as?'

'We could stop all the co-operation you introduced. Running the kitchen, looking after mail distribution, running the central-heating boiler—'

'I want the boiler kept going,' said Kruger abruptly. He stopped walking and turned to face his second-in-command. 'As for the co-operation, as you call it, Paul, it was all designed to stave off boredom. Boredom is the destroyer of morale. I put the well-being of the men above all else. That it saved the British a lot of manpower in running this camp was incidental. That the British let us do it was a victory. This morning's roll-call was also a victory, and I intend to have another.'

'How?'

Kruger told him.

Despite his reservations, Ulbrick couldn't help chuckling

as Kruger unfolded his plan. 'We're definitely going to be shipped off to Canada,' he declared.

12

The panic started at roll-call the next morning when Sergeant Finch announced to Brigadier Dayton:

'One hundred and twenty-two prisoners . . .'

'And one cat.'

'. . . present, SAAR! Ten prisoners missing.'

A frantic name call followed and Sergeant Finch reported that the ten prisoners missing were those due to be shackled for the day.

Ten new names were called for shackling, which passed off without incident even though the brigadier had arrived in his Humber without other supporting vehicles. But there was chaos in Grizedale Hall for the next two hours as guards turned the place upside-down in their fruitless search for the missing men. Telephone lines all over the Lake District hummed. Sirens sounded, summoning war reserve constables and part-time firemen to take part in search parties that combed the fells. Fire-watching towers were abandoned. Some bloodhounds drafted in had difficulties following scents and kept leading their handlers to clearings in the forest where parties of prisoners had been working.

A desperately worried Brigadier Dayton had difficulty obeying an order to return immediately to North-Western Command HQ because his Humber staff car had been left unattended long enough for it to be rendered immobile by ten leg irons that had been locked together to form a continuous chain that passed around the door pillar of his car and a tree. None of Sergeant Finch's keys fitted the leg irons' locks because Berg had jammed solder into the keyholes. A hacksaw blade skated impotently on the hardened chain. Relations between the brigadier and Major Reynolds deteriorated further with Major Reynolds's refusal to allow the tree to be harmed because it was on Grizedale Hall's

128

requisition inventory. There was nothing for it but to use the hacksaw on the Humber's door pillar. Brigadier Dayton had a draughty drive back to his HQ where General Somerfeld was waiting to ignite all manner of rockets that had been made ready for his arrival.

Attempts to play down the seriousness of the breakout to avoid panic among the local populace were not helped by evening editions of local newspapers carrying headlines such as: 'NAZI POWS IN MASS TERROR ESCAPE!'

13

Roll-call was held two hours late the next day because many of Major Reynolds's guards had been out on all-night search parties. Also he had spent a good deal of time on the telephone explaining the situation at the camp, and how it had arisen. At one point he was put through to a senior civil servant at the War Office in London and had to explain the unhappy circumstances all over again. It was not hard to divine why London was so concerned: the national newspapers had picked up the story overnight and run much the same headlines in their early editions that the local papers had used the previous day. The civil servant kept his promise and called Reynolds back within thirty minutes with the best news that the Canadian officer had received for a month. He replaced the receiver and gave the order for the delayed roll-call.

Twenty minutes later Sergeant Finch crashed to attention before the depleted parade of prisoners, saluted Reynolds, and bellowed:

'One hundred and twenty-two prisoners . . .'

'And one cat.'

'. . . present, SAAR! Ten prisoners missing.'

'Thank you, Sergeant,' said Reynolds, returning the salute and signing the offered clipboard. He cleared his throat and addressed the sea of impassive faces before him. 'I've no doubt that our ten fugitives will be rounded up very soon.

They stand no chance of getting far. The consequence of this latest piece of stupidity is that the strength of the guards here is to be increased.

'On the other matter, concerning the shackling of German officers, I shall be receiving confirmation later today that the order has been rescinded.'

The grim expressions of the prisoners relaxed. The makings of a cheer from the back of the parade was quickly silenced by a sharp word from Kruger.

'Strictly speaking,' Reynolds continued, 'the order is still in place but I see little point in implementing it now. You will please dismiss your men, Commander.'

The two men exchanged salutes. Reynolds returned to his office. His step would have been lighter but for the problem of the ten escapees.

Kruger's appearance in the boiler room caused the brawny officer feeding illicitly obtained Forestry Commission logs into the central-heating boiler to stop work and salute.

'Everything going well, Leutnant?' Kruger enquired, eyeing the huge Edwardian cast-iron boiler that stood higher than him. Getting it into working order after many years of neglect and disuse, and converting it to run on wood had been a major test of the engineering skills of several officers the previous year.

'Very well indeed, Commander. We've damped her down a little now that the days are getting longer and warmer. She's only burning just over half a tonne of logs per week now.'

Kruger nodded. 'That will help with the supply problem.'

It was an understatement. During a recent inspection several senior officials from the Forestry Commission had expressed dismay over the number of fully grown conifers that were being lost in Grizedale Forest. According to the local chocolate-dependent forestry wardens, this was due to a fungal disease. They explained that thanks to working parties of German POWs, the disease was being contained. And no, they didn't have any samples of infected timber because there was a war on and they couldn't possibly risk allowing such timber to go unburnt.

'Will we have enough fuel to see us through until June?'

'Yes, Commander. Only four more large trees should do it.'

'What I'd like you to do,' said Kruger, 'is to try burning a couple of barrow loads of wet leaves and compost. I've already got two officers rounding some up for you.'

The junior officer gaped. 'But that'll cause smoke, Commander. A lot of smoke!'

'I've no doubt that it will,' said Kruger mildly, turning to leave. 'And you would do well to remember that I don't like my orders questioned.'

There were tears in Willi's eyes as he headed across the courtyard on an errand for Kruger. Although in mourning for the loss of ten of his priceless 500 gram Toblerone bars that he had been required to hand over to each to his comrades before their mass breakout, his tears were due more to the choking white smoke that swirled across the courtyard and nearly hid the hall.

He rapped on Reynolds's door and entered when bidden.

'I was just coming to find out what's causing all this smoke,' said Reynolds testily. 'What the hell's going on?'

'Commander Kruger sends his apologies, sir,' said Willi. 'We think a bird's nest has been dislodged in the chimney. We're looking into it now and should have it cleared very soon.'

'Must be a damned big nest,' Reynolds grumbled. 'Tell Commander Kruger to get on with it as quickly as possible before we're all asphyxiated.'

14

The ten escaped prisoners of war were hiding in the forest about a mile away. They saw the dense clouds of swirling white smoke rising from Grizedale Hall to the south and began the laborious climb down from the covered shelter at the top of a rickety fire-watching tower. They dropped to the ground one by one, regrouped and set off through the pines in the direction of the Hawkshead road. The leader of the group was Leutnant sur Zee Joachim Handel – chosen not because he was the most senior ranking but because he had been the first prisoner to be shackled.

They reached the road and stood in a group, chatting and smoking, confident that they would not have long to wait because they had heard vehicles charging back and forth along the road ever since their escape had been discovered.

The sound of an army jeep approaching at high speed alerted Handel and his group. He stepped into the road. The jeep's horn sounded angrily. He was about to hold up his hand but had to jump clear as the jeep hurtled past.

'Idiot! Get your men spread out!' the sergeant driver yelled, and the vehicle vanished.

They had a ten-minute wait for the next vehicle to come into sight. It was an ancient Raleigh bicycle being pushed slowly uphill by Police Constable Ian Pritchard. He was bent double because he was having a particularly bad arthritis day – 'the screws', he called it – and due, as he told his wife, to all this chasing after those bloody escaped Jerries.

He pressed gamely on, his field of vision restricted to a small area of asphalt beneath him. At one point, where the road got slightly steeper, he actually got stuck, one leg half raised in mid step. Only by willing his weight forward was he able to complete the step. It was the same with his next step. He managed to get some sort of rhythm going that would, he reckoned, get him to Hawkshead by the weekend but further progress was interrupted by a semicircle of boots coming into his field of vision.

'Good afternoon, sir,' said a polite, slighted accented voice. 'Can we be of help for you?'

PC Pritchard felt that the question merited an attempt to straighten up, which he eventually accomplished. His startled gaze encountered a group of ten fresh-faced young men, all regarding him with some concern.

'Good afternoon, sir,' their leader repeated. 'I am Leutnant sur Zee Handel of the Kriegsmarine.' He waved his hand to the men in his group. 'There are ten of us. We have escaped from our prisoner of war camp and we are wishing to give ourselves up.'

'*You're the escaped Jerries?*' the stunned police officer croaked. 'What? All of them?'

'We are all here,' said Handel. 'I am thinking that you should be arresting us.' He reached out a hand to steady Pritchard. 'Are you going to Hawkshead, sir?'

The elderly police officer counted the men and was too shocked to speak. He nodded.

'In that case, sir,' said Handel. 'I think it best that we are carrying you. It will be no problem for us. Two each side. We can make a seat.' He felt in his pocket and produced the remains of a large bar of Toblerone. 'You must eat this, sir. It will give you strength.'

The memory of the taste of that honey-and-almond chocolate bar as he was carried comfortably in a seat made from a prisoner's jacket would live in PC Ian Pritchard's memory until his dying day.

But what was destined to become a prized memento would be a framed newspaper cutting on his mantelpiece that related the story of how he had, single-handed and unarmed, captured ten desperate, escaped prisoners of war and marched them to the police station at Hawkshead.

Part Three

The Very Important Prisoner

1

June 1942 and the morale among the prisoners at Grizedale Hall was running high. Rommel's Afrika Korps were pushing back the newly formed 8th Army, and had captured the vital port of Tobruk, taking some 35,000 allied soldiers as prisoners of war. A new German offensive had started in the Crimea. At sea, the Battle of the Atlantic was being fought by the German U-boat arm with unremitting ferocity. In the first quarter of the year over three-quarters of a million tonnes of allied shipping had been sunk, with particularly heavy losses being suffered by unconvoyed US shipping off America's eastern seaboard. Although Luftwaffe raids were not at the intensity of the London 'blitz', their attacks on British cathedral cities and industrial centres were proving effective. A good indication of Germany's fortunes was that there had been no new prisoner of war arrivals for two weeks.

Angelo Todt was a fateful exception . . .

Kruger entered his room. The earnest-looking, ill-at-ease young Heer officer sitting in front of his desk jumped to his feet and saluted.

'Have you finished, Willi?' asked Kruger.

Willi had also risen from his card-table desk. He stacked the four-page questionnaire form and placed it on Kruger's desk. 'Yes, Commander.'

'Thank you, Willi. Return to your normal duties.'

Willi left the room and Kruger broke with his tradition of always keeping his window shut by throwing up the sash.

'I didn't know England could be so warm this far north,' said the young officer. 'I used to go to a boarding school near London but we never came up here.' His garrulity was borne out of nervousness and he immediately regretted speaking because Kruger gave him an icy look and motioned for him to sit.

The senior officer glanced down at the questionnaire's first page. He lit a cheroot and studied the blue-eyed young blond perched on the edge of his chair. The intensity of the young man's blue eyes was disturbing.

'Todt,' said Kruger. 'Is that a common name around Munich?'

'I believe so, Commander.'

'Angelo is an unusual first name.'

'My father was a great admirer of Italian architecture.'

'You have an older brother – Alexander?'

'Also in the Heer, Commander.'

'Rank?'

'Oberstleutnant.'

Kruger raised his eyebrows. 'You have a long way to go to catch up, Leutnant. Not that you ever will now.'

There was a long silence. Kruger seemed to be listening. He rose, strode quickly across the room and snatched the door open. Willi was standing in the corridor, seemingly intent on his clipboard.

'Thank you for taking down Leutnant Todt's details, Willi. I am worried about your wheezing, so I think some less strenuous work for you would be a good idea.'

'I'll be pleased to obey, Commander,' said Willi, always in favour of work-reduction schemes provided that they didn't involve him having to prepare questionnaire forms.

'Perhaps you had better draw up a new questionnaire blank as a replacement?'

'I'll be pleased to, Commander.'

'Plus ten additional blanks in case they're needed.'

'Yes, Commander. Right away.' Willi moved off, annoyed at being denied the chance to eavesdrop on what promised to be an interesting interview with the new prisoner, and doubly annoyed because obtaining the paper for the extra forms was going to cost him a bar of Toblerone. The chocolate bars were his children; each one lost was a wrench that could not be healed. Several debts were still outstanding from the last consignment of parcels from the Red Cross and from sympathizers.

Kruger returned to his desk. 'You're nineteen –' he began.

'Twenty next month, Commander.'

'I'm quite capable of reading your date of birth, Leutnant. I shall make it clear when I want your comments. Your education includes a period at Harrow. You've said here that you speak good English. Is that correct?'

'Yes, Commander.'

Kruger's next question was in English. 'Did you tell the British on your capture that you could speak English? Please reply in English.'

'Yes, Commander.' Angelo looked anxiously at Kruger. 'Was that wrong? I couldn't hide it. I had to use English because no one spoke German. I needed medical help for my men.'

'It's Rommel who's doing all the capturing at the moment, so how did you manage to reverse this trend?'

'I was in charge of an ammunition truck at Galzala. It was night and we were hit by a shell from our own lines. The truck caught fire. My only concern was to get myself and my crew away from it before it blew up. We just ran without bothering to check where we were running. We were also very disorientated. We ran into a retreating British unit.'

'Unfortunate,' Kruger commented. He had listened carefully to the young man's speech. His English accent was good but his careful enunciation made his speech a little stiff and formal. He returned to his scrutiny of the questionnaire. 'Angelo Todt . . . You were sent to Harrow. Your family is wealthy?'

'I think so, Commander.'

The vagueness annoyed Kruger. 'One usually knows these things.'

'We had large estates, so I suppose we were. I never thought about it.'

A typical attitude of the aristocracy, thought Kruger. 'Your father's name is Fritz Todt.'

'Yes, Commander.' Angelo Todt's transparent face saddened. 'He was killed in a plane crash a few weeks ago.'

'Civil engineer,' Kruger remarked, looking at the questionnaire.

'Yes, Commander.'

Kruger noticed wrist bandages protruding from the young officer's tunic. 'What happened to your arms?'

'I had some burns when we were hit, Commander. Luckily I was wearing gloves, otherwise my hands would have been burned.'

'Do you need treatment?'

'The camp commandant said that there is a nurse who comes in. Brenda . . . I'm sorry – I have forgotten her second name.'

'Brenda Hobson.'

'Ah, yes. Nurse Hobson will change the dressing three times a week. The British doctors were very good. My arms are healing fast.'

Kruger tapped the questionnaire. 'You have not mentioned your wounds on here.'

'I didn't think they were important.'

'All the questions are important, otherwise they would not be on this form. The question asks about injuries received and you've left it blank. Perhaps you have something to be ashamed about how you came to be wounded?'

'No, Commander.'

'Then why the blank space?'

Angelo licked his lips. 'My father always encouraged us to make light of our misfortunes. The burns are healing. I didn't think them important. I also have a slight toothache. I haven't mentioned that either.'

The young man's unexpected show of spirit did not endear him to Kruger. 'What sort of civil engineering did your father specialize in?'

'He was an expert on new applications of concrete. He

designed the autobahns.' Angelo's look of pride died when he saw the sudden hardening of Kruger's expression. There was a long silence. Kruger's cheroot went out.

'Your father did *what*?'

The officer repeated his claim.

'Are you telling me that your father was *Reichminister Fritz Todt*?'

'Yes, Commander.'

'The head of the Todt Organization?'

'Yes, Commander.'

Kruger's expression was ice. Without saying a word to Angelo, he went to the door and bellowed down the corridor for Willi, who had been expecting a reaction and had left his door open. He materialized promptly.

'Commander?'

'Willi – I want you to remain here and keep an eye on this . . . this officer. I'll be with Major Reynolds.'

'Shall I assign him his quarters, Commander?' Willi enquired, testing waters that he sensed did not need testing. Kruger's thunderous expression answered all his questions.

'*That* is the last thing I want you to do, Willi.'

With that, Kruger clattered down the stairs.

Willi entered the office and sat at Kruger's desk. 'You seem to have upset our senior officer,' he remarked to Angelo.

'It's my father, isn't it?' said Angelo sadly.

'I think that's a safe bet.'

'But he's dead.'

'I know,' Willi answered. 'We heard the Fuehrer's oration at his funeral on the radio. It lasted about fifteen minutes.'

2

Two guards saw Kruger striding purposefully across the courtyard to the administration block and raced to place themselves between him and Reynolds's office. The German officer ignored their challenge and entered the office without knocking.

Reynolds looked up in surprise at the abruptness of the entry. He stopped himself from berating Kruger for his peremptory manner when he saw that the German officer wasn't wearing his cap – the first time he had ever appeared in his office without it. Also he had no wish to bawl out Kruger in the presence of the two guards, who had crowded in behind him, loud in their apologies for failing to stop him. In truth Reynolds had been expecting this reaction. He dismissed the guards and gestured for Kruger to sit. The invitation was curtly rejected.

'Oh, for Chrissake, Otto. Don't go all stiff-necked on me. You've come to see me about Leutnant Angelo Todt. Right? So sit down and let's talk.'

Kruger's face remained impassive but he yielded enough to sit. 'Why wasn't I told about him?'

The German officer's tone annoyed Reynolds. 'I didn't know myself until yesterday. I decided not to prejudge the issue until I'd seen him. We're under no obligation to provide you with advance information on new arrivals.'

'You told me that this camp is for politically colourless officers. Has there been a change of policy?'

'There has been no change of policy, Commander. And that's as far as I'm prepared to go in discussing policy regarding the dispersal of prisoners of war.'

'Angelo Todt cannot possibly be politically colourless.'

'He must be, otherwise he would not have been sent here.'

'He is the son of Reichminister Fritz Todt,' said Kruger coolly. 'One of the chief architects of the National Socialist Party and a close friend of the Fuehrer. He cannot possibly be accepted into this camp.'

'*Was* a close friend,' Reynolds pointed out. 'His father was killed earlier this year.'

'A state funeral,' Kruger snapped. 'The Fuehrer delivered a long oration.'

'Now how do you know that, Otto?'

Kruger realized that he had gone too far. The British suspected that the prisoners had crystal-set radio receivers – they were easy enough to make – but they had never found

139

them despite frequent snap searches. He thought quickly. 'From recent arrivals who heard the broadcast.'

Reynolds flipped his intercom and asked for the file on Angelo Todt. Private Knox brought in a sheaf of papers.

'I'm sorry, sir,' said the private. 'I've not had the papers long enough to raise a new file.'

Reynolds accepted the apology and dismissed him. He flipped through the documents. 'There is very little about Todt from his interrogation. But it is clear enough that he has no interest in politics and never has had.'

'That would be easy enough for him to hide.'

'They're not fools in London, Otto, as you well know. Their findings were that young Angelo wasn't very bright and was a disappointment to his family. His older brother is a colonel. Did he tell you about his capture?'

'Yes.'

'Getting himself captured by a unit that's in retreat wasn't exactly clever, and surely you've wondered why he is only a leutnant? Your army's lowest officer rank? Infantry. Don't you think his father could have done better for him?'

Kruger was undecided. There were issues involved that he wasn't prepared to discuss with the enemy. He decided to bring the meeting to an end and stood. 'I request, Major, that Todt is kept separate from other prisoners until I've had a chance to confer with the other senior German officers here.'

'Request refused,' was Reynolds's crisp response. 'Have you assigned him his quarters?'

'No.'

'Please do so, otherwise I'll do it for you.'

For a moment it looked as if Kruger was going to argue. It was clear that he wanted to say something but thought better of it. He left the office and went in search of his principal confidants: Hauptmann Paul Ulbrick and Oberleutnant Karl Shriver. He found them sunning themselves on the terrace, watching a brisk game of table tennis while sampling a fine Riesling that Ulbrick's wife had sent him. They found a cup for Kruger and listened as he outlined the problem of Angelo Todt.

'So where is he now?' Shriver asked when Kruger had finished.

'Willi's keeping an eye on him in my office.'

'You're going to have to assign him quarters,' said Ulbrick. 'I don't see that you have any choice. Okay – so maybe his father did come from our leader's top table, but from what I've heard of Todt, he was a good engineer and an efficient operator. The autobahn network was a remarkable achievement.'

'Things are different now,' said Kruger. 'The Todt Organization uses slave labour.'

Ulbrick looked doubtful. 'I've heard this rubbish before. I think you must be mistaken, Otto,' he said. 'What evidence do you have for this?'

'The evidence of my own eyes,' said Kruger coldly. 'The Todt Organization was building the U-boat pens at Lorient when our flotilla was transferred there. They're vast things that can hold several boats. Reinforced concrete roofs ten metres thick. There were thousands working on them. Mostly Poles.'

'Good workers, the Poles,' Ulbrick replied. 'And no doubt glad of the work and the pay.'

'They were not paid,' said Kruger. 'One of my crew got friendly with them. They lived in a camp outside Lorient under appalling conditions. They were given barely enough food to live on. After a raid by the RAF, their women and even children were brought in to help clear up. They were some of the most wretched people I've ever seen. I wouldn't treat rats the way they were treated.'

'Did your crewman actually see their camp?' Ulbrick enquired.

'No. It was strictly out of bounds.'

'Not a bad idea. You said yourself once that a big worry was what your crew caught off French girls; God only knows what Polish girls would give them. As for allowing women and kids to help out after a raid, there's a *Picture Post* in the library with photographs showing women and children helping clear rubble after a bombing raid on London.'

'There is a difference between voluntary labour and slave

labour,' said Kruger dispassionately. 'I daresay that the women and children in *Picture Post* are well fed. The women and children I saw at Lorient were half-starved wretches.'

Ulbrick sipped his wine. 'So far nothing you've said has convinced me that this Angelo Todt's father used slave labour.'

'There was absolutely no doubt about it,' Kruger replied. 'Ask Hans Schnell. *U-497*'s second watch officer. He's in that group on the lawn.'

Shriver and Ulbrick glanced at the small knot of prisoners and guards in earnest conversation in the middle of the lawn.

'Schnell befriended a Polish girl,' Kruger continued. 'She and several of her friends were being routinely raped by Todt officials.'

'Proof?'

'Two of the girls committed suicide by jumping off the roof of a pen at Lorient. They held up a banner saying that they were slaves. Then they held hands and jumped together. One of them was the girl that Schnell was friendly with.'

Shriver broke the silence that followed. 'Did you report your suspicions?'

'They were more than suspicions.'

'But did you report them?' Shriver persisted. 'To your senior officers? The OKM – your naval high command?'

Kruger didn't answer the question immediately. Instead he lit a cheroot, hiding his face with his hands to cup the match even though it was a still day. He stared at the group of prisoners and guards. 'No,' he admitted at length.

'Why not?'

'I did raise the matter, but it was pointed out to me that we needed those pens finished.'

'Nevertheless, you did nothing?'

'This has nothing to do with the immediate problem. I have certain suspicions about Angelo Todt. I believe he deserted.'

Shriver was tempted to comment on Kruger's changing of the subject but decided to remain silent. He suspected that he would have done the same. Instead he asked, 'Did he tell you he did?'

142

Kruger outlined what he knew of Angelo's capture, concluding with: 'So there you have it: an officer captured by the British when the British were in retreat.'

'It can happen,' Shriver remarked. 'How serious were his burns?'

'I didn't look. He made light of them.'

'Which means that they may have been serious,' Shriver observed.

'I doubt it,' said Kruger dispassionately. 'He kept quiet because he didn't want anyone asking too many questions about how he got them.'

After a year and several battles Ulbrick had got to know Kruger and had learned to respect his integrity. He had always thought of him as a fair-minded man. He found this new blind spot disturbing. 'Perhaps a second opinion might be an idea,' he suggested. 'Would you like me to have a word with him?'

Kruger considered the offer and accepted.

'Give me thirty minutes,' said Ulbrick rising. 'And don't drink all that wine.'

Shriver took Kruger's mind off the problem of Angelo Todt by bringing up the subject of the camp's next drama production, of R. C. Sherriff's *Journey's End*.

'An all-male cast, Otto. I've got an English-language text. Your English is better than mine, so I'd like you to translate it into German. I might miss some of the subtle nuances.'

They were locked in a heated discussion about the suitability of a play set in the British trenches of the Great War being performed before a prisoner of war audience when one of the prisoners who had been talking in a huddle of guards and prisoners in the middle of the lawn left the group. He hurried across the lawn and came up the terrace steps two at a time. His expression was tight with barely controlled anger.

'Sorry to interrupt, Commander,' he said brusquely, without formality, 'but we've just learned that we have a new arrival. A prominent party member. Very prominent – Angelo Todt of the Todt Organization.'

'A member of the Todt family, Schnell,' Shriver observed.

'Not quite the same thing as being a member of the Todt Organization.'

'The son of Fritz Todt!' Hans Schnell retorted. 'Commander – if you welcome this vermin—'

'Save your threats, Leutnant Schnell,' said Kruger. 'I understand exactly how you feel. I will not be welcoming Angelo Todt into the camp at dinner, and I will do all I can to ensure that he's moved to another camp.'

Schnell was undecided for a moment. 'If you fail, there are quite a few of us who will do all in our power to have him moved to a hospital, or worse.' With that the naval officer turned on his heel and went down the terrace steps.

Shriver fully expected Kruger to take exception to the officer's behaviour, but he remained silent, watching Schnell as he strode across the lawn to rejoin the group. Ulbrick returned. He poured himself a cup of wine and looked sadly at the level in the bottle.

'You should've looked at his burns, Otto. They're serious – or were. He's young, fit and healthy so they're healing well.' He sipped his wine while he collected his thoughts. 'Angelo Todt is a personable enough young man but not very bright.'

'Bright enough to provide a story to cover his desertion,' said Kruger dryly.

Ulbrick shrugged. 'I think you're seriously misjudging him, Otto. The lad's open and disarming. His story holds up. What he does try to conceal, and not very well at that, is that he's a disappointment to his family, particularly his father. They virtually disowned him and packed him off to the infantry. All the family pride and adulation was showered on his brother.'

'What's more to the point, has he disowned his father?' said Kruger pointedly.

'Would you disown *your* father?'

Kruger regarded Ulbrick coolly. 'I would if he became a user of slave labour.'

'Which Angelo Todt refuses to accept.'

'My brother's working on the design of a production plant in the Hartz mountains,' said Shriver. 'He wouldn't say what

144

it was for but he did say that the Todt Organization have provided over a thousand slaves and that they were treated abominably by overseers. Some were even shot if they were too weak to work.'

The three men lapsed into silence and watched the table tennis game.

'The chances are that we've all heard rumours about what's going on,' said Ulbrick at length. 'Some of us have heard and seen things more tangible than just rumours – such as Otto and Schnell's experiences at Lorient. Yet we've done nothing about it. We feel guilty therefore and we jump at the chance to assuage that guilt by focusing it on Angelo Todt. Holding our hands up in horror and pointing shocked fingers makes us feel better. It distances us from what's going on. The guilt doesn't go away, but it helps us to ignore it.' He poured himself the last of the wine and drank it. 'It's a good job we're going to win this wretched war. Otherwise there would be a lot of awkward questions to answer when it's all over.'

3

Dinner in Grizedale Hall's dining hall, formerly the great hall, was at six o'clock and was the main event of the day.

Hilgard's kitchen assistants set up numbered trestle tables and chairs in neat lines and the prisoners filed into the great hall in the order of table numbers that had been assigned to them. Every month was the ritual of drawing numbers for a new table – one of Kruger's innovations so that the prisoners got to know each other.

Angelo hung back. He had already learned the routine at lunchtime but had lacked the courage to go up to the serving table with a plate. But now he was hungry and the food smelt good. He entered the dining hall when all the prisoners had taken their seats. He was surprised that none of them had gone up to the serving table where two prisoners and Hilgard in grimy white aprons stood waiting behind their steaming cauldrons and serving trays. Then he remembered Willi telling him that the evening meal was when Kruger made announcements and welcomed new arrivals.

A sea of silent, hostile faces stared at him while he looked frantically around for somewhere to sit. There were ten prisoners sat around each table. As far as could make out, there was no vacant place and he doubted that he would have the courage to sit at it if there had been. Instead he unfolded a card table and a chair and set them up well apart from the others, near the entrance.

Kruger rose and rapped the table with a spoon for attention. 'Very little news today, gentlemen. The drama group still can't agree on whether we should go ahead with a play or a revue. They may well decide to inflict both on you.' Kruger waited for the laughter to die away before he continued, naming the vegetable plot of the week and that his English classes had a vacancy. He thanked everyone and sat.

'Tables One, Two, and Three!' Hilgard bellowed.

Thirty men rose and formed a queue at the serving table. Their plates were quickly loaded with stew, mashed potatoes and dumplings. Hilgard's machine for feeding over 200 prisoners of war was efficient.

'Tables Four, Five and Six!'

Angelo was surprised. His hope was that Kruger had made a mistake and forgotten to welcome him. When all the men were eating, he rose, collected a plate, and approached the serving table. He was about to speak but the mighty ex-*Bismarck* chef looked at a clipboard and roared, 'Leftovers! Table Ten's turn today!'

Angelo was shouldered roughly aside as ten men rushed to the serving table for extra helpings. The serving trays had been scraped clean when he presented his plate to Hilgard.

'May I have some dinner, please.'

Hilgard folded his brawny arms and stared right through Angelo. A hush fell. Angelo was scared but not intimidated. Conscious of the eyes of all the prisoners on him, and feeling like Oliver Twist, he repeated his request.

'You've got eyes. There isn't any more.'

'I haven't had any lunch. I am very hungry.'

Hilgard shrugged and said nothing.

Angelo flushed with anger. 'I am entitled to food! If you do not serve me, I will go to the Commandant!' With that he threw down his plate and strode determinedly between the rows of tables to the double doors.

'And that will be the end of our running of the kitchen,' Ulbrick said quietly to Kruger.

'Todt!' Kruger snapped.

Angelo stopped and turned to look questioningly at Kruger.

'You will remain here,' said Kruger curtly. 'Leutnant Hilgard – give this man a dinner. You will have plenty for your helpers. He can be fed in the kitchen. He will take all his meals in the kitchen with your staff until further notice.'

'Very well, Commander,' said Hilgard in bad grace. 'But I'd like my objection noted.'

'It's noted. Please do as I say.'

Hilgard shrugged and spoke to one of the helpers, who beckoned to Angelo and led him to the kitchen.

Ulbrick looked Kruger in the eye and said mildly, 'That lad is no deserter. He's got more courage than all of us put together.'

There were two assistant chefs in the kitchen. Big men who regarded the new arrival with undisguised hostility.

'Gunter and Kurt will feed you,' said the helper, and returned to the great hall.

Kurt banged down a large, well-filled bowl in front of Angelo and told him to sit at the far end of the long, food preparation table. Angelo thanked him and wolfed the stew and dumplings, too hungry to notice that the bowl was unlike the plates that the kitchen staff used when they sat down to eat at the far end of the table. He was scraping the bowl clean when he saw Hermann slinking in. The cat investigated a food splattered newspaper spread on the floor in the corner.

Gunter snapped his fingers at the cat. It ignored him and sat staring at the newspaper as though expecting a miracle.

'That's Hermann,' said Kurt.

The two kitchen assistants almost choked with laughter. Angelo turned the bowl around. It had 'Hermann' written on the side in crude, painted lettering. At this point Kurt and Gunter became almost paralysed with hysterics, especially when Hermann jumped on to the table beside Angelo to express profound grief at this misuse of his property.

Angelo's response was to lift the bowl to his face and lick it. He offered it to Hermann who licked it and then Angelo had a lick. Cat and prisoner took it in turns to lick the bowl until it was whistle clean. Angelo kept grinning at the two men all through the ritual. They had stopped laughing and looked ashamed of their prank. Gunter shook his head, and filled a clean plate with a generous helping of stew, which he placed before Angelo.

4

That evening Angelo tapped tentatively on Willi's door. He had to identify himself. There was the sound of a lock being turned, the door opened and Willi's moonlike face appeared.

'Please, Willi. Where do I sleep?'

'I've received no instructions from Commander Kruger,' said Willi. 'I can't assign you quarters without his authority.'

'In which case I will have to see Major Reynolds.'

'You'd better wait here.'

Willi locked his door and went along the corridor. He knocked on Kruger's door and entered. He emerged a few minutes later, signalled to Angelo and showed him to a small, cold, unused room on the same floor. It had a bare bed with a stained mattress, a narrow north-facing window, a blackout board, and that was all.

'You can have this or you can be assigned to a dormitory on the first floor. Big rooms – twenty prisoners to a room.'

'This will do fine, thank you, Willi.'

'Having your own room will cost you.'

'But I don't have anything.'

'You'll be getting parcels?'

'Yes. I filled in the Red Cross forms. I'm sure my family will see that I have everything.'

'You're entitled to one sheet, one blanket, and one pillow. You get an extra blanket on the first of September. You can have extras of everything now on account, but there's a charge. I'll give you a list.'

'I think I would like two sheets and three blankets and two pillows, please.'

'How about a reading light? Expensive but it will make life more bearable.'

'Yes, please.'

Willi made some entries in a notebook. 'Okay. We can work out what you owe when we've seen what you've received. Usually new prisoners need so many extras to start them off that they have to hand over their first parcels to me.'

'I understand, Willi,' said Angelo, thinking that all this was part of the camp's economic structure, not realizing that it was a cornerstone of Willi's economic structure. The families of captured prisoners were so relieved to hear that their loved ones had been taken prisoner that their first parcels were generous. As the weeks went by the drain became a chore and the parcels shrank accordingly.

The following morning Angelo stayed in the kitchen after breakfast had been served and offered to help Kurt and Gunter with the washing-up and cleaning. They accepted, Hilgard had no objections, so Angelo spent the rest of the morning doing several jobs that had been neglected such as scrubbing the flagstone floor and cleaning the walls.

It set the pattern for Angelo's first week at Grizedale Hall. He was content to spend all his hours in the kitchen, working hard and helping with food preparation, peeling mountains of potatoes without complaint. Hilgard, Kurt and Gunter and the rest of the kitchen helpers soon learned to like the personable young man and to respect his courage and indomitable spirit. When they saw the extent of the burn scars on Angelo's arms they accepted his account of how he came to get such injuries and rejected the stories about the young man's desertion.

'He's not clever enough to lie,' had been Hilgard's verdict. 'And he's that trusting, it would be easy enough for his father to keep anything from him.'

And so the kitchen became Angelo's home and sanctuary. On the third day, all three heavies accompanied Angelo to the library to suggest to the librarian that he reconsider his decision not to allow Angelo to borrow books because he wasn't an 'officially' registered prisoner.

When he was not in the kitchen Angelo felt vulnerable and exposed. There was no let-up in the tension. Conversations would cease at his approach; calculating, hostile eyes followed him. Particularly those of Leutnant zur See Hans Schnell, the second watch officer of *U-497*.

When Schnell and two fellow prisoners made their move during Angelo's second week at Grizedale Hall, it was swift, it was brutal, and at night.

5

'Four stitches needed to a cut above his left eye,' said Nurse Brenda Hobson, reading from her notes. 'A wisdom tooth broken. Two stitches needed in his upper lip. Severe bruising about the temples, and to his chest. Fortunately the burns to his arm are nearly completely healed, so at least he was able to defend himself up to a point, but he's suffered some lesions to the new skin.'

'We don't know that he was attacked,' Kruger objected, filling Reynolds's office with cheroot smoke.

Brenda's tone was scathing. 'Credit me with some sense, Commander. I've been a nurse long enough, and I've patched up enough brawlers, to know the difference between fight injuries and those caused by people suffering falls – even bad falls. From his injuries, I'd say that Angelo Todt was attacked by two men – possibly three.'

'As long as he insists that he fell down the stairs leading from the third floor to the second floor, then we have to go with that,' Reynolds commented.

'A short, narrow flight,' Brenda replied. 'Plenty of banisters and uprights for a fit man to grab hold of. That's not what happened, Major, and both of you know that. One man held him and two took it in turns to punch him.' She turned to Kruger. 'Brave men, your prisoners, Commander. It was touch and go if I sent him to hospital.'

'But he's comfortable now?' Kruger enquired.

'No – he's not comfortable,' Brenda retorted angrily. 'Nor would you be. But at least he's out of danger in the sickbay.'

'How long before he's fully recovered?' asked Reynolds.

'A week to ten days.'

'Thank you for your report, Nurse Hobson,' said Reynolds. 'And for your frankness.'

'I take it that his name means nothing to her?' said Kruger when he and Reynolds were alone.

'It means nothing to me either,' was Reynolds's brusque reply. 'To me he's a captured German POW officer that I'm responsible for.'

'So you're not going to recommend his transfer?'

'And pass the problem on to another camp? I don't work like that. The problem isn't Todt – it's you and your lack of discipline.'

The barbed comment did not perturb Kruger. 'You know that that's not true, Major. Todt is a special case. There are feelings against him that are too strong for even me to control.'

'From what Sergeant Finch has told me, and what I've seen with my own eyes, you've done nothing to contain such feelings or even accord Todt a measure of justice. The bully boys have taken their cue from you.'

'I have incited no violence towards Todt, Major.' Kruger hesitated. 'I don't like to have to admit to this but the problem is getting worse. Contrary to what you might think, not every hand is against Todt. The kitchen team have befriended him and they're upset over what has happened. They're threatening to give short-measure meals to those they suspect of harming Todt. There was an ugly scene in the dining hall this morning. Luckily it didn't get out of hand.'

Reynolds leaned forward. 'Now listen, Otto. So long as this camp ticks over on the cheap without trouble, it'll be left alone because accommodation for POWs in Canada can't be built fast enough. But if things go wrong here, the War Office will close it down tomorrow and you'll all be shipped off to Canada – huts or no huts. Neither of us want that, so I've worked out a compromise solution.'

6

Charlie Fox eyed Angelo up and down. 'Welcome to Spauldings Farm, Mr . . .' He looked at the typed notes that Private White had left him when the prisoner had been delivered into his care. '. . . Todt? So what do I call you, Mr Todt? Angelo?'

'At school in England they called me Andy,' said Angelo, wondering if he would ever get used to the smell of pigs.

'Andy it is then.'

'What would you wish for me to call you, Mr Fox?'

Charlie shrugged. The young man's command of English, although slightly clipped and formal, unsettled him. 'Don't matter to me. The Jerries we've had so far on working parties from your hotel have usually called me Charlie.'

The two men shook hands. Charlie Fox was short and balding, with a permanently dour expression that cloaked an otherwise easy-going, kindly nature.

'Right,' he said. 'Best I show you round first.' He pointed to a small farmhouse in need of repair. 'That's where the Land Army girls live. Strictly out of bounds. They looks after themselves and the pigs. Nearly five hundred of them.'

'Five hundred girls?'

Charlie's lugubrious expression broke into a grin. 'No, thank Christ. Five hundred pigs. There's four girls. Sometimes more. They comes and goes and mostly goes because they get fed-up looking after pigs. Me and the missus have a cottage just over there.'

'Are you the owner, Charlie?'

'No. He's dead. I was kept on by his solicitors to run the place until his will's sorted out. That were two year ago. Got your stuff in your kitbag?'

'Yes. And I've my food rations for this week that I have to give to your wife.'

'Best go and see her first. She's sorted you out our son's bedroom. He's in the army.'

Charlie's wife, Edna, had never had much to do with the occasional working parties of German prisoners of war. They arrived in the morning, bringing their own lunch boxes, and left in the afternoon. Angelo was the first German she had ever spoken to, or even shaken hands with, therefore she was wary of him at first. For her to be captivated by his engaging smile, blue eyes, blond hair and courteous demeanour, took all of two minutes. She showed Angelo up a narrow flight of creaky stairs to a tiny but pin-neat, clean bedroom, and afterwards made all three an urn of tea. Charlie's bucket-size mug held most of the urn's contents. The three sat around a table in the parlour drinking while Charlie read through a list of notes.

'Says here that you have to leave here each morning to go to roll-call and come straight back,' said Charlie. 'Will someone fetch you?'

'I will walk,' Angelo answered. 'It will take only ten minutes.'

'Seems silly to me,' said Mrs Fox.

'The whole thing's silly,' Charlie observed. 'Whoever heard of a prisoner of war living on a farm?'

'It's only for a month,' said Angelo. 'While they make up their mind what to do with me.'

Mrs Fox looked worried, wondering if Angelo was some kind of criminal. 'What did you do, Andy?'

'We're not supposed to ask questions,' Charlie warned.

Angelo smiled and sipped his mug of tea. 'It is all so silly, Mrs Fox. The other prisoners think I deserted. I hope in four weeks they will have the evidence that I did not.'

'Is that how you got that cut on your head?'

'It has nearly healed, I think. It won't stop me working.'

'Work,' said Charlie, downing his bucket. 'Only two rules

here, young Andy. Work hard and stay away from the Land Army girls. That's really for your own safety.'

'Man-mad, useless lot,' Mrs Fox snorted. 'Although that Doris seems more sensible than most. Better educated.'

'My mother is always complaining about her staff, especially maids,' said Angelo cheerfully. 'In her last letter she said how difficult a new maid was being.'

'Maids?' said Mrs Fox, raising her eyebrows. 'Your mother has maids?'

'Why, yes.'

'How many, for goodness sake?'

Angelo frowned and started counting on his fingers. 'Ten, I think, Mrs Fox.'

'Ten!'

'That is not including the kitchen staff or the gardeners. It is a big estate.'

7

Angelo settled in quickly at Spauldings Farm. He enjoyed the work because it was varied. Helping Charlie clearing ditches one day, fencing the next, and even sitting on the saddle and driving a gang-mower or a harrow when Charlie discovered that Angelo was experienced at handling horses.

He saw the land girls in the distance on occasions when he had to pass the farmhouse and the piggery buildings on errands to the cottage for Charlie. They always stopped work and stared at him when he walked by, sometimes shouting coarse comments, but he always kept his eyes down. They seemed big, rough-looking creatures, and they scared him a little. Angelo had good reason to be wary of women.

'You really must get the girls to start on clearing the cherry trees today,' said Mrs Fox to her husband at breakfast. 'They're more than ready and the birds will have had the lot if we don't bring them in.'

The afternoon was warm and pleasant. Charlie and Angelo

made such good progress on a new fence that they were likely to run out of posts.

'I'll take the cart over to Sam Kidock and pick up those chestnuts he promised us,' said Charlie. 'We'll need some chicken wire, too. Reckon you'll be okay on your own for an hour?'

'I'll be fine, Charlie.'

'Bloody stupid splitting this field,' was Charlie's comment. 'Best done with a wall to keep sheep in, but the men from the bleedin' ministry must be obeyed.'

Angelo set to work by himself. He could hear occasional shrieks of laughter and snatches of singing from the Land Army girls, who were working the cherry orchard two fields away. It was the closest he had ever worked to them and their proximity made him uneasy.

He was about to swing the pickaxe to break up a buried rock when he heard screams of terror from the girls. One of them was sobbing hysterically. Angelo dropped his tools and raced across the adjoining field. The orchard was surrounded by a high hedge to protect soft fruit from the wind. Rather than waste time hunting for an entrance, he plunged into the hedge at a thin spot and fought his way through.

He darted between the fruit-laden trees in the direction of the girl's sobs of terror and stumbled over overturned baskets of cherries. The cries of distress were from a terrified girl, standing on top of a high stepladder and clutching a branch of the cherry tree. The stepladder was wobbling dangerously.

'What is the trouble, please, miss?' Her jet black hair intrigued Angelo. The women who used to enjoy tormenting him had been blondes.

The girl seemed unable to speak and unable to let go of the branch. She nodded frantically at the ground.

Angelo looked around and could see nothing to account for the girl's terror.

'Snake!' she managed to blurt out. 'There!'

This time Angelo caught a glimpse of bluish silver in the long grass. He picked up the slow-worm and held it up for the girl to see. It was a good-size adult nearly half a metre long. 'It is not a snake, miss. It is a slow-worm. A lizard that looks like a snake. It is harmless. It cannot hurt you. Can you see from there? Look. It can blink. A snake cannot blink.'

The girl was not interested in the ocular capabilities of the creature. 'Kill it!' she sobbed. 'Just kill it . . .'

'I do not think that would be right—'

'For God's sake kill it!'

'I will release it a long way away from you. It would not be right to harm it. Keep still. I will come back and hold the ladder.'

Angelo strode quickly away and placed the creature in long grass in the shade of the hedge, handling it carefully the way a groundsman had shown him on his father's estate to prevent it shedding its tail. He returned to the girl. She had refused to budge from the wobbly safety of her perch.

'It has gone now, miss.' He gripped the ladder. 'You can come down.'

The girl gave no sign of moving but stared down at Angelo with wide, terror-filled green eyes. She shrank away when he stepped on to the ladder's lower rungs and held out his hand, but her sobbing had stopped.

'You didn't kill it,' she accused.

'I took it a long way away,' said Angelo, smiling encouragingly. 'They are well named. They are so slow that it will take it a year to get here. But it will not want to. It was more scared of you than you were of it.'

His reassuring tone settled the girl's nerves.

'Please, miss. Take my hand.'

'I can't move, stupid!'

Angelo went up another rung and saw that in her panic to climb as high as possible, a slender branch had jammed itself under a lower button of the girl's blouse and reappeared at her neck. She was trapped, unable to take her hands off the branch she was hanging on to to free her blouse.

'Your blouse is caught on a branch, miss. You must please keep very still so that I can free you.'

'I can manage!'

'I do not think so, miss. Please keep still.'

Angelo eased himself up the ladder, one rung at a time until he was facing the girl. The prettiness of her grimy, tear-streaked, elfin-like face was lost on him but not her almost jet-black hair. Her blouse was pulled up on the branch, exposing bare skin above the waistband of her slacks. She did not appear to have anything on under the blouse. The branch looked too thick to bend back and forth to break.

'I must undo the buttons on your blouse to release the branch,' Angelo explained.

Despite her fear, the girl was not happy with the suggestion. 'Can't you pull it out?'

'It is too long, miss.'

'For God's sake,' the girl muttered. She sounded quite refined now that the panic had gone from her voice.

'I will close my eyes tightly like this,' said Angelo, suiting his actions to the words. He supported himself with one hand and unfastened the buttons with the other. The branch sprang clear. Angelo was as good as his word about keeping his eyes shut as he groped for the free ends of her blouse to refasten it.

'For God's sake, this is ridiculous,' the girl muttered.

Angelo found one side of the blouse but his hand accidentally brushed against her exposed breasts as he groped for the other side.

'Keep your filthy hands off me, Jerry!' the girl spat. Her sudden wriggle nearly sent the ladder toppling. Angelo felt a tear splash on his arm.

'I'm sorry, miss – really I am.'

Only when he had managed to secure two buttons, albeit through the wrong buttonholes, did he dare open his eyes. Persuading her to release her grip on the branch one hand at a time took several minutes. At one point she had another panic attack and froze. Angelo moved gingerly down the ladder and grasped the girl around the waist. He steered her foot on to a lower rung. His tight hold gave her confidence and eventually they reached the foot of the ladder and safety. She shook his arm away and sat on a tree stump, her hands clasped over her face. She was trembling violently and crying. Not understanding the effect of delayed shock, Angelo thought her reaction was because he had touched her. He was terrified. He wanted to comfort the girl, to beg her forgiveness but there was a distant yell. He wheeled around. It was too late to speak to the girl now. Mrs Fox and the three land girls were running towards him. The farm manager's wife was carrying a shotgun, out of breath. The land girls were big, chunky wenches. They comforted the girl while Mrs Fox listened to Angelo's account.

'Slow-worms,' she scoffed. 'The sun makes them active. We get them in the farmyard. I did warn them but they take no notice. City girls.'

'Mrs Fox . . . Edna . . . She was trapped at the top of the ladder and—'

'That's what Janet said.'

'I had to help her down. I did not mean to but I touched her. It was—'

But Mrs Fox wasn't interested. She berated the four girls for their stupidity and ordered them to gather up the spilled cherries.

Angelo endured three days of misery before he finally accepted that the girl was not going to complain about him. The warm weather continued.

The following morning Charlie jumped down into an overgrown ditch at the edge of a field and declared that it was bone dry. 'Be good to get it cleared, Andy.'

He pointed out the course of the ditch where it skirted a drystone wall that led down a steep slope to a broad stream that was almost a river. 'Come autumn and the real rain and it always floods down there. This dry spell would be a good chance to get it cleared at last. Big job but at least it'll be a good start if you could clear the worst bits down near the stream. No deeper than half your spade's length otherwise the bloody sheep will never get out if they fall in. Don't make the sides steep either. Do you mind being on your own for a few days? Got a lot to see to.'

Angelo was happy working alone with mattock, billhook and spade. The silt came out easily. He piled it up away from the ditch so that it wouldn't be washed back in when the rains came. The sun climbed higher making him glad of the battered straw hat that Mrs Fox had insisted he take with him. He worked steadily through the morning, pausing only to swig occasionally from a water bottle, and took a short midday break to sit in the shade of the wall to eat his spam and homemade chutney sandwiches. In the afternoon he could hear the land girls, shrieking and splashing in the stream. He guessed that they were in the next field but he couldn't see them, and they wouldn't see him if he stayed in the ditch.

The sun beat down. He peeled off his clothes and worked in just his underpants, boots, and straw hat. Sweat streamed down his torso, his blond hair was matted, but he enjoyed the hard work and hoped that Charlie would be pleased with his progress.

'You look as if you could do with a swim.'

It was the girl's voice! His head snapped up. She was standing a few metres away, watching him, a half-smile playing at the corners of her mouth. She was wearing a chemise-like garment, soaked and clinging to her slim body. Her impossibly black hair was wet, hanging in strands.

Panic filled Angelo. He was half-naked and embarrassed, his clothes some distance away. He raised his hat, bid the girl a good afternoon, and held the hat in front of himself.

'You're Angelo, aren't you?'

'Yes, miss.'

'I'm Doris. Doris Blake. Never call me Dolly. You're from that POW holiday camp down the road?'

'Yes. I work here on parole.'

'Can I sit down?'

Angelo couldn't think of what to say. He nodded and began edging towards his clothes. Doris sat and leaned back on her hands. 'I want to say sorry for shouting at you the other day.'

'It doesn't matter, miss,' said Angelo, praying fervently that she would go away. 'You were frightened.'

'I was stupid. I called you names. I'm very sorry. And please call me Doris.'

'I am glad you are okay now.'

The girl looked puzzled. She sat forward, her arms around her knees. What Angelo could see of her from his position in the ditch almost unnerved him. 'You seemed frightened, too. Why was that?'

'I touched your breasts while I was trying to untangle you.

159

I didn't mean to. It was an accident. I was frightened in case you complained.'

The candour of Angelo's reply astonished Doris. She looked carefully to see if he was mocking her, but his expression was serious.

'Why should I complain?'

'Well . . .' Angelo didn't complete the sentence.

'And why are you so frightened now?'

'It is forbidden for me to talk to you.'

She wrinkled her nose. 'Oh, that's just Charlie. He has to be like that – regulations, but he doesn't really mind so long as you work hard. And it's not a condition of your parole, is it?'

'No. But—'

'Are you forbidden to swim in the river?'

'No. But it isn't deep enough for swimming.'

'It is where we are.' She jumped to her feet and held out her hand. 'Come on, Angelo. You'd love a swim.'

That was true enough but Angelo held back, not knowing what to do other than that he had to get his trousers on somehow.

'If you don't come for a swim, I really will complain. Now come on – out of that ditch.'

The threat was accompanied by a lovely smile but it awoke too many humiliating adolescent memories for Angelo to respond with matching good humour. He stayed in the ditch and reached for his trousers. The girl planted a sandaled foot on them. 'You won't need those for swimming. Now come on.' Before he could raise further objections, he found himself being hauled out of the ditch. She was surprisingly strong. She scrambled over the drystone wall giving Angelo another brief glimpse of bare thighs as he followed her, still clutching his straw hat in front of himself. Her three companions were up to their waists in the stream, their chemises ballooning around their thickset bodies. They stopped splashing and watched Doris and Angelo's approach.

'How did you know my name?'

Doris laughed. 'It was easy enough to find out. Would you prefer to be called Andy?'

'I do not mind.'

He avoided looking at the three girls in the water, uncomfortably aware that they were staring at him. 'But you are right about the stream. It is almost a river here.'

Doris kicked off her sandals and raced into the water. 'Get those boots off and come on in! It's lovely!'

There was nothing for it but to pull his boots off and wade quickly into the stream to get himself immersed securely up to his waist. The water was cold but refreshing once the initial shock had worn off. Doris introduced the other girls as Janet, Ann and Julia, but Angelo didn't take anything in. He nodded to them, turned and swam a little way upstream until the water became too shallow to swim properly. He felt safer swimming apart from the group but Doris came after him, kicking strongly, her black hair streaming in the water. She insisted on him joining in a game in the deepest part that involved him having to carry a girl on his shoulders to wrestle with another shoulder-mounted girl.

The game got noisy and enjoyably boisterous. Each girl insisted on a turn on his shoulders. Getting rid of his mounts was achieved by heaving them into water by grabbing their feet. The frequent glimpses of breasts and pudenda were too much and, to his mortification, he suddenly realized that he had a decidedly unwanted erection. Worse, Doris brushed against him when she climbed on to his shoulders for another round. To his relief she didn't seem to notice. Once it was safe to leave the water, he thanked the girls for inviting him for a swim, saying that he had to get on with his work.

The four girls watched him walking away.

'Wow!' breathed Janet. 'Those eyes. I went all gooey every time he looked at me.'

'They were a shock when he opened them up that tree, I can tell you,' said Doris.

'Funny thing to do,' opined Julia. 'Most blokes would just gawp.'

'Maybe he's a pansy?' Ann offered.

Doris smiled and shook her head. 'I don't think so.'

Over dinner that evening, Charlie dropped a minor bombshell.

'Saw you swimming in the river,' he said, forking mashed potatoes into his mouth. 'Can't say I blame you. Stinking hot today and going to be the same tomorrow.'

Angelo was alarmed. 'You don't mind, Charlie?'

'Mind? Why should I mind?' He said to his wife, 'He's cleared at least twenty yards – the worst bits all dug and clear as neat as you like. All by himself, too.'

'You mustn't work if it gets too hot, Andy,' said Mrs Fox reprovingly. 'I've told the girls to knock off early.'

'I think Andy could do with a pair of swimming shorts,' said Charlie.

'I'll cut down a pair of old trousers for you,' Mrs Fox offered.

Angelo started work the next morning as soon as he returned to the farm after roll-call. He was surprised with himself for not being able to get the picture of Doris's elfin face out of his mind. It was a little after two o'clock when he heard the girls in the stream. He changed eagerly into the shorts made from a pair of old flannels and jumped over the drystone wall to join them.

'You seem more relaxed today,' said Doris, splashing him playfully.

'I don't think Charlie minds me swimming with you.'

'What did I tell you?'

For the next hour the land girls heaved their bulks on and off Angelo's shoulders for their wrestling contests. His heart pounded harder each time it was Doris's turn to wriggle herself into position, always pressing herself hard against the nape of his neck. At one point she even teasingly yanked her chemise over his face to blindfold him. The brief glimpse of her breasts when he looked up made his head spin.

'I bet you didn't close your eyes that time, Andy.'

Angelo tumbled her into the water and admitted that he hadn't.

'Come on,' said Doris, swimming away from him. 'Let's go downstream. You can swim quite a long way – right around that bend. Race you!'

The other girls paid no attention to them when they swam away but carried on splashing each other and laughing.

162

Doris was a strong swimmer. Although Angelo could have overtaken her easily, he let her lead, wholly fascinated by her hair streaming between her shoulders and the seductive swell of her buttocks, showing clearly through the thin cotton of her chemise. She swam into the screening foliage of an overhanging weeping willow. Her arms went around Angelo's head and she pulled him close for a tentative kiss.

'That's for rescuing me from the snake.'

Angelo smiled. His eyes dazzled Doris. 'But it wasn't a real snake.'

'And that wasn't a real kiss. But this is . . .'

Angelo would never be able to recall how long that first real kiss of his young life lasted but he would never forget its heady passion or its inevitable consequences. He pushed Doris away. 'I'm sorry,' he blurted. 'I didn't want to embarrass you . . . Or me . . .'

Doris studied him quizzically. 'You're a funny bloke, Andy. How could you be embarrassed by a kiss?'

'I was getting an erection. I thought it would make you angry.'

It was the second time that Angelo had astounded Doris with his unbelievable frankness. She gave a little gasp and had to work hard to stop herself laughing.

'And now I have made you angry,' said Angelo sulkily.

This time Doris did give a little laugh. She stroked his hair. 'Of course you haven't, silly. It's just that your honesty is a little bit . . . Well . . . Surprising.'

'You asked me why I was embarrassed, so I told you.'

'You're an amazing bloke, Andy. Do you always tell the truth like that?'

'My brother always says that I am too stupid to lie. I think he is right. I always get found out, so it is easier to tell the truth but I make people angry.'

'But you haven't made me angry, Andy,' Doris assured him. 'Just very surprised.' She reached for him underwater and smiled impishly. 'Yes – you were telling the truth.'

Now Angelo was really embarrassed and a little afraid. 'We must get back,' he said and broke away, swimming in the direction of the land girls' shrieks.

Doris followed him, her breaststroke languid, her expression thoughtful. She wondered if the other girls were right about Angelo and was determined to find out.

Just before they parted company and Angelo was about to return to his ditch, Doris gave him a peck on the cheek and pressed a note into his hand. He unfolded it before starting work. It was torn out of a pocket diary. Doris had made a rough sketch of the front of the farmhouse and marked a downstairs window with a circle and an arrow. In the circle was written: 'My bedroom. Everyone is asleep by 1 a.m.'

8

The alarm clock went off under Angelo's pillow at a few minutes to one o'clock. He stopped it. He had hardly been asleep anyway, agonizing about Doris's message and what he should do about it. He would have been happy for the afternoons by the stream to continue, but the spell of good weather looked about to break and other pretexts for seeing Doris were unlikely to arise. The thought that he might not see that lovely elfin face and her wonderful black hair the following day was unbearable.

He came to a decision, slipped from his bed, opened the bedroom door and listened intently. Charlie's deep snore was unmistakable. He had to listen hard to detect Edna's regular breathing. All was well. He pulled a coat over his pyjamas, picked up his boots, and crept stealthily down the cottage's creaky stairs, avoiding the steps that made the most noise.

Ten minutes later he was crouching by a hay wain in the farmyard, marshalling the courage to tap on Doris's window. The farmhouse had an unoccupied feel, not as much as a chink of light showing around the blackout blinds. He crept nearer, listening, and decided that there was no point in further hesitation. The window flew open in answer to his tentative tap on the glass.

'Andy?'

'Hallo, Doris.'

'Andy!' She leaned out of the window and they kissed. They were content for an hour to pass like that in almost total darkness, sometimes kissing, most of the time talking in whispers.

'I feel like Romeo in *Romeo and Juliet*,' said Angelo sheepishly, wishing he could get closer to Doris yet glad of the wall.

Doris kissed him again. 'You want me to let down my tresses for you to climb up to my balcony?'

'That was not Shakespeare – I think it was the Brothers Grimm. But I do love your hair. I wish I could see it.'

'I'll let it down tomorrow,' Doris promised.

'Tomorrow.'

Their final kiss lasted five minutes and was their most passionate. Angelo didn't panic, not even when Doris worked her tongue into his mouth. He returned to the cottage wishing it had lasted five hours.

The next day was chilly and overcast. Angelo worked all day on the ditch, praying for the sounds of the girls but they never came.

That night Angelo was tormented with doubts when he crept up to Doris's window. They hadn't seen each other for twenty-four hours – long enough, he reasoned, for Doris to have second thoughts about the stupidity of risking an affair with a prisoner of war – particularly an affair with the son of a man who had been one of Hitler's confidants.

But her window was flung open in response to his nervous tap. The warmth of her against him, and the intensity of her work-broken nails digging into his shoulders banished his fears. She helped him climb through the window. He stood in the darkness, feeling helpless, while she wedged a blackout board into place. A match flared, a candle was lit, and he was so overwhelmed by her beauty and the outline of her body through her nightdress that he almost fainted. The only furniture in the cramped room was a single bed, a tiny dressing table and a marble-topped washstand with a china basin and a ewer. There were clothes hanging everywhere.

'It's cold,' said Doris, helping him out of his coat. 'Let's snuggle under the eiderdown.'

'Snuggle' was a new word for Angelo, but he soon learned the enjoyment of holding Doris close under the covers on the narrow bed, facing her, one arm pinioned by his own weight, the other around her waist. The candlelight flickered on her hair and he kept reaching up to touch it.

'Where did you get those amazing eyes, Angelo Todt?'

'From my mother.'

'Tell me about her.'

'I want to learn about *you*.'

'There's nothing to tell. Mum and Dad worked as tenants on a farm near Devizes. General farming. About twenty acres. They had a cottage about the size of the Foxes' place. I went to the local Holy Cross until I was fourteen and I was entitled to help from the manorial fund to pay for me to go to boarding school. After that I ended up at Woolworth's in Devizes. It sounds dead-end but it wasn't. I was going to be an assistant manageress when the war started. I didn't want to work in a factory, even though the money was good. I'd been used to working outdoors, so I joined Lady Denham's Women's Land Army. The pay's terrible – only thirty-five shillings a week. A bit extra for working on a pig farm like this dump, so I manage to send Mum and Dad a postal order for ten shillings each week, and I saved a bit in the post office. I've always saved.'

'No brothers or sisters?'

'An older sister,' said Doris, feeling warm and secure in this strange man's arms, not having to fight him off. She wondered if she would ever have to fight him off. 'She's married with two children. She and her husband run a boarding house in Littlehampton.'

'Where is Littlehampton?'

'It's a little resort town on the south coast. What's your brother like?'

'Clever. He is an oberstleutnant. That is like a lieutenant-colonel. Only a few ranks below a general. They are all very proud of him.'

'And you're a lieutenant?'

'Leutnant. Many ranks below a general.'

'And they're not proud of you?'

'No.'

Doris giggled. 'You're allowed some little white lies, Andy. You don't have to be so honest.'

'It is all I want to be with you, Doris.'

She tugged playfully at his ear. 'Nothing else?'

His answer was to kiss her, nuzzle her hair. He slid his hand up her leg, drawing up her nightdress. He had touched her many times when swimming and wrestling but this was different. Excitingly, frighteningly different. He was almost relieved when she caught hold of his hand and squeezed it, holding it hard against her leg.

'I am sorry,' said Angelo awkwardly. 'I have upset you. I did not mean—'

Doris pressed a finger to his lips. 'You haven't upset me, silly. It's just – oh, I wish I could be as open as you, Andy. I've got tomorrow off, so I'm going shopping in Ambleside. If they haven't got what I want, I'll get the bus to Windermere. In fact, I might as well go to Windermere. They're all so bloody nosey in Ambleside.' She pulled him close and kissed him. 'It'll be all right tomorrow night, I promise.'

9

Angelo worked the next day on the ditch, his emotions such a mixture of dread and heart-pounding excitement that he worked without thinking.

'That's too deep, Andy,' said Charlie on an inspection visit in the afternoon. 'You're doing a bloody good job though. Could never have done it myself. I reckon you'll be done in a week but don't go making work for yourself. You'd better fill that length in a bit. Stupid things, sheep.'

Angelo worked on. Dreading yet welcoming each passing hour. When he tapped on Doris's window at one o'clock and it flew open, all his worries evaporated the moment he held her in his arms.

He undressed in the dark because she didn't want a candle lit. There was the shock of discovering that she was naked

167

when he wriggled under the bedclothes but it hardly had time to register such was the passionate intensity of her smothering kisses. He hardly knew what happened during the next ten minutes. Doris was kissing him and touching him. He reached up to caress her breasts, entwining her hair in his fingers and wishing he could see it, and her movements blotted out all the individual sensations of her wonderful presence, merging them into one that ended with her collapsing on him, her head to one side as she crammed the sheet into her mouth while making little mewing noises deep in her throat. The paroxysms that raked her body frightened Angelo at first. He ran his hand down her spine, wet with perspiration, and that resulted in several more spasms before she became still, her breath rasping in his ear. He could even feel her heart through her breasts that were pressed against his chest. He found he could move again and this time it was only a minute or so before she gave those strange little cries again and clenched him tightly.

She was still for a few minutes before she moved off him. He wriggled over to make room but she sat up and struck a match to light the candle. He eased himself up, marvelling at her glorious hair as she filled a tumbler with water from a jug and drank. She offered it to Angelo. He realized that his mouth was dry and gulped it down.

Doris blew out the candle and slipped down beside him. 'It's been a long time,' she said quietly. 'I usually get a bit carried away but never as much as that. Did I shock you?'

'You could never shock me, Doris.'

'Oh, I think I could,' she replied mischievously.

'Have you . . . Have you known many . . .' He could not finish the sentence and regretted starting it.

Her fingers tugged playfully at the hairs on his chest. 'Many men?'

'I should not have asked. It was rude of me. It is just that I want to know all about you.'

'Four,' said Doris abruptly. 'And not one of them was a bit like you.' She slipped her hand down and took hold of him. 'Now it's your turn. Come on, Honest Andy. How many women has this little chap known?'

'I don't know. I think you are the first.'

Doris used his chest to stifle a laugh. 'You *think*? Surely one knows these things?'

Angelo's reluctance to reply earned him a dig in the ribs. 'We used to have some chambermaids who liked to make my life a misery,' he said. 'There were three of them. Blondes. All with long hair in plaits. They would come into my bedroom early in the morning and . . .' His voice faltered.

Doris was agog. 'And what?'

'They would tease me. One would sit astride me and one would hold my feet down. While the third played with me. They would change places – taking it in turns.'

The pain in his voice was too real for Doris to think of making a ribald comment. 'How old were you, Andy?'

'Fourteen. Only six years ago.'

'Couldn't you have called for help or something?'

'One always sat astride my face. All I can remember is nearly suffocating all the time. But the other two used to make me stiff. I tried not to be but I could not help it. I was always like that in the morning anyway, and they seemed to know. They were big – always a heavy weight on me, so I never really knew what was happening.'

'Couldn't you have told anyone?'

'I suppose so, but I felt so . . . so . . .' He groped for the right word.

'Humiliated?'

'Yes. But it only lasted two weeks. They were temporary staff taken on for all the weekend house parties that my mother loved organizing.'

Doris was silent. It had never occurred to her until then that women were as capable of sexual assault as were men.

'Ever since then I have been a little scared of blondes. But you are a beautiful brunette, Doris. The most beautiful girl in the world and I love you very much.'

They made love again and fell asleep, and awoke in a near panic because it was an hour before dawn.

Alone in her bedroom, Doris collected her thoughts and had to accept that she could not imagine life without her beloved Angelo.

They made love again over the next few nights although not with the same unleashed abandon as their third night together. They discovered that they enjoyed being in each other's company, holding each other close and learning about each other. Doris was entranced by Angelo's stories of his late father's estates. The weekend house parties, the balls, the hunting trips, visits to the opera – how his mother loved opera and even had famous singers staying at their summer lodge in the Tyrol. She gasped when Angelo told about the time when his father had designed a raft big enough to hold an entire symphony orchestra so that it could be anchored in the middle of their lake to entertain guests. This young man opened doors on to a fairytale world that she thought existed only in her wildest fantasies. And yet it was real, so incredibly, sparklingly, marvellously real – a million miles removed from her own drab life.

'So what happens to your father's estates now that he's dead?' she asked one night as Angelo was preparing to leave.

'He read his will out to us once. His main intention was to keep the estates together, intact, in a trust. Alexander and I have equal administration and share the income from the farms. He gets two thirds and I get a third. My mother has money of her own.'

'So you're rich?'

Angelo smiled at her as he buttoned his trousers. 'I think I am,' he agreed.

10

The blow fell after breakfast.

'I'm sorry to have to tell you this, Andy,' said Charlie. 'But you have to go back to Grizedale Hall.'

'But I have two more weeks here, Charlie!'

'I'm really sorry, Andy. Major Reynolds's scheme for prisoners to board out has not been approved. You have to return. They wanted you to go back tomorrow but I've persuaded Major Reynolds that you can stay to finish the ditch. Thursday.'

'Thursday!' Doris exclaimed when Angelo told her that night. 'But that's terrible . . . Terrible . . .'

'I have to take my things when I go to roll-call on Thursday morning, and they won't let me out.'

'But that means we have only two more nights together!' With that Doris started crying, burying her head against Angelo's chest, sobbing uncontrollably. 'Oh, Andy – you're the first man I've ever met that I really love. I hate all this meeting like this . . . I want to be with you always. For ever.'

'And I want to be with you, darling. When this war is over—'

'It'll *never* be over!' said Doris bitterly. 'You've only got to read the papers. It just goes on and on and on.'

They clung to each other in the candlelight, their shared misery made no less painful by their closeness.'

'We could run away together,' said Doris between sobs. 'I can't bear the thought of being apart from you.'

'I will be very close at the hall.' Angelo realized that it was a feeble thing to say; he had said it without thinking, unable to face the reality of the finality of his return to Grizedale Hall, and hating seeing his beloved Doris so distraught.

'You might as well be a million miles away!' She stopped crying and stared at him. 'Yes – we could do it.'

'Do what?'

'Run away.' And then her mind was racing ahead. 'If we could get to France, you could telephone your mother to send us money and we could be at your family's estate in a few days.'

'Doris, darling. We would never—'

But she wasn't listening. She pulled on a dressing gown, lit another candle, and told him that she would only be a few minutes. Angelo waited. He heard the creak of a floorboard immediately above. Moments later Doris returned with a bundle of men's clothes which she dumped on the bed and started sorting through them: shirts and ties, trousers, jackets, even a complete suit. They reeked of mothballs and were all good-quality garments.

She held up the suit. 'Try this on. It's Mr Humphreys's stuff. From his best wardrobe. He won't need these things now – he's been dead two years. Now try it on!'

Not quite sure what was going on in Doris's mind, he pulled on the trousers.

'A bit loose,' she said. 'But that's better than being too tight. You'll have to wear braces. Everyone's clothes are loose since this bloody war started. Now the rest.'

The late farmer's clothes were a good fit. A pair of patent leather shoes fitted perfectly.

'Thank God for that,' said Doris. 'What time do the Foxes go to bed?'

'About ten.'

Doris thought hard. 'You'll have to pretend to be tired and go to bed before them. Do they ever look in on you?'

'Never. Otherwise I would not be here now . . . Doris—'

'I'm thinking. I'll take tomorrow afternoon off and draw some money from the post office in Hawkshead. There's about forty pounds in my account. I can only draw some out each day but it should be enough to last us a month if needs be. I'll book a taxi while I'm there to pick us up and take us to Windermere. I'll check the times of London trains—'

Angelo had to interrupt her. 'Doris – what are you thinking of?'

'I'm thinking of us! We could be in London and on our way to Littlehampton before we're missed. There'll still be lots of people on holiday there. We'll be part of the crowds.'

'But why?'

There was a wild look in her eyes. 'To steal a fishing boat, of course! There's dozens of them there. Little things like rowing boats. They go out and catch crabs or lobsters or something. You said you could sail.'

'Only on our lake.'

'It's the same thing, isn't it? It's not far to France. Some of those little fishing boats have even got outboard engines as well as sails. I've watched them coming and going often

172

enough. Listen carefully, darling. This is what we must do.'

11

'I'm not surprised,' said Edna Fox sympathetically when Angelo said he was tired and would have an early night. The couple wished him goodnight and continued listening to the radio.

In his bedroom Angelo changed into the clothes that Doris had sorted out for him. Everything he needed, including shaving tackle, was packed into a battered suitcase that she had found on her second upstairs forage the previous night. The flannel trousers, shirt and tweed jacket were a good fit but the brogues were on the tight side. The alarm clock's time was right because he had set it by the radio earlier that evening. It was still twilight when he opened the bedroom's sash window and climbed on to the roof of the outside lavatory. The biggest risk was that Charlie or Edna would use the toilet. Within minutes he was clutching his suitcase and walking rapidly through the farm's front entrance. He turned left and saw Doris, standing by a smaller suitcase. She looked bewitching in a black and white print dress and high heels. They stood back from the road, hugging and kissing for ten minutes, until it was dark when they heard the sounds of an approaching car.

'It must be the taxi!' Doris whispered. She stepped into the road when she saw the cowled headlights and waved. It was the taxi. They piled into the back with their suitcases. 'We thought we'd save you turning into the farm,' Doris explained.

'Right-ho,' said the driver. 'Have to step on it a bit to get the overnight down.'

'An extra five shillings if you make it,' Doris promised him.

They made it with five minutes to spare. The train was crowded with noisy airmen from the flying training school at Carlisle, all sporting their new wings and talking in high spirits to cover their mixture of nervousness and excitement about what the future held in store for them.

Doris and Angelo folded themselves into each other's arms in the corner of a third-class compartment, oblivious of the world about them. Their whispered conversation sometimes trailed into silence as they thought about their uncertain future. The journey to Euston was the longest period they had ever spent together. Doris refreshed Angelo's memory about the coinage because he hadn't handled English money since his schooldays and had always had trouble understanding it.

'You'll be all right so long as you remember that there are twenty shillings to the pound,' Doris explained. She offered him her open purse. 'Now – pick out two and sixpence.'

At Euston there were red-capped military police at the station barrier but they weren't interested in young couples.

During their breakfast at the station's milk bar, Angelo looked at Doris's watch and commented that they'd be taking roll-call at Grizedale Hall. Doris squeezed his hand. 'And Janet will be knocking on my door with a cup of tea.'

Angelo toyed with the reversed ring Doris was wearing to serve as a wedding ring. 'If only it were real.'

'It soon will be,' said Doris. 'But you'll have to buy me two rings.'

'Two?'

'A wedding ring *and* a diamond engagement ring.'

They took the underground to Victoria Station and arrived at Littlehampton at midday. Angelo had changed into the suit during the journey.

'It would be awful if we met your sister,' he said worriedly when they emerged from the station into bright sunlight.

'Don't worry – we won't. Not where we'll be staying,' Doris replied, looking for a taxi. 'She lives at the posh end.'

The taxi dropped them at the end of a nondescript road where all the Victorian terraced houses seemed to have boarding room signs in their windows. Angelo paid the driver using money that Doris had given him. When he concentrated, he could manage the same accent as his former school friends at Harrow.

Doris chose a large house that seemed unable to make up its mind whether it was a hotel or a boarding house. They registered for three days as Mr and Mrs Fox, for bed and breakfast only. A longer stay would have required the production of ration books. Their well-dressed appearance made a good impression. For a pound tip, plus a five-shilling charge because they hadn't brought their own sheets, the manageress accepted that they had left their identity cards behind in the excitement of going on holiday but they would have to pay in advance. Doris had chosen well: the manageress made good money on the side by being discreet and not too demanding. And, no, there was no objection to guests using their room during the day. She quite understood that Mr and Mrs Fox had had a long journey and needed to rest. Hot water available two hours in the morning and evening and please observe the Battle for Fuel five inches of bathwater rule.

They coaxed just enough warm water out of the hand basin tap in their room for them to wash with flannels and a piece of Lifebuoy soap that Doris had thought to pack. They were hungry, but even hungrier for each other. They made love and dozed on a mattress that felt like it contained a cache of knobkerries but they didn't care. They were alone, facing an exciting adventure together, and the smell of the sea was a reminder that their road to freedom and riches was close to hand.

12

They ventured out at six o'clock. It was a fifteen-minute walk to the seafront despite a sign in the boarding house claiming half that. Doris was disappointed at the relatively few holidaymakers about. She knew that the traditional resort towns on the south coast were less popular now because the beaches were closed, isolated with barbed wire and mines; most people preferred the quiet of the country and the absence of air-raid sirens. Nevertheless there were enough families about to make the couple feel less conspicuous. Their evening meal in a grubby cafe consisted of fish-cakes, more potato than fish; and chips, more grease than potato. Doris counted what was left of her money on the oilcloth-covered table. She grimaced, remarking that it had been an expensive day but at least the worst of their costs were behind them.

Afterwards they walked in the failing light along the path flanking the River Arun and stared down at the crabbers' cobles – open clinker-built boats, some piled high with crab pots. It was low tide and many of the craft were pulled up above the high water mark on a shingle bank. Other fishing boats were lying on the mud at the foot of a small quay. They strolled casually arm-in-arm on to the shingle and stood locked in an embrace, leaning against one of the craft while Angelo sized it up. Close to, they were quite large but, in answer to Doris's anxious question, he said he was sure the two of them could drag one into the water when the tide was in. The one they were leaning on had a Seagull outboard motor and a stout mast lying across the thwarts together with a paddle. Angelo guessed that the padlocked locker that formed the craft's foredeck held a sail. Everything was splattered with droppings from the wheeling black-headed gulls.

'Look at all the seagull mess,' said Angelo. 'Hardly any of the boats seem to have been used for a long time.'

'I expect the fishermen have all joined up,' Doris replied. 'I don't suppose running these tiddly little boats counts as a reserved occupation.'

The next morning was cold and wet. From the esplanade the sea looked calm. With so few people about Doris decided that they would be too conspicuous near the fishing boats, so they walked into the town centre. Doris bought a school exercise book containing a map of Southern England, the English Channel, and Northern France at W. H. Smith. At the post office she withdrew another five pounds from her savings and picked up a free tide table. A secondhand shop sold her a boy scout's pocket compass for ten shillings. A torch proved much harder to find. They eventually tracked down a bicycle lamp with a new battery that cost one pound.

'Nearly half a week's wages,' said Doris ruefully while they were having a mid-morning coffee dash and a bun in a cafe to supplement their meagre boarding-house breakfast of porridge and toast.

'I feel bad living off you like this,' said Angelo.

As always, Doris's lovely smile allayed his concerns. 'I was the one who pushed you into this, darling.' She added teasingly, 'Besides – you'll be the one who will end up keeping me in a manner to which I'm unaccustomed.'

The buzz of conversation died away when the cafe's owner turned up the volume on his radio for the news.

'The English live for news on the wireless,' Doris observed.

That there was nothing about them was a tremendous relief. The bulletin ended and they looked at the map of the English Channel. Angelo expressed his concerns when he worked out from the rough scale that it was at least seventy miles to France.

'But look how big France is,' Doris reasoned. 'The weather's settled. We've got a compass so all we have to do is keep heading south. We can't miss it. Easy-peasy.'

Angelo had doubts about getting a strange boat out of the Arun estuary at night into the south-westerly prevailing wind. 'It's hard enough in the daytime with a dingy, you know.'

'If we took a boat when the tide was turning, wouldn't that carry us out?'

'I suppose it might,' said Angelo.

'Look at this,' said Doris excitedly as she studied the tide-table leaflet. 'It's high tide at quarter past one tonight. And look – it's high tide now. It looks brighter out so let's go and see what it's like.'

The weather had cleared when they left the cafe and more people were about. Fifteen minutes later they were looking down at the cluster of little fishing boats and measuring the distance they would have to push the boat that was nearest the water – the one that they had taken a close look at the previous evening.

'At least twenty metres,' said Angelo. He grinned suddenly. 'We are both strong. I think we will manage.'

'Of course we will. Listen, Andy. We've got to picture everything clearly in our minds now. Remember where everything is. This isn't like Cumberland. They're really strict on the blackout down here. We've got to go back to the boarding house to get plenty of sleep. But we need to get a big dinner inside us first.'

Their big dinner was provided by Littlehampton's British Restaurant. The civic-run cafeteria was crowded and with good reason: for eleven pence each, not even a shilling as Doris commented, they were provided with roast beef and two generous portions of vegetables, two thick slices of bread spread with National margarine, rounded off with treacle pudding and coffee.

They returned to their boarding house, calling in at some shops on the way back to buy four bottles of lemonade and some apples and pears. 'Our sea voyage supplies,' Doris explained.

Once they had got all their purchases in their room, Doris tracked down the manageress.

'I'm awfully sorry,' said Doris apologetically, 'but we have to leave you tonight. I've heard that my mother is ill. My dad's coming to pick us up after he's finished his shift. Will it be okay if we leave here after midnight? We don't want a refund.'

'Of course, Mrs Fox. I'm sorry about your mother. The front door is always on the latch at night. Just make sure you close it firmly behind you.'

One problem less, thought Doris as she returned to their room. Any irritation she felt because she had to think of everything was soon dispelled once she was in bed with Angelo with his arms around her.

13

They rose and got ready for their great adventure just after midnight. Everything was packed into their suitcases. Doris ruled that they should wear their best clothes because a well-dressed couple with suitcases, looking like late arriving or departing holidaymakers, was less likely to attract attention. They would be finished if a policeman wanted to see their identity cards.

But no one did stop them despite the long walk through the blacked-out streets. An ARP warden passed them and merely nodded. They reached the river but the darkness was so total that it was necessary for Angelo to risk very quick flashes with the torch to get their bearings. Their shoes sounded deafening as they crunched across the shingle to the boats. Another quick flash located the boat they had earmarked and they piled their suitcases on the duckboards. They could hear the water lapping. It sounded very close. There was a gentle breeze off the water. Doris stumbled on a large stone which she heaved into the boat.

'What is that for?' asked Angelo.

'To break the padlock.'

On the count of three they pushed together but the boat refused to budge. Angelo rocked it back and forth and this time they succeeded in sliding it a little way down the shingle. It took them thirty minutes to get it on to the mud. The flat-bottomed craft was designed to be manoeuvred on tidal estuaries and, to their relief, it slid more easily than they had expected. Nevertheless it was hard work because the mud was getting softer and they had to keep stopping to unglug their feet. Angelo was pulling on the bow when he felt water around his ankles.

'We are nearly there!' he exclaimed. 'A few more metres!'

'How many times have I told you to talk in yards?'

Quite suddenly the boat was moving easily. It was afloat. Angelo helped Doris to scramble in and kept pushing the boat until he was up to his waist. Doris grabbed him by the waist to help him over the gunwale and into the boat. They moved quickly, having already gone over several times what they had to do and the order in which they had to do it. Angelo pulled off his jacket and used it as a cloak over his head to inspect the outboard's petrol tank with the torch. As they expected, it was dry.

Two hard blows with the stone was enough to break the

hasp on the sail locker's padlock. Angelo felt inside and was relieved to encounter sailcloth.

'It's here!' he exclaimed. Working by feel, he found the keel socket for the short mast and stepped it into position. He couldn't find a boom for the sail and assumed that the inshore fishermen didn't use them – that they relied on fastening a sheet to a cleat. Without a boom tacking would be difficult but not impossible. The sail itself was provided with wooden rings that simply dropped down the mast. He was working entirely by feel, so it was hardly surprising that he got the sail upside-down on his first attempt. Once it was on the right way and he gripped the sheet, the breeze filled the tiny sail immediately. The sheet tugged firmly on his arm and the boat was moving. The next problem was the tiller or, rather, the lack of one.

'There must be a rudder!' Angelo exclaimed.

Doris crouched as low as she could and flashed the torch quickly around the duckboards. There was nothing. Angelo secured the sheet and joined her. After a few minutes searching with his hands he found the fold-down arm on the Seagull outboard. He laughed, swivelling the motor from side to side. 'Look – it is so simple. The outboard engine acts as the rudder.'

He went back to the sheet. Water was rippling past the hull, which made him think that they were going too fast, so he stood, shortened the sail by a ring, and stood staring in the darkness for a hint as to where they were.

The hooded headlights of a vehicle turning on the opposite side of the river briefly illuminated the white chevron marks on the mole near the mouth of the river. He was elated. 'Doris! We're going in the right direction!'

She came forward to kiss him. The boat heeled.

'No. No. You must hold the tiller. Keep it in the centre.'

'Angelo – there's a light – straight ahead.'

But Angelo had already seen the dim green light. It was perhaps a mile ahead – he couldn't tell with certainty – but he could tell that it was moving from left to right. As he watched it a red companion light appeared beside it and he realized that what he was seeing were port and starboard navigation lights. There was a fainter white masthead light above them. They formed a perfect triangle, which meant that the boat they belonged to was heading straight towards them.

'What is it, Angelo?' Doris whispered fearfully.

'Perhaps a fishing boat coming in. They cannot have seen us because we are not showing lights. They will pass us by.'

A few moments passed and they heard the beat of a diesel engine. The triangle of lights became bigger, the note of the diesel engine got louder.

And then a powerful beam of light stabbed out from the approaching craft. The light scoured the estuary, briefly illuminating buildings and moored boats. It passed across them, blinding them momentarily, and then swung back to pinion the runaways with a fixed, unblinking glare.

14

The court bailiff signalled to Angelo to stand when the magistrate and the clerk re-entered the courtroom and took their seats.

'Lieutenant Angelo Todt,' said the magistrate frostily, 'you have pleaded guilty to all the charges against you and this has been taken into consideration when deciding your sentence. Count yourself lucky that owing to a quirk in English law, there is no offence of attempting to steal a boat. But the laws and defence regulations you have breached are enough to be going on with. You will go to prison for three months. When you have served your sentence, you will be handed over to the military authorities, who will deal separately with the questions of the breach of your parole and your fruitless escape bid. Do you have anything to say?'

'Yes, your worship. Please can you tell me what has happened to Doris Blake? I have heard nothing about her since we were arrested last week.'

'Well, you'll hear nothing from me, even if I did know, which I don't. Next case, please.'

Angelo was taken out to a waiting police car. He repeated his plea for information to a police constable.

'Sorry, mate,' said the policeman sympathetically but I don't know anything either. Chances are that she'll get much the same sentence as you and be sent to Holloway.'

'Holloway?'

'A women's prison in London.'

'Where am I going?'

'Somewhere in England. I'm sorry, mate – but you're a German, though you don't sound like one – so I can't tell you anything.'

Despite being in the depths of despair, Angelo managed to settle well into the routine of making soldiers' kitbags in Maidstone Prison's workshops. The frugal pay was enough for him to send two letters a week. The ones he addressed to Doris Blake, care of Holloway Prison, were always returned a week later marked 'not known' but he kept sending them in case she was transferred there. After two letters to Charlie and Edna Fox he got a curt reply saying that they didn't know where Doris was and didn't care. Angelo was told in no uncertain terms that his escape had caused them a great deal of trouble. A letter that he addressed to 'Janet – the Land Army Girl' at Spauldings Farm got a reply from her, printed with block capital letters, to say that no one had heard from Doris. On the advice of a warder, he started sending letters for Doris through the Home Office's prison department. They were not returned, which gave him hope, nor were they replied to.

The weeks slipped by. The dreary workshop routine meant that he had little to do but think. Instead of fading with time, his fond memories of Doris grew stronger by the day.

By the time he finished his civil sentence and was handed over to the army, he was in a state of depression at the thought that wherever he was sent, his family background would follow him and there would be more bullying.

'Where are you taking me?' he asked the military police sergeant who signed for him and changed his handcuffs to army-issue pattern.

'Can't say,' said the sergeant. 'Somewhere in England.'

15

The 'somewhere' turned out to be Grizedale Hall.

Major Reynolds berated him for ten minutes on his return. 'I can understand chasing after a girl – every man has it in him to make a fool of himself over a girl but one expects an officer and a gentleman to remain an officer and gentleman. You failed to do so by breaking a solemn parole and in so doing, all paroles here given by your fellow officers were suspended for a month. If you get bullied again by your comrades when you've finished your thirty days solitary, then I, for one, won't blame them.' He handed Angelo a package. 'Your mail. You've got some catching up to do. Dismissed.'

Alone in his cell, Angelo's fingers trembled as he opened the package. All the letters had been slit open by War Office censors and bore their date stamps. He went quickly through the envelopes, recognizing the handwriting of his mother and various relatives, until he came to handwriting that he did not recognize. It was from Doris and was a mass of neatly cut rectangular holes. The censors were efficient – they were not content with mere obliteration.

He started reading and almost wept when he saw the hole that could only have been her return address:

My Dearest Andy

After our arrest I was *[blank]* and sentenced to *[blank]* at *[blank]*. This farm is wonderful and I'm so happy here. I did get your letters, which were sent to me here. It's taken me so long to reply because I didn't know what to say to you and I hated myself because I knew that what I had to say would hurt you. You were always so honest with me and I could not bring myself to lie to you.

Dear Andy – Roger is like you – kind and understanding. It will be difficult for him to come up to the standards that you have set in my mind as to what a man should be but I know that he will succeed. We are to be married in November. This is a huge farm that belonged to Roger's father. When the war is over we plan to sell it and buy an orange plantation in Florida. But wherever I am, I will always think back with great fondness to our wonderful times together.

Curiously, Angelo realized that the letter wasn't the terrible blow that he might have expected. The futility of his longing for Doris had been brought home to him so brutally and so decisively, like the sure sweep of a surgeon's scalpel that minimized bleeding. The longing had been a black torment, a constant pain twisting his soul back and forth, and now it was gone.

16

Kruger was shown into Reynolds's office.
'I think you had better sit down, Otto. Some bourbon?'
'Thank you, no, Major.'
'I guess you'd better have some anyway.' Reynolds poured two glasses and pushed one across his desk.
'So what are we celebrating, Major?'
'The end of a big problem, Otto. Angelo Todt ends his solitary tomorrow.'
'I would've thought that that was the renewal of a problem – for both of us.'
Reynolds opened a desk drawer and passed a stout blue envelope to Kruger that bore an embossed swastika.
'That was sent by the German High Command to us through the Red Cross in the same way that we received the diamonds for your Knight's Cross last year. Maybe you would be so kind as to read the citation certificate for me. My German isn't up to it although I can work out that *Eisernes Kreuz 2nd Klasse* means Iron Cross Second Class.'
'Indeed it does,' Kruger answered absently, intent on the citation. 'The Second Class Iron Cross is awarded for single acts of great courage in the face of enemy action.' He stiffened in shock and reread a passage. 'My God!'

'Something wrong?' Reynolds enquired.

'It's been awarded to Leutnant Angelo Todt! At Galzala he was in charge of an ammunition truck that caught fire. He carried two of his injured comrades to safety and went back to drag two soldiers clear of another truck that had also been hit. Despite being badly burned, he insisted on going back to rescue a driver when he was caught by a British unit in retreat.'

Kruger stopped reading and shook a small packet out of the envelope. He opened the little case and stared at the Iron Cross, gleaming in the case's satin lining.

Reynolds leaned back in his chair and regarded Kruger speculatively. 'So I take it you'll be welcoming Angelo Todt to the camp tomorrow?'

Kruger downed his glass of bourbon and could think of nothing to say.

Part Four

A Stately Home of England

1

Ulbrick had a theory that there were Belgian genes in Kruger's ancestry, because the senior officer seemed to savour, if not actually enjoy, being miserable.

'He's like all Belgians,' Ulbrick had declared. 'He hates having a good time – he's only really happy when he's utterly miserable.'

On that basis, it was generally agreed among the prisoners of war that Kruger's happiest moments were during his morning and afternoon constitutional walks around the perimeter of Grizedale Hall's grounds. They usually consisted of four circuits and lasted an hour. Sometimes more if he found it necessary to stop to berate or fine a rogue vegetable, or its grower, for being out of line in the neat rows on the vegetable plots. Compost heaps were required to rot down evenly. Weeds were strictly forbidden. A footprint that hadn't been raked over could result in a deepening of his black scowl and an identity parade of feet to pinpoint the prisoner responsible.

The manner of his deliberate, seemingly measured paces, were a sure indication of his mood, which was usually bad. They were a particular source of considerable vexation for Sergeant Finch, who was convinced that Kruger was measuring the progress of a tunnel.

A collective sigh of relief went up from all those prisoners whom he passed without commenting on their work. All gaped in horror one morning when a new arrival, U-boat first watch officer Leutnant Josef Hinkel, fell in step beside Kruger and engaged him in conversation.

'I just want to say how happy I am to be here, Commander,' said Josef cheerfully. He was a bright, personable young man. His artistic sensitivities were reinforced by his total insensitivity to atmosphere. Kruger quickened his pace but this didn't register with Josef, because he bobbed along beside his senior officer and added, 'I consider myself very lucky.'

'You must be the only prisoner who thinks that,' said Kruger sourly. He reached the southernmost corner of his walk, turned towards the hall, increasing his stride yet again.

'Oh, but I am, Commander,' Josef exclaimed happily, matching Kruger's pace. 'Grizedale Hall is a wonderful building. Magnificent.'

Kruger wondered how this bouncy, irritating prisoner had got past the British psychiatrists, unless they'd seen Josef Hinkel as a means of making his life miserable. He stopped walking and lit a cheroot. He inhaled deeply and stared at the unwanted madman beside him.

'What is so wonderful about Grizedale Hall?' he demanded.

Josef was gazing, rapt, at the mansion, blithely unaware that he was being skewered by a stare that could send grown men howling for their mothers. 'Its elevation is a perfect golden rectangle, Commander.'

'It's a *what*?'

'A golden rectangle.'

Against his better judgement because it sucked him into Josef's crazy world, Kruger felt impelled to ask, 'And what is a golden rectangle?'

'It's a ratio that was thought to have been discovered by Pythagoras. You take a square – height and width being equal – and add the radius of the height to the width and you end up with a golden rectangle. Actually it's a lot more complicated than that, but that's roughly what it is. It's known by the Greek letter tau.'

Kruger decided that resistance was useless: he was ensnared. 'And what has this golden rectangle got to do with Grizedale Hall?'

'It's a shape that is pleasing to the eye although no one knows why. Greek architects used it for the Parthenon. The Romans copied them, of course. Did you know that the Brandenburg Gate is based on the golden rectangle, Commander?'

'I had no idea,' Kruger admitted. He continued his walk, hoping that the routine would help preserve his sanity.

'Oh yes, Commander,' Josef bubbled, breaking into a trot to keep up with Kruger. 'But they ruined it with the Quadriga – that dreadful war chariot drawn by stallions that's perched on top. It completely destroyed the elegant harmony of the golden rectangle.'

'Disgraceful.'

'Absolutely. But the architect of Grizedale Hall didn't make that mistake. He designed it so that the tops of the chimneys are within the golden rectangle and define its boundaries.'

'Leutnant Hinkel – when I interviewed you yesterday on your arrival here, you said that you trained as an architect, but you made no mention of the wondrous beauties of Grizedale Hall.'

'That's because I hadn't had a chance to look at it properly, Commander.'

Kruger grunted. 'To me it's an ugly pile of slate which I always avoid looking at on my morning and evening walks – which I like to take alone.'

Kruger's latter point went straight over Josef's head – he was suddenly busy effervescing on Kruger's first point. 'Slate . . . Yes – of course. Slate. It's a wonderful building material, Commander. A metamorphic rock with perfect parallel cleavage caused by pressure over millions of years. All you have to do when quarrying it is to cut it square and you have perfect building blocks. It's as if you have God on hand as bricklaying partner. We have so little of it at home. I think the hall is built of Skiddaw slate – the best in the world. The British don't know how lucky they are. They have virtually every type of rock imaginable within their shores. That lovely, white Portland stone from Dorsetshire, some of the oldest igneous rocks in the world from Devonshire—'

'Leutnant Hinkel,' said Kruger firmly. 'I hadn't been able

to make up my mind what work would best suit you. Well, I've now decided. I want you to spend all your working hours preparing a complete report on Grizedale Hall. Its history, its construction. I want detailed drawings and a five-thousand-word description. Do you understand?'

Josef's face lit up. 'Everything, Commander?'

'Everything,' Kruger affirmed. 'I must congratulate you, Leutnant – you've aroused my interest in this quite fascinating building. Leave no slate block unturned. I want you to make a start now. Willi Hartmann will be pleased to supply you with plenty of foolscap paper.'

Josef could scarcely believe his good fortune. 'I'll get started after lunch, Commander.'

'You weren't listening, Leutnant. I said that I wanted you to make a start *now*. Every minute you waste talking to me, is a minute in which I'm deprived of your report. And that means yet another minute spent by me looking upon the hall as a pile of slate. That would never do, would it?'

'No – of course not, Commander. Forgive me. I'll go and see Willi Hartmann for supplies.' With that, Josef saluted and took off in the direction of the architectural marvel of Grizedale Hall.

2

K ruger's ruse to keep Josef occupied did not work. The young architect fell in step beside him the following morning.

'I've made a start, Commander,' he declared brightly, and gaped in surprise when Kruger pointedly turned on his heel and walked in the opposite direction. Josef did likewise, bobbing alongside Kruger like an animated yo-yo, and repeated that he had made a start.

'I heard you!' Kruger snapped. 'I'm not interested in your starts. I'm interested in your finishes.'

'I need your help and advice, Commander.'

189

'My help you've already received. Willi is in a state of shock over the amount of paper he's supplied you. My advice is that you don't trouble me until you've finished the task I set you.'

Josef was undeterred. 'One of the guards told me that there's a file in the admin offices that contains information about the hall, Commander. It would help if you would approach Major Reynolds and ask him if I could take a look at it.'

Kruger had a strict rule that all dealings with their captors on policy matters should be through him. On this occasion breaking with protocol seemed a sensible option. 'You speak good English, therefore you have my permission to approach Major Reynolds directly.'

'Thank you, Commander.'

'But only on the matter of Grizedale Hall. Explain to him about golden rectangles. I'm sure he'll be fascinated.'

3

Major James Reynolds's first love had been a tall, flaxen-haired, green-eyed Icelandic goddess whom he had met at university. He had been so besotted with her that he had pretended to be wholly fascinated by her favourite subject: the Icelandic sagas. Her idea of a fun evening in was for him to sit in her apartment listening to her reciting the Eddic or Skaldic epic poems; her idea of a fun evening out was to drag him to a recital of the Eddic or Skaldic epic poems. In retrospect it seemed to him that the recitals had dragged on for weeks, with breaks only for meals, that left no time for any other activities that he had set his heart on. He had eventually ended the affair and taken up with a plump girl reading law who knew by heart all seventy-five verses of the *Ballad of Eskimo Nell* and was happy to re-enact most of them with him.

Listening to Josef Hinkel enthusing at great length about Grizedale Hall and expounding on the ratios of Fibonacci's consecutive numbers that contained the underlying mathematical structure of golden rectangles had Reynolds looking back with longing on those heady days with his Icelandic goddess.

He was a decent man who liked to encourage his prisoners to pursue harmless interests, which was probably why he had allowed Josef to drag him out of the security of his office to admire Grizedale Hall at a distance on three consecutive mornings.

On the third morning his will finally snapped. Josef's rambling discourses made the terrible fate of the Ragnarok in the Icelandic sagas – when the gods would fall, the sun become black, and smoke would gush forth to sink the earth into total and everlasting darkness – as an event to be looked forward to.

'Now look, Leutnant,' he said, standing at the far end of the lawn near the watchtower where Sergeant Finch was perched, looking down on the activities of the prisoners, convinced that every seemingly inconsequential action was part of a mass escape plan. 'I can't possibly let you see the plans of the hall. For all I know this might be part of an escape plan you have in mind.'

'Escape?' Josef echoed. 'Why would I want to do that? Actually, sir, it's not the plans I'm interested in, because I've drawn up my own. What I would love to see are any associated documents you may have about the hall's history.'

Reynolds gave in. 'Okay. Call in at the office after roll-call tomorrow and I'll have Private Knox dig out what he can.'

Josef was so overwhelmed that for a terrible moment Reynolds thought he was about to receive a hug and a kiss. 'One thing,' he warned. 'You can copy documents but you can't take them out of the office.'

'I understand, sir. I've got plenty of paper.'

'You have? I'm sure Private Knox would be grateful for any spare sheets.' Reynolds made a move to return to his office but Josef fell into step beside him.

'Some have got my golden rectangle calculations on one side, sir. All in pencil so that I can rub them out. Before I do, do you think Private Knox will be interested in them?'

Reynolds paused and glanced up at Sergeant Finch glowering down from the top of the watchtower. 'Would you like to see the hall from up there, Leutnant?'

'If it's possible, sir, I'd love to!'

Reynolds cupped his hands to his mouth and hailed Sergeant Finch. He explained that Leutnant Josef Hinkel was to be allowed up the watchtower for fifteen minutes. 'Should be long enough for you to interest Sergeant Finch in golden rectangles, Leutnant,' was his parting shot to Josef as he retreated to his office.

4

The week that followed was one of relative peace in Grizedale Hall because Josef was too busy prying into the intricacies of the hall's construction with his measuring stick, notebook and sketching pad to talk to anyone. Those prisoners who had rashly asked Josef what he was doing during the early days of his investigation had acquired detailed knowledge about golden rectangles, which they generously shared with those prisoners who had not spoken to Josef, thus deterring further enquiry. Also Josef's good command of English coupled with his willingness to spread enlightenment ensured that the guards left him alone as well. Normally any prisoner going around taking notes and measurements would have been certain to incur Sergeant Finch's suspicions, but he, too, seemed content to leave Josef to his own devices. In fact he had only to see Josef to be reminded that he had pressing business elsewhere.

Berg actually found Josef useful. Having him near his workshop was far more effective than any number of lookouts, which meant that he and his assistants could make good progress without interruption on whatever clandestine project they were engaged on. The intricate task of carving fonts for the printing press he and his assistants were making demanded a high degree of concentration.

The halcyon days ended on a cold day in late September

in the dining hall when Kruger and Ulbrick were sitting in battered armchairs, discussing the forthcoming production of the camp's play – R. C. Sherriff's *Journey's End* – which Ulbrick would be producing and Shriver directing.

'I agree that it's an excellent play, Paul,' Kruger was saying.

'Thanks to your translation, Otto.'

'But what concerns me is that its simplicity means that few of the men are involved. One set, a small cast. The purpose of these entertainments is not so much to entertain but to provide something to occupy the men during the winter months.'

'You want us to put on a revue?' said Ulbrick dispiritedly. 'I hate revues.'

'It would have the advantage of involving everyone.' Kruger waved a hand at the trestle dining tables that were folded and leaning against the walls around the big room. 'Especially if every table has to produce their own five-minute sketch. We could turn it into a competition.'

'A revue,' said Ulbrick glumly. 'Hardly fulfilling stuff.'

'Why not do both?' Kruger suggested. 'Let's do *Journey's End* in November and a revue at Christmas.'

Ulbrick brightened. 'That's not a bad idea, Otto.' His face darkened. 'It doesn't look as if this damned war's going to be over by Christmas now, does it?'

Kruger shook his head. 'Perhaps not by Christmas. But it'll be over in the new year.'

Ulbrick said nothing. He did not share Kruger's confidence and didn't wish to start another argument.

'But not even a revue will be enough to keep the men occupied during the winter months,' Kruger was saying. 'We need a project – something big, grandiose.'

Ulbrick was about to speak when four trestle tables leaning against the wall behind Kruger suddenly moved half a metre of their own accord, making a teeth-gritting squealing noise as they slid on the parquet floor.

Kruger gave Ulbrick a puzzled look. He rose and pulled his armchair to one side. Both officers contemplated Josef who, oblivious of their attention, was stretched out on the floor, digging a screwdriver into the plaster in a window corner just above the skirting board. A small chunk came loose. He peered closely at the wall, bit a piece off the plaster he had prised free and chewed it, his expression thoughtful.

Kruger enquired politely, 'Are you planning to eat all of Grizedale Hall, Leutnant Hinkel, or will you be satisfied with just the dining hall?'

Josef looked startled. He jumped to his feet and gave Kruger a clumsy salute. 'I'm very sorry, Commander – I didn't mean to disturb you.'

Kruger repeated his question. Josef's eyes widened in alarm. 'Eat Grizedale Hall?' He smiled sheepishly and took the piece of plaster out of his mouth. 'Oh, no, Commander – I was just tasting the plaster.'

Kruger looked questioningly at Ulbrick. 'Do I ask him why?'

'Risky,' said Ulbrick worriedly.

'Fraught with danger,' Kruger agreed.

'There's oak panelling under this plaster, Commander,' Josef volunteered. 'Real oak panelling carved in the style of Grinling Gibbons.'

Kruger was about to ask who Grinling Gibbons was but he sensed more danger. Instead he asked if the discovery was important.

'Very important, Commander. In fact I'd say that—'

'In that case, I suggest that you waste no time in reporting the matter to Major Reynolds.'

Josef looked doubtful. 'Do you think he'll be interested, Commander?'

'I'm sure he'll be quite fascinated,' Kruger replied. 'There's no time like the present, Leutnant . . .'

'Yes – of course. It's definitely in the style of Grinling Gibbons. He's certain to be interested.' With that Josef scurried from the dining hall.

'A narrow escape,' Kruger remarked as he and Ulbrick settled in their armchairs to resume their discussion.

'Narrow indeed,' Ulbrick replied. 'For a moment there I thought we were done for. Who the hell is Grinling Gibbons?'

5

'Who the hell is Grinling Gibbons?' Reynolds demanded. Josef was shocked. 'One of world's most famous woodcarvers, sir. Seventeenth century. He received commissions from Charles the Second, Christopher Wren—'

'This hall was built at the turn of the century, so how can it contain the carvings of someone who lived over three hundred years ago?'

'I think the carvings are in the style of Grinling Gibbons's work, sir,' Josef explained. 'His cascades of flowers and fruit were brilliant and are still popular today. Just before I joined the navy, my company received a commission to—'

'Is this something I need to know?' Reynolds asked, feeling trapped.

'But of course, sir! The plaster that's been slapped over the panelling and carvings in the dining hall is very acidic – you can taste it.' Josef produced his lump of plaster. He broke a piece off and offered it to Reynolds, but it was declined. 'Normally plaster is lime-based and therefore alkaline,' Josef continued, 'but not this plaster. It's eating away at the wood underneath – slowly destroying everything.'

'Maybe you're right,' said Reynolds. 'But there's nothing that can be done about that right now. There is a war on, you know.'

'But something must be done!' Josef protested. 'One of the documents you let me see was a schedule of dilapidations that was agreed between the War Office and the owners of the hall when it was requisitioned. It says that the carvings and panelling in the main hall are to be kept well protected and in good order, but they're being destroyed and the War Office will be responsible for putting it right. It could cost more than the hall is worth.'

Reynolds was damned if he was going to get involved in a discussion about War Office legal responsibilities with a

German prisoner of war. He said so in a forthright manner and dismissed Josef.

The matter weighed on the Canadian officer's mind for the next two days because much of the responsibility for the care of Grizedale Hall rested on his shoulders, as Beatrix Potter often reminded him on her visits. She was chairman of an influential advisory committee on the care of buildings of merit that had been requisitioned by the government. Why the hell did the British use stately homes for their prisoner of war camps? In the end he got Private Knox to word a 'guarding our asses' signal, which he sent to North-Western Command HQ. It provoked an indignant telephone response from Captain Moyle.

'What's all this nonsense about, Major Reynolds?'

'It's clear enough. I'm merely putting on record a confirmation that as commanding officer of Grizedale Hall, I cannot accept responsibility for hidden structural damage to the building or its decorations.'

'This is rubbish! The hall is structurally sound! It was properly surveyed by a firm of local architects on behalf of the War Office before the compulsory requisitioning order was made.'

'Then get them to accept responsibility,' Reynolds suggested.

'It's your responsibility!'

'Captain Moyle – with due respect – I cannot be expected to accept responsibility for things that are hidden from me, such as damp rot, dry rot, tommy rot, acid rot et cetera. My signal is merely a request for clarification of my orders and responsibilities.'

'Your signal is not accepted, Major Reynolds.'

'But you've got it and have to process it, Captain Moyle. It's in the camp log, so it's now on record. All you have to do is issue a warrant to those architects for them to take another look at the great hall and issue a brief report.'

'That would require General Somerfeld's authorization. My job is not to waste his time with such trivial matters!'

'One of your brief memos to him would suffice. You could even surprise him by issuing a warrant on your own initiative and sending an architect along. I'm sure the General would understand.'

'What is understood, Major Reynolds,' said Captain Moyle bitingly, 'is that you don't seem to know that there's a war on!'

'Oh, but I do know, Captain Moyle. I've got your memo.'

The line went dead but Reynolds's concerns seemed to have provoked some reaction, because the following day the gatehouse called Reynolds on the intercom to let him know that Beatrix Potter had arrived to see him on a matter concerning the hall's care and maintenance.

Reynolds groaned. Captain Moyle was getting his revenge. He quickly straightened his tie and greeted Beatrix Potter as her chauffeur-driven Rolls-Royce purred into the courtyard. She bustled into Reynolds's office – a swirl of tweed skirts and moth-eaten cardigans. She declined tea, accepted a measure of Canadian bourbon, and got straight to the point.

'What's this I hear from Captain Moyle about this magnificent building falling down owing to your disgraceful neglect, Major Reynolds?'

'I merely expressed my concern to him about possible deterioration that may be taking place and suggested that an expert should take a look at it, Mrs Heelis. That's all.'

'He referred the matter to General Somerfeld – an old friend – and he asked me to take a look as a favour before we start thinking about wasting money on architects' reports. So what's the problem?'

Reynolds was five minutes into his explanation when Beatrix Potter interrupted him. 'The name is *Grinling* Gibbons, Major – not Grinning.' She drained her glass and rose. 'Right. Let's take a look at the main hall. And please send for this Josef Hinkel.'

'He's a prisoner, Mrs Heelis,' Reynolds pointed out.

'So what? You said he speaks good English. He sounds a remarkable man.'

197

A table tennis tournament being held in the dining hall between the Luftwaffe and the Kriegsmarine was interrupted by the arrival of the deputation with its escort of two guards, and Private Knox bringing up the rear with his shorthand pad to take 'guarding our asses' notes for Major Reynolds. Tables and armchairs were pushed to one side and the prisoners heeded Kruger's order to keep a polite distance, although all looked on with interest as Josef went down on his knees to show Beatrix Potter his findings. He prised away another large lump of plaster to expose some badly pitted woodwork underneath.

'It's very strange, Mrs Heelis,' said Josef politely. 'The damage definitely looks acidic. What puzzles me is why the walls and ceiling have been covered up like this. Papier mâché seems to have been packed into the carving and a thick layer of plaster slapped on top. Why hide what must be some wonderful work?'

'Wonderful is right,' said Beatrix Potter emphatically. 'The carving was carried out by Hardwicke Rawnsley and his apprentices from the School of Industrial Art in Keswick that he founded. He was also a founder member of the National Trust. A wonderful man . . .' Her tone softened. 'I first met him when I was sixteen and what he did for me changed my life.'

Reynolds's interest perked up.

'He was the Vicar of Wray, you know,' Beatrix Potter continued. 'He encouraged me to write and draw. He even helped get my first book published. He also taught me to share his love of the Lake District, and he fought every intrusion – even the building of this magnificent hall. But Harold Brocklebank hired a first-class architect and gave Hardwicke a free hand with the panelling and carving in here. This was the banqueting hall, you know.' She looked sharply at Josef. 'It was very astute of you to spot that the work is based on Grinling Gibbons's style, young man.'

Josef smiled sheepishly. 'This is a good building. The architect used a true golden rectangle for the outline of the building, Mrs Heelis.'

The old lady looked admiringly at Josef. Reynolds cursed inwardly.

'Indeed he did,' said Beatrix Potter, warming to Josef. 'You certainly seem to know your stuff.' She turned to Reynolds. 'Get this young man to tell you about golden rectangles some time, Major Reynolds. It's a fascinating subject. Anyway, the reason why the panelling and carving has been plastered over is because the Holiday Fellowship breached the terms of their lease by not looking after it. As chairman of the trustees, I carried out an inspection at the end of their first season and was appalled at the damage.' She pointed to the end wall. 'Some wretched mill workers had carved their initials there. There was a communist slogan between those windows, and an obscene drawing underneath. The mindless vandals had even broken off a cascade of fruit. Disgraceful. We called in one of our National Trust experts. We couldn't remove the panelling or the carvings, nor could we close this hall because it was needed as a dining room, so he suggested covering the entire hall with papier mâché and plastering over it for the duration of the Holiday Fellowship's twenty-year lease. It wasn't the best solution but it was better than seeing everything destroyed, so that's what we did.'

'That might account for the acidity, Mrs Heelis,' said Josef. 'Were old newspapers used to make the papier mâché?'

Beatrix Potter smiled graciously at Josef. 'Why, yes. When I arrived for an inspection, the workmen were making papier mâché, using a cement mixer to shred and mix the paper. Bales of old newspapers were arriving by the lorry load.' She gestured to the uneven walls. 'In some places the plaster overlay was slapped on over the papier mâché to at least three inches thick to protect the more ornate carvings.'

'Newspapers can be very acid, and the ink certainly is,' said Josef.

'In which case,' said Beatrix Potter, turning to Reynolds,

199

'it is imperative that immediate steps are taken to correct the situation. Come, gentlemen. To battle.'

Reynolds told Josef to remain and the rest of the party followed in Beatrix Potter's formidable wake.

Kruger beckoned to Josef. 'I got most of that, Leutnant. I gather that something about this hall has upset Mrs Heelis?'

Josef briefed the senior officer on what had happened and concluded that he thought Mrs Heelis a remarkable lady.

'Do you know who she is?'

Josef was puzzled. 'A local landowner, Commander? She seems influential.'

Kruger smiled. 'You don't know how influential. She's Beatrix Potter.'

Josef blinked. 'Peter Rabbit? Mrs Tiggy-Winky? My mother used to read them to me.'

'The same.' Kruger stooped and pulled at the plaster where Josef had been working. A large piece came away quite easily. He examined it, picking at shreds of newspaper, and looked around the hall, at the high, unevenly plastered walls and vaulted ceiling. 'I imagine that stripping all this off will be a big job?'

Josef agreed that it would be a major job.

'In which case,' said Kruger thoughtfully, 'we need to have a serious talk.'

7

After a week of phone calls and tetchy signals from North-Western Command HQ as a result of Beatrix Potter's bullying, Major Reynolds came perilously close to losing his temper with the obdurate Captain Moyle. He pressed the telephone harder to his ear and gritted his teeth.

'Several points, Captain. Firstly, it wasn't me that chose to stir up this hornets' nest, as you call it. I merely wanted my concerns put on record. Secondly, I have not hired an architect without authority. That report was prepared by a prisoner who was an architect in civilian life. It cost nothing. We merely typed it out and sent a carbon flimsy to Mrs Heelis, as she requested.'

Captain Moyle was incensed. 'What? You're telling me that this Josef Hinkel is a prisoner of war?'

'I would've thought that "Leutnant Josef Hinkel, Kriegsmarine" typed at the foot of the report would have been seen as a bit of a giveaway,' Reynolds remarked dryly. 'Also, you should have his name on your lists of prisoners of war.'

'This is absolutely absurd, Major Reynolds!' Moyle rasped. 'Are you seriously expecting that we should accept the calculations of a German prisoner of war regarding the number of man hours needed for this remedial work?'

'Of course not, Captain. There's nothing in my covering memo that says that we should. The wording in my covering signal was simple enough: "Please find enclosed report from qualified architect Josef Hinkel." Please read it again. Move your lips at the same time if it helps.'

'Two thousand man hours! Have you any idea of what that will cost?'

'I've no idea, Captain. I'm not a surveyor or an architect. Why not call in a firm for an independent report?'

'Mrs Heelis has already been on the phone to General Somerfeld today demanding immediate action. She's been on the phone every day!'

'Perhaps she doesn't realize that there's a war on,' said Reynolds sympathetically.

'That's what it looks like,' Captain Moyle muttered.

'Perhaps she never got your memo?'

The conversation ended in the manner that Captain Moyle was used to end most of his phone calls to Grizedale Hall: the line went dead.

Reynolds sent for Josef and regarded him with a particularly unfriendly eye when he was marched in to his office between two guards.

'Leutnant Josef Hinkel, if I could think of a charge that would result in your receiving indefinite solitary confinement, I would be a happy man. But I am not a happy man. I am a very unhappy man. Can you guess why I'm an unhappy man?'

Josef looked anxious. 'My report, sir?'

'It has spread alarm and despondency,' said Reynolds. A look of hope came into his eyes. 'In fact that is in itself an offence. Defence of the Realm and all that.'

'I didn't mean to upset anyone, sir.'

'It never occurred to you that quoting two thousand man hours would cause an upset?'

'I tried to be accurate, sir.'

'And I'm trying to be patient!' Reynolds snapped irritably. 'Do you have any idea of what the repair work will cost?'

'There's not much involved in materials, sir. I've listed quantities in the appendix—'

'I'm not interested in materials! I'm interested in finding two thousand hours of skilled labour in wartime and worrying about who is going to pay for it if it can be found!'

'I have a suggestion about that,' said Josef tentatively.

'Let's hear it.'

'Why not ask Commander Kruger if us officers would do the work?'

'Out of the question.'

Josef fidgeted. 'May I ask why, sir?'

'No!' Reynolds regretted the snapped answer and unbent. 'Because he would never agree, because my senior officer would never agree – it would seem like we're using you prisoners of war as captive labour.'

'Not if the work was the practical side of a training course on building restoration. Commander Kruger likes his training courses to keep us occupied – especially with winter coming on. I could easily draw up a syllabus.'

Reynolds was about to dismiss the idea out of hand but changed his mind. He glared at Josef, not certain how to react.

'There would be a lot of spoil,' said Josef. 'All that waste plaster would be ideal material to repair the driveway to the main gate. Provided it's well pounded home, it could be used to fill in all the potholes, and it would consolidate the surface and provide good drainage . . . The papier mâché would make good boiler fuel. I could have a quiet word with Commander Kruger if you wish, sir.'

'I'll do all the quiet words, if you don't mind, Leutnant.'

Reynolds spoke to one of the guards outside the door to his office. Kruger strolled in a few minutes later and accepted a seat and an offer of bourbon. He sipped his drink and looked questioningly from Reynolds to Josef.

'I suspect that Leutnant Hinkel's presence means that this meeting has something to do with your problems with the great hall, Major?'

Reynolds outlined Josef's idea but Kruger interrupted him. 'My apologies, Major Reynolds, but I cannot permit my officers to carry out such an absurd plan that benefits the British.'

'You agreed to the outside farm working parties.'

'Because it gets my officers out of the camp now and then.'

'You had no qualms about getting them to convert the boiler to burn wood.'

'Because that benefited my men as much as it benefited you. More so because there are more of us. But restoring the great hall would not benefit them. Quite the contrary. The hall is used for table tennis tournaments. That won't be possible if we have to concern ourselves with worrying about the carvings and panelling.'

'Ping-pong balls won't cause any dam—' Josef began but was trounced into silence by a steely glance from Kruger.

Reynolds shrugged. 'Fair enough, Commander. I can't make you agree, of course, but—'

'However . . .' Kruger held up his hand. 'Running a training course on building restoration with some practical work included as part of the syllabus does have its attractions.' He lit a cheroot and studied Reynolds through a cloud of smoke. 'But there are problems.'

'Such as?'

'The work will be long and arduous. It will probably take us until Christmas to complete the project. A modest increase in rations will be necessary. Nothing excessive. Two eggs a week per man instead of one, for example. Some extra meat.'

Reynolds made a note.

'Flour . . . Sugar . . .'

'Okay. Okay. I'll do my best, but I can't promise anything.'

'Sheets.'

'Sheets?'

'Bedsheets. At least a hundred. We'll need to continue to use the great hall as our dining hall and common room while work is in progress. The sheets will enable us to contain the dust and we'll need them as safety nets to catch debris when we're working on the ceiling.'

'Anything else?' Reynolds enquired, tight-lipped.

Kruger felt in his pocket, unfolded a piece of paper and studied it. 'As you know, Major, Oberleutnant Karl Shriver was a civil engineer. He calculates that we'll have to cut at least fifty young pines in the forest to make the scaffolding.'

The meeting ended ten minutes later with Reynolds wondering who had manipulated whom. His parting admonishment was that under no circumstances should work start until he had cleared the project with General Somerfeld.

8

Along with being the only prisoner to gain weight, Willi Hartmann's other great, but less visible, achievement was that his wheeling and dealing activities in prison had amassed him a fortune of just over forty-five pounds – mostly in one pound and ten shilling notes. He always carried twenty pounds about his person to finance any potentially lucrative deals that might come his way during the day. The remainder of this considerable sum, which represented nearly a year's pay for a private soldier, was in an alcove behind a detachable length of skirting board in a corner of his room. He was the only one that knew about it. His intangible wealth was in the form of chocolate bars, soap, cigarettes, cigars, wine and a hundred and one other scarcities garnered from fellow prisoners as payments for dubious services rendered. Their value varied according to the frequency of Red Cross supplies and parcels from pro-German sympathizers – mostly those in neutral countries such as Uruguay, which had a large German-descent population. His precious stock of Toblerone bars always held their value.

Each evening, before lights out, he would visit his bank, taking great care not to disturb the cobwebs and dust in the corner, and do his accounts. The most enjoyable part was paying in the day's takings. It could vary from as little as two shillings as part of his cut from the sale of one of Berg's cuckoo clocks through a guard, to as much as five shillings for a toy locomotive. Toy sales were picking up now that autumn had arrived and people's thoughts were turning to Christmas.

The bank balance had mounted steadily, but Willi wasn't satisfied. It rankled that there was real money being made on the black markets of wartime England and that he wasn't part of them. The guards on his payroll talked about the crazy prices that a few eggs or rashers of bacon were fetching. Willi had experimented with vegetable sales but that had proved a loss-making venture because it seemed that every householder in England had turned their gardens over to raising crops or were renting allotments from their local council. The fine summer had knocked the bottom out of the onion market.

And now Willi's fertile mind had come up with a scheme that he was sure would treble his fortune, provided it was carefully planned. He had done his research, questioning fellow prisoners of war who were members of the farm working parties, and had gleaned information about the local farmers, their habits, their produce and, above all, their weaknesses.

Once armed with all the information he felt he needed, he waited until late afternoon and went in search of Kruger and found him by following the sound of hammering and sawing coming from the dining hall.

Progress on building the scaffolding that Karl Shriver had designed had been rapid. The first of two tapering lattice towers was complete, and work on the second tower was nearly finished. The remarkable progress had been helped by the enthusiasm of the prisoners, who welcomed the break from their routine.

Six men were busy sawing slender, debarked pine trunks to length and cutting tenons on the ends while three other prisoners were using broad chisels and braces and bits to cut matching grooves in the second tower's uprights. Willi was proud of himself for not being a part of this buzz of activity.

Kruger and Shriver were sitting at a trestle table at the far end of the hall, going over Shriver's professional-looking drawings of the scaffolding. Willi drew nearer and waited for the right moment to accost Kruger. The two senior officers knew he was present but ignored him. Willi liked being ignored when it suited him. It helped with his eavesdropping activities.

At ten minutes to six o'clock Sergeant Finch marched in, accompanied by two guards carrying a large toolbox. He glowered at the lattice-work towers, convinced that they were really intended as part of a massed escape that the prisoners were planning, and blew on his whistle – the signal for work to cease.

'Right, you lot!' he roared. 'Let's be having them tools!' He ticked the returned tools against his clipboard as they were dumped in the toolbox. His parting shot of 'Get this mess cleared up!' as he and the guards marched out was hardly necessary because the prisoners were already sweeping the floor and clearing up in readiness for dinner. On a signal, two men on each leg of the towers slid them hard against the wall. There were some loud comments about Willi's laziness as prisoners started unfolding and setting up rows of trestle tables and chairs. Willi was about to speak his piece to Kruger but Major Reynolds strolled into the hall.

The Canadian officer looked up at the completed tower. The workmanlike efficiency of the sturdy-looking structure worried him. Where the tenons of the cross-braces protruded from their grooves, they had been bored through and wedged with short lengths of ash. The result was a rigid tower held together without metal fastenings, yet which could be easily

206

dismantled. The same tusk-tenon principle had been used for a robust ladder. The ingenuity and efficiency of the German prisoners concerned him. Simple structures such as this and the speed at which they had been designed and were now being built offered an insight into the ingenuity of an enemy for whom he was supposed to harbour enmity yet could find only respect.

He exchanged salutes with Kruger and Shriver, and commented, 'You guys have made amazing progress in four days. But why two scaffolding towers?'

'There'll be one each side, Major,' said Shriver in slow German. 'They'll be spanned with a cantilever arch that supports a railed platform for four men to work at the apex of the ceiling. Their weight will make the towers press outwards against the walls and increase the scaffolding's rigidity and safety. A principle invented by Elisha Otis for his elevators.'

All three men looked up at the high, vaulted ceiling.

'It's eight metres to the apex,' Shriver continued. 'That may not sound much but it'll seem three times that to the men up there. Not only must they be safe, but it's vital that they feel safe, as we discovered when working on Cologne Cathedral. It improves efficiency.'

Reynolds nodded. The tame architect from Bowness that Beatrix Potter had unearthed had confirmed that the Germans' plan was sound. 'I thought I'd let you know that the sheets you requested have arrived, Commander.'

Willi was interested. He had heard about the bed sheets and hoped to get hold of some.

'But only thirty,' Reynolds concluded.

'Thank you, Major,' Kruger replied. 'I daresay we'll manage.'

Willi closed in when Reynolds left. 'May I have a word please, Commander?'

Kruger's cold eyes regarded Willi. 'Thirty new bed sheets, Willi. We'll need every one as dust sheets. I will count them personally, and demand your miserable hide if any go missing.'

'Yes, Commander. I wouldn't think of touching them.'

'Then why are you hovering?'

Willi patted his paunch. 'Nurse Hobson says I should lose some weight. I've been worried about it, too. I would like you to put my name forward for inclusion on a farm working party, Commander.'

Kruger could barely conceal his astonishment. 'You? Work?'

'I'm ten kilos overweight, Commander. Nurse Hobson said it could shorten my life.'

'In which case your overweight condition is a highly desirable characteristic, Willi. You don't have many. Best you hang on to it.'

'*Please*, Commander,' Willi implored, contriving to look suitably crushed. 'I'd love to get the chance to work on Mrs Heelis's farm.'

'Officers for the farm working parties have to give their parole, Willi. That is, give their word they will not escape. The names I put forward are officers whom I consider to be men of honour and integrity.'

'Yes, Commander,' said Willi glumly, sensing what was coming.

The double doors leading to the kitchen opened. The huge frame of Walter Hilgard entered the hall. His biceps bulged from the weight of a witches' cauldron of bubbling stew, which he placed reverently on the serving table. Several of his helpers followed, bearing smaller catering pans filled with boiled potatoes. Prisoners began filing into the hall in the order of their table numbers to collect plates and cutlery.

'Honour and integrity are words that are quite alien to you, Willi,' Kruger continued. 'You are an unscrupulous thief; a devious, scheming liar, and a conniving blackmailer. Your word of honour is worth as much as a snowflake in a blast furnace. But these are qualities that make you a good executive officer.'

'I will give you my solemn word that I will not escape, Commander.'

Kruger regarded Willi dispassionately. 'I believe you, Willi. I don't think you see any profit in escaping. Very well, I will put your name forward to Major Reynolds.'

'Thank you, Commander.'

Kruger took Willi by the arm and guided him to the serving table. 'The smell suggests you've surpassed your usual excellent standards, Leutnant Hilgard.'

The mighty ex-*Bismarck* chef grinned. 'More meat than usual, Commander. A good yield from the rabbit snares and a couple in the hutches were ready.'

'A pity, because we have to help out Willi. He wants to lose weight and needs to cut down on his food. Isn't that right, Willi?'

'Yes, Commander,' Willi agreed sorrowfully.

Walter Hilgard gave Willi a smile as broad as himself. 'You want me to reduce your portions, Willi? Consider it done. I'll pass the word to my team.'

9

Josef avoided looking down and took care not to lean against the platform's safety rail. Watched by Kruger and Shriver, who were with him on the scaffolding's platform, he reached up and used the handle of a large screwdriver to tap the rough, thick coating of plaster that covered the hall's ceiling.

'It sounds hollow,' Kruger commented.

'Which is what I was hoping for, Commander,' Josef replied. He then tapped his way down the curve of the ceiling. The hollow note remained unchanged.

'Sounds promising,' Shriver observed.

Josef worked the screwdriver's blade cautiously into the plaster at the highest point and levered gently. An area the size of a dinner plate bulged outwards. A little more pressure caused the plaster to craze and large chunks to drop into the sheets that were suspended under the platform. He examined the smooth plaster underneath and turned to the two senior officers, grinning happily.

'I think we're in luck. The workmen who slapped on this plaster didn't bother to clean the ceiling.' Josef wet his finger, rubbed it on the bare patch and tasted the residue. 'Tobacco,' he declared. 'Soot and God knows what else.' He dug a little more with the screwdriver and an even larger chunk of plaster struck the edge of the platform and fell into the sheets.

'Look's like you were right, Josef,' said Shriver, picking up a piece of plaster that had fallen at his feet. 'It hasn't bonded to the ceiling properly.'

Josef turned to Kruger. 'If the ceiling is the same all over, then this stage is going to be easy, Commander.' He pointed to where the ceiling's downward curve joined the vertical surfaces of the wall. 'But the panelling ends there – you can see the bulge of the frieze, and the tests I've done show that the plaster has taken well to the carving. We should be able to strip the ceiling fairly quickly, but stripping the plaster from the panelling is likely to be very slow going.'

Kruger nodded and glanced down. Their height above the floor made him uncomfortable. 'But at least the men will be working lower down when we get to the panelling.'

'We'll alter the scaffolding to suit,' said Shriver.

'What are the chances of getting the job finished by Christmas?' Kruger asked.

Shriver frowned. 'If extra rations are involved, wouldn't it be better to spin the job out?'

'I gave Major Reynolds an undertaking that this would be a three-month training course,' Kruger replied evenly. 'He passed that undertaking to his superiors so that there could be no question of anyone saying that prisoners of war were being used for work to improve the value of War Office property. The British are sensitive about such things.'

'So when do we start?'

'Immediately lunch has been cleared away,' said Kruger.

Two hours later the hall was buzzing with activity. Four men on the platform were creating a steady rain of plaster debris into the sheets which was raked into wheelbarrows and trundled to the drive. Sergeant Finch supervised the filling of potholes as the plaster was pounded home and inspected each barrow load in case the whole thing was an ingenious plot by the prisoners to disguise spoil removed from a tunnel.

'How would they tunnel through rock, Sarge?' Chalky wondered.

'Them bloody Jerries are capable of anything!'

'Even winning the war?'

The NCO glowered. 'That's seditious talk, Private!'

'You're the one making the claims, Sarge,' Chalky countered.

By the end of the first day's work, the scaffolding towers had been moved several times along the length of the dining hall and a broad strip of its original ceiling was exposed.

Work continued apace the following day and stopped when an unexpected discovery was made in the afternoon that resulted in Reynolds making a telephone call to Beatrix Potter. The good lady came immediately, looking like she had just stepped out of a Victorian family photograph, and bringing Cathy Standish with her.

A group consisting of Reynolds, Kruger, Josef, the visitors, plus four guards and a small crowd of prisoners stared up at the freshly exposed ceiling where it arched down to the wall. Guards and prisoners alike accorded Cathy surreptitious, appreciative glances.

'Certainly some sort of drawing,' Beatrix Potter announced, passing her opera glasses to Cathy. 'It looks like a cartoon transfer.'

'That's what I thought,' said Josef, much relieved. 'I checked the plaster we removed and there's no sign of any paint that may have come away from the ceiling. Or plaster impregnation if a fresco technique had been used.'

Reynolds frowned. 'Why would anyone want to draw a cartoon up there?'

Beatrix Potter gave him a withering look. 'Really, Major Reynolds! A cartoon is a full-size drawing prepared by an artist on stout paper. The paper is held in place, and pin pricks are made through the drawing to the ceiling so that outlines of the picture can be drawn on to the ceiling.'

'I remember that old Brocklebank had plans to have the ceiling decorated but the Great War put a stop to it,' said Cathy.

Beatrix Potter blinked. 'Bless my soul, Cathy – I do believe you're right. I seem to remember him commissioning an artist. Go up and take a look.'

None of the men present had the courage to object. Cathy was wearing jodhpurs and didn't mind strong, masculine arms helping her up the scaffolding's ladder and on to the platform, or broad, masculine hands elevating her by the buttocks. Strong, masculine arms remained around her waist while she studied the faint lines that had been drawn on the plaster.

'Looks like the masthead of a ship,' she remarked to Josef, who had also climbed the ladder but without the help of strong, masculine arms. 'Can you chip some more plaster away lower down?'

Josef lay on his stomach and reached as far as he could down the ceiling's curve. He prised several large pieces of plaster away to expose the top of a funnel. It was definitely a ship.

'A paddle steamer!' Cathy exclaimed. She pointed. 'And look – you can see the pin-prick holes.' She called down her findings to the assembly below.

'That makes sense,' said Beatrix Potter. 'It'll be a Brocklebank ship. You'll probably find a lot more drawings as you clean away the plaster.'

Reynolds was visibly relieved. 'So you're happy that there's been no damage to any paintings caused by the work, Mrs Heelis?'

'Of course no paintings have been damaged,' Beatrix Potter retorted testily. 'There are no paintings to be damaged. You might as well whitewash over the drawings and the whole ceiling when you've finished. Harold Brocklebank was not noted for his good taste. Boats indeed. Fancy wanting to paint such nonsense all over his ceiling. If one must paint on ceilings, let it be angels and cherubs.'

10

'I could do angels and cherubs, Commander,' said Hauptmann Anton Hertzog.

'I don't want angels and cherubs,' said Kruger coldly. 'I want these sketches completed.'

The two men were perched on one of the scaffolding towers while work continued on the main platform. Huge lumps of plaster thudded into the sheets.

Anton Hertzog was an infantry officer and a remarkably talented artist. Several walls in the dormitories had been adorned with his efforts. He even painted the frames, creating shadows to give them a startling three-dimensional quality. Unfortunately Anton's immovable signed originals were not eagerly sought after by his fellow prisoners of war because he was going through a Baroque phase. He was currently a great admirer of Peter Paul Rubens, and liked to paint robust-looking female nudes fighting their way out of great swirls of strategically positioned gossamer fabric. Naturally his amazons had to be surrounded by angels and cherubs.

'I'm not very good at ships, Commander.'

'You don't have to be. They're already drawn for you. There are these ships on this side, so it's likely that there are ships on the other side. We should know by tomorrow, because we hope to have the ceiling stripped by then. Your job is to complete the painting-in of all the ships.'

'From their position it's likely that they're in the form of a frieze that runs the entire length of the hall.'

'So?'

Anton studied the nearest of the drawings. They offended his aesthetic sensibilities. 'Tugs, steamboats, cargo ships are so lacking in classical finesse, Commander. How about some graceful triremes or galleys? Their sails a great swell of sensual curves as they scud across a wine-dark sea?'

'I don't want triremes or galleys scudding across wine-dark seas,' said Kruger curtly. 'I want tugs and steamboats. Turner wasn't too proud to paint a steam tug, so I don't see why you should be.'

'But Turner's "Fighting *Temeraire*" was a statement about the incongruity of the old and new, Commander,' Anton protested. 'An ugly black tug dwarfed by the ghostly white image of a mighty sailing ship – impotent yet physically dominating the tug. The triumph of brute force over the gentle forces of nature; the vanquished glory of sail being consigned to the scrap yard.'

'I am very much tempted to consign you to the floor with my boot,' said Kruger mildly. 'The purpose of the restoration of this hall is not only to occupy my officers, but equally important, it is a demonstration to our captors of the resourcefulness and talent of our country and its countrymen. It's a statement that your talent will be a part of. To ensure that, you will paint in those ships. Do you understand, Hauptmann Hertzog?'

Anton stared dejectedly at the drawings. 'Black smoke,' he muttered.

'Plenty of black smoke. I like black smoke. It gave away the positions of convoys.'

'Funnels . . .'

'Funnels, too,' Kruger agreed.

'Masts . . . Sirens . . .'

'Masts and sirens are all essential. And consider the wider audience that will be seeing your work, for years to come perhaps.'

Anton seemed to brighten. 'Very well, Commander. I will do my best.'

Kruger smiled thinly. 'Thank you, Hauptmann.' He turned to leave and paused at the top of the ladder. 'There is one other thing. I have in mind a special opening ceremony when we've finished in here. I would like you to keep your work covered until then so that as few people as possible see it. The unveiling will be a dramatic surprise. We've plenty of sheets.'

'It will be done, Commander.'

Kruger climbed down. He brushed dust from his uniform and stood surveying the activity in the hall. Most of the original, smooth ceiling plaster was now exposed. Several men were able to use tables and chairs against the walls to stand on when working. He crossed to where Josef was gently easing away plaster from some ornate carving.

'It seems to be going well, Leutnant.'

Josef stopped work. 'It's going to slow down when we get started on the walls, Commander. In places like this where the carving is particularly ornate, we're going to have to pick the plaster out piece by piece.'

'Any idea how long it will take?'

'Several weeks.'

'A more precise answer if possible. November?'

Josef shook his head. 'I'm sorry, Commander, but it really is impossible for me to say. It's going to be slow going, but that will be offset by the fact that we'll be working at ground level and can put more men on the job.'

'I have had an idea in mind for an opening ceremony close to Christmas.'

'December will give us plenty of time, Commander.'

'In that case, I'll give you a specific date for the ceremony when I want all work completed: Saturday the nineteenth of December.'

Josef grinned. 'I'll do my very best, Commander.'

'See that you do, Leutnant.'

11

W illi's hoped-for path to riches was paved with misery and the prospect of ruin. The misery was a result of having to work with pigs. After four days mucking out Beatrix Potter's sties, the smell of pigs clung to him no matter how much time he spent using his precious stocks of soap in the showers. The ruin, that now seemed inevitable, was due to the number of bars of chocolate that his plan demanded in the form of bribes – mostly expended on befriending a ten-week-old weaned piglet whom he had named Greta. As a result of Willi's frequent gifts, Greta had become addicted to chocolate and took to getting under his feet whenever he was working in the sties. After four days he was seriously over-budget and, as with all risky business ventures offering a high reward if successful, he had reached that crucial point when he had to take a decision to either cut his losses and abandon the project, or press on.

He decided to press on. There was no point in delaying his next move, so he decided to make it at four o'clock when he and the other prisoners in his six-man party stopped work and cleaned up as best they could while they awaited the arrival of the van to take them back to Grizedale Hall.

'Mr Simons,' he called out to the farm manager when the working party had finished their work for that day. 'Could I take some more of those marrows to our cook, please?' He pointed to a huge mound at the back of the rows of newly built sties. The mound was a mountain of farmyard manure that was completely hidden under a swathe of marrow foliage and bloated marrows that had lost their market value and were now fed to the pigs.

There was a chorus of protests from the other prisoners. 'What the hell are you thinking of, Willi?' one of his comrades demanded on cue. 'We're sick of the damned things.'

'Walter Hilgard has a new recipe,' Willi countered. 'He said that he'd be willing to try it. Will that be okay, Mr Simons?'

Harry Simons shrugged. 'Take as many as you like. Glad to be rid of the bloody things. Pigs have gone off them now.'

The van driven by Private Jones turned into the farmyard and stopped. The prisoners opened the rear doors and they clambered aboard except Willi, who told Private Jones that he was going to collect some marrows.

'Just so long as you're not getting any more for our mess,' Private Jones grumbled. 'We've had enough of them. Okay – be quick about it.'

Willi trotted off. He worked his way out of sight around the marrow mountain, pretending to be hunting for prime specimens, and shot off towards the pigsties while pulling a large sack from under his orange working-party blouse. Greta detached herself from the other two hundred weaned piglets in her sty when she saw Willi and needed no coaxing to dive into the open sack in pursuit of chocolate.

Willi scooped her up, cradling her under his arm, and raced back to the van, pausing only to grab a marrow and add it to the sack. Greta was happily gorging on the chunks of Toblerone and made no objection to having company. He scrambled into the van and it moved off on the five-mile drive to Grizedale Hall. With half a mile to go, Willi signalled his

216

fellow prisoners to start arguing with him over his sackful of marrows. They earned their promised chocolate because the uproar they created was enough to arouse Private Jones's anger, particularly when it seemed that his passengers were about to come to blows.

'What's the matter with you bloody lot?' he yelled above the noise from the engine and the general tumult, which drowned Greta's occasional squeals when her chocolate supply needed replenishing by Willi.

'It's Willi,' said a prisoner. 'We have threatened him with violence if he takes his marrows into the camp.'

'Please, Jonesy, turn into Spauldings Farm,' said another prisoner. 'He can give them to Mr Charlie Fox – he likes marrows.'

'I can't do that,' Private Jones protested. 'I'm not supposed to stop and we're almost home. Someone might see us from the main gate guardhouse.'

'Sergeant Finch doesn't like waste. If we refuse to eat them, he will insist that they're cooked for the guards' mess.'

The threat was enough for Private Jones to turn into the entrance to Spauldings Farm. 'Okay – get rid of them and be quick!'

Willi scuttled off, clutching his sack. Greta squealed and wriggled because she had no chocolate. Once out of sight of the van, he lobbed his one marrow into some undergrowth. He entered the farmyard and approached a Land Army girl, a brawny, muscular maiden who was hosing down cast-iron feeding troughs and heaving them effortlessly into a stack. She stopped work and regarded Willi coolly. His orange blouse marked him as a prisoner of war.

'Excuse me, please,' said Willi in his best English. 'I am from the prisoner of war camp.'

'I can see that,' said the girl, looking down on Willi because she was a head taller than him. 'A working party's not due until next week.'

'We are returning to the hall when we find one of your pigs in the road.' Willi opened the sack. Greta thrust a chocolate-coated snout out, blinked, and snorted indignantly.

217

The girl looked cross. 'Bloody new lot we've got. City girls. Useless.'

'City girl? I'm sure it is a pig,' said Willi uncertainly.

'Dead careless them daft cows are.'

'Cows?' Willi floundered. 'My English . . . I am thinking it is definitely one pig.'

'Always leaving bloody pen gates open. Give it here.'

'For them it must be difficult,' said Willi, suddenly realizing what the girl was talking about. 'You must have many pigs?'

'About five hundred,' the girl answered, confirming the information Willi had gathered about the farm nearest to Grizedale Hall. She hoisted Greta out of the sack and tucked her under a powerful arm. 'Good job you found her – she's not been tagged yet. Hey – why is she in such a mess? Looks like chocolate all over her.'

'It was the only way to catch her.'

'Dunno how it is that you Jerries always seem to have chocolate and we never see it. Okay. Thanks for taking the trouble.'

Willi returned to the van and climbed in. The first phase of his plan had been successfully carried out. There was certain to be a rumpus over the missing pig because Beatrix Potter's farm was relatively small and the loss of one pig would most likely be quickly noticed. But Spauldings Farm was a large producer; they would fatten a surplus pig free of charge between now and Christmas. They might notice if they lost a pig but it was unlikely that they'd notice that they had one pig too many. That was the big risk element in his grand scheme. At least by the time he hoped to be profiting from the pig, a satisfactory period would have elapsed from the time when it had been stolen.

12

The period that Willi had hoped for before the discovery of the loss was a week – longer than he had hoped for, not that that made much difference to the uproar that Grizedale Hall was plunged into as guards tore the place apart. They searched everywhere, not even Willi's room failed to escape Sergeant Finch's scrutiny.

'What's all this chocolate doing here?' he demanded as guards tapped the walls, searching for hidden cavities where a pig could be fattened. One of the guards used a glass tumbler, which he pressed against walls, listening for the noises that a pig might be expected to make.

'I'm the custodian of surplus Red Cross supplies,' Willi explained.

Sergeant Finch grunted. He had been tasked with finding a pig and find it he would; Willi's caches were not his immediate concern.

'Nothing, Sarge,' a guard reported.

Sergeant Finch blew on his whistle and sent a search party through trapdoors to scour the roof. Once the hall had been turned upside-down his men worked their way methodically through the grounds. They formed lines, each guard armed with a long spike to probe the ground, searching for cavities that might house a pig. They found nothing but bedrock below the thin layers of topsoil and subsoil.

Kruger viewed all the frantic activity with a disinterested eye but he decided to be helpful.

'It would be sensible to look for some sort of vent, Sergeant Finch,' he suggested. 'Pigs, like guards, need to breathe.'

When the search party checked the hutches, he described to Sergeant Finch the essential physical differences between rabbits and pigs, stressing that rabbits had long, furry ears and didn't have curly tails.

Such was the NCO's thoroughness that he even had his men carry out searches of the forest around Grizedale Hall, where working partners of prisoners had created worryingly large clearings.

At the end of a long and exhausting day he returned to the administration block, where Beatrix Potter was arguing with Reynolds.

'It's preposterous!' she was saying as Sergeant Finch entered the office. 'Those damned nosey-parker ministry inspectors as good as accused me of selling a piglet on to the black market! Absolutely outrageous!'

'Anything, Sergeant?' Reynolds enquired, knowing what the answer would be from his adjutant's expression.

'Nothing, sir.'

'You've checked everywhere?' Beatrix Potter demanded.

'Everywhere, madam. The hall, the grounds. There's nowhere that a pig could be hidden. If any prisoners did steal a pig, they must've eaten it.'

The good lady snorted. 'In which case they wouldn't have got much from it. A pig needs at least three months to fatten to a reasonable marketable size. That's assuming it's properly fed. I supposed you keep a check on leftovers after meals?'

'There never are any,' said Sergeant Finch promptly. 'If a prisoner leaves anything, the others finish it off.'

'Good to know that there's no waste,' said Beatrix Potter. 'My Land Army girls do nothing but complain and leave perfectly good food. They expected to be gorging themselves, being sent to work on farms.'

'We have an excellent chef,' Reynolds put in. 'He does extremely well despite what he has to work with, although the prisoners are experts at setting rabbit snares and they also fatten a few in hutches. Tomorrow we'll be questioning all who've been working on your farm. We'll get at the truth, Mrs Heelis.'

Beatrix Potter's expression relaxed. 'Pigs,' she said contemptuously. 'Can't stand them. I much prefer sheep but these days farmers have to do what they're told.' She rose and gathered up her belongings. 'If it's any consolation, Major Reynolds, I don't think the prisoners did steal the pig. I have the most incredibly stupid Land Army girls to cope with. Mill workers. One of them probably left a pen open and the wretched creature escaped. Probably fallen in a tarn and drowned. I'm told they're intelligent creatures but I've not seen much evidence of it.'

13

The weeks slipped by at Grizedale Hall. Morale among the prisoners of war remained high. Rommel had secured North Africa, Stalingrad had fallen, the RAF's much-vaunted 1,000-bomber raids were having little effect on war production. The British newspapers were acknowledging the grave damage being inflicted by the U-boats although they did not give specific figures on tonnage sunk.

The hours of daylight shortened, the temperatures fell, and the consumption of Grizedale Forest by the camp's boiler was stepped up from its summer level as the central-heating system was tested and brought into operation.

Willi reflected gloomily that a cold winter and the need to keep forestry wardens happy about the amount of supposedly diseased wood being cleared would seriously deplete his Toblerone stock. He comforted himself with the thought that at least the fuss over Beatrix Potter's missing pig had become a memory, and that each passing day brought Christmas nearer – the time when Greta would earn him a fortune. The one small worry was the question of how to remove the pig from Spauldings Farm, but it would be another six weeks before the problem became pressing.

Kruger was pleased with restoration progress of the main hall. The entire end wall was finished. The magnificent carved oak panelling gleamed richly under its sheen of beeswax and held promise of what the hall would look like when the work was finished.

'It's Dietrich Berg and his carvers who deserve all the praise,' said Josef during Kruger's weekly detailed inspection. 'They've repaired all the damaged work as we've uncovered it.' He pointed to bunches of grapes, their vines entwined around each other. 'Those bunches were completely missing. He copied them from the bunches on the other side. You wouldn't know it was new work.'

'Indeed not,' Kruger declared. 'I shall compliment the workmanship of his team.'

'Leutnant Willi Hartmann is concerned about the time the work is taking, Commander. He's worried about Berg's toy production with Christmas approaching.'

'I shall advise Leutnant Hartmann not to interfere,' said Kruger icily.

'Do you realize that the area of panelling on the end wall forms a golden rectangle, Commander?'

Kruger fled.

Cathy Standish was so impressed during the following monthly inspection that she carried out on behalf of Beatrix Potter that she dragged Ian Fleming along to take a look on his next visit to her. Fleming had been intending to see Kruger and took an opportunity during a quiet moment to slip the German officer a large box of his favourite cheroots.

'Nice work here, Otto. What exactly are you planning?'

Kruger frowned at Fleming. 'Planning? What should I be planning, Commander? This work is the practical side of a training course in architectural restoration.'

'Let me guess. You're preparing the ground to stake a claim to Grizedale Hall as your country seat. Do the job too well and you might find Goering beating you to it.'

Kruger's frown deepened. 'That's a monstrous accusation, Commander. The war must be going very badly for you to make it.'

Fleming gave a disarming smile and withdrew the comment. His outwardly breezy manner concealed his concern. He didn't doubt that Kruger would have an accurate figure from new arrivals that the war was going particularly badly for the allies. He knew from his own interrogations of captured U-boat officers that they tended not to exaggerate their conning tower displays of pennants indicating sunk ships and their tonnage when they returned to port. They would be much more forthcoming when questioned by a fellow U-boat officer of Kruger's stature. One U-boat first officer had boasted to Fleming that during the four months that his U-boat had been undergoing repairs at Lorient, he had counted pennants totalling 400,000 tonnes on returning U-boats. It was a pointer to the actual bleak figure of nearly two million tonnes of allied shipping sent to the bottom during the latter weeks of 1942.

To change the subject, Fleming pointed to the sheets that covered the lower part of the ceiling where Anton Hertzog was working. 'Provided my question isn't misconstrued, what's going on under the sheets?'

Kruger gave a rare smile. 'The sheets are to keep the dust off the work of our finest artist. He's painting some British ships as a memento before they're all sunk.'

The fixed nature of Fleming's smile told Kruger that he was not amused.

14

Despite the usage of a mixed metaphor in saying that Willi's pig came home to roost, this is exactly what happened with his Greta in mid-November.

'Sorry to have to disturb your morning walk, Otto,' said Reynolds when the two men had exchanged salutes. He indicated a chair. Kruger sat, lit a cheroot and waited.

'I have what may be a delicate matter to deal with. A Land Army girl, well – woman, is in the guardhouse at the main gate. A Miss Carol Bunce. She wants to see a prisoner.'

Even Kruger looked surprised at that. He forgot to inhale on his cheroot. 'One of the girls from a farm that working parties have been sent to?'

'Spauldings Farm – just over the hill.'

'Whom does she wish to see?'

'She doesn't know his name. Nor will she say why she wants to see him.'

'A delicate matter indeed,' Kruger said thoughtfully. He remembered to draw on his cheroot before it went out. 'Since that business with Angelo Todt, the new arrangements were that working parties were only sent to farms when Land Army girls had been sent elsewhere or had the day off.'

Reynolds sorted through the papers on his desk and found the one he was looking for. 'That's the odd thing. The girl said that he's short and fat and sweats a lot.'

'She doesn't sound too fussy,' Kruger observed.

'There's only one of your officers that fits that description.'

'Leutnant Willi Hartmann.'

'Exactly,' said Reynolds. 'But Willi was never on the Spauldings Farm working parties. A local wanting to visit a prisoner of war. It's unheard of. Most of them think you guys have horns.'

'Except those who have worked with us on farms,' Kruger observed, unable to hide a slight smile at Reynolds's dilemma. 'Perhaps it would be a good idea if Willi had a talk with her?'

Reynolds fidgeted, looking uneasy. 'I'm not sure I can allow that. It's most irregular.'

'Don't worry, Major. I'll be with Willi. It would be best if we saw her alone. None of the guards should be in the room, otherwise, if there is some sort of scandal brewing, it will be all over the camp in no time. I'll give you a full and confidential verbal report afterwards.' Kruger rose, put on his cap and worked his kid gloves over his fingers.

Reynolds clutched at the offered straw and agreed. He sent a guard to fetch Willi. The little Bavarian's moonlike face was a picture of worry when he was wheeled into Reynolds's office.

'Come with me, Willi,' said Kruger curtly.

Kruger refused to answer Willi's anxious questions on the short walk to the guardhouse. His spirits sank when he saw the Land Army girl from Spauldings Farm sitting at a table, and they sank even further when the guards withdrew from the tiny backroom in the guardhouse and closed the door.

The girl goggled at Kruger, resplendent in his Kriegsmarine uniform, Knight's Cross gleaming at his throat. 'Blimey,' was all she managed to say, and blurted out a second one when

Kruger spoke to her in perfect English as he introduced himself and Willi.

'Are you in charge here?' she asked.

'I am the senior German officer here, Miss Bunce,' Kruger answered, sitting and motioning Willi to do likewise. 'Now then, Carol. Do you mind if I call you Carol? Is this the officer you wished to see?'

Carol couldn't help gaping at the two men in turn. She was a big, thickset woman in her mid-twenties. Her hands, Kruger noticed, were callused from hard work. She was wearing stained dungarees over a thick woollen jumper.

'Yes,' she said. 'That's him.'

'You must appreciate that all this is highly irregular, Carol,' said Kruger gently, not wishing to intimidate the girl. 'Prisoners-of-war are not usually allowed to receive visitors, which is why I'm present as Leutnant Hartmann's confidant and senior officer. May I ask why you wish to see him?'

Carol looked uncertain but Kruger's kindly smile gave her confidence. She nodded to Willi. 'He won't get into trouble or nothing, will he?'

'That rather depends on why you wish to see him, Carol.'

'Well . . . it's silly really but about two months ago this gentleman gave me something.'

'Indeed?'

'A pig.'

Kruger fought to maintain his smile. Willi closed his eyes. 'A pig?'

'Well, a piglet really. Only just weaned, I reckoned. He said he was in a prisoner working party returning here when they saw this piglet running loose outside the farm. So they caught it, and this gentleman brought it to me.'

'Is this so, Willi? Please speak in English.'

'Yes, Commander,' said Willi miserably.

The land girl's eyes gleamed as she caught the tension between the two men. 'Anyway,' she continued, 'I shoved the piglet in with our others and didn't give it no more thought. A few days later I heard that Mrs Heelis had lost a pig but I didn't think nothing more about that neither. Her farm is some miles away. Piglets don't wander that far.

'Then yesterday we has a visit by the inspectors. You never know when they're coming. We're supposed to have four hundred and eighty-two pigs and they wants to count them. So we rounds them all up. We've got big pens. Hard to count pigs with them all running around, so we always chivvies them into the piggery one by one through hurdles. Two inspectors do the counting. They both made it four hundred and eighty-two pigs all present and correct, so they signs and stamps our books and goes away happy. Then I discovers a gilt snoozing under a pile of straw. She hadn't been counted.'

'Meaning that you had one pig too many?' Kruger suggested.

Carol looked steadily at Kruger. 'Yes. Could be trouble because that extra pig is worth a lot of money.'

'I don't follow,' said Kruger.

Carol glanced at the door and lowered her voice. 'It's like this . . . If I tells the boss, I gets into trouble. I know for a fact that he don't want inspectors jumping all over us, going through everything. Getting rid of a pig wouldn't be no trouble if it was rashers and joints but it's a bleeding live pig.'

Kruger opened a packet of cheroots and wondered if he ought to offer one to Carol but she leaned across the table and took one. He lit it for her and she drew deeply on it without coughing.

'Tar – thanks. How is that you Jer— Germans always seem to have everything?'

'I can't see that a surplus pig can be that much of a problem for you, Carol,' said Kruger easily. 'A woman in your position must know a lot of about the local meat trade.'

'I don't know enough to kill one. And I couldn't do it anyway. I can't drive, so I can't do nothing with it.' She looked steadily at Kruger. 'But I've heard that the Germans run the kitchens here. That you do all the cooking. Have a proper chef. That you snare lots of rabbits.'

There was silence for a few moments. Kruger was the first to speak. 'It seems that this officer has caused you a great deal of trouble, Carol.'

Carol glowered at Willi, now sweating profusely. 'You can say that again.'

Kruger exhaled a cloud of smoke. 'On behalf of all the officers, Carol, I would like to apologize for Leutnant Hartmann's behaviour and to offer you compensation. I will also make arrangements to take the pig off your hands.'

The girl's eyes gleamed. 'Compensation?'

'Of course.' Kruger turned to Willi and spoke in rapid German. 'Ten pounds please, Willi. Now – and no argument.'

Willi looked aghast. 'Ten pounds, Commander? But I haven't got ten pounds!'

'Now!'

Carol caught the references to the sum because the German was similar to English. She remained outwardly calm as Willi searched through various pockets and produced the required bank notes one by one, even reaching into his socks. His expression suggested that each pound note placed on the table represented a portion of his soul wrenched from his body.

'Thank you, Willi.' Kruger gathered up the money and pushed it across the table. It disappeared with great rapidity into a bib pocket in Carol's dungarees. 'And now, Willi. If you would wait for me in my office, please. Carol and I have a few details to discuss.'

It was another fifteen minutes before Kruger left the guardhouse. A keen observer would have noticed that his step was slightly jaunty. All the prisoners were keen observers of their commanding officer and word soon spread that he was 'up to something'.

He entered Reynolds's office and explained that Carol Bunce's visit was simply because it had slipped her mind to call in to thank Willi for helping round up some escaped livestock when he was in a working party returning to the camp. A much-relieved Reynolds exchanged salutes with Kruger and expressed heartfelt thanks. He had been harbouring nightmare visions of the acrimonious rows that would ensue if Land Army girls started filing paternity suits against prisoners of war in his charge. It would have been worse than the Angelo Todt affair.

Kruger paused in the doorway. 'There is one thing, Major.

I have in mind a special reopening ceremony for the hall when the restoration is finished.'

'Yes – you have mentioned it, Otto. It sounds like a good idea.'

'Would you have any objections to combining the opening with a celebratory dinner for all those who have made the task possible?'

Reynolds was puzzled. 'Well – I guess not. You run the catering side, but you'd have to do it on existing rations.'

Kruger expressed his thanks and left. His next visit was to the kitchen, where he sought out Walter Hilgard and took him to one side. The conference lasted ten minutes, during which time the chef's expression changed from its usual lugubriousness to a broad, eager grin. Hermann, the camp cat, passed the time rubbing around Kruger's legs. He believed in a reward system for training his staff and doubtless would have rubbed even more enthusiastically had he known what was being hatched between the two men.

The conversation ended with Hilgard yanking open a drawer and brandishing a large meat-tenderizing hammer in a ham-like fist. 'Killed plenty of them in my time, Commander. No trouble. One hard bash with this and that's it.' He brought the hammer down with a tremendous crash on a butcher's block. Hermann curtailed his staff training programme and fled. Kruger returned to his office to find Willi sitting at his card table desk in the depths of despair.

'I'm a ruined man, Commander,' he wailed. 'Destitute.'

'Nonsense, Willi. You've bought a large, fat pig for the bargain price of ten pounds. Thanks to me, you've made the best deal of your life.'

Willi didn't argue. Kruger could be equally intransigent in good moods as in bad moods.

'At the very least I was hoping to eat some of it, Commander.'

'But I'm as anxious as ever that you should lose some weight, Willi, although I confess that I was sorry to see that your enthusiasm for being on working parties soon waned. No matter. I'll personally see to it that you get the best cut in recognition of your remarkable effort in securing a pig for the officers. No one has done so much for them as you have.'

Willi felt a little better, his devious mind raced, thinking up schemes that might rescue the situation.

'Do you mean that you have a plan to get Greta into the camp, Commander?'

'Greta? Is that what you called her?'

Willi nodded.

Kruger dropped into his chair and leaned back, hands clasped behind his head. 'Did *you* have a plan to get her into the camp, Willi?'

'Not really, Commander. My first thought was to get her into Spauldings Farm for fattening up. I chose that farm because it's the nearest to us. I thought it would make it easier.'

'Well, I have a very definite plan.'

'Involving that Land Army woman?'

'Best I say nothing until I've worked out the details. But rest assured, we will be getting your pig back.'

A thought occurred to Willi. 'How will she know which is my pig after all these weeks?'

'You're not thinking straight, Willi,' Kruger replied easily. 'It doesn't matter what pig we get, provided Spauldings Farm end up with the right number for the inspectors to count. So . . . if all goes according to plan, we'll be getting the best and fattest pig on the farm. How much money have we got in the escape fund? About eight pounds?'

'You're going to escape, Commander?'

'No, Willi. But I am going to misappropriate some of the funds for a worthy cause.'

15

December came. With only nineteen days to go before the gala reopening dinner, Kruger stepped up his planning and machinations.

Dietrich Berg looked around the large room off the main

hall. It had once served as a cutlery and crockery store, but nowadays it was home to stacks of folding chairs and table tennis equipment.

'I think it's a good idea, Commander. Having your office down here would mean having your ear that much closer to the ground.'

'I'm confident that I don't miss anything that's going on in this camp from the top floor, Hauptmann.'

'Indeed not, Commander.'

'I want everything ready by the nineteenth.'

Berg looked at the list of instructions Kruger had given him. 'The desk will be the only problem that I can see, particularly the green leather top, but we'll do our best, Commander.'

'How about the invitations?'

'You want them by the tenth of the month, Commander. Hand lettering will take time.'

'The printing press is finished, is it not?'

Berg was doubtful. 'Well – yes. But the uniformity of the fonts would be a giveaway, Commander. The British will know immediately that we've made a printing press if they get their hands on an invitation.'

'I want them to get their hands on quite a few invitations, Hauptmann. You may go.'

Dietrich headed back to his workshop, wondering if his commanding officer had taken leave of his senses.

Kruger left the room and stood surveying the activity in the main hall with some pride. The place had been transformed. Where there had been rough, badly plastered walls there were now expanses of magnificent carved oak panelling from floor to a lime wood frieze that extended around the four walls, marking the boundary between wall and ceiling. The use of lime wood had been extended down the corners for complex bunches of grapes and cascades of fruit and flowers. There was only about five square metres of the rough plaster left in a corner where it was proving difficult to remove because the carvings underneath were ragged, badly damaged. As Josef had expected, it was restoration of the more ornate carving that was proving to be the most time-consuming.

Nevertheless the young architect had expressed confidence that the work would be finished by Kruger's deadline.

There was only one scaffolding tower left, the other one had been consigned to the boiler. Its top was hidden under the sheets that still cloaked much of the lower curves of the ceiling. Kruger walked to the foot of the tower and called up. Anton Hertzog's face appeared from behind the sheets. He spoke to his two assistant artists and scrambled down the ladder. An old shirt, streaked with paint smears, served as his artist's smock.

'How is everything going, Hauptmann?'

'We've nearly finished, Commander. There's a coaster that's given us trouble because the cartoon is very faint. But we've used a bit of imagination and licence.'

'Not too much imagination and licence, I hope?'

'No, Commander. It's an ugly little coaster. You're sure to like it.'

Kruger grunted and signalled for Anton to follow him into the room off the hall. 'This is to be my new office. I want a large painting of my U-boat on the far wall.' He unfolded a sketch and gave it to Anton. 'That's a type VIIC U-boat with the same configuration as my *U-112*. I have some more detailed sketches if you need them.'

'What size do you want the painting, Commander?'

'About one metre by two metres ought to look suitably impressive.'

Anton cocked his head on one side as he studied the sketch. 'Actually it would look quite graceful sailing across a wine-dark sea.'

'No wine-dark seas, please, Hauptmann. A grey, storm-tossed Atlantic, mean and menacing, will do nicely. My *U-112* never had the good fortune to encounter wine-dark seas.'

'Lots of sinking ships in the background?'

'Just my U-boat, please, Hauptmann. And not even as much as a hint of a trireme or a galley. *U-112* never encountered them either. I want it completed by the nineteenth.'

The next visit to Grizedale Hall was the following day when Cathy Standish arrived to check on progress in the main hall. Kruger managed to separate her from the small, admiring crowd to show her what would soon be his new office. She listened carefully as he outlined his plans for the forthcoming gala opening ceremony.

'One hundred place settings!' she exclaimed, looking at the list Kruger had given. 'Cutlery for three courses, plus napkins and tablecloths and condiments. All this for turnip soup and shepherd's pie?'

'I'm hoping that we might be able to manage something better than that,' said Kruger. 'Do you think the five pounds will cover it, Mrs Standish?'

'I'm sure it'll be more than enough. A catering firm might want a deposit. I'll ask around.'

'If you would inform Major Reynolds as soon as you can, I would be most grateful.'

Cathy looked curiously at Kruger. 'This seems important to you?'

'Indeed it is. Many people are putting a great deal of effort into restoring the great hall. A gala dinner is the least I can do.'

'Very well, Commander. I will do my best.'

Kruger bowed. 'Thank you, Mrs Standish. You are most kind.'

16

The loud hammering on his door stilled Willi's heart. For most of his criminal life, loud hammering on doors had been the precursor to a spell in custody. If this was a surprise inspection by the guards that he hadn't been warned about, then someone was going to go without their customary weekly bar of chocolate.

'Who is it?' he demanded.

The hammering was renewed.

Willi turned the key. Barely had the mortise lock's tongue slid clear of the striker plate when the door flew open. Willi staggered back, clutching his nose. Walter Hilgard stood there, his massive frame filling the doorway, with two of his assistant chefs behind him filling the corridor. They were marginally smaller than their boss, but only just.

The three men entered the room like bisons wandering into a wigwam. Hilgard looked around at the piles of goodies that included cartons of cigarettes, slabs of chocolate, cans of biscuits, sweets, condensed milk, evaporated milk, even clotted cream.

'So this is what your room looks like, Willi? A real Aladdin's cave, just like all the stories we've heard. Nice having your own room, but it's smaller than I expected.'

'It seems a lot larger without you three lugs cluttering it up,' said Willi spiritedly.

Hilgard looked sorrowfully down at Willi. 'Not a nice way to receive visitors, Willi. Especially someone as lovable as us. Kurt and Gunter are particularly lovable, aren't you, boys?'

Kurt cracked his knuckles by flexing his broomstick fingers backwards and confirmed that he was all sunshine and light. Gunter was content to stare lustfully at the chubby army officer. The stories Willi had heard about Gunter caused him some disquiet.

Willi's bed, although long used to its owner's weight, creaked as it took Hilgard's mass. The chef picked up a bar of Toblerone the size of a baseball bat. Kurt inspected a cardboard carton and found a box of fifty Havana cigars. Hilgard examined the box and was impressed.

'I don't think I want to know how you came across these, Willi.'

'What the hell do you want?' Willi demanded, the threat to his children imbued him with uncharacteristic courage but Kurt's investigation under the bed lent his voice a note of panic. The assistant chef found two bottles of Napoleon brandy, which he showed to Hilgard.

'Genuine Courvoisier 1935,' said Hilgard admiringly. 'Now I really am impressed, Willi. You're a genius.'

Willi looked upon all his treasures as his children, but with the brandy he had achieved true parental bonding. He snatched the bottles from Hilgard. 'Just say what you want and get out!'

'Being of generous natures, we've come to help you, Willi,' said Hilgard.

'How?'

'Well now . . . Ever since Commander Kruger appealed for

233

contributions to help with his gala dinner project, there have been two deliveries of food parcels. Is that not correct?'

Willi nodded.

'In particular he appealed for coffee beans.'

'And *I* made a contribution. Ask him!'

'Of course you did, Willi. And we understand that you must have found it very difficult resisting the temptation to succumb to your generous nature by giving more than one hundred grams. A real struggle for you that must have resulted in sleepless nights. We've come to offer assistance with your . . . dilemmas.'

The three men left the room a few minutes later carrying a pillowcase bulging with Willi's dilemmas.

'Good to see tears of gratitude when you do someone a favour,' Hilgard observed.

17

With two weeks to go before the gala dinner, Kruger's meticulous planning shifted into a higher gear. He went through all the questionnaires that he required new arrivals to complete and found a former head waiter of a well-known Berlin restaurant among his officers. Max Monke was summoned to his office.

He was a tall, aristocratic tank commander who managed to look like the lofty, disdainful waiter even in uniform. He listened carefully to Kruger's plans, was immediately fired with enthusiasm, and agreed to supervise the proceedings. Kruger cut short his praise, because it wasn't on the agenda.

'There will be a maximum of a hundred place settings,' he said, showing Monke a floor plan of how the trestle tables were to be set out. 'I've allowed for seventy-five officers and twenty-five guests. I'm hoping that we'll have more guests. Perhaps as many as thirty but that depends on the response to our invitations. As you can see, there is not enough room to seat all the guests at the top table. What is the usual etiquette in such circumstances?'

'You put them down an outside row, away from doors where there will be a lot of coming and going, and give them as much room as at the top table to make it easier for the waiters to serve them. The idea is to minimize the chances of accidents, and they get served at the same time as the top table, too.'

'How many waiters will you need?'

Monke gave it some thought. 'Fifteen maximum. I'd like more because of the distance between the kitchen and the hall, but none of the doors are two-way swing doors and more than fifteen would only get in each other's way. It would be useful if we had men posted at all the doors just to open and close them for the serving staff.'

'An excellent idea,' said Kruger, making a note. 'Next item – selection of and training the serving staff.'

Monke left after a further five minutes' discussion.

Kruger spent the next half hour writing out minutes of everything that had been agreed with Monke until it was time for his appointment with Reynolds.

As with all his appointments, the guards showed him into Reynolds's office at the precise moment. Kruger was never as much as five seconds early or five seconds late.

'I see that the hall is just about finished,' said Reynolds when Kruger had sat and lit a cheroot. 'I must confess, Otto, your officers have done a superb job. Mrs Heelis has written a glowing letter to General Somerfeld.'

'I'm pleased to hear it, Major. As you know, I've been planning a gala dinner reopening of the hall, to which you are invited.'

'That's very good of you, Otto. I'm pleased to accept.'

'I also wish to invite these people,' said Kruger, handing Reynolds a list.

The Canadian officer started reading through the list and his eyes widened in astonishment. 'But you said that the dinner was for the prisoners!'

'If you recall our conversation, Major, I said that the dinner was for all those who have made the restoration possible.'

'General Somerfeld and companion!'

'Without his consent, my training course would not have

235

been possible. Unfortunately I do not know if he has a wife or a mistress.'

'Mrs Heelis!'

'She's widowed. That much I do know.'

'Lieutenant-Commander Ian Fleming! What contribution has he made, for Chrissake?'

Kruger gave a thin smile and indicated his cheroot. 'He keeps me supplied with these, Major. They've helped keep me calm during the more trying moments.'

'Members of Hawkshead Council and their wives?'

'Good public relations,' Kruger replied. 'You've often expressed concern about the wild rumours that circulate among locals about this place.'

Reynolds saw the names of Captain Moyle and a few other sworn enemies on the list. 'My God – you've invited the entire North-Western Command HQ!'

'Well, not all of them, and not actually invited yet, Major. This is where I beg a little favour.' He placed a small pile of cards and some coins on the desk. 'I don't know the addresses of most of the people on the list, therefore I would greatly appreciate it if you would kindly arrange for these invitation cards to be addressed and mailed. The money will more than cover the cost of postage and some envelopes.

Reynolds picked up the top card and his eyes bugged even more at the lines of neat lettering:

Commander Otto Kruger and his fellow officers
at Grizedale Hall POW No. 1 Camp (Officers) cordially invite

Major James Reynolds, DSO, and companion

to a grand Christmas dinner and dance
to celebrate the restoration of the Great Hall.

Saturday 19th December 1942 7:30 p.m. for 8:00 p.m.
Dress: black tie. Officers – uniform

RSVP to Officer I/C, Grizedale Hall, Grizedale Forest,
near Hawkshead, Cumberland

The neatly printed card, with his name filled in using a different ink, sent Reynolds's mind into a spin. 'You can't be serious!'

'Why not, Major?'

'Because it's unheard of, that's why not!'

'Unusual, perhaps. Is there anything on those cards that's likely to fall foul of the censors?'

'Well . . . No. But—'

'If people don't wish to attend, they can always refuse.'

'There would be huge security problems!' Reynolds snapped. 'Guests coming and going. Cloakrooms. Toilets. The prisoners will be stealing everything they can lay their hands on!'

Kruger drew slowly on his cheroot. 'I give you my solemn parole on behalf of all my officers that they will do no such thing, nor attempt to escape nor do anything that will jeopardize the success of the evening. If you're not satisfied with that, I will require each officer to give his individual parole at roll-call on the morning of the dinner.'

There was a long silence, which gave Reynolds a chance to calm down. He looked speculatively at Kruger. 'Just why are you doing this, Otto?'

'Don't you think people should have a good time at Christmas? The British are having a thin time at the moment.'

Reynolds smiled at that. 'Meaning that the Germans are not?'

Kruger shrugged. 'We've anticipated all your likely and, if I may so, quite reasonable objections, Major. There will no security risk, everything is being met from our resources. Our chef has even saved some of our food issue. There is no burden on the British whatsoever. Walter Hilgard is an excellent chef. I promise you that he won't let us down.' He indicated the money he had placed on Reynolds's desk. 'We're even paying for the postage on those invitations. In view of all this, I cannot help feeling that the decision as to whether or not General Somerfeld wishes to attend is one that he should take rather than one that you take for him.'

18

'Good God,' said Fleming, as he went through the morning mail in his in tray.

Sally looked up from her typewriter and recognized the envelope that Fleming had just slit open. 'It was marked personal, so I didn't open it, sir.'

'Take a look at this,' said Fleming holding out the invitation. Sally crossed the Admiralty office and took the card.

'Lucky you, sir,' she remarked, handing the card back. 'A two-hundred-mile trip to sample prisoner of war shepherd's pie and boiled cabbage.'

Fleming laughed easily. 'That was my first thought but somehow I don't think that's our Otto Kruger's style. It would be interesting to accept and discover what he's up to.'

'You won't get a petrol allowance and you're up to your ears in work, sir.'

Fleming thought it over. 'True,' he admitted, looking closely at the card. He frowned, rummaged in a drawer and found a magnifying glass, which he used to study the invitation card under his desk lamp. He looked up at Sally. 'Ask Johnny Benyon if he's got a minute to spare. Tell him to bring the biggest magnifying glass he's got.'

Sally put a call through to the switchboard and Johnny Benyon, the crypto-analysis expert, wandered into the office a few minutes later carrying a magnifying glass as big as a frying pan. He held it up to his face and treated Sally to an enormous Cyclopean leering eye that made her shudder.

'You've got something for me, Ian?' he asked.

Fleming gave him the invitation card. 'Tell me what you think of that. And stop frightening Sally.'

Benyon went to the window and studied the card through his monster magnifying glass for a minute. 'After careful examination and due consideration, my expert opinion is that it's an invitation to a dinner, Ian,' he said cheerfully.

'There's no putting anything past you, Johnny,' said Fleming admiringly.

'It's the arrangement of the words that gives it away. In your RSVP reply you could ask our friend for the name of the toy shop with kids' printing presses in stock. My youngest would love one for Christmas.'

'So it *is* printed?'

'Oh, yes. The same imperfections occur in several letters, and so they don't have that many duplicate letters to play with either. The capital "C" is a dead giveaway. It occurs on three lines, yet they've had to use the same piece of type for each line.'

Sally received another Cyclopean leer but it was cut short by Fleming taking the heavy magnifying glass and examining the card, paying particular attention to the three occurrences of the capital letter C.

Benyon grinned at Sally and wondered if she had succumbed to Fleming's charms. He said: 'There's a tiny nick in the C's upper serif which is always the same. They've used the same piece of type three times. They had to make up the slug for the first line, fit it into the forme, print the first line on all the cards, reset the slug for the next line, run the cards through the printer again, and so on for each line. Bloody tedious, if you ask me. So don't worry, Ian – they're a long way from printing millions of pamphlets telling the world what filthy English pig dogs we are.' Benyon became more thoughtful. 'Even so, a little hand-operated press would be just the job for small-scale production of things like travel warrants, passes et cetera.'

'Which is exactly what I thought,' said Fleming.

Benyon was puzzled. 'So why would Kruger give the game away by using his press for invitation cards? He's not stupid. He must know that we would cotton on to the fact that he's got one.'

'Maybe he's cocking a snook?'

Benyon frowned. 'Is that likely?'

'I wouldn't put it past him, Johnny, the way this damned war's going,' said Fleming grimly.

Benyon gave Sally a final leer and sauntered off, carrying his monster magnifying glass over his shoulder like a vanquished tennis player leaving the Centre Court at Wimbledon.

Fleming toyed with the invitation. 'I could switch a couple of days leave around and make it a private visit,' he mused. He came to his decision and asked Sally to book a phone call to Cathy Standish. It came through five minutes later.

'Ian, darling! This is unexpected. But three minutes won't be long enough for a satisfactory amount of grovelling from you. You forgot my birthday.'

'I'm terribly sorry, Cathy. It's been a bit hectic here of late. You're fully entitled to inflict the most grievous punishment on me and you'll have an excellent chance on the nineteenth. I've been invited to a special dinner at Grizedale Hall—'

'Snap.'

'You've been invited, too?'

'I'm making a valuable contribution to the occasion.'

'Have you received a beautifully lettered invitation?'

'I certainly have,' Cathy replied. 'It's so well done that it looks like printing. Like everything those bloody Jerries do. You wouldn't believe what they've done to the hall since your last visit.'

'I'll be coming by train. Could you put me up for that night, please, my angel?'

'You mean put up with you? That depends on the grovelling lengths you're prepared to go to in your abject, crawling apology.'

'I promise to leave no toe unsucked.'

Sally sniffed and managed to make the clack of her typewriter sound disapproving.

'Not enough,' said Cathy severely.

'And I'll devote long, loving attention to anything else that's been neglected.'

Sally's sniff was slightly louder.

'What makes you think they've been neglected?'

Fleming sounded hurt. 'Surely *I'm* the only eligible bachelor in your life?'

240

'I've been married, Ian. Eligibility is not what I look for in a man these days. But I suppose you'll do until something better comes along.'

They made final arrangements and talked until the operator interrupted to tell them that their three minutes were up.

19

The hall was finished. All the newly exposed panelling had been treated with homemade beeswax polish that gave the oak a lustrous sheen. Anton Hertzog's paintings were covered with lines of clean, overlapping sheets. At dinner that evening Kruger had some announcements. He asked Leutnant Max Monke to stand and explained that he was in charge of the serving arrangements.

Monke stared around at the gathering. He looked even more like a head waiter. 'I need twenty volunteers from those officers who weren't on restoration duties to train as serving staff,' he began.

'Oh – hell, we're going to be waiters now,' a voice protested.

Ulbrick frowned and glanced sideways at Kruger.

'From tomorrow until the gala dinner, there will be a different procedure for dinner,' Monke continued, glaring around at the faces turned to him. 'The tables will be rearranged, and instead of going up to the serving table, my trainees will serve you at your places.'

'Cold stew tipped in our laps,' complained the rebel voice.

'There may be a few accidents at first,' said Monke frostily. 'But by Friday you will be served quickly and efficiently. Your meals will be hot. Now – a show of hands, please. All those on the service staff will have their dinners afterwards and will receive extra.'

More than enough hands went up, enabling Monke to select the requisite number of the slimmest men among them.

'One last point,' said Kruger rising. 'I'm sure you will all agree with me when I say that our wonderful camp orchestra is in need of some improvement.'

The comment was greeted with cheers of assent.

'Therefore I would like them to rehearse some lively dance music in readiness for the dinner. Three hours each day, please, gentlemen.' He sat amid loud groans.

'For God's sake why, Otto?' Ulbrick muttered.

'Why what, Paul?'

'All this nonsense about a gala dinner. It started out as a simple Christmas dinner for the officers, and you've gradually turned it into a massive event. We've all had to make contributions because you've invited British guests. Trained waiters and heaven knows what else, and now we'll even have a dance band! Why?'

'How many new prisoners of war have arrived during the last month?' Kruger enquired.

The question threw Ulbrick. 'Well . . . er . . . I'm not sure.'

'I always welcome them at dinner,' Kruger reminded.

'That's what I was thinking, Otto. Now I come to think of it, it must be very few.'

'I'll tell you. None. Despite what the British press is saying, the war is going our way. Every day the Ministry of Food announces more rationing cuts and yet the British claim that they're conquering our U-boats. The end for the allies is approaching, Paul. It can only be a matter of weeks now, and the British will end up as *our* captives. In the meantime we will show them that we're a civilized people, resourceful, capable of rising above adversity, and that we're not the monsters that the cartoonists in the British press portray us as. This gala dinner will be a stark reminder of our capabilities. We'll be showing the British exactly what we can accomplish against all the odds and that we're not defeated.'

'Kruger's War,' Ulbrick snorted.

Kruger did not take offence. Instead he smiled and said: 'A very small war. That's all we can do at the moment, Paul – fight a small war. But any war, no matter how small, is worth fighting when right is on your side.'

After dinner Kruger visited Berg's workshop, where four

men were busy with needles and threads in the light of the single sixty-watt bulb that the British permitted.

'Shirts make surprisingly good white jackets,' said Berg proudly, showing Kruger the results of the first finished jacket by trying it on. 'The trouble is with the weight of the material, but we'll work bits of rolled lead into the hem like this one so that they hang well. A little starch helps. Monke said that the waiters will be so busy going back and forth that no one's going to take a close look at their jackets.'

'How about their shirt fronts?'

Berg delved into a carton and produced an immaculate, professional-looking dicky. The material was stiff, and even had neat rows of buttons. 'The bed sheet you provided, Commander. Bleached.'

'Amazing, Berg. How did you manage to make sheet material so stiff?'

'Starch, Commander. We've boiled it out of potatoes.'

'And the bow ties?'

'The same material but dyed black. We're leaving them to last because they're the easiest. We're into the shortest days of the year. We need all the daylight we can get for the difficult work.'

Kruger left the workshop, well pleased with the progress being made. Everything was falling into place.

The only problem left was the biggest one of all: getting hold of Willi's pig. He expected action on that front any day now.

Solving that problem took a step nearer with a call to Reynolds's office after dinner the following evening. As luck would have it, freezing rain was tipping down, driven by a biting nor'-easterly. A blustery, moonless night. He could not have wished for better weather.

'Ah, Otto,' said Reynolds, grabbing at loose papers as Kruger leaned on the office door to close it. 'Do you remember Carol Bunce – the Land Army girl from Spauldings Farm?'

'Certainly.'

'She's at the main gate guardhouse now, in a bit of a state.'

'Oh dear,' said Kruger drolly.

'She's beside herself with worry. She's alone at the farm and some of the sheet steel plates on the roof of the main piggery house have come loose in this goddamned gale – nearly broken away. Rain's pouring in, all the heat's escaping and pigs are susceptible to cold and wet. She thinks it'll need at least six big strong guys to get it back into place before the whole roof takes off.'

'You want six of my largest to volunteer on a night like this?'

'It's a request, Otto.'

Kruger gave it a moment's thought. 'Very well. Send Miss Bunce home. I'll round up some volunteers and I'll give you their parole right now. They might as well walk as it's not far. They're going to get soaked through working outside anyway.'

Half an hour later a working party led by Walter Hilgard set off past the main gate into the driving wind and rain with an escort of two unhappy guards. All the prisoners wore long greatcoats, some even had blankets wrapped around them. They shambled into the darkness like a posse of migrating bears.

At the farm Carol Bunce kept the two guards occupied with mugs of tea in a warm parlour while Hilgard and his team set to work.

Two hours later a very different Hilgard tapped on the parlour window to announce that the roof was fixed. He was caked in pig muck and so were his companions.

'Bloody hell,' muttered one of the guards, staggering back, holding his nose. 'Have you lot been rolling in it?'

Just as the party was leaving, Hilgard slipped an envelope into Carol's hand. 'Commander Kruger's compliments,' he growled under his breath in poor English. 'Invitation to the dinner on Saturday. Can you come?'

Carol's broad face broke into a wide beam. 'I'd love to.' Her smile vanished. 'But that's only four days and I don't have a dress. Oh – I think I know where I could borrow one.'

'Come on!' yelled a guard. 'Let's be getting back, only you stinking lot all keep your distance!'

The working party shuffled back to the camp, looking even more like a posse of bears than when they had set off. All six prisoners' greatcoats and blankets had acquired a generous coating of pig manure, which resulted in the escort keeping their distance and up-wind. The rain had slackened off but the guards at the main gate were decidedly reluctant to search the leprous returnees, and the two escorts were keen to get inside in the warm.

Hilgard and his five comrades, unloved and unwanted, made their way to the kitchen. Prisoners they met on the way recoiled in horror, clutching their noses and gagging. Kruger was waiting anxiously for them in the kitchen. The scent hit him like a Panzer division rolling over a public telephone kiosk but he bore up well, threatened the lookouts with trouble if they abandoned their posts, and helped the men divest themselves of their reeking clothes.

'That Land Army wench said she'd come,' Hilgard growled. He dumped a bloodstained butcher's saw, a cleaver and a large meat-tenderizing hammer in the sink. The tools had been hanging from cords under his greatcoat, where they had been keeping a huge pig's head company, which he heaved on to the food preparation table. Hermann jumped nimbly up to investigate, decided that he was not enamoured of the pig's staring eyes and went slinking off, his natural feline curiosity about anything new and smelling of blood postponed indefinitely.

The men struggled out of their greatcoats and blankets. Two of them were custodians of two legs of pork – each one hanging from cords looped around their necks. The other two were in possession of two quarters of the carcass, each lashed tightly around their respective waists. The last man was bearer of the offal: kidneys, liver, lights, and various other stock-enhancing organs in bags made from an old cape.

'I'm no expert, Hilgard,' Kruger remarked, eyeing the dismembered carcass. 'But it appears to be a very large pig.'

'It is that,' Hilgard grunted, naked except for his underpants. He rooted in the pockets of his greatcoat and tossed four large trotters on the table. 'Biggest I've ever killed. Good, lean animal though. Shame about the blood. Could have done with it to make black pudding. Had to dig a soakaway to get rid of it. Not easy. Ground's frozen hard.'

'Why keep the head?'

'For about three kilos of brawn.'

The party departed for the showers. Kruger had arranged for the boiler officer to ensure that there was a plentiful supply of hot water. Hilgard remained to give instructions to two of his under-chef assistants, who had appeared and were gaping at the pig spread out on the food preparation table.

'The head and legs can go into outside store to freeze up,' he ordered. 'Clean the quarters under the tap and start boning. I want all the lean and fat off, separated and chopped small. It'll have to be done tonight.'

'You've done extremely well, Hilgard,' Kruger complimented.

'Thank you, Commander.' The chef's usually surly face suddenly broke into a broad grin. 'It's been fun.'

With that he headed for the showers, leaving his assistants to wrap the legs and head in greaseproof paper and muslin, and carry them to an outside storage room where they were stowed at the back behind sacks of selected, top-quality vegetables and frozen rabbits that Hilgard had been hoarding.

An hour later over mugs of hot coffee, while two of Hilgard's assistants were busy chopping up the pork into rabbit-size pieces, Kruger thanked everyone involved in bringing home the bacon. The last and most difficult part of the entire operation had been accomplished. All the pieces of his grand plan had fallen into place.

20

The two large, oval bars of geranium-scented Elizabeth Arden soap that Fleming took north with him on the Euston train not only got him into Cathy Standish's good books but much else of hers besides, including the large, decadent Italian sunken bath that Cathy's father had installed in the 1920s. It could accommodate two adults comfortably and was holding a great deal more than the Ministry of Fuel's recommended five inches of hot water.

Even after an hour's splashing and cavorting, Cathy, insatiable as ever, insisted on half-swimming on to Fleming's thighs and bouncing up and down while he was trying to shave. It was a hazardous occupation. After nicking himself twice he gave up and carried Cathy into her bedroom, to her huge four-poster, where they dried themselves by rolling and thrashing about on the sheets until it was time to get ready for dinner.

When Cathy saw Fleming in his dress uniform she was tempted to start again, and Fleming was also so inclined when Cathy presented herself in an evening gown. She looked good in anything ranging from shapeless dungarees to jodhpurs, but in a long, off-the-shoulder blue gown, she looked sensational.

They were interrupted by a car hooting outside the farmhouse. 'Our taxi,' said Cathy, disentangling herself.

'You know, my angel,' said Fleming, catching sight of their reflection in a mirror. 'We're going to look frightful chumps if dinner turns out to an enamel mug of gruel and a bowl of stew.'

'I don't think it will be,' Cathy replied. 'Damn you, Fleming – I'm going to have to change my smalls.'

'Kick 'em off and go without,' Fleming suggested, which is what Cathy did in the taxi taking them to Grizedale Hall.

They arrived ahead of the several other cars. All were allowed through the main gate so that the passengers in their evening finery could be ushered straight into the main building, out of the cold, by prisoners acting as stewards. Major Reynolds and Kruger greeted everyone with handshakes at the entrance. The central-heating system was going flat out, which prompted exclamations of pleasure and surprise from visitors unaccustomed to how such matters were organized at Grizedale Hall. The white-coated stewards spirited away armfuls of hats and overcoats.

General Somerfeld arrived with his wife on his arm. He was a tall man, three years from retirement, troubled by arthritis which played the devil with his brave attempt to maintain a military bearing, and with his temper. His chest was a Technicolor blaze of campaign ribbons and he was the only officer present wearing a sword, which had to be dissuaded from duals with ladies' dresses now and then. His bushy eyebrows provided moral support for his eyes in registering his disapproval of all this Christmas fraternizing with the enemy nonsense. He marked Kruger and his damned immaculate uniform and Knight's Cross as a troublemaker. He liked his prisoners of war in long, shuffling lines with their hands on their heads.

Beatrix Potter arrived in her best evening tweed suit. At first no one recognized Nurse Brenda Hobson out of her uniform. She had a young, local doctor in tow. Very ill at ease, not sure what was going on, what was about to happen, or who was who. He got off to a bad start by asking General Somerfeld how long he had been a prisoner of war. His nervousness was nothing compared with Carol Bunce's frantic butterflies that were urging her to take to her heels and flee. She had inveigled her big-boned body into a pink dress that was a size too small and a few inches too low to satisfactorily contain her startlingly full breasts. To her immense relief Willi appeared. Kruger had tasked him with acting as her escort if she turned up unaccompanied. Willi bowed graciously, complimented her, and offered his arm, which she nearly broke off when she grabbed it.

There was much hugging and exchanging of kisses in the corridor. Kruger made a brief speech welcoming them all to Grizedale Hall and he invited Beatrix Potter to cut a ribbon across the double doors to the great hall. The ribbon was cut, the doors thrown open and the guests filed in to behold the wonders that awaited them.

'Good God Almighty,' Fleming breathed fervently.

His astonishment was understandable. The great hall was ablaze with light from candles in silver candlesticks set out in rows down the centres of long tables covered with crisp Irish linen tablecloths. The light sparkled on silver napkin rings and created iridescent patterns of coloured light shining brilliantly from the finest lead crystal wine glasses, and created a warm, mellow glow reflected from the oaken panelling. The sheets

248

that covered Anton's ceiling paintings were still in place. There was a Christmas tree by the double doors: a fine young conifer from Grizedale Forest that had been decorated with tinsel and bells made from chocolate foil. About seventy prisoners were standing by their chairs, facing the entrance and the arriving guests, their uniforms cleaned and pressed. At intervals around the perimeter of the tables were white-coated stewards. On a signal from Monke the entire assembly clicked their heels and bowed to the bewildered guests. Stewards swooped. General Somerfeld, his wife, and Beatrix Potter were shown to the top table, where they joined Reynolds, Kruger and Ulbrick. The pretty girl Reynolds claimed was his niece lacked a Canadian accent.

'I had no idea that you treated your prisoners of war so well, dear,' Mrs Somerfeld whispered to her husband. A remark that sent the General's enraged eyebrows galloping off in all directions. Fleming and Cathy were shown to a wing table. A steward beat Fleming to guiding Cathy's chair as she sat.

'Where did they get all this mess kit?' Fleming wondered, looking at the hallmark on his napkin ring.

'You can blame me for that,' Cathy replied smugly.

'Don't be absurd, angel. All your stuff is old tat from Woolworth's.'

The comment earned him a sharp dig in the ankle from a high-heeled shoe. 'I had a word with Lady Belmonte,' Cathy explained. 'One hundred place settings, all put into storage when Belmonte Hall became a home for evacuee children.'

'First course: potage du jour,' Fleming muttered worriedly, studying the simple menu. 'May God have mercy on us.'

Once everyone was settled, Reynolds rose to welcome everyone and to thank them for turning out on such a bitterly cold night. He explained briefly about the restoration of the great hall and how everything was all the prisoners' own work. 'Even most of the vegetables they've grown themselves,' he concluded to some sporadic laughter. He introduced Otto Kruger and sat.

The senior German officer's forbidding presence was enough to silence remnants of conversation when he rose.

He spoke briefly, expressing his thanks to Beatrix Potter and everyone who had helped directly or indirectly in the restoration work. Stewards moved with precision and purpose. They flowed silently and efficiently along the tables, partially filling glasses with toast measures of white wine that had been chilled by the simple expedient of leaving the bottles outside. They left the bottles on the tables. General Somerfeld sniffed his glass suspiciously and was most displeased to discover that it promised to be a good wine.

'Major Reynolds and I discussed a suitable toast at some length,' Kruger continued. 'Neither of us could agree. In the end we both decided that the following would be the most appropriate. So, please, fellow officers, ladies and gentlemen – raise your glasses to toast the spirit of Christmas and its message of peace and goodwill.'

All the diners rose for the toast and a short grace.

'Are you sure he's a German, dear?' Mrs Somerfeld whispered. 'He speaks better English than you do.'

'A dinner without a loyal toast is not a proper dinner,' General Somerfeld grouched in reply.

With the initial ceremony out of the way without mishap, much to Monke's relief, his well-trained staff went to work. Hayboxes were carried in and pre-heated soup bowls were quickly dispensed. Tureens of soup were brought in and placed at intervals along the tables. This was the moment that Monke had been dreading. 'Half a ladle of soup and no more,' he had instructed his pupils. 'Ladling soup is when accidents happen. We leave the tureens on the tables with their ladles. After that it's up to the guests to help themselves and make their own mess.'

The technique was not up to top-class hotel restaurant standards but it was a good compromise and the first-course service seemed to be passing off without trouble.

'Oh, well,' said Fleming, picking up his soup spoon. 'Once more into the breach and all that.'

'You're being a miserable old sourpuss,' Cathy scolded. 'It smells delicious.'

Fleming conceded that it did. He took a tentative sip and was immediately transported back to fond memories of first-class hotel dining rooms, and Scotts, Pallisters, and all his favourite restaurants before they became enslaved by wartime regulations that imposed a five-shilling price ceiling on all meals. Not trusting the evidence of his taste buds, he scooped a full spoonful. The massed assault of the rich, full-bodied soup stunned his senses. Without thinking, he helped himself to two hot rolls from the basket that miraculously appeared at his side. He turned to stare at Cathy, oblivious of the exclamations of delight from other diners around him.

'My God, Cathy. This is incredible.'

Cathy nodded and kept her spoon going. 'A rich stock is the secret. What must I do to become a prisoner of war here, Ian? Try your roll.'

Fleming did so. The warm bread melted in his mouth.

Cathy helped herself to a full ladle of the soup from the nearest tureen. Other diners were doing the same. The stewards with the rolls had their baskets emptied in short order and passed the word for more. A message reached Hilgard and his perspiring staff that the soup was being well received.

'They'll be saying that that's to kill their appetites before the mediocrity of the main course,' he grumbled.

'Clever,' said Fleming, having to scrape the bottom of the nearest tureen to fill a ladle. 'They do this to make the horrors of what is to follow more bearable. A lot of restaurants are doing it.'

'You're an old misery, Ian,' was Cathy's reproving reply.

'I don't hold out much hope for lapin en croûte,' said Fleming, smiling.

Cathy studied the menu. 'This looks as if it's been properly printed. Have they got a printing press?'

'You tell me, angel. Have you noticed the labels on the wine bottles? Château Grizedale.'

'I had no idea it was home-made.'

'Prison-made,' Fleming corrected.

Further down their table, Carol had downed three glasses of wine, three bowls of soup, and decided that she was enjoying herself.

Willi's eyes popped, as did those of his neighbouring prisoner of war diners, when she suddenly reached across the table and grasped his hand in a knuckle-cracking grip. The movement caused two aureoles to appear above the top of her dress like a pair of rising brown moons. 'Oh, Willi,' she said dreamily. 'I'm so glad I came. I nearly didn't, you know.'

She caught Willi's alarmed signal, glanced down and hitched her dress up, seemingly not in the least embarrassed by the inadvertent revelation. She swallowed her fourth glass of wine, hiccupped, and smiled engagingly at her enthralled audience, including Anton, who was wishing that he could use her as a model for his amazon angels.

'Magnificent,' he whispered to a fellow prisoner. 'What is the English for breasts?'

The prisoner told him.

Monke checked with Hilgard that the main-course service was ready. He stood discreetly behind the top table, waiting until the last diner laid down their soup spoon. He could hear General Somerfeld complaining bitterly about all three of his helpings.

'Damned fishy if you ask me.'

His wife explained that it was vegetable soup.

'Have to look into their food rations. Can't have Jerries eating better than us.'

'Perhaps it's one of Lord Woolton's Kitchen Front recipes, dear? Captain Moyle's wife told me that she listens to all his broadcasts and some of his recipes are very good.'

'They're not supposed to have wirelesses!' General Somerfeld snapped.

'But you allow them to have a printing press, dear,' said his wife, tapping a Château Grizedale wine label.

The last diner finished their soup. Monke gave the signal to start the second-course service. It went without a hitch; the stewards passed smoothly along the narrow gaps between the long tables so that they avoided getting in each other's way. They served everyone with regular portions of the pie and vegetables and, as with the soup, left serving dishes on the tables for the diners to top up their plates. The service was accomplished in less three minutes so that no one got a cold meal.

Fleming eyed the generous portion of pie on his plate. It was surprisingly thick with plenty of meat and a rich sauce oozing out from under the pastry. 'There must a whole rabbit in each portion,' he remarked.

'The prisoners breed them,' said Cathy. 'Rabbits breed like . . . like . . .' She gave a little laugh, wondered if she had drunk too much wine, and tried a forkful of the pie. 'Oh, Jesus . . .'

Fleming sampled some pastry and realized that he had almost forgotten what real pastry could taste like. One taste of the meat and all his reservations were banished. The buzz of conversation died away as fellow diners made the same discovery.

'This,' enthused Cathy, her mouth full, 'is utterly and amazingly fantastic. Just look at how much meat there is! Masses of it! I had no idea that this could be achieved with rabbit.'

'My dear,' said General Somerfeld's wife, 'When I've finished this, I do believe I'm going to be a little Oliver Twist and ask for more.'

'Disgraceful.'

'But you've already helped yourself to more, my dear.'

'The amount of rabbit! Disgraceful!'

'Rabbits aren't rationed, dear.'

The bain-marie that graced the top table was raided several times and had to be replenished. Similar scenes were enacted up and down the lengths of the tables. More bread rolls were demanded and etiquette was abandoned as diners pressed their dessert spoons into service to mop up the sauce.

Beatrix Potter expressed her dislike of pigs to Reynolds, saying that on this evening's evidence, rabbit would make a suitable pork substitute.

After such a rich meal, the light dessert of apple pie was much appreciated.

Fleming's aquiline nostrils caught the scent of coffee. 'In a night of surprises, angel, I think we're in for yet another. Real coffee is on the way.'

'Real sugar lumps, too,' Cathy commented, lifting the lid on a bowl that a steward placed before them. 'I wonder how many of these will be disappearing into handbags?'

Not only was Fleming's prediction about real coffee correct, but stewards glided around offering Passing Clouds cigarettes and fine Havana cigars.

Under any other circumstances Carol choosing a cigar would have been the cause of mortification and disapproving glances, but everyone was in high spirits after such a superb meal and her smoking preference passed unnoticed. Reaching up to light the cigar from a candle caused her brown moons to rise completely – a near-seminal event for her circle of admirers. Anton came close to fainting, and General Somerfeld came close to exploding with rage when he discovered that the quality of the cognac in his brandy balloon matched the label on the bottle.

'I'm sure that the Germans know that there's a war on, dear,' his wife assured him.

Kruger rose. He was about to tap his glass but his standing was sufficient for him to command an instant silence. He thanked the guests for the many compliments about the meal. 'We will now move the tables around to create a dance floor. I can't promise that our orchestra will be up to the standards of the meal, but they will do their best. Please do not shoot the pianist.'

Cathy giggled; Fleming had to remind her that a German joke was no laughing matter.

'But before that,' Kruger continued 'there is one more small matter.' He indicated the sheets hanging down the sides of the ceiling. 'During the restoration work it was discovered that the builder of Grizedale Hall had intended to decorate this ceiling with paintings of his ships but the work was never completed. Among my fellow prisoner of war officers is an extremely talented artist – Hauptmann Anton Hertzog. He and his assistants have completed the paintings and, so far, they are the only ones to have seen them. I have seen details only.' He pointed to the anteroom door. 'That's my new office. There's an example of his work on the wall. You're welcome to go in if you wish to take a close look at his brushwork. But now for the ceiling paintings. I would like to call on Mrs Heelis to unveil them.'

Beatrix Potter had been briefed on what was expected of her. She rose, thanked Commander Kruger and his fellow prisoners for all they had done, and gave a brisk pull on the cord that had been pressed into her hand. Stewards positioned along the walls duplicated her movement by pulling on their cords and all the sheets fell as one.

There was a collective murmur of surprise. Along both ceilings was a vivid frieze of every conceivable ship. Tugs, coasters, cargo ships, paddle steamers, colliers, sailing barges, tankers, and even the faint, looming shapes of passenger liners in the mist-shrouded distance. All were spread out in a line that ran the entire length of the hall on both sides. The flickering candlelight seemed to imbue the storm-tossed seas in the foreground with vibrant life.

'They're stunning!' Cathy exclaimed. 'Not quite like the drawings I saw. These are far better. All the ships seem to be pointing towards the end of the hall.'

'What is remarkable,' Fleming commented, 'is that the paintings on both sides are mirror images of each other.'

With dinner over, the paintings provided a talking point for the sated guests as they gathered into gossiping groups while the tables were cleared and rearranged in a semicircle to form a small dance floor. An upright piano was rumbled into place.

Kruger made his way through the mêlée. He paused to have a brief word with the musicians as they set up their instruments and music stands, sometimes exchanging handshakes with guests and fellow officers. His objective was Hauptmann Anton Hertzog, who viewed Kruger's approach in some alarm. This would be the dreaded moment of reckoning but he was ready for it.

'Hauptmann Hertzog,' said Kruger genially, mellowed by wine. He waved his cigar at the paintings. 'An excellent achievement. Far better than I thought possible, and so much more dramatic to have all the ships appearing to be converging on one point. I'm as delighted with your achievement here as I am with your splendid painting of my *U-112* in my new office.'

'I enjoyed the work, Commander,' said Anton, managing a sickly smile. 'Did you notice the ship near your end? You should take a closer look.' He tried to steer his senior officer back but Kruger wanted to inspect the entire length of the frieze – particularly the point that the ships appeared to be heading towards. He ignored Anton's guiding hand on his elbow, walked to the far end of the hall and stood gazing up, his eye moving from detail to detail. His roving gaze stopped; his expression darkened. He pointed an accusing finger at the foreground, hard against the end wall.

'And *what*, Hauptmann Hertzog, are those ladies?'

'They're not ladies, Commander. They're—'

Kruger lapsed into rapid German. 'They have breasts, Hauptmann. Large, voluptuous, provocative breasts with particularly large, prominent nipples, child-bearing hips, and no obvious genitalia. From this admittedly slenderest of evidence, I deduce that they are women.'

'But—'

'You will not interrupt me.'

The object of Kruger's wrath was a group of a dozen classically proportioned naked women that would have met with Rubens's approval – Germanic blondes with impossibly long, billowing tresses. They were crowded together in the foreground, clinging to each other, and appeared to be waving at the assorted ships in the fleet heading towards them. The foredeck of the nearest vessel, an oil tanker, was crammed with sailors who were waving back.

Kruger wheeled around and saw the mirror image of the same group on the opposite ceiling. His expression paled. 'This is in direct contravention of my orders, Hauptmann.' He spoke quietly to avoid drawing too much attention but his tightly controlled anger was all too apparent.

'But, Comm—'

'Please do not interrupt. I'm extremely displeased and will require these abominations to be painted over first thing tomorrow morning. After that I will confiscate all your painting materials indefinitely. My instructions to you were most specific. No cherubs nor angels. It wouldn't surprise me if I found a trireme in the background somewhere – scudding across a wine-dark sea.'

Some prisoners had spotted Anton's curvaceous abominations. There were comments and appreciative whistles. Kruger turned and skewered them.

Anton seized the opportunity. 'They are not angels or cherubs. They are sirens.'

Kruger's icy gaze returned to the hapless artist. 'They are what?'

'Sirens,' Anton repeated defiantly. 'Sea nymphs luring ships and sailors to their destruction. You said I could paint them. Your exact words when you told me what you wanted was that masts and sirens were essential. Well, you've got your masts – and those are your sirens.'

For a moment it looked as though Kruger was about to deliver a verbal scorching, regardless of the visitors gathering nearby, but for some moments he seemed to be speechless. The camp orchestra began tuning up.

'Sirens . . .' Kruger muttered. 'Sirens!' His icy expression softened. 'Sirens.' He returned his attention to the group of voluptuous femininity.

Anton saw his hesitation and followed through with what he hoped was the coup de grâce. 'Look carefully at their hands, Commander, and you will see that what they're actually holding on to are railings. You see? The one on the left, the two in the middle? Join those lengths of railings up in your mind and what have you got?'

The swirls of blonde tresses, the crowded bodies, and the spray made it difficult to see what Anton was driving at. Then Kruger's mind performed a mental flip as though it were resolving an optical illusion and he saw everything with startling clarity.

'My God,' he breathed. 'The after railings of a Type VIIC U-boat's wintergarten deck!'

'Exactly,' said Anton, triumphant and relieved. 'And if you look at all the ships you will see that they're flying allied flags. The hidden theme in the painting is of our glorious U-boat arm about to destroy the allied fleets.'

The orchestra started up with a slow foxtrot. Brenda

257

Hobson dragged her young doctor on to the dance floor. Cathy did likewise with Fleming although he would've preferred to continue eavesdropping on Kruger's and Anton's conversation. His German was good, he had caught a few words, but the orchestra tuning up had made it impossible to follow the gist of their obviously heated conversation.

Kruger was silent for some moments. Then he put his hand on Anton's shoulder. 'Hauptmann Hertzog. Please accept my sincere apologies. I spoke too hastily. I congratulate you. Both friezes are true masterpieces.'

Anton's face broke into a broad grin. 'You wanted to surprise everyone, Commander, and I wanted to surprise you.'

'Well, you've certainly done that. It's a remarkable achievement.' Something caught Kruger's eye. He pointed to the group. 'Perhaps it's the light, but that one right on the edge appears to have the tail of a fish.'

'Actually, they all have, Commander.'

'I thought the sirens were half woman and half bird?'

Anton chuckled. 'Like angels? That's the popular belief. But you were against angels and, besides, they would have looked wrong with wings.' Anton felt in his breast pocket and unfolded a cutting from a magazine which he handed to Kruger. It was a colour photograph of a painting that showed a mermaid with her arms entwined around a shipwrecked sailor, her full breasts pressed sensually against the doomed sailor's chest as she kissed him. There was a glorious cascade of half-plaited blonde hair down her back.

'It's by the English classicist painter and sculptor, Frederic Leighton,' Anton explained. 'It's his *The Siren and the Fisherman*. It's hard to make out in that photograph, but it looks like he's depicted his siren with the lower half of her body as the tail of a fish, like a mermaid. It seemed right, so I modelled all my sirens on her.'

Kruger glanced across the hall to where a small knot was gathered around the door to his new office. 'I should've trusted your judgement, Hauptmann. Your painting of my U-boat is quite remarkable. I will put my apology in writing tomorrow. Excuse me, I think I should circulate.'

Among those who had pushed into Kruger's office to

258

admire it were General Somerfeld and his wife. The General was somewhat less filled with admiration than his wife.

'He's got a bigger office than you, dear,' she remarked. General Somerfeld was glowering at the dramatic painting that showed a U-boat ploughing into heavy seas. 'Infernal cheek!' he spluttered.

'What's the matter, dear?'

'Painting that damned thing. This is War Office property – requisitioned on behalf of His Majesty.'

'But they painted all those ships along the ceiling,' his wife observed.

'That's different. They're allied ships. That thing's an obscenity.'

'It can always be taken down, dear.'

'It's painted straight on to the wall! Including the frame!'

'They are clever, aren't they?' She ran her finger over the desk. Berg's covering of artificial green hide looked remarkably realistic, and the desk had been rubbed down and French polished. 'He's got a bigger and better desk than you, too, dear.' She tugged gently on her husband's arm. 'Shall we dance, dear?'

General Somerfeld agreed on condition that they waited for a waltz. He sat beside his wife and mentally switched off her comments about the 'Make Do and Mend' talks on the radio and how the advice seemed to have been applied to some of the evening dresses.

Willi, his belt straining against the several helpings of the rabbit pie, had been seized by Carol in an iron grip and hauled on to the dance floor like the carcass of a horse dragged into a glue factory. She clasped him to her as they moved awkwardly around the floor, a broad hand holding his head firmly between her breasts. They took it in turns to tread heavily on each other's feet but both had drunk too much wine to notice. The proximity of Carol's breasts and that he was being slowly asphyxiated did little to assuage the misery Willi felt, having seen his beloved bottles of Napoleon brandy being eagerly ravished and emptied.

Anton watched them dancing and could stand it no longer. With wine-induced courage, he threaded his way through the

259

dancers and tapped Willi on the shoulder to take over. Carol hauled her new partner to her with equal enthusiasm. Anton was taller than Willi but not as tall as Carol which enabled him to enjoy her attributes but without the facial contact. He introduced himself and struggled to make some small talk in the best English he could manage.

The dance changed to a waltz. Stewards extinguished dying candles without replacing them. The low light meant that Carol's powerful, iron-fingered hold on Anton's buttocks passed unnoticed.

'You have much beauty,' he told his partner.

Carol giggled. 'Where?'

Anton struggled to recall his recent English lesson from a fellow prisoner. 'Your tits are tremendous,' he said. Carol's renewed giggling encouraged him. 'I would be loving to paint them.'

'What with?' Carol wanted to know.

21

By eleven o'clock, the evening was winding down. There had been kisses and goodbyes. Carol had been wrapped in her horse-blanket overcoat and driven home by Reynolds's niece, thwarting Anton's ambitions towards establishing a closer acquaintance with her Rubensesque qualities. Stewards were moving around, quietly rounding up glasses and emptying ashtrays. The orchestra kept playing for the benefit of a few couples. A Hawkshead councillor and his wife had been drifting around the dance floor for an hour and seemed to be determined to go on all night.

Fleming's day had started with the long train journey from London. The warmth, the wine and brandy, and full stomach conspired to cause him to doze despite Cathy's sparkling conversation.

He woke with a start. The main lights were on, making him blink, and there was a dull pain behind his eyes. The great hall was cleared and deserted, the chairs and tables folded and stacked. Even the floor had been swept. His overcoat was neatly folded on a chair. It was nearly midnight by his watch and he felt embarrassed at having not said goodnight to several VIP guests.

There were sounds coming from the double doors that led to the kitchen. He followed them to their source and found Cathy helping with the packing of the borrowed place settings in straw-filled boxes. Reynolds was assisting by marking each item against a list on a clipboard. Kurt was washing the last of the chinaware in a zinc bath. Hermann was on the table, doing what he had been busy doing for most of that incredibly bountiful evening – gorging himself on rabbit pie.

'Ah – the slumbering sailor hero bestirs himself when the labours of lesser mortals are nearly finished,' was Cathy's unkind greeting.

Flemings apologized and asked Reynolds to convey his regret to General Somerfeld and Mrs Somerfeld for not having bid them goodnight.

'Don't worry about it, Ian. The guy was half-dead on his feet when he left. His wife made him dance.'

'It's been a good evening, James.'

Reynolds nodded. 'A brilliant evening.'

'Teutonic efficiency.'

'*And* my contribution,' Cathy put in. 'Not one breakage, thank God.'

'Christ – I'm ready for bed.'

Cathy stopped work and regarded Fleming sympathetically. 'I'm sorry, Ian, but I won't be finished for a few more minutes. The taxi will be along in about a quarter of an hour.'

'Can I help here?'

'Not the way you look. You'd break something. Put your feet up in the hall. I'll organize you some coffee.'

'Thanks. Where's Kruger?'

'Bed, I guess,' said Reynolds.

Fleming returned to the hall. He was surprised and pleased to see Kruger. The German officer had placed a chair in the centre of the great hall near the far end and was contemplating the arresting frieze of Anton's ships. He didn't

261

look around when Fleming pulled up a chair beside him and sat.

The two men sat in silence for some moments.

'It's a hell of a painting, Otto.' Fleming spoke in German.

'Indeed.' Without turning, Kruger offered Fleming a cheroot. His first inclination was to refuse – he preferred his own cigarettes – but opportunities to share anything with this aloof man were rare, so he accepted.

'Why so many sirens?' Fleming wondered. 'They destroyed ships by luring them on to a reef. There's no reef in that picture.'

'Perhaps there is? Perhaps the artist is trying to tell us something?'

Fleming chuckled. 'If he is, then I've no doubt that what he's trying to tell us is what you told him to tell us.'

Kruger looked at Fleming for the first time. 'Do you really think that?'

'It's a safe bet.'

'You speak our language; you've received some of your education in our country. You know more about us than most Englishmen. But like most Englishmen, you will never understand us. You cannot credit that we have as much spiritual freedom as the British.'

'It's been pretty much suppressed of late, Otto. You can't deny that.'

Kruger leaned back in his chair and smiled thinly. 'There's suppression on both sides. If the British thought that that painting had anything to say, it would be obliterated tomorrow.'

'And what does it have to say?'

Silence.

'You can be assured of my discretion, Otto.' Fleming immediately regretted what he had said. It was a childish response; playing along with Kruger's fantasies. He attributed his lack of judgement to his exhaustion or maybe it was the cheroot he was smoking. To his surprise, Kruger gave an unexpected answer.

'The reef is there if you look hard enough. The sirens

262

represent our U-boat force destroying allied shipping. *All* allied shipping.'

The sudden and uncharacteristic note of intense passion in Kruger's voice and his own dulled senses prevented Fleming from making a telling or humorous riposte.

'Sinking all shipping, Otto? That can never happen. Not now. Your U-boat force is spent. You're losing one U-boat a day. Thirty a month. They're being sunk faster than they can be replaced. Maybe they'll hold out for another month . . . Two months if they're lucky. And then Doenitz will have to throw in the towel. The Battle of the Atlantic – the only battle in this damnable war that matters, as Doenitz himself once said – will be lost.'

Kruger gave no outward sign that the news had affected him but Fleming sensed that he was badly shaken.

Kruger drew on his cheroot and asked mildly, 'Then where are the survivors? They're not being sent here.'

'They're sent to holding camps before being sent to Canada. Half of the U-boats are being sunk by United States warships, and the survivors are sent directly to America. If the cessation of prisoners arriving here since September has raised your hopes that we're on the point of collapse, then you're sadly mistaken, Otto. Ask yourself why you've not been receiving Luftwaffe and army officers as well. Do you imagine that the allies have lost the air and land battles too?'

Kruger didn't answer. Instead he stood and took a few paces towards the panoramic painting.

Fleming guessed that the proud officer didn't want him to see his face. He derived no pleasure from the conjecture. 'God – I'm tired,' he muttered, rising. 'This may sound trite, Otto. But I wish you a happy Christmas.'

'Thank you. I wish you the same.'

Fleming moved to the doors and paused to look at the Christmas tree, remembering that it was a German custom that the British had adopted. He glanced at Kruger, standing with his back to him.

'Do you know what happened to the sirens in the end, Otto?'

'I didn't receive a classical education, Commander Fleming.' His voice was ice.

'They failed, Otto. Parthenope, Ligea, and Leucosia, I don't remember all their names, but there were a lot of them, and they all failed and destroyed themselves.'

There was no answer.

Fleming entered the corridor, pulling on his overcoat. Maybe fresh air would clear his head but all it did was sharpen his feeling of shame.

In the darkened rear of the speeding taxi, Cathy placed her hand on his arm and asked what was troubling him.

'Why should you think something is troubling me?'

'Because I know you better than you think, Ian. I know bloody well that it's not because you're trying to summon the courage to propose to me because *you* know bloody well that I'd turn you down. It's something to do with your chat with Kruger just now.'

'How did you know about that?'

'I took you a coffee. I saw you two deep in conversation, so I decided not to disturb you. The coffee wasn't very hot anyway.'

Fleming laughed quietly and squeezed her hand. 'I could never risk proposing to you, Cathy – you'd see right through me.'

'I always feel that Kruger sees through me,' said Cathy. 'Whenever he looks at me, it seems that he's staring right into my soul.'

'A proud man with an unbreakable spirit,' said Fleming. 'He's never given up fighting his own war. Nothing could make him give up. Yet I did it tonight. I broke his spirit.'

'How?'

'With a lie.'

'Big or little?' Cathy asked after a long silence.

'He's a man of action,' said Fleming quietly. 'Decisive, clear thinking. He's had to make decisions affecting the life and death of hundreds that I know I could never make. He's the sort of man I've always admired, looked up to. I'm just a backroom clerk chasing bits of paper around. And yet I broke him.'

'Tearing down idols takes its own special type of courage, Ian. Lies, big or small, are weapons that we shouldn't be frightened to use.'

'Yes . . .' said Fleming heavily. 'That's what's making this such a damnable war. Fighting for principles that we've thrown away anyway.'

The taxi sped on into the darkness.